CROSSING LINES

ADRIENNE GIORDANO

ALG PUBLISHING

Edited by Megan Records

Copyedited by Martha Trachtenburg

Cover Design by Elizabeth Mackey

Author Photo by Debora Giordano

Print Edition ISBN: 978-1-942504-67-2

Digital Edition ISBN: 978-1-942504-66-5

PROLOGUE

VENEZUELA

KILLING A MAN HAD NOT BEEN ON LIZ AIKEN'S DAILY TO-DO list.

But she had one guard checked off and one left to eliminate. All in a barely lit basement that stunk of urine and three-day body odor after her assignment — and her cover — had been blown to hell. Her luck always did run bad.

She hovered over the guard's body, knife still in him and her hand wrapped around it. Blood soaked through his worn T-shirt, drenching her fingers in an oily slickness that would make things interesting when guard number two showed up.

Seconds.

Probably all she had until Number Two came sniffing around to join his buddy in the supposed fun. For three days the two of them had been randomly appearing. First separately, when they'd wander downstairs, *checking* on her. Did she need anything? Could they get her more water? A snack? Something to read perhaps while they kept her locked up.

That was day one.

On day two they teamed up and put their hands on her, their disgusting fingers dragging over her breasts. The one called Luca held her down and the other attempted to rid her of her jeans.

If he weren't dead right now, his balls might still be in his throat after she'd blasted him with her boot heel. Either way, after he became Mr. Broken Balls, they'd both turned tail and run. Well, Mr. Broken Balls needed his friend's assistance up the stairs. He definitely hadn't run anywhere.

Liz assumed they weren't into women who fought.

Which was why, when Mr. Broken Balls came at her again today, holding that Ka-Bar, she'd added killing a man to her to-do list.

She glanced down at him, his hateful eyes now closed.

Bastard.

The now familiar squeak of the basement door buzzed her with a fresh batch of anticipation.

One down.

One to kill.

She gripped the knife, jerked it from his abdomen and popped to her feet.

Quickly, she scanned the area, her gaze locking on the shadowed corner under the stairs where two cardboard boxes had been stashed. She'd hide the body and get a jump on Number Two.

The man Broken Balls called Luca.

Ka-Bar still in hand, she hooked her arms under the dead man's shoulders, hauled him toward the corner and used her foot to tuck him a few inches farther under the staircase. She stepped back and surveyed her work while panic kicked up her pulse. *Fight it.* When she was done, she could lose it. Allow herself a few moments to go insane. Now? No way.

She refocused on the body. Still visible, but not the first thing Number Two would see.

The *first* thing he'd see was her and the bloody knife. If she had her way, all seven inches of that blade would impale him.

She wouldn't be the one to die.

Not today.

She wiped the knife handle and then her fingers across the thigh of her jeans. A shaft of light from the upstairs doorway splashed over the staircase, illuminating it enough to track Number Two. His soft-soled boots came into view as the man slowly descended.

Step.

Step.

Step.

Liz released a long, silent breath. She'd been trained for this. The only one in her class to withstand the torment. Mind over matter. That's all.

And now she waited.

The second he hit the floor, she'd lunge, maybe get lucky and catch him off-guard before gutting him.

Were there others upstairs? She couldn't tell by the earlier creaking of floorboards overhead and the voices had been too muffled. She thought it was only two, but...

Next.

She'd deal with additional men if necessary. One thing at a time.

In front of her, Number Two's boots hit the floor and he stopped, just halted right there, staring straight ahead as if the coppery smell of fresh blood had overtaken the urine.

Now.

She charged from the shadows, Ka-Bar at the ready. He swiveled. His eyes widened and he swung a meaty arm. Force plowed her forward. She rammed her right shoulder into the support beam. Pain ripped into her neck and her vision flashed white.

Stumbling, she hooked an arm around the beam, felt the pull of muscle as her body went to war with momentum.

No going down.

Not with this asshole. Unlike his buddy, this one had more than eight inches on her and a good hundred pounds. Statistically speaking, she'd never overpower him.

But he hadn't been trained by the CIA.

And she had the Ka-Bar.

And anger.

Lots of anger.

She steadied her feet and he came at her again, moving fast. She hopped left, swung back and lunged. He leapt sideways, his lips curving into a sick — hungry — lopsided grin.

"Go ahead," he said. "Fight. All the better when I fuck you until you bleed."

One of them, without a doubt, would leave in a bag.

Not me.

Liz smiled back. "You tried that already, remember?"

Before he could process the taunt, she lunged again. Missed. For a big man, his reflexes were good.

And now he was pissed. The smile was gone, his lips pressed tight, and even in the shadowy light, his dark eyes shredded her. "You bitch," he said, his Spanish accent a little thicker than she'd grown used to.

He tackled her, knocked her on her ass — *oof* — and landed on top of her. Knife. She squeezed the handle. Without that, battle over.

Not dying in here. No way.

She jabbed at his eyes. He bobbed left enough for her to half-roll away. Still on the ground, he regrouped and reached for her wrist, keeping her on her side. She kicked out, her heel connecting with his knee. He howled.

Excellent.

Elbow. She swung it back and blasted him, taking satisfaction in the crunch of his shattering nose.

He reached up, instinctively covering his face with both hands. *Now.* Heart slamming, she leaped to her feet and sucked in a breath, tasted the dank, nasty air. The stairs were right there. *Right* there.

Freedom. So close.

She snapped one foot out, hitting him in the ribs. He howled again, but grabbed her ankle, yanked once, then again and her feet flew from under her. She hit the ground again, this time using her forearms to break her fall.

Knife. She still had it. But too quickly he was on her, straddling her. *No.* She focused on him. Throat. She'd go for the throat.

Before she could react, he drove his fist into her cheek — *pow*. Her head snapped sideways and pain exploded into her eye socket.

Jesus, that hurt.

Her vision flashed white one more time and the pain disappeared. Just...gone. It would come again. Later. Right now, adrenaline was her extremely generous friend.

Not dying here.

She peered up at him. A drop of blood dripped from his nose. She'd done that. Bloodied him.

Finish him.

He wrapped the other hand — *huge hand* — around her throat, crushing her airway. She'd given the intelligence community and her country everything she had. Including sacrificing a personal life. How much more did she have?

Not dying here. No way.

"I'll fuck your dead body, bitch."

He squeezed tighter, robbing her of air and smiling that same sick smile.

Not.

Today.

Her thoughts grew fuzzy, her vision blurring. She blinked, then blinked again.

Knife.

She lifted it. Rammed it into his side. The blade struck bone, lancing off a rib. He cried out, the piercing sound stretching her already fried nerves. She forced the knife deeper and deeper still, burying it to the hilt. Rage flooded her. Survive. That's all she had to do.

The man's eyes and mouth shot open, a gurgle bubbling in his throat.

Punctured lung. She ripped the knife free, then plunged again. His screaming filled the basement, the sound ricocheting off the walls. *Focus.* That's all she had to do.

Her mission was already toast. All she needed to do now was survive.

She yanked again, then stabbed.

Stab, stab, stab.

The bloody blade hacked away and she craned her neck, fought to free her trapped throat.

His hold, that iron grip, finally loosened and she gasped, sucking in — amazing, beautiful, air.

"Not," she choked. "Today."

She bucked and he swayed left. She bucked again, shoved and . . . He toppled. *Go.* Pushing to her feet, she risked a glance at his crumpled body and heaving chest. He let out a harsh, watery gurgle and then...nothing.

Stillness.

Absolute quiet that roared at her.

Liz released a breath, her body folding as exhaustion and pain bullied through the adrenaline rush.

Get out.

She couldn't stay here. Taking the knife with her, she hustled up the steps, her booted feet thumping against the wood. Stealth, at this point, wouldn't matter. With all the screaming that had just gone on, anyone upstairs would have investigated.

At the top of the stairs, the door sat halfway open. She nudged it the rest of the way, peeped left and right. Nothing but a narrow hallway leading to...thank you...a rear door.

A backpack hung on the knob. She'd help herself to that.

Down the hallway she went, scooping up the backpack and opening the door to darkness and a blast of humidity. Had to be ninety degrees. Not necessarily unusual for Venezuela in May. And what the hell time was it? Above her a full moon lit the path leading from the house. They'd fed her dinner hours ago. At the latest, it might be midnight. That would give her plenty more darkness.

She closed the door behind her.

Freedom.

At least for now.

1

Two Weeks Later

Shane stepped from the stale air of the convenience store into sunshine and early warmth of what would be an odd 80-degree May day. Pedestrians veered around him, some on their way to the el station half a block up. At 7:30 on a Tuesday morning, the streets of Chicago swelled with commuting warriors.

Hell, at this hour, even a man with *his* background took his life into his hands on the street.

Typically, he'd be at the bar already, prepping the kitchen for the lunch rush and checking stock on anything the cook might need. Say, the all-important cheddar cheese. Which, according to the text he'd received thirty minutes earlier, they were out of. And holy shit, how could *that* be? He got an order twice a week. One on Monday, one on Thursday. Yesterday had been busy, but not *that* busy. How the hell did they go through his entire order in less than a day?

If his biggest problem was a lack of cheese, he'd count it as a good day. Someone had probably stored the wayward cheese in the wrong spot or he hadn't received the full order. Either way, something got fucked up.

He hooked a left at the corner and headed the last two blocks to the bar. A woman fell in step next to him, impressive considering his long stride and her being at least half a foot shorter.

She stayed right with him, her gait steady.

A normal person wouldn't think twice.

Unfortunately, he hadn't been normal — whatever that meant — in two years and the hairs on his forearms danced. He gripped the grocery bag and slid his gaze in her direction. Long dark hair fell over her shoulders. Straight nose. Soft, rounded cheeks. Tiny freckle on the left. Her whole look made him think Iowa farm girl and he definitely didn't know any of those.

He cleared his throat, picked up his pace, hoping she'd get the idea that she should back. The fuck. *Off.*

And yet . . . nuh-uh. He let out a low grunt as she triple-timed her steps to keep up. Some people didn't take a hint. Now he'd have to let her know he wasn't interested in anything she was selling, handing out or preaching.

He kept his eyes straight ahead. "Do I know you?"

"Not yet."

Interesting. Sweet voice to go with the farm girl look. In his experience, those were the women to fear. The ones who'd work a man to a vulnerable spot — say *naked* — and then shove a .45 under his chin. Or other parts worth protecting. He cleared his throat. "Okay."

"I need your help."

His *help*? *What* was this now? As much as he wanted to

halt and ask her just that, he wouldn't. He'd keep moving, his mind wandering to the knife strapped to his ankle.

"Sorry," he said. "All out of help. Have a good one."

"I was told to expect surly."

Surly? *Sweetheart, you have no idea.*

"Who told you that?"

"A friend. A *mutual* friend."

Shane finally stopped, stared straight ahead at the traffic snarling the intersection. He looked down, studied her for a solid thirty seconds. The deep brown eyes that bordered on black, the fading bruise on her cheek. The scar above her perfect eyebrow. Someone had put hands on this woman. Rough hands.

As much as he hated it, not his problem. Once upon a time maybe, not now.

"I don't have a lot of friends," he said.

"You have a few. And one of them said you could help me. You know what I'm talking about."

She whipped a magazine page from her jacket pocket. A restaurant ad with a tiny map at the bottom showing the establishment's location. She pointed at it, gesturing to a spot not even close to where they stood.

Overhead came the rumble of an incoming train and a woman wearing a short skirt and blazer stormed toward them, half running, her briefcase bouncing against her hip. Shane stepped back, let her blow on through so she didn't miss her ride.

She offered a little extended eye contact. "Thank you."

He went back to the current woman occupying his mind. The one with the dumbass ad and sexy brown eyes.

"Who's this friend?"

"I can't say. Not here." She glanced to her right, then over her shoulder before going back to the map. "So, three blocks, you say?"

"Four," he replied, playing along.

Because, shit on a shingle, one thing was obvious, whoever this woman was — outside of being a lost tourist — she didn't want to be seen talking to him.

"Someone sent you?"

"Yes."

Son of a bitch. For two years, he'd been so goddamn careful. Every day, every minute, every second. No contact with loved ones. No holiday meals. No brownies from his mother.

The brownies haunted him. All hot and gooey fudge still warm from the oven. Heaven.

But...hang on. She said she needed *his* help. Not the other way around. If it were his cover blown, *she'd* be offering help.

Or trying to hack his balls off.

"Beetlejuice," she said.

Shane started moving again, faster this time, away from her. He didn't know her, didn't *want* to know her and sure as hell couldn't risk blowing cover for her.

"I'm sorry," he said over his shoulder. "I can't help you."

But he'd have a conversation with the guy who'd given her the emergency code. No doubt about that.

CEMETERIES, IN SHANE'S OPINION, WERE GREAT FOR COVERT meetings. No security cameras, no guards stationed at the gate, no nosy employees after five. Yep, pretty much, St. Augustine's Cemetery fit the bill just fine. Particularly at night.

He parked his nondescript — vanilla, no sprinkles —

Chevy on the street behind the cemetery, hopped the iron fence and made his way across an open area where gravesites had yet to be claimed. At the southernmost point of the field stood a mammoth mausoleum painted a bright white and finished off with decorative columns along the facade. He took his time, enjoying the comfort of warm night air. Here, city chaos didn't exist. Here, in the blackness, all was quiet and for the brief minutes it took to cross the cemetery, his mind absorbed the peace. Took it in. Reveled in it.

Soon enough, that calm would be gone.

At the back of the mausoleum, away from the security cameras that only monitored the public areas, he unlocked the employee entrance using the key he shouldn't have kept from his maintenance job two years earlier. On the other side, a wall of damp heat welcomed him. No air-conditioning in the stairwell. Only in the mausoleum itself. Which, Shane supposed, made sense for the folks visiting loved ones. The loved ones most likely didn't give a shit. They were, after all, dead.

He jogged to the basement level, then used the flashlight on his phone to guide him along a narrow walkway beside stacks of grass seed, fertilizer and other supplies. At the support beam, he hung a left and hustled to the long-ignored three-foot air vent built into the cement.

He'd discovered this little gem one morning while searching for an extra shovel. To this day, he wasn't sure what had made him pull the louvered grate from the wall and inspect behind it. Then again, his curiosity — er, nosiness — had made him one hell of a Recon Marine.

The vent, as evidenced by the stuck grate he almost broke his hand trying to budge, obviously hadn't been used in years. Still, he'd forced that sucker off and peeked inside at the metal ductwork that ran straight up. At that point, he'd abandoned his search for a shovel and jumped straight into the mental rabbit hole that led him to an air vent big enough for someone to crawl through. Six inches above the opening, on the back part of the shaft, he'd found a rusted, quarter-sized hole and man-oh-man the curiosity hog inside him went ballistic. He had to know what was back there. Had to. He'd jammed his six-foot-three body into the confined space and poked his finger through the hole. Rust flaked away and the dirt behind it collapsed, revealing a dark, hollow space. Shane had retreated, grabbed one of the shovels he'd come to the basement for and opened that hole wide enough to fit his body through.

Exactly what he intended to do now.

He climbed in, resetting the grate behind him. On the opposite wall, he removed the second grate he'd installed to cover his handiwork and climbed through to the tunnel on the other side.

Back in the day, coal mining wasn't uncommon on the outskirts of Chicago and Shane had discovered part of an abandoned mine.

Now, failing to appreciate the dank, closed-in space, he picked up his pace, marched into the tunnel's darkness with only his phone lighting the way. *Another ten yards.*

But, damn, he hated tight spaces. No. Wrong. Confined spaces weren't the problem. Being trapped was the problem.

And wasn't *that* a pisser, considering his current life circumstances? Nothing like being a prisoner in one's own life.

At the end of the tunnel, he reached a door he'd installed a lock on. Just in case, you know, someone like him stumbled upon his super-secret hidey hole. He checked the knob. Unlocked. *Crazy son of a bitch is here.* Shane pushed the door open, stepped into the storage space, complete with old tools and blasting caps, and found Dustin — Dusty — slouched in one of the fold-up soccer chairs. Couldn't exactly squeeze office furniture through a barely three-foot opening. An oversized camping lantern threw shadows over the walls and illuminated Dusty's ever-present *I'm-slightly-amused* look.

He didn't move from his spot. Just sat there, long, jean-clad legs stretched in front of him, as he stared out from under his sideswept bangs and the bill of his ancient ball cap.

And as happy as Shane was, and always would be, to see his old friend, he'd sent him a text via their emergency-only burner phones, summoned him to this place that ensured privacy and lessened the risk of being seen together, to rip him one. "How many times I gotta tell you to lock this door?"

"Wha, wha. How many times *I* gotta ask *you* who the hell cares? If someone we don't know walks through that door, we're screwed anyway."

Shane tromped across the fifteen-foot room. Along with the soccer chairs came a portable table with a canvas top. He'd like to lean on it, get right in Dusty's space, but the table would definitely collapse under his weight and he'd wind up doing a face plant. At which point, his friend would laugh his ass off.

Instead, Shane propped his hands on his hips, took a long pull of damp air and focused on a crack in the cement. Part of why the CIA had once loved Dusty was he could work a man's nerves. Absolutely burrow under the skin in record time. He screamed surfer dude with that shaggy hair and easy gait. Throw in the laid-back attitude and all of it wrapped around a brain that knew how to make the sanest of the sane go abso-fucking-lutely nuts.

"You flaming asshole," Shane said. "You stole my cheese."

In response, Dusty made a noise. That cross between not laughing and laughing. The *you-bet-your-ass-I-stole-your-cheese* laugh.

Shane waggled a hand. "Don't try to deny it. I pulled my security video. You broke into the bar last night. I saw you walk straight to the cooler."

"I didn't break in. I have a key. And the code to your alarm. Not exactly high-level operative shit."

"I'm changing the locks and code. And speaking of codes, you gave our emergency one to that sexy brunette. I can't believe you sent her to me."

"You'd rather I sent her in your front door? Maybe made her an appointment?"

And there it was, the admission. Crazy fucker trying to get them all killed.

"I'd rather you not send her at all."

"Exactly! Dude, I needed to get you out of the bar to talk to her and you always hit the market in emergencies. You should vary your pattern."

Ha. Now, he'd get a lecture from the guy who'd put all of them in jeopardy? "Fuck off. My patterns were great until you got involved. It's not enough we're watching our own sixes, you want us to watch hers too?"

"It's a damned fine six."

Shane squeezed his eyes closed, prayed for patience — and his mother's brownies. His mother's brownies always made a bad day better. He'd kill for one of those effing brownies.

He opened his eyes again, gave Dusty the mother of all

death glares. They'd met six years ago at Fort Huachuca during training for the CIA's Special Activities Division. Shane, then a Recon Marine, had been on loan to the CIA and serving as a member of SAD's Ground Branch. Dusty, two years younger, had been recruited from his position as a CIA field operative because, in short, he was a flipping engineering genius. They'd been friends, *brothers,* ever since.

And right now, Shane was pissed and like any brother would, he'd summoned his buddy to their hideaway for an ass-kicking. Typically, they met here only when the stresses of living undercover became too much. When they needed a few minutes with someone who knew them as Bobby MacGregor and Terrence Whitley, their birth names. That's what normal people did. They socialized with friends. They *connected.*

Only Shane and Dusty and their other friend, Trevor, did it in a drafty room at the end of a forgotten tunnel under a mausoleum.

What a life.

Shane held his hands out. "Are we running a charity for wayward operatives? Hell yes, I'd say no. It's me, you and Trevor. That's it. We start helping people, word gets out and we're toast. You wanna die? Because I don't. Whoever this chick is, whatever her problem is, talking to her compromises us."

Because the badasses looking for a couple of blown CIA guys and a former DEA agent would pay a mighty sum for the opportunity to scrape the skin off their bones.

Layers at a time. Until they sucked their last goddamn breaths.

"Sully sent her."

Shane's head dropped forward. Just...bam. *Sully.* Otherwise known as Jonathan Sullivan. That asshole had been part of Dusty's last SAD team and hadn't done him any favors.

"Sully? Are you serious right now? How can you trust that guy?"

"Oh, hey, now. He's an asshole, but trust is different. He wouldn't sell out an agent."

What complete and total crap. On their last mission, Sully and Dusty had been holed up on a mountain in Pakistan waiting on a target when headquarters got a bogus tip that their location had been compromised. HQ ordered them to abort. With months of work about to be blown, Sully, the more experienced agent, knowing full well he couldn't ignore an order, let HQ know that overcast skies prohibited flying out.

A total lie considering the stretch of blue overhead. All he'd done was buy the team another twelve hours to complete their mission.

Which they did.

Too bad HQ checked the weather at the team's location and that led to a brutal tongue-lashing for disobeying orders. Dusty still winced when he talked about it. What came next was a craptastic display of bureaucratic bullshit the agency liked to unleash on their faithful. Sully, as the senior field agent, received a promotion for completing the mission, while Dusty took a grade reduction. And in the CIA, grade reductions stayed in a personnel file.

Forever.

Shane scoffed. "Please. He didn't waste time selling you out."

"He didn't sell me out. Not intentionally. He got a bump and I didn't. No harm, no foul. This is different. He's helping her."

"And what, you trust someone *Sully* sent?"

"Hardly."

"Then why are we here?"

From his abused messenger bag, Dusty retrieved a tablet, poked at the screen a few times and tossed it on the canvas table. Any other table, it would have landed with a statement-making *fwap*. Here, like every other aspect of their lives, it was a mind-shredding silent landing. "After she made contact, I had Sully send me her file. It's encrypted."

Jesus H. Christ. Now he was having the not-to-be-trusted one smuggle files out of Langley. Who knew what kind of heat that might bring? "Dude, you're killing me right now."

"Don't care." He pointed to the tablet. "Read it."

"No."

"Read it, you jackass, and you'll know why I sent her. I'm not letting you leave until you read it."

Then the asshole flashed an all-teeth smile that made Shane want to bust those teeth out.

Except, down deep, the truth was, he didn't mind Dusty's threat. As much as his friend made him crazy, these clandestine meetings were the only direct contact either of them had — well, were supposed to have — with anyone from their former lives. At the very least, it reminded Shane of who he used to be. That he'd once lived an existence where he socialized with friends, called his brother on his birthday or took his niece for ice cream just because he damned well wanted to.

Those simple events, the emotional ties he'd taken for granted and now craved, absolutely hungered for, were gone.

But he was still breathing.

He stared down at the tablet. *Don't look.* He knew. Without a doubt, whatever it contained would change things. As much of a pain in the ass as Dusty was, he'd never, not for a second, put Shane or Trev in danger unless it meant something.

To Shane.

And that scared the shit out of him.

How had his life turned into a circus that had him standing in an abandoned coal mine, pining for the company of friends and terrified to read a file?

An itch traveled along the back of his neck and he dug his nails in good and hard, more to feel the pain, to experience something, anything, that proved he was alive and well and thankful for it.

"Goddamn you, Dusty."

"Just read it."

Whatever that file contained, Dusty had gone to some trouble making sure Shane saw it.

And Dusty wasn't a pushover. His cover was as tenuous as Shane and Trevor's. Sure, they'd gotten new identities, but at any time, one of them could run into an old chum and the lives they'd spent two years building would have to be abandoned. Discarded like used paper.

Dusty had been willing to take that chance.

Why?

The answer was in that file.

Goddamn Dusty.

Shane stared down at the screen that would probably rip his life apart and — *Jesus* — before he thought too hard about it, picked the tablet up. Done.

A color photo — leave it to Dusty to go for the drama — of a dark-haired woman, her face all kinds of banged up, was the first thing Shane saw. Someone had worked her over. He focused on her eyes and the intense brown he'd seen that morning.

A woman shouldn't look like this. Ever.

Scrolling to the next page, he found a CIA personnel report. An eyes-only file. Elizabeth "Liz" Aiken had been hired as an analyst straight out of college. After eighteen months, she'd been promoted to fieldwork and by all accounts, she'd been a damned good agent.

At least until two weeks ago when she'd been working an op in Venezuela and had her cover blown.

"Venezuela," Shane said.

Shit.

2
___

THE FOLLOWING DAY, AFTER A SERIES OF ENCRYPTED EMAILS, Liz stood in line at the Navy Pier Ferris wheel. She wore a tie-dyed purple shirt Dustin Osbourne had gotten to her via a dead drop at a park on the North Side. The emails had sent her on a journey around the city, the last one bringing her to the park and the large rock fifty paces from a tree with a missing dog flyer stapled to it.

So far, their covert communications had accomplished getting her to the target point at exactly 1:30. Without incident. Meaning she'd hadn't been captured or killed.

Yet.

Midday sun glinted off the giant wheel and the lake breeze tickled her cheeks like gentle fingers.

When had she last been touched with affection? Long time. That's when. Too long to do the math on. So, she'd stand in line, another person with her gaze hidden by sunglasses, blending into the crowd.

Her instructions had been to wait in line for a man to join her and present her with the code word.

The line nudged along. Another three people and she'd

be next to board the ride. What then? Did she get on? Step out of line and wait? What?

Dammit. Resisting the urge to once again scan her perimeter, she kept her gaze straight ahead, focused on the wind-blown auburn hair of the woman in front of her.

And then someone nudged her elbow. Could have been an accident. Another tourist getting bumped and setting off a chain reaction. Happened all the time. Plus, no code word.

"Hi, babe," a man said from behind her. "Sorry I'm late. Got hung up near Wrigley."

Wrigley.

Code word.

She angled back, smiled up at Shane Quinn, the mountain of a man — nicknamed within the agency as Viper — she'd ambushed the day before.

"Hi, sweetie," she said. "I'm glad you got here."

Only a man in his position would understand how true that statement was. Playing her role, she boosted to tiptoes and kissed him on the mouth, lingering for a second because, why the hell not? She'd just been lamenting the lack of affection in her life and maybe this little charade wouldn't fix that, but it sure wouldn't hurt.

The Ferris wheel attendant cleared her throat and Liz pulled away from Shane. The attendant, a young woman with impossibly long legs and a too-sugary-smile, ushered them to the next car and held the door open. Sparing a glance at the woman, long enough to be kind, but short enough to be forgotten, Liz stepped into the air-conditioned, glass-enclosed car and settled onto one of the seats. Shane slipped the attendant some cash to ensure a private car and sat beside Liz, resting his arm over her shoulder and kissing the top of her head.

All apparently for the attendant's benefit, given her

blatant staring at the jacked, smoking hot guy in front of her.

Shane needed to turn the volume down on his looks. Big time. Even in a baseball cap and aviator sunglasses he grabbed attention.

Their car began to rise and Liz took in the whitecaps and sun-touched swells of Lake Michigan. Sailboats and yachts cruised the lake, their passengers completely clueless about the privilege of having their own names.

Using his thumb, Shane tapped the side of Liz's arm. "Here's the deal. We'll get you new IDs, new social, education and employment history. In exchange, you never mention me or Dusty to anyone. Understood?"

"Or what?"

"Honey, your life is in my hands. Don't fuck with me."

She shifted sideways, looked up at him, feeling only slightly insulted he expected her to expose him or his friends. "Of course not. And I'd never jeopardize you. Or your friends."

"Then we won't have a problem." He looked out at the lake. "I should have everything by tomorrow. You know the city at all?"

"No. First time here."

"I'll check into apartments for you. Get you set up."

"Thank you."

"Tell me about Alfaro."

Liz flinched. When she'd been captured, she hadn't known Number Two's last name. All she'd known was that she'd been snatched off the street and tossed into a filthy basement. Later, after calling in every favor owed, she made it back to the States and was informed she'd taken out the son of Venezuela's president, a man with connections to the

Liborio drug cartel, the country's most violent criminal organization.

"My assignment," she said, "was to dig up intel on the chargé d'affaires."

"The K and R case?"

Apparently, the man stayed up on Venezuelan news, because not many folks were aware the senior American diplomat had been kidnapped and held for ransom three months ago, presumably by the Liborio cartel. The CIA had been tasked with locating the missing woman. Enter Liz, posing as the daughter of a Cuban businessman.

"I was only in Venezuela a few weeks when my name was leaked. I still don't know who or how, but my identity made it to the cartel."

Someone, more than likely at the agency, had probably made a bundle by selling her out.

Traitors everywhere.

"I saw that in your file," Shane said.

He had her file? She looked up again. "They gave you that?"

"Hell no. Dusty got it. We still have friends inside Langley. Otherwise, we couldn't do this for you. Or for ourselves."

"Why are you helping me? There are other burned agents."

"Mainly because Dusty is a sucker for a pretty girl."

"Oh, please."

He smiled briefly. "Maybe that's crap."

"Maybe?"

"Sully reached out to Dusty. Thought I might have an interest in your situation."

"Why?"

He looked down at her, pulled his sunglasses off to

reveal those sparkly blue eyes she'd first seen in a photo two nights ago.

"I've never done this for anyone other than Dusty and Trevor. Had no interest either. It was bad enough I got burned. When it happened to Dusty with an unrelated case, I helped him out."

"Why?"

"Simple. He's my friend. We met at Fort Huachuca during our Special Activities Division training six years ago. Trevor was part of Dusty's mess, so he got a pass. We're all in Chicago but spread out. Close enough to help, far enough to not be connected. It's just the three of us. You make four."

"Why me?"

"Because Alfaro is after me too."

GODDAMN IT FELT GOOD TO SAY IT. TO BLURT IT OUT LIKE IT hadn't been trapped inside him for two years. Outside of the agency and Dusty and Trev, Shane had never spoken of it. To anyone.

Even the most well-meaning people tended to have loose lips and he'd refused to risk it.

Until now.

And what the hell had gotten into him, letting that factoid fly? Beyond Liz Aiken's agency file, he didn't know jack about her. Hell, she could climb off this Ferris wheel, go right to Alfaro's father — or the cartel — and cut herself a deal by sacrificing Shane.

He averted his eyes and concentrated on the John Hancock Center and its antennas jutting up into a cloudless blue sky.

For a few seconds, he blocked out the panic and took in

the perfection of the moment. The freedom of discussing his past.

He glanced back at Liz and her crazy-beautiful dark eyes that made his brain ping. Forget about what kissing her did to him. That, along with everything else about Liz Aiken, had been careless. Careless, but enjoyable.

"You know Alfaro," she said.

Statement, not a question. And, oh, yeah, he knew him. "Last time I saw him I was having breakfast with his family."

"*Really?*"

"I was a Recon Marine recruited for SAD."

"Impressive."

He shrugged. "I love my country. I love serving. And I was good at what I did. It still took me three years to get inside Alfaro's circle." Shane held his fingers up, pinched them together. "I was so close."

"What happened?"

What didn't happen? "I went into Colombia under the guise of teaching English to wealthy students. I hooked up with a professor, also a member of FARC. A little moaning about my hatred of capitalism and he took me to the rebels."

"You *joined* FARC?"

"Yeah. It worked for my mission. We left Colombia and set up camp just over the border in Venezuela, running drugs in and out of the country. Dabbled in illegal gold mining, too. Anything to get some cash rolling."

"How did you get to Alfaro?"

"I met Andres while doing a drug deal."

"He's the older son," she said. "I took out Luca, the younger one."

"Yeah. They were both involved with the Liborio Cartel's drug smuggling. Daddy gets a piece of the action so he lets the smuggling — and his sons' involvement — go."

Liz shook her head. "Lets it go? Please, he does more than that. His sons were members of the cartel."

"Which is how I got to Andres. I met him and worked him for months. Got him to trust me."

Shane sat back, rested his head against the glass and formed a mental picture of Andres. His twisted attachment to the kid's wit and generous heart — at least materialistically speaking — still haunted him. When Andres loved someone, he trusted completely.

A fold Shane had managed to worm his way into.

Liz shifted, propped her head against his arm and once again, he paused to appreciate the absolute normalcy of what could never be normal.

"That's why you're nicknamed Viper. You got them to trust you."

"Always hated that nickname. But, yeah, that's where it came from."

"What happened?" she asked. "The op fell apart?"

"Big time. I was staying inside the compound with Andres when one of the staff caught me messing with his phone. He left it on the table when he went to the john. I took the opportunity to look. He had this crazy coding system he used for names where he'd spell the name backward and then toss in some symbols. I was trying to figure it out when I got busted. With the help of an asset I had inside the compound, I talked my way out of it, but let Langley know that same night. They weren't risking it and SEALs pulled me out the next morning. It took seconds. Boom. One minute I was having breakfast with the fam and the next I was hustled into a waiting helo. Along with me, they grabbed Andres."

Liz nodded. "He's in a CIA prison in Europe now. They keep moving him."

"Yeah. I heard." He glanced down at her, still snuggled under his arm. "Alfaro got over me getting inside his organization. He couldn't handle his son being captured. That, he pegged me for."

"God, this world we live in. The two of us should be dead. Thank you for helping me."

"I know what it's like to be hunted by this guy. He's a vicious prick. If he finds you — "

"I know."

The two of them stayed silent while the last minute of their ride wound down. Fourteen minutes of semi-normalcy. Of two supposed lovers enjoying a spring day.

As their car approached the jump-off point, Shane pulled Liz close, made a show of kissing the top of her head again. Just a guy and his girl. He nuzzled her ear.

"When we get off, I'll grab your hand, we'll walk to the entrance of the pier and split off. I'll contact you tomorrow about your new setup."

She nodded. "Thank you," she said again. "You have no idea."

"Yeah, I do. Don't thank me yet. You're not nearly secure."

THE FOLLOWING MORNING, AFTER THREE BUS CHANGES AND A cab ride, Liz sat on the designated bench in a park on the city's northwest side. Her instructions, via another set of encrypted emails, instructed her to find the red bench two hundred yards from a brass dedication plaque. From there she counted three more benches to the left for her meeting spot.

And she'd managed to be on time. Not bad for a girl who'd been on the move for two hours.

She unzipped her backpack, that same one she'd swiped from the hellhole in Venezuela. Most would think her nuts for keeping it.

Her?

She considered it a badge of honor. The reminder that she'd survived.

The battle she'd won.

Under bright morning sunshine that would fry her skin in twenty minutes, she pulled a *People* magazine — excellent prop — from the backpack and stole a peek at her surroundings.

Tall European buckthorn and green ash trees lined the pathways, offering shady spots to rest or take a break from the hot sun. Big park with just the right amount of pedestrian traffic, cyclists and happy kids. As with Navy Pier, the perfect place to get lost in plain sight.

She slid her gaze right — no Shane — then left to where a young guy, maybe early twenties, approached, his focus solidly on her.

She wore jeans and a short-sleeved Henley. Throw in the backpack and the cute wispy bangs she'd helped herself to the day before, and she'd nailed the college-girl look.

Before going back to her magazine, she met the guy's stare, hitting him with a quick and universal I'm-not-interested smile.

Taking the hint, he cruised right on by.

These were the moments she'd miss about fieldwork. The rush, no matter how small the victory, that came with succeeding.

Once again, she scanned the area. Her focus landed on Shane, his big body moving down the path at a pace that wasn't quite leisurely but far from hurried. He wore baggie black cargo shorts and an untucked tan T-shirt that neither hugged his big body nor hung loose. Nothing to draw attention. Just an average Joe cutting through the park.

Blending.

He nudged his sunglasses up, hunched his shoulders — blending, blending, blending — and angled around two women pushing baby strollers. Lord, he must have been a good operative. The two of them together? That would have been fun.

He reached the bench, braced one hand on the back of it and dropped a quick kiss on her lips. "Hey, sweets," he said.

Sweets. Funny. She'd been called many things — bitch, whore, conniver — and now she could add sweets to her stable. If only it were true.

He dropped beside her. Still playing the role of attentive lover, he set his big hand over her thigh. She glanced down, spied the corner of a folded note peeping from under his fingers. Casually, she slid her hand under his, burrowing into the warmth of handholding. Along with the note was something hard. Metal.

He nuzzled up to her ear. "Your key and apartment address. Nothing fancy, but it's clean. Good neighborhood. There's an envelope there with everything you need. Including a job lead."

Wow. He worked fast. In less than two days, he'd built her a new life and hooked her up with a potential job.

"That's great. Thank you."

"I know a professor at Northwestern. He mentioned he needs a research assistant. Tell him I sent you. Pay is for shit, but it's enough to get you by for a while."

"I'll work it out. Do I have a work history?"

He nodded. "We didn't have a lot of time, but there's enough to pass a cursory background check." He withdrew his hand. "I should go."

"Yes, you should."

He needed to get up and leave. Just walk away from her because two people on the run from a sadistic foreign leader shouldn't be seen together. It was, in fact, a disaster waiting to happen.

Walk away.

He stood, but — wait — she grabbed his hand, clutching his long fingers while she rose from the bench and ensured no one was in earshot. "What's my name?"

"Faith Burgess."

Faith? Was he kidding? Way too optimistic for her. All she wanted was to survive. She didn't consider that faith. Stubborn, yes. Faith? Not so much.

She shook her head, let out a small snort and stood. "That's funny."

"I thought it fit."

This man didn't know her at all. "Who is she?"

"Three-week-old infant. Died twenty-eight years ago."

She closed her eyes a moment, let that sink in. "A baby."

"Yeah. Took three hours of schlepping through a cemetery looking for someone about your age. I was about to give up and there she was. Faith Burgess. Gotta say, I haven't missed that part of the job."

"The part that requires you to hunt down the names of dead children so you can steal their identities?"

"Exactly."

"Thank you. You saved me."

"You saved yourself. You can find me at my bar — the Corner Tap — if you need something, but unless you're in deep, try not to contact me. Or Dusty."

Liz — *Faith* — nodded. Of all the cover names she'd had, this one would be permanent. As much as it hurt, that letting go of Liz Aiken, she owed it to him to disappear. To sever ties that would get them all killed.

She stepped back, one stomach-shriveling step that left her once again alone. Tipping her chin up, she set her shoulders and her mind ticked back to that first foster family. She could do this. Just like every time she'd started over before.

"Bye, Shane. Take care of yourself."

SHANE PUSHED THROUGH THE BAR'S ALLEY ENTRANCE AND forced his thoughts to the day's tasks rather than Faith Burgess and her Iowa farm girl sweetness.

God willing, he'd never see her again.

Not seeing her brought safety. And maybe her carving out a life for herself. As much as someone could, anyway. The relentless pressure of an assumed identity meant constant scrutiny, checking surroundings, mistrusting new people, wondering if they were the ones sent to kill him.

Or her.

Yeah, not a great life.

But it sure beat dead.

He waved a greeting to the kitchen staff and retreated to his cluttered office, a shoebox of a room barely big enough for a desk and two chairs, never mind the filing cabinet he'd crammed into the corner. Whatever. It was his. And from the hell he'd come out of, even a cramped office and some beat-up secondhand furniture could be considered paradise.

His cell phone rang. Private number. Maybe Dusty or Trev — both cover names like his — calling from a burn phone.

Not a lot of people rang up Shane. Mainly because he

didn't give out his number. If people wanted him, they found him at the bar.

"This is Shane."

"Hey."

Dusty. His voice didn't have that deep baritone of Trev's. Made them easy to identify by one syllable.

Shane closed the office door, eased into his desk chair and propped his feet up. Helluva day so far and he still had fourteen hours until closing.

"What's up?"

"You back from your errand?"

Meaning, was he back from giving the former Liz Aiken a life. Yeah, he was back and in a piss-poor mood.

He should have been happy that he'd helped her. Or, as she put it, saved her. But had he? Most likely, it hadn't hit her yet that he'd just wiped away the last twenty-nine years of her existence. Sure, he'd helped her get a new name and history, but taking on a stolen identity permanently was a whole lot different than doing it for an undercover assignment.

And that nagged at him, bit right into the back of his neck because not only had he wiped away her life, he'd told her to get lost. Even if his intentions were to keep them all safe, he'd abandoned her.

"Yeah, I'm back," he said.

"It go okay?"

"She's probably heading to her place now. What are you up to?"

"I'm at work."

Dusty, the engineering genius, had landed a nine-to-five job — murder for guys like them — at a Chicago trading firm. Shane wasn't sure what the hell Dusty did all day, but it had something to do with managing the company's computer servers. Whatever the job, it paid the bills and kept him out of sight.

"And?"

Dusty never called to make small talk. None of them did. Wasn't their style. When they called, they had something to say and if Shane knew his friend at all, Dusty had more on his mind than checking on Liz-now-Faith.

"I got a call. About Brutus."

Son of a bitch.

Brutus. The nickname the CIA had given Luis Gustavo, an assassin rumored to have ties to the Liborio Cartel. And President Matias Alfaro.

When the cartel wanted someone dealt with, they rang up Luis. It cost them a healthy chunk of their misbegotten profits, but what did they care? Plenty more cash rolling in from their drug and arms smuggling.

If Dusty had received a call about Brutus, chances were that call came from somewhere inside Langley. Specifically Sully, Liz's former coworker who'd sent her to Shane by way of Dusty.

Because, hey, kids, it was no coincidence that they'd provided Faith with a new life and Dusty suddenly had intel on a man associated with a cartel that kicked money up to the corrupt president of Venezuela. A man who'd placed a bounty on not only Shane's head, but now-Faith's also.

Oh, the tangled web...

"Where is he?"

"They tracked him to a town in Ontario. Sault Ste. Marie. Located on the St. Mary's River. Close to the US border. A mere seven-hour drive from our fine city."

Shit.

"Any idea what he's doing there?"

"Nope."

Terrific. "Keep me posted."

Shane disconnected, opened his top desk drawer and grabbed a piece of hard candy out of the bowl. Some people smoked, some drank. Shane? Hard candy. The root beer barrels from the shop near his apartment were his favorite, but he'd run out of those the day before and hadn't had time to buy more. Not yet anyway. He'd been busy giving Faith Burgess a life.

One that, on freaking day two, might already be compromised.

LIZ — *FAITH, I'M FAITH NOW* — SET HER DUFFLE ON HER new bed and plopped down next to it. As Shane had promised, the tiny attic apartment above a two-story single-family home provided a private rear entrance. It was also clean and orderly with a queen-sized bed that appeared lump-free. One long dresser stretched along the wall, anchored by a wicker rocking chair. A woman must have lived here before. Most men didn't buy wicker rocking chairs.

None she knew anyway.

She stretched out on the bed, stared up at the freshly painted ceiling and breathed in.

Home. For a while at least. With little money and even fewer resources, she'd have to stay put for now. In a few months, after working and saving, she'd move on. Maybe find a quiet island somewhere.

Life in the foster system had trained her for solitary existence. That early experience honed her skills for fieldwork. No emotional ties, no hesitation when it came to risks, no pull from home.

A noise below — a chair scraping on a wood floor —

shot her upright. She got to her feet, already reaching for her compact 9mm.

She stood in her new bedroom, weapon aimed at the open doorway. *Wait*. The whoosh in her ears died down, allowing her to focus. To listen for any movement in the apartment.

A five-hundred-square-foot space offered limited hiding places and the inability to move around without being heard. Good for locating bad guys. Bad for getting away from them.

The tick, tick, tick of an analog clock sounded from somewhere. Otherwise?

Silence.

She let out a forced laugh and lowered her weapon. Weeks she'd been on the move, barely sleeping, her mind on alert and now, somehow, she had to manage that, had to stop the constant anxiety, because she couldn't spend her life on edge.

Waiting for a killer.

Cautious, yes. But the stress of a full-blown, hyper-paranoid state would put her in a grave long before Alfaro ever did.

She shook her head and set her 9mm on the bed within reach. Time to get settled. To unpack and grab groceries. Explore the neighborhood. Even if she didn't make friends, knowing her surroundings and where the streets led could save her life.

In the small galley kitchen, she examined the contents of the large envelope Shane had provided. New passport and driver's license. Birth certificate. Cell phone. The all-important cash and a neighborhood map. Look at that, Mr. Thoughtful had marked little x's where she'd find a grocery store and a clothing boutique.

Handy since her only clothes were two pairs of jeans and a few shirts. Sully had promised he'd pack up her apartment in DC and send some things when he felt it was safe, but she'd been rotating the same clothes for two weeks and needed a fresh wardrobe. Her limited funds wouldn't allow for a shopping spree at a boutique, but she could probably swing a few things from a less expensive big box store.

Faith leaned against the counter and stared beyond the breakfast bar big enough for two. An upholstered sofa — a decent caramel one with nicely stuffed cushions — and a metal framed coffee table filled the small living room.

Her new home.

For now, anyway.

Tick, tick, tick. There it was again. That clock might drive her to madness. Given the current circumstances of her life and the fact that a vicious — not to mention pissed-off — corrupt politician wanted her head on a stick, she didn't need the drama of a ticking clock. She turned toward the sound, found the bugger on a small shelf above the sink and removed the battery.

Done.

She set the ceramic clock back on the shelf and placed the battery in the drawer. Now it was time to survey her new neighborhood, discover possible escape routes and hiding places. Maybe she'd stop at the bank on the corner and open an account. Get on with life as Faith Burgess.

She wandered five blocks — all of them lined with bumper-to-bumper parked cars capable of hiding attackers — in search of a coffee shop. According to the app on the phone Shane had given her, she'd find one at the end of the street. She tucked the phone in her jacket pocket and peeped over her shoulder, checking behind her, beside her, everywhere she could sweep a casual glance.

No one following. At least not that she could see. Her pulse kicked — that instinctive paranoia she'd grown used to making itself known.

Now, thanks to Shane Quinn, she could relax. Even if only a little bit.

She'd never be completely safe. Alfaro wasn't a man to give up, but part of Faith's anxiety over the past weeks grew from her lack of a plan. She was no good to the CIA anymore and they'd sent her on her way.

Nice knowing you, thanks for your service, good luck.

That was the risk that came with fieldwork. When you were blown, you were blown. US citizens couldn't foot the bill for every compromised agent.

Faith reached the corner and found the Daily Brew. Quaint little place. Not a typical storefront, but a squat brick building with large windows in front. She pushed through the heavy wood door — nice touch that — and stepped inside. The barista, a woman in her thirties with blond dreadlocks tucked under a bandana, wiped down the counter.

In the far corner, a man sat on a cushioned chair while he pounded the keys on his laptop. Two women with baby strollers occupied one of the three larger tables in the middle of the room.

The long hallway toward the back was troublesome, but she couldn't clear every building she entered. She'd keep her eye on that hallway. Make sure no bad guys came from the back entrance.

"Hi there," the barista said. "Welcome to the Brew. What can I get you?"

Faith stepped to the counter. "Vanilla latte, please. Make it a skinny."

Who needed all the extra calories?

Actually, *she* probably needed them since her jeans hung on her, but she'd worry about her weight later.

"You got it," the woman said. "First time here?"

"Yes."

Why bother providing details? Fieldwork had taught her to keep it simple and concise. Made the lies easier to remember.

"Thanks for coming in. I'm Darla. The owner."

The owner. Good to know.

While Darla prepared the latte, Faith scoped out two empty tables by the front windows. *Not there.* Anyone on the street would have an easy shot.

"That's the Corner Tap," Darla said. "Great cheddar burgers. It's their specialty."

Huh?

Faith looked back at her. "The Corner Tap?"

"The bar."

The Corner Tap.

Across the street, emblazoned with large green-and-white block letters on the window was indeed the Corner Tap.

That fool.

Darla put the finishing touches on the latte and handed it over. "On the house," she said. "A welcome gift."

Well, that was nice. And a terrific way to gain repeat customers. "Thank you." Faith smiled. "I'll definitely be back."

Disregarding her earlier hesitation about the windows, she slid into one of the front tables, her gaze glued to the nicely stained entry door on the bar across the street.

The one owned by Shane Quinn.

3

AT 10:05 ON A STICKY EVENING THAT LEFT SWEAT ALREADY running down his back, Shane squeezed his big-ass body through the mausoleum wall and made his way down the tunnel to their makeshift meeting room.

He checked the door handle — unlocked, of course — and pushed the door open.

"You're late," Dusty said from his usual spot in his soccer-mom chair.

"You're breaking my balls about five minutes? Some of us work evenings. Not exactly easy to take a few hours off when I own a bar." He jerked his chin at Trevor, sitting in his own chair. "Hey, Trev."

In the three weeks since he'd seen his friend, Trev's curly dark hair had grown an inch. Unusual for the usually squeaky-clean former DEA agent. Trev hopped up and they exchanged their typical combo fist-bump-man-hug. Unlike Dusty, Trev was the affectionate one and always, every time, offered up some sort of physical contact.

As men separated from loved ones, they'd become family. A twisted one, but still family.

"Good to see you," Shane said.

"Always."

Trev took his seat again and rather than sit, Shane leaned against the wall, hands in pockets. The cool cement was a welcome relief from the sticky June heat outside. It also helped knock back his aggravation.

Dusty had called this little impromptu meeting — on a goddamned busy night with the Cubs in town — when Shane needed every pair of available hands at the bar.

"What'd you drag me out here for? Guessing it's not a run-of-the-mill kumbaya moment."

"You checked on our girl at all?"

"When did she become *our* girl?"

Dusty shrugged. "How about when you planted her five blocks from the bar and a mile from your apartment?"

Shane gave him a hard look. "I know the neighborhood and needed to place her fast after *you* came to me with her sob story."

Trevor waved them both off. "Relax."

A middle child who came from a family of five kids, Trev had taken on the role of mediating when Shane and Dusty got their shorts in a wad. All in all, the dynamic worked. Otherwise, with the number of times they'd gone at it, either Shane or Dusty would be dead.

Or at least hospitalized.

Brothers to the core.

However, Dusty had a point. When Shane had helped the two men in this room take on new identities, he'd placed them across town, away from each other. And more importantly, away from him.

And then Faith Burgess happened and he'd...? What? Gone temporarily insane?

Shane held his hands up. "What's done is done. And to answer your question, she's okay."

"And you know this how?"

"I've spotted her in the coffee shop across from the bar. She's there way too much."

"Shit," Dusty said. "You're sure it's her?"

"Positive. I gave her a cell phone with her new creds."

Trev let out a snort. "You're tracking her."

"Bet your ass. I helped her. Doesn't mean I trust her. I check her movements every day. She's damned good with varying her pattern and wearing disguises, but she's risking her cover." Shane waved a hand. "Not to mention mine. Maybe that's the point."

Dusty scoffed. "You think she's letting you know you're just as vulnerable if you decide to sell her out? That's horseshit. Sully said she's solid. And, hello, she's not stupid. She probably assumed you're tracking her. She could dump that phone if she wanted."

"Have you talked to her?" Trev asked. "Any contact?"

"Not since I left her in the park. She got that job at Northwestern though. The guy is a regular. He came in the other night. Said he hired her."

"Well, then," Dusty said, "Brace yourself, ladies, because we got a problem."

Not a surprise with the sudden meeting request. On a busy night.

"Spill it so I can get back to work."

"I got word from Sully."

Sully again. That guy was becoming a regular pain in the ass. A bigger pain in the ass than normal.

"And?"

"Brutus left Canada. They think he's in the States."

Well, shit. If Alfaro's assassin left Canada via his original location of Sault Ste. Marie, he could be just hours away. "How does he know?"

"They tracked him when he crossed the border, but lost him. Now he's in the wind."

Shane tipped his head back, resting it against the wall while he ran scenarios. "He probably stole a boat."

Dusty shrugged. "A boat *was* found docked at a Michigan marina. No one aboard. They ran the serial number."

Shane met Dusty's gaze. "Let me guess. Wrong boat."

"Correct-a-mundo. The vessel assigned to that serial number is sitting in dry dock in Ontario."

"Knew it. He found a similar one, hot-wired it, painted the serial number on it and sailed to Michigan."

Fucking Brutus. So damned predictable and yet no one could catch him.

Trevor held his hands up. "Let's not get ahead of ourselves. They lost him in Ontario, right? No one is saying *he* stole that boat. Could be anyone."

Trev, always Mary Sunshine. Always wanting to give people the benefit of the doubt. For a hardened DEA agent living undercover, the guy was almost annoying with how much he saw the bright side.

But Shane loved him for it. Of the three of them, Trevor still had hope.

"He's right," Dusty said. "Sully is trying to confirm it was Brutus. But, yeah, could be someone else."

These boys were full of wishful thinking today. Shane let out a sarcastic grunt. "And if it's not, why is Alfaro's number one muscle in Michigan?"

The two of them stared at him, neither willing to accept

the inevitable. Well, Shane would have to help them. "Face it. Michigan is easy access to Chicago. *Someone* leaked her location."

Probably that dickweed Sully.

Apparently reading Shane's mind, Dusty shook his head. "Not Sully. He swears it. Could be someone on his staff." Dusty sat forward, propped his elbows on his knees. "Does it matter? I mean, we don't know if it's Brutus. I'm just passing info along. Could be nothing."

He was right. Could be nothing. But if it wasn't?

Shane boosted off the wall, headed for the door. "I need to warn her."

AFTER A NIGHT SPENT CRUISING BY FAITH'S HOUSE AND getting zero sleep, Shane arrived at the bar at 7:40 the following morning.

Battling the weighty press of fatigue, he stood by the back door for a few measly seconds, his face tipped to the sun's warmth.

Combat nap. At some point, he'd stretch out on his office floor and sleep for twenty. Just enough to sharpen him again. Now he'd head over to the coffee shop where the handy app on his phone indicated Faith's presence. She should know better than to frequent any location.

Damn, the woman. The whole situation irritated him, but her being so close gave him the opportunity to make contact while staying undercover.

He pushed through the shop's entrance and the instant aroma of fresh ground beans sent his internal circuits firing. Typically, he drank his own sludge in the morning and treated himself to the good stuff in the afternoon.

A pattern, he supposed, he'd fallen into. Just like Faith. Damn. He was as guilty as her. Between the two of them, they were lucky they hadn't gotten cozy with a bullet.

This time of morning on a Saturday, a few early risers in varying states of dress sat at tables or stood in line. Some in business clothes, some in workout gear, a few college-aged kids who looked like they hadn't made it to bed yet.

He took his place at the back of the line, fiddling with his phone, scrolling through emails while he waited. From the corner of his eye, he spotted Faith sitting at a table three back from the window, her shoulder-length hair pulled into a ponytail that accentuated her sweet face.

She kept her head down and her nose in her phone. Who the hell knew if she was reading or, like him, trying to look busy?

Either way, she'd seen him come in. Good field operatives kept an eye on their surroundings.

The line whittled down and he stepped to where Darla ran the register.

"Well, hey, Shane. You're in early today."

He offered up a smile and limited eye contact. Friendly, but not too friendly. "I couldn't take my sludge this morning. Figured I'd swing in."

"The usual?"

"Yeah."

The usual for him was the dark roast. Black. Full firepower. And yet another pattern he hadn't realized he'd established.

Darla snagged a sixteen-ounce cup from the stack and handed it off to the barista. "I have a new blend I want you to try. It's strong and barely drinkable."

At that Shane chuckled. "Hell of a recommendation, Darla."

"I know. It's a Colombian bean with a hint of jasmine. Maybe a little vanilla thrown in. A guy came in the other day and suggested I order it. He said it's the best coffee he's ever had. I'll use you as my test subject. If you like it, I'll start carrying it."

"Ooh, the pressure."

Darla laughed. "Somehow I think you can handle it. Faith," she called over her shoulder, "this is Shane. He owns the bar across the street. He's the burger guy."

And thank you, Darla, for making my life a shit-ton easier right now.

He handed Darla a ten and glanced over at Faith who finally looked up from her phone. Her eyes held that oh-shit stare that should have been funny, yet wasn't. What the hell did she expect when she squatted ninety feet from his front door?

"Faith is new in town," Darla said. "I was telling her about your cheddar burgers. Told her to check 'em out."

Shane smiled. "Thanks. Appreciate it. I'll stop and say hello."

"Sure thing. God knows you've spent enough money in here for me to return the favor."

Darla handed him his change. He threw the coins and a buck in the tip jar and shoved the rest in his wallet. While in there, he grabbed one of his business cards and snatched a pen from the cup near the register.

Card in hand, he moved to the end of the counter. The barista slid the cup to him and he headed straight for Faith.

On his approach, she peered up at him and hit him with that same sweet smile. Her eyes though, the deep brown that bordered on black, turned hard. Dangerous.

Yeah, sweetheart, this isn't a social call.

"Hi." He set his coffee down, made a production of

shaking her hand in case any busybodies watched. "I'm Shane."

"Hi, Shane. Pleasure to meet you."

"You too." He wrote a note — time and place she should meet him that evening — on the back of the card he'd pulled from his wallet and set it on the table. "Come by the bar. Give this to the server and they'll take care of you."

She picked up the card, studied the front, then casually flipped it, reading his note. "I'll take you up on that. I'm always up for a good burger."

"Shane," Darla called, "did you try that coffee yet? Tell me what you think."

He picked up the cup, took a sip. Strong. Really strong. He didn't know about the jasmine-vanilla tones. He couldn't think that hard, but for a guy who liked his coffee with a kick, it did the job. Hell, he hadn't had coffee this potent since...

Shit.

Darla passed the register duties off to one of her employees and wandered to the end of the counter just across from where Shane stood.

"How is it?"

"Wicked good. Colombian, you said?"

Colombia. Right next door to Venezuela.

"It is. The guy who requested it has a Spanish accent."

Come on. Could this be? He stood for a second while his blood pressure spiked high enough to give him a stroke.

Couldn't be Brutus. No way.

But...

Shane held one hand out just above his head. "Tall guy? Dark hair? Scar above his eyebrow?"

Darla cocked her head. "His hair is blond, but he has the scar. You know him?"

He sure did.

4

FAITH STEPPED OFF A CURB IN A QUIET NORTHSIDE neighborhood filled with elegant brownstones and neat row houses. She paused while a black cargo van cruised thru the intersection. She checked the street sign, its letters barely visible under the darkening sky. According to her phone, one more block and she'd be at the gyro place Shane had written on the card.

Odd meeting point in the middle of a residential neighborhood, but she supposed he had a plan. And a reason for calling this meeting. Maybe he'd simply spotted her at the coffee shop each day and wanted to ream her.

If so, she'd tell him to conserve his energy. Anything he'd say she already knew and berated herself over since that first morning a couple of weeks back when she'd woken up early and the apartment walls, the unfamiliarity, closed in on her.

Suffocated her.

Then she looked at the clock and knew, based on what Shane had told her about where to find him, he'd probably be heading to the bar at some point.

And she could see him. If only to catch a glimpse of someone who understood. Someone who'd lived this life.

A compatriot.

A hot compatriot she'd been fantasizing about since he'd first set those icy blue eyes on her.

That was all it took to get her out of the house and to the coffee shop. Each day after, she'd made the same careless decision, justifying it by telling herself that she was keeping tabs on him. Searching for anything suspicious. Making sure he was safe while all that time she put him in danger simply by being there. Oh, the vicious cycle.

At least now she did it around her work schedule at the university rather than sitting like a shut-in all day.

Her job. Something else Shane had helped her with. The favors she owed him continued to stack up. Someday, she'd figure out a way to repay him.

Beside the parked vehicles lining the street, a small gray sedan slowed. She shifted her gaze, peeping out of the corner of her eye. She picked up her pace and sucked in the sticky humidity of a ninety-degree evening near the lake. A bead of sweat slid down her neck as she moved her hand closer to the trusty 9mm under her shirt. If that failed, she'd go for the knife at the hem of her jeans.

"Excuse me," a man called.

She kept walking, trudging through the thick, heavy air while taking stock of the space ahead. A metal garbage can. A decorative planter in front of a house two doors up. A pile of bricks. All makeshift weapons.

"Excuse me," the man said again.

Now this guy was becoming a pain in the ass and it fired every one of her nerves. She kept walking, ignoring him while eyeing the bricks just ahead.

"Lady, are you leaving?"

Was she *leaving*?

She glanced over at his car, creeping along the road beside her while traffic built up behind.

Parking spot.

Ohmygod. He wanted her damned parking spot, not to kill her.

Great life, Liz.

Faith. Her name was Faith now.

"No," she said. "Sorry."

The man waved and gunned the gas, the other cars following as some of the tension left her.

She kept walking. Another half block and she'd be at the meeting point. She checked her phone. No calls or messages.

A cargo van — same van? — halted beside the fire hydrant to her left and the ka-chunk of a moving door drew her gaze.

The side door slid open. A tall man wearing a balaclava hood leaped out. Charged toward her.

Cold numbness froze her.

Run.

Scream.

Yes, she'd scream. On a city block like this, there'd be hundreds of people sitting in their homes.

"Help!"

Run.

She backed up, swiveled right, peered up the block. Shane. He'd be at their meeting point. He'd help her.

She took one step — *too late.* An arm clamped around her waist, squeezing so hard the pressure sent a sharp breath through her lips.

Fight. Scream. Draw attention. Anything to scare him off.

"Help!"

She kicked out, throwing elbows, trying to get the right angle. *Fight, fight, fight.*

No good.

She kicked again, connecting with his shin, but he had that iron arm around her, lifting her clear off the ground as he dragged her toward the van.

Too strong.

But if he got her inside that vehicle...game over.

"Help!"

Someone had to hear her. In this neighborhood, on this upscale, well-tended street with pretty potted flowers, screaming couldn't be common.

She kicked again, connecting with her attacker's knee.

"Ow. *Mierda.*"

Spanish. No, no, no. They'd found her. She'd been too careless. Too damned careless.

Panic consumed her and she fought her spinning thoughts. Focused on the bricks just ahead.

And escaping.

"Help me! Someone!"

"Hurry up!" a man inside the van shouted.

"No," she said. And then she gave up on the help-me's and let out a long, he's-attacking-me scream that would scare the ever-loving shit out of *someone* and get them on the phone to 911.

She reared back and — *bam!* — elbowed him on the side of the head.

"Ow! Stop," he gritted out, his English clear but heavily accented.

"Never."

Memories of that nasty basement, Alfaro's son on top of her, his grip on her throat...

She kicked again, her heel connecting with his shin as he reached the van.

Too strong. He was too damned strong. *I'll never win.* If he got her to that van, another man would join the fun and it would be that dank, smelly basement in Venezuela all over again.

Knife. She needed the knife. Or her gun.

"Get her in here," the man in the van said.

The second man, also hooded, reached out and she swung at him. Feral. Wild.

"Look out," the driver said, half laughing. "She's swinging."

"No shit, Sherlock," the second guy said. American. The two guys in the van were definitely American.

He reached for her and she swung again, both hands moving, blocking, punching. *Win.*

"Jesus Christ."

"Hey!" a voice sounded from somewhere behind her.

A man standing at his front door, the overhead light shining on him as he leaped off the porch.

The iron grip around her loosened and she ripped off another kick, connecting with her attacker's shin again.

"Help me!"

"Leave her alone!"

The guy from the house was at the curb in seconds and horns behind the van sounded.

"Leave her," the driver said. "Too much attention."

"It gets worse from here," she told them and kicked again.

Then the guy from the house was at the rear bumper of the car parked near the curb, his arms extended, reaching for her.

"Let's go!" the driver hollered.

The pressure at her mid-section released — just gone — and her body was in a free fall.

Ooofff, she landed on all fours and pain shot from her knees and wrists straight up her limbs.

The tall guy hopped in the van and she bolted to her feet. The door slid closed, the ka-chunk once again breaking through the panic devouring her.

And then the van was in motion, roaring down the block. The man from the house reached for her.

No, no, no. No touching.

Still on her knees, she whipped her arm away and he threw his hands up. "Sorry. Sorry! Are you okay? You're safe now."

That's what he thought.

Still trembling, she set one foot on the ground, levering up to both feet. "I'm...fine. Thank you. I...have...to go."

Shane. By now, he'd be at their meeting place. He'd help her.

She ran, her feet pounding against the sidewalk, further angering her already aching knees.

"Wait," the guy said from behind her. "My wife called the cops."

Terrific. Damned do-gooders. But those do-gooders had probably just saved her life.

She kept running. Using the last of her adrenaline to storm by the homes. A few more and she'd be at the corner. And right around that corner would be the restaurant.

Shane.

She picked up speed. Please, please, please. Let him be there.

She reached the corner, made the turn and — *crash* — slammed into someone a whole lot bigger than her, sending her bouncing off his much bigger body.

He looked down, his hands immediately steadying her.

Shane. Relief poured over her, knocking her tension back enough to focus on her next move.

"Oh my God," she said. "We have to get out of here. They found me. Three guys in a van. They took off."

He gripped her arm and did a visual sweep of her body. "Are you all right?"

"Yes."

"Then let's go."

5

LIZ — _FAITH_ — DOUBLE-TIMED HER STEPS TO KEEP PACE WITH Shane who might possibly be breaking speed-walking records while they traversed an open field in the pitch black.

After the almost-abduction, he'd hustled her to his car, a white sedan they'd driven in for nearly thirty minutes until he'd parked across from an iron fence surrounding a vast field. He'd given her a boost over the fence to speed the process. She'd climbed many a fence in her day and could have easily done it on her own.

But this was different. Help. Support. Camaraderie.

And that, she hadn't had a whole lot of recently.

If ever.

Aside from her grandmother, that saintly woman who'd taken in a wild-child ten-year-old whose mother found it fitting to join a religious cult. This after not being totally sure who exactly Liz's father might have been.

For all her faults, Mom had had the good sense to leave Liz — _Faith_ — behind. And wasn't that name ironic considering the whole religious cult thing?

"Um," Faith said. "Where are we going?"

He neither slowed nor looked at her.

"It's safe," Shane said.

Total non-answer, but at this point, did it even matter? Clearly, he had a plan. All well and good, but hey, this was her life too.

The last time she didn't know her destination she'd wound up in a basement with a couple of guys who tried to gang rape her so, yeah, she wanted to know where the hell he was leading her.

In the blackness, she halted. "I get it," she said. "I've compromised you. I'm sorry for that, but this isn't working for me. I need to know where I'm going."

Shane stopped too. For a few seconds he tipped his head back and stared up at a starlit sky.

"You read my file," she said. "You know what happened to me in Venezuela."

She couldn't see his features clearly enough in the dark, but he looked at her for a few long seconds. "Over this hill. See the lights? It's a mausoleum. When I first came to Chicago, I worked here while figuring out how to open the bar. I found an abandoned coal mine underneath the mausoleum. When we want privacy, we come here."

They were in a cemetery? That was once a coal mine? Well, *that* she hadn't expected.

"Who's we?"

"Me, Dusty and Trevor."

Okay. That was...okay. She supposed. She hadn't met either man, but Dusty had been instrumental in getting her to Shane.

"How the hell did you find a coal mine?"

He laughed. "I'm nosy. Recon Marines tend to be that way."

She cocked her head, refusing to let him off the hook that easy.

He waved a barely visible hand. "My job here was grounds maintenance. One day I found a grate. The wall around it was deteriorating. I pulled it out and found a shaft." He shrugged. "I was curious and crawled around in there. Now, if we can stop talking, you'll see where we're going."

Five minutes later, after coming over the hill and meandering through some gravestones, they reached a giant building with carved marble columns along the facade.

Shane led her around back and used a key to open the door, making sure it locked behind them. She followed him into a narrow hallway stuffed with lawn care supplies. Whether it was the gardening tools or the supplies, a pungent, earthy smell — fertilizer — permeated the confined air. She held her breath for a few seconds, letting her senses adjust while walking.

"Aren't you worried about security cameras?"

"Cameras are only on the entrances and the front of the buildings. I avoid those areas."

They stopped at an air vent covered by a grate he promptly removed.

"Tail me," Shane told her. "Once we're in there, it would help if you could reach back and pull the grate back into place. No one has ever come along, but the way things are going, we're not risking it."

He squeezed his enormous body through the opening — no easy feat, that — and fired up his phone's flashlight, illuminating the enclosed space. Faith stayed close, following him through yet another opening into a dusty tunnel.

"Unbelievable," she breathed, not bothering to hide her wonder that he'd uncovered this hidey-hole.

As a field agent, these types of discoveries always mesmerized her. In Venezuela, illegal gold mines operated in jungles lined with underground tunnels. All equipped with makeshift pulleys to move product.

On her escape, she'd hidden in one of those tunnels while waiting for her military escort — a Venezuelan soldier she'd aided with food and water for his family prior to her abduction — to smuggle her out of the country. Favors equaled currency. Always.

The thought brought her back to that place and the gut-shredding fear over being discovered.

She shook the thought away. Here and now. That's what she needed to focus on. Staying alert and strong and finding a way to be rid of Alfaro.

Shane unlocked another door and opened it.

Pitch-black.

Once again, her mind tripped back to Venezuela. To being shoved into a dank basement that reeked of piss.

No way.

No.

Way.

Light illuminated the area and she blinked, letting her eyes once again adjust to Shane, who'd turned his phone's flashlight off and lit a lantern that sat on the floor in the small room.

"You're safe," he said when she refused to enter the room. "I promise."

Somehow, when he said it, she believed it. After all he'd done for her, he deserved as much.

She needed to settle down. Get focused. She forced a

breath. A long, slow one that knocked her pulse down a few beats.

She nodded. "I don't know why you brought me here. Alfaro has found me. The quicker I leave, the better off we'll all be."

SHANE DIDN'T KNOW WHAT THE HELL HE WAS DOING, BUT ONE thing he did know was that Liz — Faith — wasn't going anywhere.

And what the frig was that about? He should be handing over another pile of his emergency cash, driving this woman somewhere far away and telling her to watch her cute little ass.

"Come in," he told Faith who was still out in the hall. "Grab a chair. It's not the Ritz, but it's private. And safe."

She stepped inside, her gaze darting over the dirty walls and dusty floor before taking the soccer chair closest to the exit.

Shane closed the door, then leaned against the side wall, giving her plenty of space. After the ordeal she'd just experienced, he'd keep his distance. Let her settle in and get comfortable again.

"Just so you know," he said. "Dusty and Trevor are on their way."

"Why?"

He kept his hands at his sides. No folding his arms, no stiff body language that might freak her out. "Because they might be exposed, too. Especially Dusty, since he communicated with Sullivan. If they're vulnerable, they need to decide for themselves what to do. Have you heard of Luis Gustavo? He's known as Brutus."

"In our line of work, anyone who's come close to Venezuela knows Gustavo does Alfaro's wet work."

"Sully alerted us that Gustavo was in Canada. They lost him, but a boat that disappeared from Canada was found in Michigan. Then, this morning, Darla gave me that damned coffee."

Faith narrowed her eyes. "Coffee?"

"Yeah. The one she asked me how I liked. When I was in Venezuela, I was addicted to a Columbian blend Alfaro served in the palace. What Darla had me try this morning? Columbian. And *really* similar to what Alfaro liked. Darla special-ordered it for some dude with a Spanish accent. I'm concerned it's Brutus — Gustavo — who attacked you."

FAITH'S HEAD DIPPED FORWARD. TOO MUCH. ALL OF IT. SHE'D been so careful getting to Chicago, covering her tracks, staying off the grid, only using cash and burner phones and now Alfaro had tracked her.

More than likely at the coffee shop. Her own fault.

How, how, how did she think she'd be able to get away from that man? That ruthless, power-hungry, vengeful prick.

Shane had done it and his success, if abandoning his life and living under an assumed name could be considered success, had lulled her into thinking that she'd pull it off.

But Shane hadn't killed the man's son. She had. She'd taken a life, even though it was to save her own, and Alfaro wouldn't stop until he took hers.

An eye for an eye.

She let out a sharp huff. "They found me."

Still leaning on the wall, Shane nodded. "Based on what just happened to you, we have to assume so." He held up a hand before she could respond. "By the time Brutus checks in with Alfaro and tries to locate you again, we'll have you somewhere else."

"No. We can't risk your cover. Or Dusty and Trevor's. I'm not worth it." She headed to the door. "I grabbed my backup creds before I left my apartment. Since you'd summoned me to a meeting, I figured something was up. I grabbed my backup creds before I left my apartment. It's one of my covers from an op two years ago. I brought it from DC just in case. I'll use it to get...somewhere...and then get new creds."

"No," Shane said. "We're not there yet."

"Um, yeah, we are. I'm better alone anyway. I'm used to it."

Finally, he moved. She hadn't missed his attempt to stay glued to the wall. Being the smart man he was, he'd given her space. Enough of it to get her focused and not worried about the fact she was cloistered in an abandoned mine where anyone could walk in and eliminate her.

He stepped closer, then stopped, still leaving three feet between them. "I have an idea. If you don't like it, you can go. At least listen first." He held one hand out, waiting for her to grab hold. "Trust me. I've got you."

Trust him.

So far, he'd done nothing but help her. If she *was* being followed, all her trips to the coffee shop could have gotten him killed. And yet, he hadn't abandoned her.

Lord, what had she done to this man? She grabbed his hand, gave it a hard squeeze.

At least with him, she already knew he wouldn't turn her over to Alfaro. Turning her over meant blowing his — and his friends' — cover.

That, Shane had told her, he'd do anything to protect.

Even if it meant her going along for the ride.

. . .

A DOUBLE, THEN TRIPLE KNOCK — THE SAFE SIGNAL — sounded on the door before Dusty and Trevor strode through.

"Hey," Shane said.

The two men nodded at him and turned their gazes to Faith, who'd claimed her seat again.

Shane waved his hand between them. "This is Dusty and Trevor."

"Hey, girl," Dusty said, "good to meet you in person."

"You too. Thank you. For everything." She lifted her hand, then let it drop. "I'm sorry I dragged you into this. All of you."

"No worries. Sully says you're good people. And he doesn't like a lot of people, so that's saying something."

Trevor snorted and held his hand to Faith, who returned the gesture.

"Glad you're okay," Trevor said. "Hopefully, we'll get you out of this."

"What's the plan?" Dusty asked.

Hell if Shane knew. All he had was an idea and, at this point, there was no controlling his thoughts. This woman had him rolling. Rolling, rolling, rolling. And that wasn't like him. The constant mental chaos and conflict.

But he'd been — some days still was — in her place. Alone, scared and running. Trying to figure out how to stay alive.

"Between the intel from Sully, the boat, the coffee and someone trying to snatch Faith, let's assume Brutus is in Chicago."

"Which means I need to leave," Faith said. "I won't risk all of you. Not after what you've done for me."

"No," Shane said.

She rose from the chair, shaking her head. "I don't know if you've got a hero complex or what, but I've been on my own a long time. I can deal with this."

Hero complex? What the fuck? He cocked his head, gave her the squinty-eyed stare his former teammates said made them piss themselves. "You don't know shit about me."

"I know you should get your head out of your ass. Doing this on my own is the way to go. I need to disappear."

Dusty snorted. "Great plan, baby girl. However, this isn't about just you anymore."

She faced Dusty, giving her own death glare and Shane understood what his former teammates felt because, yeah, he might piss himself.

"I know that, baby *boy*."

Eee-doggies, she had a solid set of balls. Before the two of them got scrappy, Shane put his hands up. "If we're assuming Brutus is here, we're further assuming he's frequenting the coffee shop. Right across from my bar."

"Shit," she said. "I led Alfaro straight to you."

"Technically," Dusty said, "Shane helped. I mean, dumb ass that he is, he planted you smack in the middle of his neighborhood."

Shane grunted. Leave it to Dusty to point out the obvious. "I can't believe I haven't kicked your ass yet. However, you are correct. Call it a lapse in judgment. I thought I could keep an eye on her."

He'd gotten too complacent. Too comfortable in his everyday routine. It might prove to be his biggest mistake yet.

"Alfaro," he said, "wants both our heads. We're not giving them to him."

"Of course we're not," she said. "But how do we accomplish that?"

"We find Brutus."

She gawked. "And what? Invite him to Darla's for a cup of that coffee he loves so much? What's the point? As long as Alfaro is alive, he'll keep sending people after me."

Shane clucked his tongue. "True. Brutus may have found *you*. What we don't know is if he found *me*. I need to know if I'm blown. We have to locate Brutus and question him."

"And then what?" Faith asked. "Wish him bon voyage and send him on his way?"

Another smartass. Excellent. "Funny," he said, "but no. Once we have answers, we kill him."

6

DID HE JUST SAY . . .

Shane Quinn might be a man after her own heart with these ambitious ideas.

Faith folded her arms, tapping her right index finger against her biceps. "Even if we pulled that off, there are a thousand more Gustavos out there. Alfaro will send another one."

"But it'll buy us time to regroup. Brutus is independent. I met him at the palace a couple of times. Rumor had it he's good, but drives Alfaro nuts. He doesn't check in enough. Disappears for weeks at a time and then shows up when the job is complete. They're used to him going dark. If we eliminate him before he finds us, we'll buy ourselves a couple of weeks to regroup. You got a better idea?"

She wished she did. Maybe he was right. Killing Brutus wouldn't solve the problem, but a few weeks would give her enough time to settle somewhere else. And what the hell kind of lives were they living where calmly discussing ending a man's life was the best option?

She continued tapping her finger against her arm. *Tap-*

tap. Tap-tap. Tap-tap.

"Hey," he said. "We're working this on the fly. I don't have all the answers."

"I get that. Believe me. It took me days with no sleep to get out of Venezuela. I'm good on the fly. My boss didn't call me Queen of the Pivot for nothing. But I'm not risking your lives anymore."

"We're not leaving you," Dusty said.

Great. Now him too?

Dusty clapped his hands together. "We're wasting time. How do we find this guy?"

She eyed him, took in the set of his jaw. She'd learned enough about men to know he wouldn't be swayed. She went back to Shane, who wore the same stubborn look.

"Come on," she said. "You can't do this."

Shane cocked his head. "If we do, we'll all be safer."

God, these men. As much as she hated it, they were right. And this was her fault. In her quest to keep herself safe, she'd brought heat to Shane.

Still, she couldn't have known Alfaro was after Shane as well. Sully should have warned her.

Sully. He could help them. She waved a hand. "I'll ask Sully how we find Brutus."

"Shane doesn't trust him."

Interesting. She faced Dusty. "Why?"

The two men exchanged a look. "Sully," Shane said, his gaze still on his friend, "you will learn, has a big mouth."

"Not that big," Faith said, "because he never told me Alfaro was after you. If he had, we wouldn't be in this mess. What's your problem with him?"

He finally broke eye contact with Dusty and gave her his attention. "Dusty got caught in a jackpot that involved Sully. Miraculously, Sully came out unscathed."

"It wasn't a big deal," Dusty added. "Shane's *sensitive.*"

"When my friends get fucked? Bet your ass." He faced Faith again. "*Your* relationship with him, however, seems solid."

Oh, no he didn't. "If you're implying I'm screwing him, you're way out of line."

Dusty let out a snort. "That's exactly what he's implying. Our guy here is trying to ascertain your loyalty to Sully."

She supposed she couldn't blame him for that. Considering Sully had risked their safety by sending her to them. "He's a friend. If he's interested in more than that, it's not my problem and it's definitely not something I've encouraged. I don't need the drama."

She reached into her back pocket for her phone — the burner she carried in addition to the one Shane had given her — and checked the signal. Nothing. Not a surprise since they were in a damned coal mine.

She held the phone up. "When we get outside, I'll call him. See what he's got on Brutus."

Shane stepped back, leaned against the wall and propped one foot on it. "There might be another option."

Excellent. Considering they seemed to be short on options. "I'm all ears."

"There was a woman. Leslie Larshot. She worked for Alfaro doing intelligence work. She's beautiful and charming. If Alfaro needed intel from world leaders, he invited them to his compound and unleashed her on them. At the time, her brother worked in the compound as well."

Not uncommon considering men — at least in Faith's opinion — habitually let their sexual urges overrule their common sense. Just ask the two guys she'd gutted on a basement floor.

"What does she have to do with Brutus?"

"After seeing her in action, Alfaro realized she could help Brutus on certain jobs. She'd lure men in and Brutus took them out."

"She traveled with him?"

Shane jerked his head. One solid nod. "She did. Knows his quirks. The types of places he likes to stay, restaurants and such. She knows our enemy better than the agency or Alfaro."

Finally, Dusty boosted himself off the wall. "How do we find her? We can't exactly reach out on Twitter."

At that, Faith laughed. Good one.

"When I was in Venezuela," Shane said. "I flipped her. Made her an asset. She wanted out and we promised we'd help. By then, she'd seen enough and wanted a better life for her and her brother, Reynaldo, but he refused to leave."

Now this might be a promising lead. If nothing else, a way to take an offensive stance rather than a defensive one.

"Can you still make contact?" Faith asked. "We could talk to her. Maybe she'll tell us how we find Brutus and get ahead of him. It'll save us time if she can give us a lead. She probably also knows his weaknesses. We can exploit those."

Shane shook his head. "Yeah. If we can find her. After the agency got what they needed out of her, she was given a new identity. Last I heard she was in Alabama. That was right before I got burned."

Whether Shane liked it or not, if this woman was a CIA asset, Jonathan Sullivan could help them. "We need Sully. I'm calling him."

She headed out the door into the dirt-strewn hallway, heard the swish of fabric behind her and peered back to find Shane and Trevor on her heels and Dusty quickly locking the door.

Uh, no. She wouldn't do this with an audience. *Sorry,*

boys. "Are we making this a conference call?"

"We'll give you privacy," Shane said, "but you're not standing out there alone."

Excellent. Now they were chained at the hip. Time for her to set these boys straight about a few things. She reached the hole they crawled through to enter the mine and spun back. "We need to be clear on a few things."

"Uh-oh," Trevor said. "It's the mom tone."

Shane made no attempt to hide a sigh.

"You're not calling the shots," she said. "I've been working solo a long time. Personally and professionally. I don't need a bunch of alphas taking over. I'm grateful for the help you've given me, but this is my life and if you're expecting me to fall in line, it won't happen."

"Fall in line?"

Shane stepped closer, his gaze pinned to hers and the confined space grew...small. Really small. *Whoopsie.* She'd apparently hit a nerve. She held her breath and waited for the yelling to start.

"We *know,*" Shane said, "what it feels like to have no control. To feel trapped. If anyone should be laying down demands, it's us. You could seriously fuck us over."

No yelling. But his quiet tone, the punch of the words, had an equally devastating effect.

"I wouldn't do that," she said.

His hand shot up. "How about we agree that we're all in this for the right reasons? And, yeah, there will be times when one or more of us will try to take over. That's what we do. You don't survive in our line of work without being aggressive. And that goes for you too. Don't lose your shit when it happens. We operate as a team. That work for you?"

A team. Yeesh. She sucked at teamwork. Supremely sucked. It wasn't that she didn't appreciate a team environment. She simply did better on her own. Pivoting was so much easier without a partner. Or three.

She nodded. "Fine."

"Good," Shane said. "Now let's call that prick Sully and see what he can tell us about Leslie Larshot."

THE SECOND SHANE CRAWLED OUT OF THE AIR DUCT, HIS phone dinged. Three times. His bartender letting him know they were short on olives, bitters and the all-important straws. He'd deal with that in the morning.

Faith followed him through the opening, her phone in hand. He waved her down the hall and walked while checking his texts. "Let's get out of here before you call Sullivan. I don't like lingering. You never know if someone'll come in."

"I can call while we're moving. I'd like some privacy though."

And why would she need privacy unless his suspicions about her relationship with Sully might be spot-on? Could he trust this woman?

Hell, it was probably way too late to think of that now.

"You can walk ahead of us," he told her. "Is that a burner phone?"

"Yes. I carry this and the one you gave me."

"Good."

"I feel bad enough dragging you into this situation. I won't further compromise you by calling the CIA on the phone you gave me. Besides, I think of that phone as Faith's. The burners are about my former life. Liz's life."

He glanced over at her. "I get that. It sucks that we live this way, but..."

"It's safer. We both know it."

True 'dat.

Once outside, Faith picked up her pace, leading the charge across the vast cemetery. Shane, Dusty and Trevor hung back, but kept her in sight in case they had to reach her in a hurry. Say, if a psychotic serial killer working for Alfaro popped up in the middle of a cemetery.

Jesus, the paranoia. Total killer.

Beside him, Dusty stared up at a sky dotted with stars, then brought his attention back to Faith, walking ahead of them. "What're you thinking?"

"Besides that this day won't end and my paranoia might get me committed?"

"Yeah. Besides that."

"She can't go back to her apartment."

"No way." This from Trevor on the other side of Dusty. "Hotel?"

Damn, Shane didn't know. Hotels had cameras. Plus, Brutus might be making calls to see if she was in residence.

Assuming he knew her new name.

That's what Shane would do. Just start calling hotels and asking for her.

Then again, there were so damned many hotels in the city, it'd be easy to hide. Except...cameras. Was it worth the risk?

The implications bounced around in his mind, ping-ponging in all directions.

Like Dusty, he peered up at the starlit sky, drew a long pull of fresh air to settle his mental bedlam. *Concentrate here, buddy.*

"Wait," Dusty said. "You're not —"

"Taking her to my place and risking both of us? Yeah. What option is there?"

Trevor peered around Dusty. "Dude, that's *nuts*. What

the hell are you thinking?"

As they walked, he held up a finger. "It *is* nuts. But, I live in a first-floor unit where every window and door is armed. If anyone so much as touches something, the alarm goes off."

"Shane, I'm—" Dusty ran one hand down his face. "Fuck. I shouldn't have—"

Shane stopped walking and faced his friends. "No. No way. You did the right thing sending her to me. If you hadn't, she might be dead now. It's our rotten luck Brutus is that damned good. How the hell did he track her? I mean, how many people know where she is? Far as I know, only us and Sullivan. Someone who knew where she was leaked it to Alfaro."

"It's not Sully."

"How do you know?"

"I don't. Except, I do. He's not *that* guy."

Shane didn't believe it. Not for one second. Jonathan Sullivan would sell his soul if it got him promoted.

"I don't know what it's gonna take for you to realize he *is* that guy. And I'm not letting him fuck us over. That's not happening."

"It's me." Faith said when Jonathan Sullivan answered his cell phone. "Virginia."

Her code name, inspired by wartime spy Virginia Hall, came in handy when she needed to reach Sully. He'd been her coworker, her mentor and, she liked to believe, her friend.

Was he ambitious to a fault? Probably. In DC that described ninety percent of the sharks she'd come in contact with. Kill or be killed environment, that one.

"Virginia." The name rolled from his tongue slowly, the disbelief evident. "Nice to hear from you. How are you? "

Simply on the basis of this phone call, he knew damn well she wasn't any good. Why else would she be risking her apparently already compromised new identity.

Still marching through the grass, she swung a look over her shoulder where Shane, Trevor and Dusty trailed behind, shadowed in darkness.

She went back to Sully. "I've had better days. Bad news from my brother. You remember Rodney."

Before she'd come to Chicago, they'd agreed Shane's code name would be Rodney.

"Is he off the wagon again?"

Off the wagon. What the hell was he talking about? Had they discussed code for that? She thought back to their last conversation. Nothing. Whatever. "Rodney's marriage fell apart a few years ago. Ugly split. Now, his ex appears to be back. And, you know she hates me as much as she does Rodney. We're both having to deal with her nastiness."

A long pause ensued. Was he even understanding her reference to Alfaro?

"I'd heard about that," he said.

Excellent. Somehow, he'd deciphered her hints. "It's a shame."

"I'm sorry to hear that." He paused for a few seconds, the line filling with silence. "Virginia, someone is at my door. Can I call you right back?"

Calling her back meant ditching his cell phone for an untraceable burner he'd toss after the call.

She hung up and glanced back at the three men trailing twenty feet behind. She kept moving, tromping through a patch of longer grass in the open field where graves had yet to be dug.

If she could focus on the good, on the kindness of people willing to help — the positives — she'd be okay. She'd find a way out of this and once again escape from Alfaro and his henchmen.

A fresh start. For her? No big deal. Between her mother walking out, her grandmother's death, bouncing from foster home to foster home, she'd learned to navigate ever-changing landscapes.

In Faith's world, love wasn't important enough for people to stick around.

Her phone rang, shattering her miserable thoughts. "Hello?"

"It's me," Sully said, his voice more clipped than a minute ago. "Secure line. What the hell's going on?"

They hadn't come up with code names for Alfaro and Brutus yet and she needed him to understand. Quickly. She didn't have time to mess with code names and explaining things.

He'd already told her they were on a secure line and she knew she'd be ditching her phone. Screw speaking in code. "*Rodney* thinks Brutus found me. There's a coffee shop. Some foreign guy who likes the same coffee served in Alfaro's compound showed up. *Rodney* recognized the coffee."

Even on a secure line, she wouldn't share that Shane's bar was across the street. Some details didn't need to be revealed.

"Hang on," Sully said. "You're freaking out because Rodney thinks some guy who requested a cup of coffee is an assassin?"

"This coffee is from Colombia and the owner of the coffee shop described the guy who requested it. Rodney thinks it's Brutus. He's got the scar on his eyebrow. And you told, um, that other friend, about the boat. Between the coffee and the boat, it's a pretty good bet he found me. Let's not even talk about who may have leaked where I was. Or the fact that Rodney and his friends could be exposed."

She shook it off. Who had time for these thoughts? Later they'd figure out who ratted her out.

"We're on the move," she said, "and looking for a woman who worked with Brutus. Rodney says she was an asset."

"Leslie Larshot."

Good; he remembered her. "Yes. That's her. We need to find her."

"Why?"

"Because she knows Brutus's habits and can fast-track our reconnaissance. If we find *her,* maybe we find him."

"Six months ago she was in Alabama. Or Kentucky. Let me poke around. You know this is dangerous. Talk about opening Pandora's box."

Oh, she knew. She was the one running from that box. What choice did she have? She'd done her job, worked for years improving her craft, mining countless amounts of critical information regarding national security and now, as the government's way of saying thanks, they'd discarded her. Sent her on her way because she was no longer of use to them.

That alone should fry her ass. Never mind all this sneaking around trying to stay alive.

"Leslie Larshot," she said. "Help me find her. The agency owes me that much."

SHANE, DUSTY AND TREVOR CAUGHT UP TO FAITH, WHO'D apparently ended her call because she stood in the middle of the field, hands loose at her sides, but still holding her phone.

"I talked to Sully," she told them. "He said Leslie was in Alabama or maybe Kentucky as of six months ago. He said he'd dig around. But let's face it, the agency hasn't exactly been fair to us. I'd say we need a plan B."

Plan B. Lucky for them Shane had gotten pretty fucking good at Plan B. Two years of living under a fake identity tended to sharpen survival instincts.

"Let's see what he comes up with. If I had to, I could probably scrounge an address or phone number for her."

The moon bullied its way from behind a cloud and a shaft of moonlight threw shadows over Faith, who flapped her arms. "Then why did I call Sully?"

Now she wanted to get testy with him? He started walking again, angling around her. "I didn't say I had an address. If necessary, I can make some calls. If your buddy can help, I won't have to risk any of our safety by making inquiries."

"Let's give Sully until tomorrow morning," Faith said when she fell in step beside him. "Let him get to the office and see what he can dig up. In the meantime, I'll lay low somewhere. Drop me at a motel outside the city."

As if. Someone had attempted to snatch her off the street and now she expected them to leave her alone?

"Too risky," Shane said. "You can come home with me. And before you start screaming about me bossing you around, I'm not. I've got my place wired so tight the alarm goes off if someone breathes. You'll be safe there. And so will I because, hell, I go to Darla's for coffee, too. Brutus may have seen me. We don't know. And, if Sullivan has intel, we'll mobilize faster if we're together. Unless Sully tells us Leslie Larshot is dead, we may be calling her tomorrow."

_____

7

AFTER STOPPING AT ONE OF THE BIG BOX STORES TO PICK UP clothes and toiletries for Faith, Shane parked three blocks from his place. They cut through patches of yards and alleys, zigzagging from block to block to confirm they didn't have a tail.

Oddly, it fired him up. Brought him back to his Ground Branch days when he thrived on the excitement and constant challenge. The adrenaline rushes that came with being of service. He'd loved that job. He'd _loved_ having a purpose greater than himself. Now?

As fast as the thought entered his mind, he pushed it away. Getting nostalgic about life as Bobby MacGregor, his birth name, didn't lead anywhere good.

Ever.

As he walked, he casually checked his six, scanning the decently lit street and sidewalks, thanks to lamp posts and porch lights. This time of night, bumper-to-bumper cars lined the curbs, the residents grabbing street parking for the evening.

Everyone was tucked inside, enjoying the comfort of

home and family and the lives they should be so goddamn grateful to have, but probably weren't.

What the hell was wrong with him? Judging people. Prior to becoming Shane Quinn, he'd been one of them. Living out his days not even thinking about what it would be like to not be Bobby.

Across the street, a woman came out of a house, leash in hand and a puppy scampering down steps. For effect, he grabbed Faith's hand. Yep. That was them. A couple out for a late-night stroll.

The woman — definitely not Brutus — led the puppy to the giant tree in front of her house and let him do his business while she peered over at Faith and Shane, making sure they knew she'd seen them. The neighborhood watch in action.

Good for her. What she didn't realize was that if he wanted her dead, she'd already be dead.

At the corner, he checked behind him. Nothing. The woman must have returned to the house. All was quiet, not even a car in motion. Good.

He pointed to his left. "We're cutting through here. My place is on the backside of this house."

The people living behind him either didn't have a rear light or never used it. Something that typically irritated the shit out of him because he couldn't see what was going on in their yard. A guy never knew when an assassin might be lurking in the neighbor's yard.

This time, he didn't mind so much because all that darkness allowed him and Faith to be the lurkers. If they got caught, he'd explain they were too lazy to walk around the block and shortcut it.

They reached the rear stoop of his place and climbed the two steps. As opposed to the front entrance that shared a common hallway and stairs leading to the second and third-floor units, the rear had dedicated entrances via the fire escape. It was, in fact, one of the main reasons he'd rented this place. Easy escape out the back.

Shane unlocked his door, pushed it open and the beep-beep of his security system welcomed him home.

Twenty seconds. That's how long he had to disarm the system. He waved Faith into the entryway that was lit up like O'Hare at night because he refused to walk into a dark house when any number of bad guys could be waiting for him.

Faith stood just inside the door and he reached around her, flipping the lock and catching a whiff of her scent. Something soapy and clean and altogether female.

Jeez, why did his mind go there? The last thing either of them needed were distractions. And thinking about Faith as anything more than a teammate? Total distraction.

"Give me a sec to turn the alarm off."

He hustled through the hallway to the keypad, punched in the code that he changed every couple of days and turned back to Faith. Her presence alone was...weird. For two years, he'd avoided bringing a woman here. The few women he'd dated had wised up enough to move on when he didn't share his address. These days, smart women figured out a guy who wouldn't show her his home was either married or up to no good.

Now, Elizabeth Aiken/Faith Burgess had just walked into his home and Trevor's words from earlier came back to him. What the hell *was* he thinking?

FROM HER SPOT AT THE BACK DOOR, FAITH WAITED FOR SHANE to disarm the security system. To her left, the kitchen was small and neat with a round table only big enough for two, possibly three. No surprise considering the life he led. Living in hiding didn't lend itself to large gatherings.

The incessant beeping of the alarm stopped and she peered down the narrow hallway where Shane waved her in.

"Come in." He pointed at two adjacent doorways. "Bedroom and bathroom. Help yourself."

"I'm good. Thanks. I'll shower in a bit. If you don't mind."

"Not at all."

She angled around a small entry table compact enough to pick up and throw at someone — or crack over their heads — and moved past the bedroom. What sort of bedroom did Shane have? Neat and tidy like the kitchen? Or clothes strewn about? And what about furniture? A mishmash of different pieces or one of those complete sets bought at furniture stores.

In front of her, Shane entered the living room and snatched a pair of socks off the floor. A tablet sat on top of a glass coffee table with a *Sports Illustrated* underneath it. At least it wasn't porn.

"Have a seat," he said.

The closest spot was an end seat of his gray upholstered couch, so she grabbed it. "Thanks. You didn't need to bring me here. I would've gone to a hotel."

He gave her a small smile. "I know."

"If Brutus finds me, we'll both be dead. It's a risk for you."

He met her gaze, holding it for a few long seconds. "Maybe. But you, of all people, know how this works. This is my space. I know every window and door. I've practiced escaping countless times. Everything is situated so I can use it."

She followed his gaze to a dining chair near the mouth of the hallway. And then there was the side table she'd walked by. Both placed where they'd be of use.

The two of them were a pair. Constantly on alert.

"You're prepared. Thank you."

"No prob. You can have the bedroom. I'll sleep on the pullout."

Bad enough she'd risked his cover and now he wanted to give up his bed to her? But, God, she hadn't had a decent — never mind good — night's sleep in weeks. Maybe months. Even in her cozy apartment, her mind spun and sleep came in restless bursts.

With Shane here, knowing she wasn't alone, she might actually manage REM sleep. *Safety.*

Gaze still on his, she sat back, slouching into the sofa. "I want to tell you that I'll take the couch. That you don't have to give up your bed. I should insist on it, in fact."

"But?"

She shook her head, fought an unexpected tightening in her throat. "The idea of sleep, actually shutting my brain off enough to rest, won't let me. Does that make me horrible?"

"Not at all. You know your body. Know what you need to stay sharp. Getting rest makes you an asset instead of a weakness."

He waved a hand toward the kitchen. "You hungry? I didn't have dinner. I brought some stew over from the bar earlier. There's plenty."

"I'm okay." She swung her thumb toward the bathroom. "I'll shower while you're eating?"

. . .

After a thirty-minute piping hot shower, another luxury she hadn't afforded herself in years, she found Shane at the kitchen table scrolling his phone. An empty plate sat in front of him along with an open plastic container filled with...brownies. And they looked homemade. *That* she wouldn't mind snacking on.

He glanced up, took in her leggings and the long-sleeved yoga top they'd bought at Target on the way over.

She pointed at her wet hair tucked into a ponytail. "I didn't want to search through your cabinets for a hairdryer."

"You could've. Not that you'd have found one." He mirrored her gesture pointing to his close-cropped blond hair. "No use for one and I don't exactly have houseguests."

He scooped a brownie out of the container and held it up. "Brownie?"

She slid into the chair across from him and took the generous — man-sized — serving along with a napkin from the stack on the table. "Thank you. Was my love of sweets in my file?"

"No. At least not that I saw."

She took a bite, let the rich, dark chocolate melt on her tongue and closed her eyes. Holy smokes. Whoever made these had mastered the art of just the right amount of gooey. "Wow. These are really good."

"Thanks. My mom's recipe. I'll be damned if I can get it right though."

He made them? Ha. This giant, alpha male who could slay any enemy liked to bake. That alone might force her to love him. "Seriously? Because these are amazing. What can possibly be wrong?"

He laughed. "That's the problem. I don't know. I follow the recipe exactly, right down to hand mixing the batter.

The only thing I can think of is the vanilla. She uses a local brand I can't get. I'm not in a position to call her."

She took another bite, enjoying the buzz of a sugar rush while she contemplated overdosing on brownies and her mother walking out on her. She'd grown used to her mother's absence. Long ago, she'd given up the pity parties over not being able to seek her mom's advice. Some people just weren't built for parenting and her mother easily qualified for president of that organization.

"It's hard," she said, "Isn't it? The separation. My mom was never really part of my life, so I don't feel that particular aspect. But I know when my grandmother died, it crushed me."

He shrugged. "It takes getting used to. I'm a family guy. Holidays, birthdays, Sunday dinners. Playing with the kids. My nieces and nephews are growing up. I'm missing it."

"You have to stay away."

"I'll never regret that part. As long as it keeps them safe." He sat back, set his hands on his thighs. "I saw in your file you were an only child."

How much more did he see in her file? Did he see the mother who'd walked out and never looked back?

She set the brownie on her napkin and propped her chin in her hand. Over the years, she'd learned to deal with the emotions surrounding her upbringing. The grief counselor she'd seen on campus after Gram died told her she had *abandonment* issues.

No.

Kidding.

As if she hadn't known that? As if every time she left Gram's house, she didn't wonder if Gram too would get sick of her. Tell her to never come back. Or when she dared to make friends, but never fully trusted them, assuming they'd bolt if Faith allowed herself to get attached.

Yeah. Abandonment issues galore.

"As far as I know, I'm an only child. My mother took off on me when I was twelve. I guess you saw that too."

"Yeah. You were raised by your grandmother."

"If ever someone should be a saint, it's my gram. I was a handful."

Shane opened his mouth, let out an exaggerated gasp. "You? I'd have never guessed."

Faith laughed.

"I mean," he said. "you kicked the shit out of two guys and then managed to get yourself out of Venezuela safely. The average person doesn't have the balls — or the survival skills — for that."

She shrugged. "People are capable of more than they know. Escaping Venezuela was choosing who lived and died. I think my learning to deal with disappointment at a young age groomed me for the agency. I didn't have a family at home to worry about."

"You're a loner."

"Not intentionally. My grandmother died when I was a freshman at Michigan. After that, I figured it was easier, way less turmoil, to be on my own."

"We come from totally different backgrounds and here we are in the same place. Running from the same guy. It gets old."

She had no doubt. "Is there a choice?"

"Not when my family is at risk."

He took a second to analyze the brownies still in the container, seeming to choose his next victim carefully before biting off half and swallowing. Lord, did he even taste it?

"You have no contact with them at all?"

He eyed her, obviously considering how much to tell her. "Once a year I get a message to them. I vary it. Sometimes it's spring, sometimes fall and it's always different. Email, snail mail. I mix it up."

"And what about them? How do they reach you?"

"They can't. If there's an emergency, there's someone they can call — a former teammate — who'll reach me, but otherwise no contact. I hate it. There's not a lot I can do about it." He pointed at the brownies. "So, I try to nail my mother's recipe. We entered them in a baking competition once and I helped her. Won a blue ribbon too."

Faith laughed. "No way."

"Bet your ass. We killed it. Now, I'm getting ready for the day where I can walk up to her and hand her a brownie I made."

"I hope it happens. You deserve your life back."

He lifted the cover to the container. "You want another?"

She shook her head. "I'm good. I may have one for breakfast though."

"You can do that." He sealed the lid and sat back, his big shoulders relaxing. "Whatever happens tomorrow, it won't be easy. If Brutus is in Chicago, Dusty, Trevor and I are at risk. We've built lives here. Maybe they're not great lives, but it's something. And starting over again isn't in the plan. We're getting rid of him before he finds us."

8

THE WOMAN WAS MAKING HIM NUTS.

Shane had no problem admitting that to himself as he lay sprawled against the back of his crappy pullout mattress with the busted spring that, no matter how many times he flip-flopped, he couldn't get away from. As soon as they settled this deal with Brutus, he'd fix that damn spring.

Or buy a new couch.

In the beginning, the first few months he'd lived here, he'd bought as little furniture as possible until he got a feel for whether he'd be staying. Six months of sleeping on the pullout — and the busted spring — convinced him he should buy a bed. And dressers to put his shit in.

He shifted and the spring poked him in the lower back. No wonder he couldn't sleep. Yeah, the spring was his problem. He'd keep telling himself it had nothing to do with the brunette currently snoozing away in his bed.

Alone.

And wasn't that a damned shame.

With her crazy mix of toughness and vulnerability, Liz-now-Faith crawled into his bed and under his skin. Throw in the fact that she was cute as hell and had that petite body he wanted to tuck next to him and he was screwed. Totally hosed.

Worse, it felt good — comfortable — to talk to someone. Really talk. About his family and the brownies he'd become obsessed with for no other reason than they gave him hope that maybe, someday, he'd go back to being Bobby MacGregor.

That was the dream.

The squeak of his bedroom door sounded and he bolted upright. What the hell? If someone had gotten in the back door, the alarm would have sounded.

Had to be Faith. He turned to where the nightlight illuminated the hall. Faith, looking adorable in her yoga pants and T-shirt and rumpled hair, stood there and nothing about her being in his space in the middle of the night felt wrong.

That? Problem.

She looked straight at him. "You're awake."

Sure am.

He cleared his throat. "Yeah. Winding down."

She headed straight for him and — shit. He'd taken his damned shirt off, as he did every damned night before going to bed. And somehow, the idea of him being shirtless in a bed sparked a supremely excellent vision of Faith flat on her back, bare-assed naked and under him. Call him lonely. Call him horny. Call him whatever, but he liked that vision.

He shook his head, half-laughing to himself. He'd be up all night after this.

"I can't sleep." She waved one hand around her head. "Too much going on."

Despite his own warnings, Shane scooted over, reached

for the T-shirt he tossed on the opposite arm of the couch and grabbed the remote. What the hell was he doing?

Putting clothes on. Good first step. He shoved his arms into his shirt, moving way faster than he probably needed to, but hells bells, half naked in front of Faith combined with the way her eyes were on him? Not good.

T-shirt on, he glanced over at her, found her with a wicked half-smile. She waggled her eyebrows. "You didn't need to do that on my account."

"Believe me," he said. "I did. Now — " He flipped the sheet open. At least he'd been smart enough to leave basketball shorts on. "I can't sleep either. Climb in and we'll find a movie."

She slipped under the covers, tucking the sheet around her. "Do I need to put pillows between us to make sure there's no funny stuff?"

At this, he let out a full-on laugh. Growing up, when he and his brothers had girls over, his mother would make them stay in the living room where she'd shove throw pillows in the middle of the couch between them. Good luck with that trick keeping hormonal teenagers at bay.

"God," he said. "My mother would love you."

"From what you said about your mom that's a great compliment. Maybe, when this is over, I can meet her."

He doubted that. Considering he hadn't seen her in two years.

"Faith, if that could happen I'd be the luckiest guy alive." He gestured to the television. "What do you like to watch?"

"This time of night? *I Love Lucy* reruns."

Of all the things he expected her to say, that wasn't it. He snorted and she drove her elbow into his arm. "Don't judge. They relax me."

"I'm not judging. My folks grew up watching that show

and if they had it on when one of us came home, they'd they make us sit through it. Quality television, they'd say, as compared to the crap we liked to watch."

"If that's the worst thing your parents did, you were living large."

"For sure. But we were kids. What did we know?"

How things changed. Back then, watching television with his folks had been torture. He'd had better things to do. Hang with his friends, play football or basketball. Watch the cheerleaders practice.

Now, at thirty-three, he'd like to hit rewind. Just jump back to sitting with his parents in that living room he'd never realized he'd miss. Rather than brood over the injustice his folks were inflicting on him, he'd say thank you. He'd appreciate parents who loved their kids even when they were pricks.

Too late.

He hit the power button on the remote. "After the day we had, we could use a laugh."

THE SOUND OF A CELL PHONE RINGING CLAWED FAITH FROM A dream. A weird one to boot. Something about mountain climbing in freezing temperatures while wearing flip-flops. What that meant she had no idea, but *a dream*. She'd actually had one.

More than that, she'd achieved REM sleep. A solid miracle.

And someone dared to wake her. If she wasn't so happy about sleeping, she might tear the offender a new one.

She forced her eyes open. Stared straight up at a white ceiling. White ceiling? A second later, the fog of that miracle REM sleep lifted and her brain engaged. Shane's ceiling.

The phone rang again and her body suddenly dipped left. *Whoa.* She whipped her head around, found Shane slapping his hand over the arm of the sofa in search of his ringing phone and...

Ohmygod.

Lucy reruns. Pullout bed. She was still in the pullout bed.

With Shane.

He picked up the phone and stabbed at the screen. "What's up?"

His morning voice — oh, wow — had that gravelly, rough edge and . . . nope. Not going there. She scooted sideways, putting at least another three inches between them. She could do this. Just play it casual. After all, nothing had happened. For confirmation, she looked down at her yoga top, still in place. Good.

She sat up, gathered her hair and tucked it into a loose knot high on her head. Beside her, Shane kept his gaze straight ahead as he listened to the caller.

The TV was off. That had to have been Shane's doing because the last thing she remembered was snorting at Lucy and Ethel shoving candy in their mouths.

Shane swung to her, his sleepy blue eyes suddenly sharp. "Her phone must be off. Or the battery died. I'll have her check...Yeah...Thanks." He disconnected, tossed the phone on the bed between them.

"That was Dusty," he said. "Sully can't reach you."

Her burner phone. She patted the mattress in search of it. Nothing. She checked under the sheet. Nope. The pillow. Zip. Where the hell was it? Maybe it fell under the pullout bed? Still, she'd have heard it.

"I didn't see you bring it out with you last night," Shane said.

No way. Nuh-uh.

That phone, or any phone for that matter, had been glued to her hand for years. Shower, potty break, you name it, a phone was within reach. She never knew when it might mean survival. Or the lack thereof.

She flipped the sheet off and scrambled to her feet. "I left it in the bedroom. I can't *believe* it. I take a phone everywhere."

Something about Shane Quinn had her totally off her game. Could be any number of things, including the jacked body, the crystal blue eyes and movie-star handsome face or that all-important trait that Faith had been missing since her grandmother died.

Shane, at the core of all that hotness, was a protector. Someone willing to sacrifice himself for the greater good. For a stranger.

It might be the biggest, baddest weapon this man carried. Most women, she imagined, probably dropped at his feet.

She marched into Shane's bedroom, where the sheets on the massive king-size bed lay rumpled from the night before. Beside the bed, her phones — the burner and the one Shane had given her when she'd become Faith Burgess — sat on the nightstand. Right where she'd left them.

She picked up the burner and the screen alerted her to a voice mail. Private number. She tapped the button and lifted the phone to her ear. "It's me." Sully's voice. "Call me back. Got info for you."

She tapped the callback icon.

"Hey," Sully said. "I've got thirty seconds so listen up. I'm sending you an address in Alabama."

Yes! Whoa. Wait. He said an *address*. Did that mean...?
"What about a phone number?"

"No. The one we have isn't valid."

"Meaning she didn't answer? Or it belongs to someone else?"

"I called it and got some guy. She probably got rid of the phone."

Her initial excitement sunk like lead. "Crap."

"Yeah. Sorry. I'll keep working it, but for now, all you have is an address. I'll text it to you. Gotta go."

The line went dead.

She tipped her head back, stared up at the ceiling and said a silent thanks for even the smallest lead. Sully had found an address for Leslie Larshot. It might not get them to Brutus — the woman would be crazy to even talk to them — but it was a morsel and sometimes that was all Faith needed. Morsels gave her hope.

"Everything okay?" She spun back to where Shane stood in the hallway. She held the phone up. "He has an address for Leslie. And, before you ask, no phone number."

"Well, *that* sucks."

"Sure does. Sully called her old number and it belongs to a man."

Shane leaned against the doorframe, his gaze on Faith, but his eyes clouded over. As if he was looking at her, but not focused.

"You're thinking. What is it?"

"We should get you out of the city. Take some heat off."

"No."

He lifted one hand. "Just listen a sec. Please. Leslie, if we can locate her, can help us."

"Unless we're driving to freaking Alabama, we can't reach her."

When Shane didn't respond, Faith gawked at him. "You're not serious."

"About a road trip? Yeah, I am."

Oh, now the man had completely lost it. It would take them all day to get to Alabama and it might be a bust. They'd spend two days on the road and for what? Failure.

"Believe me," Shane said. "I know it's not the best option. *However,* it gets you out of the city and we might find her. Otherwise, we're calling hotels asking for Luis Gustavo."

Faith waved that off. "Talk about a waste of time. He'd never use his real name. And there are a million hotels in this city. We need to narrow it down. Can Darla help us?"

His eyebrows hitched. "Coffee shop Darla?"

"He told her to get that special coffee. Maybe he's coming in regularly."

Considering it for a few seconds, Shane rolled his bottom lip out, then nodded. "I'll call her. See if she has any intel on him. Jesus, I hate bringing her into this. I still think Leslie is our best option. She traveled with him. Can help us with the types of places he likes to stay. His aliases too. She can give us intel it'd take us days, maybe even a week, to gather."

She couldn't argue it. But a day to drive south and then a day to get back? Was it worth it? If Leslie got them to Brutus, most definitely. And randomly calling hotels didn't seem like a great option.

She moved to the shopping bags she'd thrown on the floor and pulled out her newly acquired clothes. She'd have preferred to wash them first, but...whatever. "I guess if Darla can't help, we're heading to Alabama."

By 7:30, after ascertaining that Darla knew zippo about the Spanish guy who'd suggested that special blend of coffee, Faith sat in the passenger seat of Shane's no-

nonsense Chevy as they cruised West Madison Street. In the weeks she'd been in Chicago, she'd memorized various routes to the expressways, Union Station and El train stops. All to help her leave the city in a hurry.

If her memory served, they'd hop on I-94 east to I-90 and then make their way south through Indiana.

Except...Shane just blew by the I-94 entrance.

Faith pointed. "Uh, you missed it."

"What?"

"I-94. You went right by the ramp."

"We're not going that way. I need to make a stop."

A stop? What stop?

He'd been the one telling her to hustle up so they could get on the road. Now he wanted to run an errand?

"Care to fill me in? Considering I'm on this trip too."

He shrugged. "We're switching cars. I have one I keep in storage."

Un-huh. A car in storage typically meant no way of it being traced back to him. "It's not registered to you?"

"Correct. Casey Irvine owns it."

"And he is?"

"No clue. Been dead since 2007."

Shane kept his eyes on the road while Faith studied his profile. How many backup identities did the man have? "He's your backup identity in case you have to run again."

He didn't respond. Really, he didn't need to. She herself had at least a dozen identities she'd used throughout her career. Some were simply names she had fake credentials for while others had a complete personal and work history that could easily be checked online if someone wanted to dig.

Shane hooked a left onto S. Halstead and Faith finally gave up on waiting for an answer. Another few turns on streets she didn't recognize led them to the gate of a seven-story storage facility.

After punching in the gate code, he drove through, passing two long rows of outdoor garages before making a right. At the fourth unit he parked.

"Stay here a sec."

She waited, watching as he moved around the front of the car, unlocked the storage unit door and rolled it up. A few seconds later, the sound of an engine roared and — *hello, baby* — out came what Faith recognized as a black Dodge Challenger that gleamed under bright morning sun. One of her coworkers at the agency had a Challenger and droned on endlessly about it.

She supposed she couldn't blame the guy because this car? Total beast.

Shane parked beside the Chevy and they both hopped out, ready to switch vehicles so he could store the one she'd just exited.

Being nosy, she checked the Challenger's rear tag. Wisconsin plate. Once inside, she popped the glove box finding an insurance card and registration for Casey Irvine. Milwaukee address.

The driver's side door opened and Shane slid in, spotting the documents in her hand.

She held them up. "I was curious."

"No prob. I'd have done the same. I found him in a cemetery in Milwaukee. The age was close enough, so I went with it."

"I assume you have creds for him?"

He gave her a rueful smile. "I keep them under a loose floorboard in my bedroom. I grabbed them before we left."

Not a shock since she'd grabbed her own set of backup credentials before leaving her apartment the night before.

At the time, she hadn't known why Shane summoned her to a meeting, but assumed it wasn't for happy hour. If she had to run again, she'd need identification in a hurry, so she'd brought along a passport and driver's license from one of her old CIA cover names.

It wouldn't have worked permanently, but the alias would have bought her time until she'd been able to set up another identity.

Faith buckled her seatbelt and settled back into the soft leather of the seat. "I'm fascinated that you keep this baby locked in storage while you drive the Dad-mobile every day."

"*Dad*-mobile? Ouch."

"Sorry," she said, "but it's true."

"And exactly the point. The Chevy blends better." He tapped the steering wheel. "I took a chance on this one. Crazy-assed risk, but I figured if I had to run again, I might as well do it in style. It was a screaming good deal. A guy Dusty knows has a gambling problem and needed cash fast."

He went through the usual routine of checking his mirrors and plugging his phone cord into the jack.

"When's the last time you drove it?"

"When I bought it."

Oh, man. The guy was killing her. "Seriously?"

"Faith, it's my *emergency* vehicle. I come by every week and start it. Other than that, I have the Chevy."

"I get that you don't want your neighbors oohing and aahing over it, but you could drive it outside the city."

"Trust me, I've been tempted. It's not worth the risk."

"It's worth it now?"

He shifted the car into gear, but before taking his foot off the brake, met her eye. "We don't have a choice. If we're followed, no one can tie this car back to me. Or Dusty or Trevor."

"I'm sorry."

"For what?"

"All of it. The car, risking your identity, this damned road trip. It sucks."

She shook her head, stared out the windshield to a blue sky too perfect for what they were doing. They should be walking along the lakefront, grabbing a coffee, chatting with strangers and possibly making friends. That's what people did. People unlike them anyway.

"What's your point?"

If she only knew. Actually, no. She did know. She peeled her gaze from the beautiful spring morning. "I don't think I can do this. What you, Dusty and Trevor do. Constantly on edge, thinking ahead, working on escape plans. Storing a stunning car because I'm too afraid of being discovered. In the field it's different. That's temporary. I eventually get to come home and decompress."

"Beats dying."

Did it?

He released the brake and hit the gas. "You're thinking too much. Sit back and relax. It's a long drive."

NINE HOURS INTO A NEARLY TWELVE-HOUR DRIVE, SHANE followed Faith from a quiet roadside restaurant she'd found a few miles off I-65 near Huntsville.

All he wanted was to get to Montgomery, find Leslie Larshot and get the hell back to Chicago, where they'd hunt down Brutus and eliminate him.

Except Faith had needed to pee. And eat. Of course she

did. One would think, given her experience with fieldwork, she could control her bladder and stomach better.

So...dinner. Which, he had to admit, turned out to be a good idea. An abundant and hot meal of meatloaf and mashed potatoes — ultimate comfort food — and good conversation did a man good. Playing the role of attentive significant other wasn't exactly taxing. For a minute or two his mind had actually given him a break and let him relax. As Daffy Duck would say, *woo-hoo!*

Even if he'd been on high alert the entire meal, it got them out of the car and geared up for the last leg of the drive.

As he left the restaurant, Shane scanned the rear lot where the Challenger sat hidden from the road. He opened the passenger door and waited for her to climb in.

She buckled in and peered up at him. "Don't you feel better now?"

With all the bitching he'd done about making this extended stop, there'd be no way — no way — he'd respond to that loaded question.

"Ha!" she said, "Of course you do. We've eaten, stretched our legs and our minds are sharp again. Now we can make a plan for finding Larshot. I'm thinking we check out the address tonight. The darkness will be good cover for us. Then we'll get some rest and sit on the place in the morning. Would you recognize her?"

Hell yeah he would. What man wouldn't? He glanced around for any busybodies. No one. Good. Still, he didn't want to stand around having this conversation.

"She's tall. *Really* tall. Even if she changed her hair color, not a lot of women are six-foot."

Leaving it at that, he shut Faith's door and walked around to the driver's seat. A minute later, he pulled onto the rural route that led back to I-65 and hit the gas. The speed limit sign said thirty-five. Jeez-a-lou. Pushing his speed on the interstate was one thing, but he wasn't interested in messing with local cops.

He checked the speedometer. Twenty-five.

At the traffic light, he hooked a U-turn in the intersection and checked the rearview mirror for a tail. Faith peered over her shoulder.

"We're good," Faith said, facing front again.

He pressed the gas. The speedometer leaped, then immediately dropped. "What the hell?"

"What?"

He eased off on the gas and checked the dashboard where the speedometer continued to fluctuate. This car was fucked. And it had happened suddenly.

While they were chowing.

A burst of adrenaline poured into his body. *Focus.*

All day, the Challenger had been a rock star. Not one issue. As each mile passed, the car responded to his demands and he'd fallen so in love he'd considered switching the Dad-mobile out. Risky as it might be.

The speedometer leaped again.

Before they'd gone into the restaurant, everything was good. None of this quirky shit. Which meant . . .

He inhaled, breathing in the fading scent of leather cleaner from the car's last detailing. Adrenaline did this to him. Sharpened his senses. Brought him to a heightened alertness that later exhausted him.

He could be wrong. They hadn't been in the restaurant *that* long. *Long enough.* Shit. His mind raced, offering visions of the two of them being blown sky-high, limbs flying off.

Not worth the risk. If wrong, the worst that would

happen is he'd look like an idiot. Definitely not the first time that happened.

"Faith," he said calmly, his gaze ping-ponging from the road to the mirror while he kept his foot on the gas. Steady speed. Steady. Steady. Steady.

A half mile ahead a car turned right. Other than that, no other cars on the road.

"What is it?"

"Don't freak. Just do what I say. Grab our backpacks from the backseat."

"Shane — "

Dammit.

He gripped the steering wheel, all his contained energy shooting into his fingertips. "Faith! Do it. This fucking car might blow up and we need to jump out. Grab our shit."

Quickly — *thank you, God* — she unbuckled and reached behind her for their packs, placing his on his lap. "Use it when you jump. It'll cushion the fall."

This woman. Not only did she trust him when he told her she'd have to jump from a moving vehicle, she'd slipped right into operative mode, offering suggestions. Not one argument or a slew of questions. Total buy-in.

Road sign dead ahead. He'd have to clear that so Faith could jump without hitting it on her way to the ground.

"When I pass this sign, we go."

Once past it, he eased closer to the shoulder where the soft grass might keep Faith from serious injury.

Jesus. She could whack her head on the pavement. But blowing up wasn't a great alternative. He squeezed the steering wheel again, kept his foot on the gas. If he went any faster, they might turn into fireworks. Clearly, he hadn't reached the speed where the bomb would detonate. Sweat ran down the back of his neck and his pulse thumped.

"On three," he said. "We jump."

In unison, they opened the doors and a blast of air and wind noise filled the car. *Jump, don't jump, jump.* He shook his head, concentrated on keeping his foot steady on the gas. It'd be a miracle if they got out of this without breaking bones.

"Jump at an angle," he said. "Away from the car."

"We practiced this during my training. I'm pretty good at it."

"Good. On three. One, two, three."

He set his left hand on the door, lifted his right from the steering wheel and gripped his backpack. Easing his foot from the gas, he dipped his chin and . . . rolled.

Air whooshed, smacking at his ears as he fell from the vehicle and tucked himself into a ball, readying for impact.

Ooff! His shoulder hit the ground. Pain shot straight down his arm and he rolled. And rolled and rolled, coming to a stop in the street under a stream of waning sunlight. A breath shot from his mouth. *Made it.*

Move.

Scrambling to his knees, he scanned the area for Faith.

"Faith!"

"I'm okay," she called.

Ahead of him, the car — still intact — had veered to the right and down a slope on the shoulder where it picked up speed as it rolled toward a clump of trees.

What the fuck? Had his paranoia sent him completely over the edge, making him imagine the car had a bomb on it? The speedometer thing though. He'd seen it. Talked extensively with a teammate about electronic detonation devices being attached to speedometers and at a certain speed — *boom.* Bye-bye car.

Except, nothing. Maybe he'd imagined this whole thing? Risked getting them hurt over nothing?

Ten yards to his right, Faith got to her feet, holding up a hand and waving.

Boom!

The force of the explosion blew him straight back, knocking him on his ass. He rolled to his feet, charging straight for Faith. On the ground and flat on her back.

9

WHAT THE HECK?

Faith lay in the grass, her body aching from the fall —
both of them — while the acrid stench of burning rubber
assaulted her senses.

"My God."

She inhaled and rib-shredding pain shot straight up her
back to her shoulders.

Relax.

She knew what this was. Had felt it before when she'd
taken a hard fall and had the wind knocked out of her.

Slowly, she drew a few soft breaths while wiggling her
fingers and her toes. Everything in working order. Next, she
lifted her extremities and besides a bit of minor pain, all
good.

Excellent.

She moved to her side and paused for another breath.
Just ahead, bright orange and yellow flashes engulfed the
Challenger, the flames twisting and contorting in an oddly
beautiful dance.

"Run!"

Shane sprinted toward her, backpack in hand. Thank goodness for those backpacks. Although it'd be a miracle if her laptop had survived.

"Are you alright?" she asked.

He reached her, latching on to her arm and dragging her to her feet and holy hell her body rejected *that* in all sorts of ways.

"I'm good. You're okay?"

"Yes."

"Then haul ass," he said. "We need to get out of here before the cops and whoever planted that bomb show up."

Minus a car, the swath of woods beside them would be their best option for staying out of sight.

"We can cut through the trees," she said. "Once we get some cover, I'll check my phone and see what's on the other side."

Shane's longer legs carried him easily across the grass while Faith double-timed to keep pace. Her foot landed in a hole and sent her stumbling.

"Ow. Shit."

Momentum carried her and she fought against her shifting weight. No going down. Not again. Another fall meant potentially breaking something and they didn't have time for that.

Shane spun back, spotted her going over and halted. She tumbled forward, but the solid wall of him kept her upright.

"Whoa," he said.

"I hit a rabbit hole or something."

"Can you still run?"

She lifted her foot and circled it. It hurt like hell, but she could move it and, more importantly, put weight on it. If she'd broken a bone, they'd be screwed.

The trees were *right* there. Maybe another twenty yards.

Once they got there, they could huddle up, take a minute to rest and let the adrenaline rush subside. Maybe get their bearings.

What kind of life was this?

Not one she wanted. But . . . Shane.

He'd helped her. Literally just saved her life and God only knew how he'd recognized the car was about to blow. His paranoia had prevented them from becoming kindling.

"I'm good. Let's get to those trees."

She hobbled along, the kink in her ankle having mercy and working free with each step.

Life in the field had taught her to be grateful for the little and not-so-little things. Not only was she still mobile, she wasn't charred from that explosion.

They walked farther into the woods, each checking behind them until the street disappeared. If they couldn't see the street, no one on said street could see them.

"We should be good for a few minutes." He pointed to a tree stump. "Take a seat."

"I'm all right."

"Sit."

Bossy, bossy. Still, she wouldn't mind a look at her foot. She set her backpack down and dropped to the ground beside it. Shane squatted in front of her, his hands already in motion yanking up the hem of her jeans.

He wrapped his fingers around her ankle, the heat from his touch shooting straight through her sock and up her leg. She flinched.

"That hurt?"

"No."

"You flinched. If it hurt, tell me."

"It didn't hurt. I'm not . . ."

"What?"

"It's . . . nothing." Dammit. How to explain this without it being a thing. "Really. I'm fine."

He gave her a look. Maybe irritation. "Don't do that," he said. "I need to know your status. Are you good or not?"

Her status. Ha. Terrified, confused . . . needy. And for someone who'd survived on her own for so long, that needy thing was a pisser. She grabbed her backpack, dug through the front pocket for her phone. "I'm fine. I wasn't ready for you to grab . . . no . . . not grab. I didn't . . ."

She shook her head, closed her eyes for a second and focused. She opened her eyes again, found him staring at her, his crystal blue gaze direct. "I wasn't ready for you to touch me. That's all. After Venezuela, I'm jumpy."

He kept his hand in place — at least he hadn't snatched it away like she'd fried it. "I'm sorry. I should have — "

"Don't apologize. You've been nothing but kind. I know you wouldn't hurt me. I just reacted."

"I'd *never* hurt you," he said. "At least, not intentionally. Can I look at this ankle?"

She nodded because, really, what could be so wrong with her partner, her *teammate,* checking an injury? And, at the same time, getting her comfortable with a man having his hands on her again.

A double win.

Gently, he worked her sneaker off her foot and rolled her sock down.

She lifted her phone. "I'll see where we are and how we can get out of here."

He squeezed her ankle. "Does this hurt?"

"No."

Another squeeze. "What about this?"

And, holy cow, the man's hands were magic. All calloused but gentle and sending tiny shock waves to parts of her that hadn't had that particular yummy feeling in way too long.

She gave up on her phone and looked at him. His gazed was fixed on her ankle, those amazing hands moving over her while his bottom lip slightly protruded.

For the most part, Shane kept his features neutral, never giving away his thoughts. But there were times, like now, when he offered glimpses of himself.

Couple that with sleeping next to him after watching *I Love Lucy* reruns and her hormones were unleashing some kind of weird venom that made her want things she couldn't have.

These thoughts. They wouldn't do her any good. As much as Shane *affected* her, as much as she wouldn't mind a little passion . . . No future.

The two of them combined? Emotional nightmare. After the lives they'd led, they'd never be comfortable letting their walls down.

And that was a damned shame.

She went back to her phone. "How did you know about the bomb?"

"The speedometer."

"What about it?"

"It was acting weird all of sudden. Fluctuating."

Oh, come on. "And that immediately made you think it was a bomb? No offense, but that's scary."

He snorted. "When I was Ground Branch, our explosives guy messed around with reverse engineering an electronic detonation device for speedometers. He finally figured it out, but it was screwing with the car's performance. Frustrated the crap out of him. When the Challenger started acting weird, I panicked."

"You didn't panic. You used your experience and came to

a correct conclusion. And lucky you did or we'd be dead. I'm sorry."

"For what?"

"How about nearly getting you killed? How about insisting we stop for a sit-down dinner when we only have a few more hours on the road? I was watching for tails the entire day. I missed it. Now, I've brought Alfaro right to you."

He gave her ankle a gentle squeeze before resetting the hem of her jeans and peering at her. "I think you're good here. And I knew who you were running from. I *chose* to help you. That's on me. If this plan works, we'll both stay alive."

SHANE GOT TO HIS FEET, SCANNING THE AREA AROUND THEM. Thick, towering trees kept them hidden from view, but shrieking sirens drew closer. The fire department and cops, no doubt. Someone must have driven by, seen a random car in flames and called 911.

They had to move before cops came looking for the owner of the now toasted car. His foresight on taking the car registered to a dead guy from Wisconsin was a good one.

But what the fuck happened? He'd been careful. Jumping on and off highways, taking rural roads, all the while continually searching for possible tails. And not just him. Faith had been diligent as well. They'd *both* missed it.

What did that say about their reconnaissance skills?

Eyes still on her phone, Faith pointed to her right. "There are railroad tracks on the other side of these trees. If there's a station nearby, we can jump on the next train. Maybe it'll get us to Montgomery."

After shouldering his backpack, he held out his hands to her, giving her a boost to her feet. "Sirens are getting closer.

We'll get to the tracks, hunker down for a minute and see if we can find a train station."

Before the car had blown to bits, he hadn't noticed any activity behind them. Whoever tailed them and blew up his awesome fucking car might not have seen them run into the woods. He hoped.

Faith tapped at her phone. "Tracks should be just ahead."

They came to a clearing where in another thirty minutes darkness would make the tracks all but invisible. On the other side, the woods continued so they walked on, into the cover of the trees.

"I'll keep watch," he said. "See if you can find the nearest train station or car rental place."

She dropped to her knees, slid her backpack to the ground and used it to block the light from her phone in case anyone might be watching.

"Ugh," she said. "The nearest car rental is ten miles north. A town called Edingville. The closest southerly one is fifteen miles."

Damn. The closer one was the wrong direction. "What about train stations?"

Faith grunted. "The good news is, according to this map, the tracks go right through the town where the rental place is."

"What's the bad news?"

She gestured to the tracks. "These are for freight. No commuter stations close."

It shouldn't have shocked him. Why should anything actually go their way? He couldn't get hung up on it. Bitching about their rotten luck wouldn't get them a rental car. Shane ran one hand through his hair and blew out a breath.

"We're fine." She covered her phone with her hand, then stood and tucked it into her back pocket. "We'll hoof the ten miles north. It's not the worst idea. Whoever followed us won't expect us to double back."

God, he loved a smart woman. "Good. Once we get there, we'll rent a car and finish the drive." He pointed north. "Let's do this."

FAITH WALKED BESIDE SHANE, BOTH STAYING MOSTLY SILENT to avoid possible detection on the off chance that someone might be wandering the woods or walking along the tracks in the darkness. They'd been on this path an hour and all she'd seen were trees, trees and more trees. All of them now casting towering shadows from moonlight.

Hello? What kind of wildlife did Alabama have? Would they get eaten out here?

It should have been creepy, but somehow, the quiet — along with two ibuprofen for her sore ankle — soothed her. Calmed her rioting nerves and chaotic thoughts regarding being hunted by a vicious killer.

"It's peaceful," Shane, the mind reader, said.

"It feels—"

She took a second to organize her thoughts. To figure out what the heck this feeling was. Good? Yes. But it was more than that. Something she hadn't experienced since . . . when? She thought back. Since Gram died. "It feels simple. Normal."

"We don't have a lot of either in our lives."

A clanging noise halted them. A second later the clang turned to a rumble. *Rumble, clang, rumble, clang.* In unison, they turned. A circle of bright light coming around the bend they'd come from minutes earlier shattered the blackness.

Train.

"We should duck out of sight," Faith said. "When the train gets here, we'll be lit up like Broadway."

Shane's expression may have been shadowed, but she'd spent enough time with him to recognize his silence, that vast cavern of emptiness between them, meant active thoughts.

"Shane? What are you thinking?"

"I'm thinking we can give that bum ankle of yours a break *and* cut our travel time."

Clang, rumble, clang. Clang, rumble, clang. The train and its glowing light drew closer. It didn't take a rocket scientist to figure out he wanted to turn this thing into a Hollywood stunt by hopping aboard.

"It's probably not moving that fast," he said. "And we're traveling light. If your ankle holds up, we'll run beside it and grab on to one of the handrails. We can cruise along until we get to Edingville. I don't see a downside."

At that, she laughed. "You mean other than one of us possibly falling off and winding up dead from a skull fracture? Or being sliced in half by a train wheel? You don't see that as a downside?"

He waved off those minor issues. "If you can get out of Venezuela with zero resources, you can hop on a train."

True.

She peered back at the train. The easy, rhythmic ka-chunk-ka-chunk of churning wheels indicated slow speed. As much as falling off that thing terrified her, they could probably jog beside it and leap right up. It had already been a long few days. Schlepping another five or so miles in pitch black where she might step in another hole and break her already sore ankle wouldn't conserve her energy.

"If hitching a ride on that thing will get us to wherever we're sleeping tonight, I'm game."

Shane lifted his curled fingers for a fist pound. "I like your style. This'll be easy. Freight cars usually have steps and a handrail. I'll use the flashlight on my phone so you can see where you're going. Once you're on, you do the same for me. "

They ducked into the trees out of sight of the conductor until two, three, four cars passed. Whatever this big guy was carrying was liquid because the containers were all round with ladders leading up to the top.

Good news for their purposes.

Shane led her toward the moving train. "Heads up. Not this car, but the next one. There's a handrail. You grab hold and hang on."

He fired up his phone's flashlight and swung it to the next car, identical to the one that had just passed.

"On three," he said, "start running. Grab that ladder."

He counted down and they ran as Shane held the flashlight steady. Faith's ankle? Not a fan as evidenced by the incessant pin pricks shooting up her leg. No time for that now.

Faster. *More speed.*

Eyes on her target, she pumped her legs harder, sucking a breath each time that ankle nearly gave out. Lord, that hurt.

The rail.

Right . . . there.

She reached up, grabbed hold with one, then the other hand and her legs flew out from under her. Whoa! The immediate flying effect made her gasp and a burst of energy sent her system buzzing.

Pull.

Her shoulders seized and her muscles stretched and tightened rebelling against the pressure. *Hang on, hang on, hang on.* This train meant the difference between resting and not.

Rest. She wanted it. She gripped the rail harder and yanked, dragging her body up, ignoring the ripping sensation in her back. She swung her feet, searching for purchase and — *yes!* — her sneaker hit something. She peered down to where Shane's flashlight lit the ladder and its glorious steps.

Holy cow. She did it.

Below her, Shane, still running beside the train, let out a whoop. Clearly, the man was enjoying this. She stepped to the middle of the ladder, gripping the left side, nearly wrapping her body around the rail, praying he had enough room to squeeze behind her. Before she could even get her phone out — *ooff* — Shane slammed into her from behind, momentum carrying his much bigger body forward. In the darkness, his left hand closed over hers, crushing her fingers while he held on to the opposite rail with his right, all of him cocooning her and her backpack between his arms.

Yowzer.

"Shit." He let go, moving his hand higher so he could grip the handle. "Sorry. Did I hurt you?"

"No. Are you on?"

"I'm good."

"Oh my God," she said, laughing. "We just did that."

"I know! Wicked fun."

"Says you. You need help, my friend."

"Probably. But now we get to hang on for the ride."

Hang on for the ride. Hadn't she been doing that for weeks now? Each day, waking up, flying solo and hoping she'd stay alive long enough to see nightfall. Now, with

Shane tucked behind her, she couldn't deny the difference. *This* time she wasn't alone.

How was it possible that they were hanging off the side of a moving freight train and she somehow felt safer than she had in years?

"Hey," he said, his lips right next to her ear. "Look up."

She tilted her head up, bumping against his chest. *Not alone.* A blanket of stars twinkled in a sky so clear no artist would do it justice.

"Wow," she said. "Stunning."

She closed her eyes, let her mind and body be still, soaking in the gentle swipe of a warm Alabama wind against her cheeks. Fresh air and the woodsy scent of nature blanketed her and for the first time in weeks her mind slowed. She inhaled and focused on the moment. On being present and thankful for being alive. And for Shane, a man she barely knew but who had risked his own safety to help her.

She peeled her gaze from the sky and peered up at him over her shoulder. "You were right. I'll enjoy the ride."

10

_____

WHEN THE TELLTALE CLANG OF A RAILROAD CROSSING sounded, Shane peered over the top of Faith's head to where red lights lit up the darkness. He checked his watch. Over nine miles since leaving the restaurant.

Dang. The last five miles of Faith snuggled in front of him, their bodies molded together under stars might be the closest thing he'd had to actual fun in a long time. Too bad her backpack sat between them, but still, he liked the closeness.

After this, no matter what happened, he needed to get a life. Change his fucked-up existence and lack of emotional connections. He wasn't sure how to do it while staying safe, but it needed to happen.

He'd learned not to think too far ahead. Why risk disappointment? For now, he'd concentrate on getting off this train and finding a rental car to get them the last 180ish miles to Montgomery. Who the hell knew if the rental car place would even be open? Even if it was, it'd be late by the time they got to Leslie Larshot's and Shane was already dog-tired. After rolling from that moving car, his body was bull-dozed and in need of rest.

The immediate plan, if Faith agreed, would be 1.) rental car and finishing the drive and 2.) finding a hotel so Operation Leslie could roll first thing in the morning.

He dipped his head, putting his mouth just next to Faith's ear. "I think this is Edingville."

She nodded. "The train is slowing down. We should jump."

"Let's do it before we get to the crossing." He glanced down at the ground. "The grass'll cushion us when we hit the ground. Don't lock your knees."

Jesus, another roll from a moving vehicle. They'd be lucky to get through this day without broken bones.

They neared the crossing and by the mercy of whatever god paying attention, the train slowed to a crawl. He'd never considered himself a lucky guy until now.

Faith angled around and peered up at him. Even in the darkness he saw her smile. "Can you believe it? We can step right off. The universe is definitely on our side."

"As my mother likes to say, from your lips to God's ears. Let's do this."

Shane held on to the rear rail with both hands, then hopped off, sticking the landing. Easy. He walked beside the train, waving Faith to jump. "Hop off. I've got you."

He held his arms out and she stepped off, landing in front of him so he set his hands on her arms, steadying her.

She turned and faced him, tipping her head up and hitting him with another smile that blew his chest open. Just — wham. When she looked at him like that, everything got lighter. And he hadn't had much of that recently.

Leaving his good sense on the train moving past them, he dipped his head, half hoping she'd back away and remind him this whole situation was fucked and they shouldn't mix pleasure into the mess. But she was here, smiling that smile and making him feel like a man should feel. Making him want things a man should want.

Not only did she not step back, she went up on tiptoes helping his cause. Their lips met and his body did that crazy blown-open thing again. Then her hands slid up his chest and — oh, yeah — this was what he wanted. Heat and action and fun. *All good here.*

She wrapped her hand around the back of his neck, dragging herself flush against him and deepening the kiss. Her tongue played hide-and-seek with his and he met her stroke for stroke. He set his hands on her ass and scooped her up, holding on as she tucked her legs around his waist.

A horn blared. The train clearing out. Damn. Once it was gone, they'd have to get their asses moving or draw attention from anyone waiting at the crossing. She leaned back an inch. "We should stop."

"Yep."

Except, she kissed him again. "I don't want to."

He laughed. "Honey, me neither."

"To be continued? In private?"

Shit on a shingle. He'd be crazy to agree to that. And yet . . . "You know it."

She dragged her legs from around him and he set her on the ground knowing full well the two of them had lost their fucking minds. Getting emotionally involved while running from an assassin wasn't exactly the best operational plan.

"Stop thinking, Shane. This isn't good. We both know it. No sense in obsessing over it." She dragged her phone from her back pocket and put her thumbs to work. "The car rental place is three blocks down on the left."

While waiting for the train to clear, they made quick

work of straightening hair and shirts as best they could after leaping from a car. Hopefully, in the dark, the dirt smudges on their clothing wouldn't be as noticeable.

As soon as the clanging stopped and the gates rose, they crossed over the tracks, walking along a typical small town Main Street. Barbershop, beauty salon and hardware store on one side. All closed. Across the street, a few cars were parked in front of the corner bar. A shot-and-a-beer joint with a red neon Open sign. Otherwise, the only lights were streetlamps.

He'd anticipated this, but his mood still plummeted. "Guessing the rental place is closed?"

She kept her gaze straight ahead. "Based on the lack of activity, I'd say you're correct."

In which case they were basically screwed because their ride had literally just left the station.

"Shit."

She stopped walking and faced him, her face lit by the overhead light. In case she got any ideas about touching him, he crossed his arms. Totally closed posture.

"Let's go into the bar," he said. "If we can't get wheels, we'll go to plan B and find a place to crash. Small town like this? There's probably a B and B in need of guests."

"That's all we can do. Hopefully, we won't have to use plan B."

Shane wasn't counting on that.

BEFORE HEADING INTO THE BAR, FAITH WENT BACK TO HER phone. "Hold on. We need a cover."

She tapped on the map she'd used to find the car rental and zoomed out. The closest interstate was fifteen miles. *Too far.* She checked the north-south routes for possibilities.

They'd be a couple passing through. Visiting from . . . Where? Someplace north, but not Chicago.

St. Louis.

Yes. That'd work.

They'd be heading to Montgomery to visit friends for a few days. Not a total lie and with the size of Montgomery, folks wouldn't ask too many questions.

She held the phone up for Shane. "Route 84 is a few miles up. We're from St. Louis on our way to visit friends in Montgomery. Our car broke down."

"Where on 84?" He snatched the phone and tightened the zoom. "Mangler. 84 and Mangler. The tow truck driver gave us a lift to town so we could rent a car."

"Perfect." She plucked the phone back and tucked it into her pocket. "Let's go."

Holding the door open for her — such a gentleman — Shane waved her inside where four tables sat along the far wall, one of them occupied by two guys — maybe mid-twenties. They gave her a once-over, spotted the enormous guy behind her and went back to their conversation.

The oiled oak bar and a row of stools stretched along the adjacent wall where the bartender spoke with a couple sitting at the end. He stood tall, eyeing them as they approached the empty stools four down from the couple.

"I'm Ray." He slapped coasters on the bar. "What can I get you?"

Shane pulled a stool for Faith and she hopped on.

"I'll take whatever you have on tap," Shane said.

"I got Coors or a craft beer from a local place. It's pretty good."

"The local one." He turned to Faith. "Honey?"

Honey?

Clearly, he wanted to avoid using names. The less they

said, the better. But there was something sort of amazing about him calling her honey. Particularly after that scorcher of a kiss they'd just shared.

"Club soda with lime," she told Ray. "Thanks."

Never a big drinker, this definitely wasn't the time to put alcohol in her system. Between fatigue and anxiety, God knew the chaos alcohol might create.

Ray set about pouring Shane's beer and flicked a glance their way. "You folks passing through?"

"Yeah," Shane said. "Car broke down on 84. Tow truck driver gave us a lift so we could rent a car." He jerked a thumb toward the door. "Rental place is closed, but I guess you know that."

Ray gently placed the beer on the coaster, managing not to lose a bit of the foam over the rim. "They close at five sharp. Open to seven on Friday. My brother-in-law owns it."

"Does he live nearby?" Faith asked, a renewed hope sparking inside.

"'Bout a mile. Knowing that miserable son of a bitch, he's half into his six-pack already. But that's a whole different story. You want me to call him?"

Oh, small towns. A girl had to love them. "That would sure help. We were hoping to get to our friend's house tonight."

Ray reached for a cordless phone next to the cash register. The country song streaming through the speakers slid into another and Faith tapped her foot to the fun beat. Something about a honky-tonk woman.

Shane eased toward her, nuzzling her ear and playing his role to perfection.

"We might get lucky here," he whispered.

Big boy, you have no idea. Playing along, Faith cupped his cheek. "That would be nice."

Ray turned back to them. "Good news. He's only half drunk. He'll be here in twenty minutes. "

11

NEARLY THREE HOURS LATER, AFTER SECURING A RENTAL FROM the only-half-drunk owner, Shane pulled into the parking lot of what his mother would call a rattrap motel.

If murderers and drug addicts didn't live here, he might be Mr. Rogers. And there was no way in hell he was Mr. Rogers.

Beside him, Faith made a humming noise. "I guess we know why it's only sixty-nine bucks a night."

He couldn't let her sleep here. No way. Him? He'd had way worse. Caves, condemned, mice-ridden houses, moldy warehouses, he'd seen it all. Given her CIA experience, maybe she had too, but — no. Not happening.

"There's got to be another place," he said. "Anything."

"Not within ten miles. There are three," she made air quotes, "hotels in this town. The other two were booked. This one had a vacancy and it's only eight minutes from Leslie's address. But hey, after the day we've had, if you want to schlep another thirty minutes to a Marriott, let's do it."

When she put it that way, the rattrap suddenly had a certain character to it.

If he had to drive another mile he might put his 9mm under his chin and — *pow* — end this whole nightmare. In his former life, he'd go days on a combat nap. Now? Mental and physical fatigue had gnawed him to a stub.

Yes, it was confirmed. He'd gone soft.

And that pissed him off, but he knew enough about his own stamina to know if he didn't get some shut-eye, he'd be no use to himself or Faith. And God only knew if Larshot still lived at the address Sully had given them. This could be a giant goose chase.

He eased his foot off the brake and pulled into an open spot in front of the office where a vacancy sign flashed. From inside, he'd be able to see through the plate-glass window if anyone approached the car.

"Stay here," he told Faith. "I hate leaving you alone, but the less people who see you, the better." He pointed at the glovebox. "There's an extra weapon in there if you need it. Lock these doors behind me."

Faith saluted. "Sir, yes, sir."

Jesus. Now she was gonna give him shit for bossing her around? He didn't mean to be an overbearing asshole, but if it kept her safe, it'd be worth it.

He exited the vehicle, made sure his T-shirt covered the 9mm holstered at his waist and shut the door, pausing a second until he heard the locks engage.

An older guy in his sixties with slicked-back gray hair and three days' worth of beard sat behind the desk messing on the computer.

He sized Shane up with dull eyes that had probably seen way too much in this hellhole. "Help you?"

"Yeah. My friend called and reserved two rooms."

"Sorry. Only got one left."

Seriously? This guy wanted to jerk him around? Shane

cocked his head. "She called an hour ago and reserved *two* rooms. Or do I need to explain what a reservation is?"

The guy shrugged. "We had a walk-in. I don't think they're staying all night. I figured they'd be gone by the time you got here, and I'd clean the room. Sorry, but I gotta take what I can get here."

A walk-in. If Shane wasn't so damned tired, he'd laugh. By the looks of this place the walk-in was probably a hooker and her John. Or some guy — or woman — cheating on their spouse and looking for a quickie.

"All the rooms have a pullout couch," the guy said. "If you take it, I'll give it to you for forty-nine bucks and when the other one comes available, I'll clean it."

Shane glanced outside where Faith sat in the front seat of the rental. The red flashing vacancy sign illuminated her face as she watched him watching her. Her sleeping at his place was one thing. They'd had an entire apartment to separate them even if she did wind up crawling into bed with him and falling asleep. That had been an accident.

This?

This would be three hundred square feet of space.

And the way he was feeling after that smoking hot kiss they'd shared, all churned up and needing some sort of release, it didn't bode well.

Fuck it. They were grown-ass adults. They'd have to control themselves. And they'd save money on the second room.

"Forget the second room. We're too tired to wait. Can I get fresh sheets for the couch?"

Because God only knew when those linens had been changed last.

After paying cash and receiving fresh sheets along with a plastic key chain with the motel's name emblazoned in gold,

Shane headed back to the car. Faith unlocked the door and he hopped in, handing over the linens.

"Minor hiccup," he said.

She snorted. "Why does that not shock me?"

"He only had one room left. They had a *walk-in.*"

Faith snorted. "Lord, they gave our room to a prostitute."

He gave her the quick rundown on the walk-in situation. "My guess? The random person who got our room isn't Brutus. If it was, he wouldn't bother with a room. He'd kill us in the parking lot." He waved a hand. "Our room has a pullout, we're good. You take the bed."

"Because that worked so well for us last night?"

At that he had to smile. He did love her quick wit. "Something like that."

He drove around the side of the building to room twenty-seven. Above the door the spotlight was burned out. Shit. He did *not* like that. What were the chances, after hustling through the woods, jumping on a freight train and renting a car, that Brutus *had* tailed them?

They'd taken every rural road possible checking for headlights behind them. At one point they'd turned down a dirt road that wound up being a driveway.

They'd been careful. Extra careful. But he'd felt that way prior to the Challenger being blown to hell. And dammit if he hadn't liked that car.

"It's a coincidence." Faith gestured to the building. "The light. There's no way we were followed."

Only one way to find out.

He slid the key out of the ignition and grabbed his extra gun from the glove box so he could store it in his backpack. "Let's check out our new digs. Don't expect too much."

They grabbed their backpacks from the rear seat and moved quickly to the hotel room door. Standing close to the doorframe, but far enough not to appear odd to any onlookers, he unlocked it, pushed it open and stared into complete darkness. Between the lightbulb being blown out and the pitch black in front of him, his temples throbbed.

He shifted sideways, nudging Faith farther out of view before snaking his arm around the doorframe and slapping at the wall. Bingo. He flipped the switch and light flooded the room.

No bad guys.

That he could see.

He drew his weapon and stepped in, waving Faith in behind him as he scanned the room and headed to the bathroom to clear it. One thing they shouldn't do was stand outside drawing all sorts of unwanted attention.

The room had a classic seventies vibe. Brown paneling, shag green carpet, a small closet with no door that made his life easier because it made hiding impossible.

"It's not that bad," Faith said. "We've both slept in worse, I'm sure."

"Not by choice. But I like your optimism."

He stood to the left of the bathroom, giving it a quick peek while she waited, her own weapon in hand just in case. The ancient mirror over the pedestal sink helped his cause, revealing nothing but white tile. Still, he swung in, weapon raised and pointed at the tub.

Empty.

Thank you, Jesus. He might actually get some sleep.

He holstered his weapon, found Faith standing in front of the bed already rummaging through her backpack, pulling out tights, a shirt and leather flip-flops she'd picked up on the way to his place last night.

She tossed the flip-flops on the ugly carpet and made quick work of changing out of her sneakers. "I need a shower. My new sandals will be ruined, but I'm not stepping barefoot on any surface in this place."

"No problem. Take your time."

She nodded. "I won't be long."

When she passed, his gaze shot straight to that cute little ass of hers. Jeez, the woman fascinated him. He hadn't yet learned all the details of her being attacked in Venezuela, but he knew she'd kicked the crap out of two men. One of whom had grown up under the tutelage of the most violent, bloodthirsty dictator Shane had ever encountered. And that was saying something.

Faith? Total badass. Which, in his own twisted way, turned him on. He pounded his fist against his forehead. He needed to focus here. Get his mind right.

He stepped over to what he'd loosely call a loveseat and dragged the cushions off, tossing them aside.

The bathroom door swung open again and Faith came out. "Forgot my toothbrush."

He gripped the mattress frame and pulled. Before the legs even hit the floor his insides curled.

"Dammit."

Not bothering to unfold the frame — the *empty* frame — he set it down.

Toothbrush in hand, Faith used it as a pointer. "That's a problem."

"Ya think?" He waved her off. "Go shower. I'll call my buddy at the front desk and tell him we're missing a mattress."

Faith headed back to the bathroom and Shane dropped on the bed scooping up the phone — something he probably should've disinfected before touching — and hit zero.

"Front desk."

"Yeah. I just checked in. Room twenty-seven. The pull-out? No mattress."

A short pause ensued. "What do you mean there's no mattress? Are you sure?"

"Dude, kind of hard to miss something like that. You got another one?"

"Why would I have another one?"

"Uh, because you're missing one?"

"Well yeah, but I didn't know that. Someone stole it. Goddamn lowlifes. Now I'll have to buy another."

Shane pinched the bridge of his nose. So effing tired. "I feel you, but it's not my problem. How am I supposed to sleep on a pullout with no mattress?"

"I'm sorry about that, but it's late. I can't be banging on doors and disturbing guests asking if I can take their couch's mattress. I won't charge you for tonight and I'll fix it in the morning. That work?"

From the bathroom, a whistling noise sounded as the shower came on. No mattress and whistling pipes. Good thing this guy already comped them for the night.

Shane glanced over his shoulder at the supposedly queen-sized bed that was clearly a full. Unless he wanted to sleep on the floor — and who knew the last time that had been cleaned? — he'd have to share the bed with Faith.

He dragged a hand over his face. It was gonna be a long night.

SOMETIMES A HOT SHOWER WAS ALL FAITH NEEDED TO RESET her mind. After all, things could definitely be worse. She *could* be stuck in that dank basement being gang-raped by violent drug dealers.

Odd how everything was now measured against one

experience. All she could hope was that eventually the event, like the other unpleasant ones, would find refuge in some shuttered place in her memory and she'd avoid the constant reminders.

After draping her towel over the shower curtain rod, she gathered her dirty clothes from the floor. They'd have to find a laundromat tomorrow. Traveling light didn't offer a lot of options for clean clothes.

She swung the door open, letting a burst of steam escape and already thinking about dropping her exhausted body into bed.

Upon exiting the bathroom she found Shane sitting on the bed, staring at the couch.

"Uh-oh," she said. "No luck on the mattress?"

"Nope."

She dumped her dirty clothes next to her backpack and joined an obviously miserable Shane. She settled next to him, bumping her shoulder against his.

"If this is the worst thing that happens tonight, we're in really good shape."

"Believe me, I get that. But, that kiss? The whole 'to be continued' thing? We're both tired. We should sleep. Not," he rolled his hand, "you know."

She laughed. "Agreed. Allow me to point out that I assumed we'd be staying in Edingville for the night and that was three hours ago. Now, I need sleep. Besides, we shared a bed last night and managed to control ourselves."

"Last night was an accident. You fell asleep."

"What are we, fifteen? Our parents aren't going to yell at us."

He stood up. "We're not sharing this bed."

She laughed. This man. So cute. "I'm wildly impressed that you find me, in my yoga tights and oversized T-shirt, so tempting, but I'm exhausted. Rest assured, that hot body of yours is safe with me." She grinned up at him. "At least for now."

"It's not the sex, smartass."

"The sex we're not having?"

"Exactly."

Lord, why did the man have to complicate this when she was so damned tired? "Then what is it, because I'd like to get to sleep and as stubborn as we both are an argument with you could take all night."

He shook his head, scrubbed his hands over his face. "I don't know. I guess, all that talk about my family last night has me screwed up."

"It's understandable. You miss them. It probably stirs up a lot. Honestly, I don't know how you've separated yourself from your family and your friends for so long."

"You get used to it."

Not for a second did she believe he'd gotten used to it. He'd all but admitted it a minute ago. "Yes, but can you do this for the rest of your life? Miss out on all the milestones your family has?"

He blew air through his lips. "I don't know. I don't think that far ahead. That was Bobby MacGregor. Shane Quinn doesn't make plans. Shane takes it day by day."

Faith's shoulders flew back. Did he just...

Ohmygod.

"Bobby MacGregor. That's your name?"

He told her his name.

After two years of locking that shit down, of making sure the name Robert Charles MacGregor couldn't be found in his apartment, his place of business, his car and safe deposit boxes — three of them that he'd spread his personal documents in — he'd just blurted it out.

Compromised himself.

And it was pretty damned easy.

Something about this woman made him take risks. Made him open up in ways he hadn't done since this whole nightmare started.

He wanted her.

And not just sexually.

He *liked* her. Enjoyed her company more than any woman he'd met in . . . hell . . . he couldn't remember.

He met her gaze, fought a wave of emotion because, goddamn, he missed having loved ones. "Yeah," he said. "I'm Bobby. At least I was."

For a few long seconds, she sat there, staring at him like he'd lost his mind. Which, in reality, he probably had. She, of all people, knew you don't share your deets.

"You're still Bobby," she said. "And thank you. For trusting me with that. It means ... a lot."

A loud bang sounded from the room next door. Shane bolted upright, the blood rush sending him to his feet and reaching for the weapon he'd re-holstered.

The bang sounded again, but it wasn't exactly a bang. A pound maybe. Something hitting the wall.

Pound, pound, pound.

And then . . . shit. Were they *moaning*?

Still on the bed, Faith stared at him with wide brown eyes that sparked with humor. Her mouth fell open and she slapped her hand over her it.

"Jesus," he said, when the pounding started again. "I bet it's the hooker. Apparently, they're finding paradise."

More moaning ensued and Faith swiveled around, staring at the wall as if she could miraculously see beyond it.

"John!" a woman shouted. "John, John, John!"

"Holy shit," Shane said. "Is his name seriously *John*?"

Faith faced him again, her lips rolled in, stifling a laugh and her eyes? They were the killer. All wide and lit with amusement that made him think of rollercoasters and fun he hadn't had in too long.

"Maybe she calls them all John," Faith said. "*Maybe,* she doesn't get personal. You know, like when we're in the field. No emotional ties. No intimate moments. It's all about the mission. Keeps her focused on the job."

Shane cracked up. "Are you insane? You're comparing a hooker to a highly trained government operative?"

"Hey, Leslie Larshot made a career out of it."

Well, she had him there. "Huh. You might be on to something there."

A loud cry sounded, then a grunt and...silence.

"I think they're done," Faith said.

Again, Shane laughed. "They must've exhausted themselves."

While they were at it, they'd totally derailed the conversation on this side of the wall. *Thank you, Hooker.* But there was most definitely an elephant in this room. The one that had him revealing way too much about himself. And wanting things he shouldn't want.

"Look, Faith."

She held up a hand. "Your secret is safe with me. I promise you. If we manage to eliminate Brutus, assuming it's Brutus who followed us, and Alfaro has found me. I'll leave Chicago. Staying puts you Dusty and Trevor in jeopardy and I won't do that."

If there was an argument, he couldn't summon it. Had it been only him taking the risk with Faith staying in Chicago, he'd do it. But Dusty and Trevor? No. He wouldn't compromise them.

He walked toward the bathroom, grabbing his backpack on the way.

Time for a long, cold shower.

"This," he said, "is why Shane Quinn doesn't plan ahead. I'm hitting the shower. Get some sleep. Tomorrow might be a long day."

12

AT 6:30 THE FOLLOWING MORNING, FAITH SAT IN THE passenger seat as Shane pulled into the parking lot of an apartment complex that wasn't quite seedy, but far from luxury. The front of the building revealed crumbling bricks, dented gutters and white trim that had long since faded to a putty color.

Aside from the chipped paint, the arched entry doors would be considered charming. Now? It all seemed... worn.

Tired.

Kinda like her. And what a thought that was. After this was over, she'd start fresh somewhere. Find a new place to live. Maybe near a beach so she could sit in peace. Lake Michigan, in the short time she'd been in Chicago, had offered refuge. After work, she'd cop a squat on a bench and just breathe for a few minutes. She liked it.

A lot.

"Cool building." Shane swung into a spot in the second row of the lot. "Too bad nobody's taking care of it."

"I was just thinking that."

She checked her notes on her phone. "We're looking for

One C." She pointed to the third door on the right where a black number one and a C hung. "That one."

A half-filled row of assigned parking spots lined the front of the building and a beat-up Nissan occupied 1C's.

She snapped a picture of the license plate. "I'll send this to Sully. Maybe he can run it for us."

"You should be careful with him."

Now he wanted to start in with the Sully subject? She didn't need the two of them to be best friends, but a resource was a resource. "I know you don't trust him, but he's all we've got at the agency right now."

"And it didn't occur to you that besides us there are only three people who knew we were coming here?"

"You think Sully sent Brutus to follow us? "

He killed the engine and kept his gaze straight ahead. "Jonathan Sullivan has a history of selling out his supposed friends."

She shifted sideways and lifted her chin, giving him her battle glare. "That's your opinion. He helped me get out of Venezuela and away from Alfaro. Why sell me out now?"

Shane went back to watching the building. "Please. If it involved a promotion, he'd do it. Ask him how the hell Brutus found you."

"I will *not*. Hypothetically, how do you know Dusty or Trevor didn't slip and tell someone where I was? I'm sure they still have government contacts."

He snorted and the whole condescending sound of it ignited a blood rush that made her cheeks hot. "Don't be an ass. I'm not accusing them. I'm pointing out that Sully isn't the only one who knows my whereabouts."

"All right," he said, "I'll play. They could have slipped. But that would make them the two most stupid men alive.

Outing you puts them at risk and we've busted our asses staying under the radar. Highly unlikely."

Her phone buzzed an incoming text. Sully. She held the phone up, gave Shane a sarcastic smile. "*Sully* is running that plate for us."

"Oh. *Goodie.*" He went back to staring out the windshield. "Whoa. Heads up."

The door to apartment 1C opened and a man wearing khakis, loafers and a button-down shirt under a blazer stepped outside.

"Look down," Shane snapped.

They huddled together, heads tipped to the floor. "Maybe she got married," Faith said.

"Or she moved."

Faith snuck a peek. The man climbed into the Nissan and backed out of the parking space, paying them no mind as he left the lot.

"Follow him?" Shane asked.

She considered it for a few brief seconds, then shook her head. "I don't think so. If she got married or is living with that guy, she might still be inside. I say we wait."

No activity.

Zero.

Had Faith not insisted on staying, Shane might have given up by now. They'd abandoned sitting in the parking lot three hours ago, opting for getting out of the car because — yeah, two strangers sitting in a parked car for hours wasn't suspicious. They'd taken up hiding in a clump of trees at the back of the lot that still gave them a view of apartment 1C, but kept them out of sight.

This entire trip was a bust. And he was down a supremely sweet car.

He let out a frustrated grunt.

"Don't get pissy," Faith said. "You know how this goes. We've only been here a few hours. Maybe she works second shift and doesn't leave until mid-afternoon."

In which case, they'd be here for — he checked his watch — another five hours. Five hours in which Brutus, if Sully were double-crossing them, would show up, blow both their brains out and hightail it back to Venezuela on Alfaro's private jet.

Done and done. Two birds. One stone.

Lucky Alfaro.

"We can't sit here another five hours," he said. "The cars probably all have parking permits. Ours doesn't. It's too risky."

His stomach let out a rumble. Chow time. If he didn't feed his system in the next hour, he'd have the mother of all sugar crashes. And he needed his mind and reflexes sharp.

"I need food," he said.

She gawked at him. "Now?"

"We haven't eaten yet. I'll stay here while you do a food run. Or you stay here and I'll go. I don't care. In fact, see if you can park the car somewhere on the other side of these woods and double back. Less conspicuous."

This time, she didn't gawk, but the way she stared at him? All dull-eyed and with her lips slightly parted? She definitely thought he'd lost it.

"Shane, you're killing me."

"Nourishment-starved people running from an assassin isn't exactly a great combo."

The lack of an argument clued him in that she, even reluctantly, agreed.

He flashed a smile. "I'll take a double-cheeseburger. A side salad with grilled chicken, if they have it. I need protein. And a couple of waters."

He dug into his wallet, but she put a hand up.

"I've got it."

Before she could stand, the sound of a car pulling into the lot drew their gazes beyond the trees.

The Nissan returning.

Of course. Just as Shane's body might fail him.

"He's back," Faith said, the words rushing out.

They hunkered down, peering around the side of a giant oak. The man parked in the same spot, exited the vehicle and quickly scanned the lot, pausing in the direction of their rental.

Crap. Could he have made them? Or was the strange car tripping his radar?

Either way, it wasn't good.

The dude gave up on the car, glanced around the lot again, surveying the trees.

"Look out," Shane said. "He knows something is up."

They huddled closer, but he could only make himself so small and this tree wasn't nearly big enough to keep them both out of sight if someone came looking.

They waited a solid minute before Shane took another quick peek. "He's gone. Car is still there so he must have gone inside."

Snap.

Shane froze at what sounded like twigs breaking. He whipped his head around. Something was out there. Animal?

If so, a very large one. And that would make them well and truly fucked because he'd have to shoot it and draw all sorts of unwanted attention.

"Don't move," he mouthed.

Another twig snapped, closer this time. Shane pulled his weapon from the holster, holding it in the general direction of the sound. He eased out a breath and slid his gaze left to right, doing a visual sweep. Nothing.

But something was out there. His instincts roared, his skin buzzing like a loaded beehive. He fought the adrenaline rush, concentrated on the area dead ahead where the sound had come from.

Where are you?

A man's head — the Nissan guy — shot up from behind a bush. In less than a second, he trained a gun trained on them. This guy was good. Fast and sneaky.

"Fuck," Shane said, scrambling to his feet.

Shane never considered himself an egomaniac, but his radar ran hot 90 percent of the time, so someone sneaking up on him? Didn't happen a lot. Which meant.

A professional.

The guy's hair was short and dark, like Brutus's the last time Shane had seen him, but the features were all wrong. No wide chin and thick nose.

"Drop that gun," the guy said, his voice somehow . . . off.

The tone. Something about it didn't quite jive.

Shane did as he was told and he and Faith held both their hands in front of them.

"We don't want any trouble," she said. "We're looking for someone."

"I see that," the guy said. He stepped out of the bushes, coming closer, his steps light but swift. "Take your cap off," he told Shane.

Slowly, Shane lifted his baseball cap. The one he'd bought at one of the rest stops along the way. The guy's head craned forward, his gaze locked on Shane.

"Oh, my God. George?"

GEORGE. HIS COVER NAME FROM VENEZUELA.

What.

The fuck?

Shane studied the guy's features, looked straight into his eyes searching for something recognizable. Anything that might clue him in as to an identity. It could have been someone who knew Leslie, but how would he know Shane?

"Come with me," the guy said.

"My ass," Shane shot back. "We're not going anywhere until you tell me who you are."

If he worked for Brutus, they'd already be dead. The buzzing under Shane's skin eased as the adrenaline rush subsided.

Whoever this guy was, he knew Shane. "How do you know me?"

"Who's George?"

This from Faith, whose gaze bounced like a rubber ball between them.

The guy stepped closer, lowering his weapon. Good start. At least they weren't full of holes.

Now barely five feet away the guy halted. "It's me," he said, his voice softening.

Beside him, Faith gasped. She clutched Shane's forearm and squeezed, but kept her gaze on Nissan Guy. "Oh, my God," she breathed. "You're a *woman*. Are you Leslie?"

Shane did a double-take. What the hell was she talking about? The last time Shane had seen Leslie, she'd had a massive mane of red hair, enough makeup to rival any Hollywood actress and had been wearing a short black miniskirt and sky-high heels.

He swung his head back to the guy, his gaze shooting straight to his chest where the loose button-down gave away nothing.

The face though? Could it be? He thought back to Leslie's angular cheekbones and full, heavily lipsticked lips.

This guy's face was more filled out, but a few extra pounds could do that.

"It's me," the guy whispered in that soft voice again. "We can't talk out here. Let's go into my apartment."

"No way," Shane muttered. He turned to Faith. "There's no way this is her."

"Batman," the guy said.

Shane's head snapped back. *Holy shit.*

"Huh," Faith said, staring straight at him. "I see a trend here."

She wasn't stupid. The codeword Dusty had given her was Beetlejuice and now the codeword this person had offered up was also a movie title.

Shane might have to change things up. Damn, he was slipping.

"It's me. Leslie. Now, please, let's go inside before someone sees us."

Faith followed Possibly-Leslie and Shane through the front door of apartment 1C. Inside, the place was small and neat with a white leather sofa, upholstered gray side chair with funky geometric shapes, a metal coffee table and a widescreen TV mounted on the wall.

The opposite wall featured a contemporary print of a woman wearing a wide-brimmed hat. The rich blue background brought her back to a painting she'd spotted in a gallery in Spain a few years earlier. She'd been on an assignment and heading back to her hotel after a meal. A painting just inside the gallery's doorway drew her inside where she'd fallen in love with the works of Manolo Valdes.

"It's a Valdes print," Possibly-Leslie said.

Faith nodded. "I thought so. I discovered his work a few years ago. I love the colors."

"He's a master. One day, I will own an original."

Possibly-Leslie waved them to the sofa and she took the side chair. "It's me," she told Shane.

He held his hand out, palm up. "Prove it. I need more than the codeword."

"Ah, George. You always were so suspicious."

Her voice was softer now, less gravelly, as if she'd given up trying to alter its tone. "When I was ready to leave Venezuela, you were kind enough to vouch for me with your government. After they were done with me, I was given a new identity — Stephanie Turnbull — and left at a Hampton Inn in Montgomery."

"And what was your cover story?"

"I grew up in Louisville, Kentucky." Her voice shifted again, this time easing into a sultry femme-fatale lilt. "My parents owned horses. Thoroughbreds. I went to Western Kentucky University and moved here to escape an abusive relationship. I'd be happy to show you the documents, but they're locked in a safe deposit box. I felt it was safer to start over with a new identity that no one knew."

Her lips lifted into a crooked smile. "Do you really not recognize me?"

Shane sat, clearly shellshocked that the woman they'd been looking for had so thoroughly disguised herself as a man.

"I can't believe it," he said. "Take out your contacts. Then I'll know."

She popped out a set of contacts revealing wide emerald-green eyes. Amazing eyes that transfixed Faith.

No wonder she wore contacts. Those peepers would be a dead giveaway.

"Jesus." Breathy wonder filled Shane's voice. "I knew you were good."

Leslie smiled. "You always were a charmer."

And something about the way she looked at him — heat — set Faith's nerves on edge. Between the sultry voice and the intense green eyes locked on Shane, there was something there.

None of my business.

Whatever had gone on between them was long before Faith's time. Besides, she and Shane had already established that this was a business arrangement. Anything more would be a suicide mission.

Faith pressed herself into the sofa, lifting her chin slightly. Even disguised as a man, Leslie Larshot was stunning. A woman who understood how to use her beauty.

Those haunting green eyes darted to Faith. "What is your name?"

Shane put up a hand. "Don't worry about it. She won't cause you any trouble. We need your help though. I'm not with the agency anymore. After you left Venezuela, I got burned. "Shane held his hands wide. "I've been living the same way you have."

"It's lonely, isn't it?"

"It is."

She faced Faith again. "I assume, since George has brought you here, you're somehow involved in whatever this mission is."

George. How odd to hear someone call Shane by yet another alias. "Yes," Faith said. She wouldn't be too forthcoming about her circumstances, but the quickest way to gain someone's trust was to give them a little something to nibble on. "We're trying to find Brutus. We think you can help us."

"Brutus?" Leslie said. "Why would I do that? If he ever found me he'd torture me for days, maybe weeks, dragging it out slowly before allowing me to die."

"That's why we need to find him," Shane said. "So we can all be free."

Leslie eyed him. "The only way we'll be free is if that son of a bitch dies."

"Exactly."

Leslie threw her head back, letting out an enthusiastic laugh that filled the quiet room and reverberated off the walls. When neither Shane or Faith joined in, she sobered and faced Shane again. "George, you can't kill that man. You'd be a fool to reveal yourself."

"I don't have a choice." He glanced at Faith. "*We* don't have a choice. Like you, I've built a life. Not the one I ever intended, but it'll do. I'm not starting over. From the intel we've obtained, we believe he's in the States. We need him gone. For good."

She dragged her gaze from Shane to Faith, studying her for a moment. "George still can't resist a damsel in distress. For him to risk coming here, you must be some piece of ass."

Refusing to take the bait, Faith met the woman's stare. "It's all about sex with you, huh? This *piece of ass* killed Luca Alfaro. I gutted him and his buddy on the floor of a basement after they tried to rape me. Now, Alfaro wants *my* head. In this little game of can-you-top-me, whatever you've got, it doesn't beat eliminating the man's son. As for George, he may not be able to resist a damsel in distress, but he doesn't deserve to have a psychotic assassin on his doorstep because of me. Please give us both a break and tell us what you know about Brutus so we can get out of here and avoid any of us being discovered."

Leslie offered another crooked smile. The "you've-got-me" one. "So, *you're* the one? Brave soul, killing Luca."

"Not that brave. I didn't know who he was."

"Still. It takes a strong woman to do that. What do you want to know?"

"We believe Brutus is in Chicago," Shane said. "You traveled with him. Know the places he stays. His aliases. We need anything that will help us find him."

"Chicago?" She lifted one shoulder. "I've never been there, but he likes luxury. Smaller, boutique hotels. Whatever is the finest in the city, that's where you'll find him. It's his one weakness. No. I'm sorry. His second. The first is his dinner habit."

Oh, this sounded like something. "What habit?" Faith asked.

"Dinner is at 6:30. Every night."

Shane shook his head. "Seriously?"

"Unbelievable, isn't it. As careful as he is, he allows himself to be vulnerable for a meal and a good bed. He grew up in the slums with a blanket over concrete for a mattress. Some nights, dinner was his only meal. By 6:30 he'd be starving. As of two years ago, his body craved food at 6:30."

"It's a mental flaw," Faith said. "Regardless of the time he eats lunch, his brain tells him he's hungry. Fascinating."

"Perhaps. When we were together, we had to be at a table and eating at precisely 6:30. And if they botched his order, he took it as a personal insult and let them know."

Shane inched forward on the sofa. "What about aliases?"

"He has plenty. When he came to the States, he'd

pretend to be royalty or a corporate heir. Once it was diamonds, another time textiles."

"Do you remember any of the aliases?" Faith asked.

"Of course. I had to write them down, along with a brief history so I could keep them straight. I still have my notes. For leverage — bargaining, if you will — in case he finds me."

"But you won't give them to us."

Shane glanced over and shot her a warning glare. "We've surprised her. Let's give her a minute."

"I don't need a minute." Leslie leaned in, held a steady pointed finger at Faith. "I can see why the agency hired you."

"We never said the agency hired her."

"You didn't need to. My guess is she was a field operative trying to insinuate herself into Alfaro's world. Something went wrong and here we all are."

She wasn't that far off, but Faith wouldn't confirm or deny. "It doesn't matter. What matters is the three of us are in the unenviable position of Alfaro wanting us dead. We can either sell each other out or work together and maybe get on with our lives."

Leslie's gaze pinged between Shane and Faith, finally landing on Shane. "She's got a spine, this one."

"She does. She wants the same thing we do. If you help us find Brutus, we all get our freedom."

13

AFTER MEETING WITH LESLIE, EXCHANGING PHONE NUMBERS and leaving her to consider whether she'd help them or not, Shane and Faith hit a drive-thru for food and spent the majority of the ride back to the motel in silence. Every second of it grated against his already shredded nerves.

In his opinion, silent women, particularly this woman who was never shy about speaking her mind, meant he was either A.) in trouble or B.) in trouble.

What the hell he might be in the doghouse about was beyond him.

"Thinking," Faith said.

"About?"

"A number of things. Leslie living as a man. And if she'll give us Brutus's aliases. She was actually somewhat open for someone in her position."

"I helped her."

"I'm sure you did."

Whoa. He pulled the car into a parking space around the back of the motel, killed the engine and looked over at her. "Excuse me?"

Ignoring his inquiry, she waved him from the car. "Let's not make ourselves a giant target."

Following her through the breezeway in the center of the building, he dug the room key from his pocket. "I have the key."

She held hers in the air. "Got mine."

He waited while she unlocked the door, the stiffness in her shoulders doing nothing to hide her pissiness. What the fuck?

Once inside, he cleared the room — no bad guys — then flipped the safety lock and leaned against the door, arms folded. "What was that crack you made in the car?"

She whipped around, mirroring his stance and crossing her arms. "Maybe you could have told me the two of you had been lovers?"

What now? He almost laughed. "*Lovers?* You think I screwed her?"

"Come on, Shane. Happens all the time. All I'm saying is that we're partners in this. It would have been nice to know the relationship went beyond professional and, oh, you know, maybe she goes nuts or something because you broke her heart."

Priceless.

Women. Funky creatures. "That's what you're worried about? That a *relationship* puts our mission at risk?"

"Of course."

"Liar."

"*Excuse* me?"

"You're so full of shit, Faith. You're jealous."

Did it make him an asshole that it amused him? Probably. But hell, it'd been so long since he'd cared it was almost a relief.

"You could have told me."

She didn't even try to deny it. Fascinating.

"I could have," he said. "But it would have been a lie and I've been straight with you every step."

"You—" She shook her head. "Please. With the way that woman looked at you? There's something there."

"No. There's not. Think about it. She spent years with Alfaro, first as his mistress, then being groomed to do his wet work. He trusted her. She was tasked with keeping an eye on Brutus, who tended to go off-leash too often. Leslie Larshot knows how to play anyone with a dick. With me, she tried. When it didn't get her anywhere, she gave up and saw me the way I saw her. As an asset. We had an understanding."

"What understanding?"

"If she got into trouble, I'd help her. And vice versa."

"How?"

"Her brother, Reynaldo, worked in the palace. Remember I told you an asset I had in the palace helped me when I got busted with Andres's phone? It was Reynaldo. Leslie had told me he could be trusted. Without her and her brother, I'd have died that night. Instead, the SEALS got me out."

She stood unmoving for a second and then her posture changed. All that stiffness sliding out of her shoulders. "That's why you helped her. You owed her."

"Yes. The relationship was professional. That's it. And, so you know, if it had been more, I'd have told you before we left Chicago. I'm not gonna let you go into a situation blind. But, hey, next time, maybe you could ask before rolling with sarcasm and accusations."

"Sarcasm is my weapon."

Well, *that* he didn't expect. His mind tripped back to the conversation in his apartment. To her mother walking out on her. Her grandmother dying. Being a loner because it was easier.

He took a step closer, focused on her eyes. "Why? Because you think no one loves you enough to stick around?" Her eyes snapped, but he continued before she could get a word in. "You blow shit up so the other person won't have to."

HE'D FIGURED HER OUT.

In record time.

Not only had he determined her weak spot, he'd thrown it in front of her, laying it bare. A ball of heat shot into Faith's chest and she threw her shoulders back.

All these years, she'd been dealing with her abandonment issues on her own, steering clear of getting too close, too emotionally wrapped up in relationships of any kind.

No one had ever called her on it. Not once.

"You don't know me," she said.

He shrugged like it was no big deal. Like he hadn't just firebombed her.

"I know enough," he said. "And I'm sure as hell not blind. I've been living undercover for two years, keeping people at a distance because everything and everyone jeopardizes my safety and Dusty and Trevor's. With you, it's different, but the same. We're both too fucking terrified to let anyone see us. Really see us. And it makes you crazy that I pegged you."

It was a damned shame his cover had been blown because he'd probably been an excellent operative. "God, you're full of yourself." She laughed and headed to the bathroom. "I'm taking a shower."

"You do that. I'll be here."

She whirled back, ready to blast him. Ready to verbally rip him apart and shut this whole thing down. "What does *that* mean?"

"You got nowhere to run, Faith. Sooner or later, you'll admit I'm right. You were jealous."

Bastard. "That's what this is about?" She waved her arms. "Then by all means, let's settle it. Let's give you the ego boost you seem to so desperately need. It's like high school all over again, but hey, why not? You're right, Shane. I'm *jealous*. I didn't like the way she looked at you, that tone she took. There was an intimacy to it that made me feel . . ."

Ugh. Why bother. She swung back, headed to the bathroom.

"Not a chance," he said.

Sensing him behind her, she quickened her pace, got to the bathroom and swung the door shut.

Her rotten luck that he had long legs that moved fast, catching her and wedging his enormous body in the doorway. Now she'd never get rid of him and the panic took hold. *Ignore him.*

That's what she'd do. Turn to stone and straight up pretend he didn't exist. Eventually, he'd give up and go away.

"It made you feel what?" he said. "Tell me."

"Get out. I'm showering."

"Tell me what you felt."

She yanked on the shower faucet and whipped the crappy, half-torn curtain closed. God, the place was a shithole. "Get out."

"Tell me."

He wouldn't leave? Fine. He could stay. Wouldn't be the first time a man saw her naked. Besides, it might just be shocking enough to get him the hell out of her space.

Ignore the crazy woman taking her clothes off.

"Well, since you're not leaving, I guess I'm showering in front of you."

She toed out of her shoes, tore her socks off, kicked out of her pants, then ditched her shirt and bra.

Shane's eyes bugged out. "Are you bonkers?"

"Ha! You have no idea how bonkers I am."

She checked the water temperature, found it just shy of scalding and stepped in, snapping the curtain closed behind her.

"I know what you're doing," he said through the curtain. "I'm not leaving. Tell me what you felt. For fuck's sake, just say it. You'll feel better."

Faith tipped her head back. A weak stream of hot water washed over her, but she'd need more than that to fix her problems. To *feel* better. Not only had she been alone her entire adult life, if she had to live on the run, she'd spend the rest of it on her own too.

And didn't that sound peachy? No friends, no family. No intimacy of any sort. Living a constant lie.

Jesus, how did she get here?

She couldn't do it anymore. Nope, nope, nope. Couldn't keep pretending having no family or loved ones was reasonable and convincing herself that she was somehow self-protecting by not forming relationships.

What kind of crap had she been spewing to herself all this time? The lies, the emotional suppression, the self-talk about feeling empowered because she lacked any ties to family.

No more.

Done. Time to be honest. With herself and with Shane.

She whipped the curtain back and stood there, soaking wet and staring at him. Points to him for keeping his gaze above her shoulders.

"I've never had an emotionally intimate connection to a man. I've never *looked* at a man the way she looked at you. Like she knew what your body felt like on top of hers and she loved it. And the more I thought about it, it sent me spiraling down a rabbit hole thinking about all the things I've missed. Sitting there? I realized I want that and I might want it with you. God help us both. Happy now?"

She jerked the curtain closed again, only to have it reopened. "She doesn't know what being in bed with me feels like."

Leave it to a man to be so literal. Hot water continued to spray out of the ridiculous shower head. That showerhead? The CIA should use it as an interrogation device. Completely maddening. "God, Shane! That's not the point."

"Then what the fuck are we talking about?"

She might have to kill this man. "I *thought* she knew and that made me feel . . . alone. Which is totally normal for me. But, when you're around, I like the companionship. I like that I have someone to talk to and bounce ideas off. Today, when I thought you and your *asset* had been lovers, it scared me. Today, for the first time with you, I felt adrift again. Like I was separated from you and I hated it."

She spun back to the showerhead, lifted her face to the wimpy stream, ignoring the fatigue pressing in on her. This would be why she avoided emotional connections. The physical and mental exhaustion wrecked her. "Please, Shane. Just . . . go."

He reached in, shut off the water — of course he did — and grabbed one of the crappy towels with the worn edges. When she got home — wherever the hell that wound up being — she'd buy herself the softest Turkish cotton towels she could find. He handed it over and she wrapped herself in it.

He stepped into the tub.

What the heck? "Um, what are you doing?"

He stayed silent, just looking at her with those crystal blue eyes that, no matter his mood, sparkled. Magic eyes that literally slayed her.

He waited for her to secure the towel, then stepped closer, reaching his arms out and drawing her close.

And, oh, God. Why was he hugging her? Try as she may, she couldn't help flinching.

"I know that fear," he said. "It's different for me, but the same. I left everyone I love behind. All the people I call when something big happens. None of them are available to me. I'm terrified they'll get hurt. Or worse. I brought danger to the people I love. I'm scared of that connection too."

Different, but the same. What a mess. Two people, wildly opposite backgrounds and yet, both afraid to get attached.

Of all the people to fall for, Shane Quinn was probably the worst.

Epic disaster.

So why did being in his arms feel so safe?

She turned her head, pressing her cheek against the soft cotton of his shirt where his heart thumped in her ear.

"This is bad."

"Really bad," he said.

HIS PHONE RANG. LESLIE'S RINGTONE HE'D ASSIGNED AFTER she'd given him her number.

Talk about a sign from the universe.

Well, shit.

He pulled back from the hug and squeezed Faith's arms. "I'm sorry. But that's Leslie's ringtone."

"Answer it."

Sliding the phone from his pocket, he poked the screen. "Hello?"

"It's me."

The throaty, seductive voice. Leslie's voice. A callback this soon might not be good news. Not that he'd blame her. Not only had they risked her cover by coming here, they wanted her to betray a psychotic serial killer. He wouldn't blame her if she told him to shove it up his ass.

He stepped out of the tub, forcing himself to focus on the call. "Hey."

"I'll give you aliases that I know of."

Yes! He spun back to Faith, giving her a thumbs-up.

"You helped me once," Leslie said. "Saved me. This makes us even. But my brother—"

"Reynaldo? What about him?"

"He wants out. Can you help him?"

Jesus. How the hell was he supposed to pull that off? It wasn't as if he could call Langley's switchboard and ask for a favor.

Still wrapped in the towel, Faith stepped out of the tub and Shane followed her out of the bathroom. She stopped at the bed, standing beside it.

He brought his attention back to Leslie. "I'll do whatever I can. No guarantees."

"I'll trust you."

"Thank you. How do you want to do this?"

"It's done."

"Come again?"

"Go to the front desk. There's a bakery box — the Boston creams are my favorites — that was just delivered. Inside the box, you will find the list. And then you leave. Understand?"

She'd been here? Sure, he'd told her where they were

staying, but he didn't expect her to actually come here. "You—"

"No questions. Do you understand?"

He sure did. The more he talked, the longer he and Faith were in town, the more risk it created.

"Got it," he said. "I know what I'm asking of you."

"I know you do. As I said, consider the favor repaid and if you can assist Rey, I'm sure he'd be willing to help in whatever way needed."

The line went dead. Boom. Over. He disconnected, tossed the phone beside him on the bed. His mind spun. The possibilities. Oh, man, the possibilities.

"That sounded promising," Faith said.

"She's giving — correction, gave — us a list of aliases."

Faith's mouth dropped open. "Wow. She's brave."

"You don't know the half of it. I'll explain when I get back." He shoved his feet into his sneakers and jerked his thumb toward the door. "The list is in a box she had delivered. Unbelievable. If they find her . . ."

He shook it off. Neither of them needed him to finish that sentence. They both knew what Brutus was capable of.

"Stay here. I'm gonna grab that box."

"We should get out of town. "

"I agree. You've got 'til I get back to finish showering. I'll call Dusty and Trev. See if one of them can meet us in Edingville after we drop off the rental."

"Should we risk that?"

"No. But we shouldn't have risked this whole thing. And if they don't come get us we're stuck with keeping the rental or public transportation. Depending on train and bus schedules, it could take us two days to get back to Chicago. And I'd rather not keep the rental. We'll either have to return it or get charged a mind-blowing drop-off fee."

"I agree, but I don't want Dusty and Trevor in danger either."

"We'll leave it up to them. If they say no, no harm no foul. My guess? They won't say no."

THE LIST, FORTUNATELY OR UNFORTUNATELY, WAS PLENTIFUL. An hour into the ride, after various detours to ensure a tail — or two — didn't exist, Faith sat in the passenger seat of the rental while Shane kept to the speed limit. Given their anticipation of returning to Chicago, his attempt to avoid getting pulled over might be killing him.

She checked her sideview mirror. The silver car that had pulled behind them miles back was still there. She'd keep her eye on it. She held up the handwritten list Leslie had left them. "There are thirty-one aliases on this list."

"Those are the ones she had. There's probably more. What about hotels?"

Wasn't he just Mary Sunshine? Shaking her head, Faith skipped down the page. "Nothing specific for Chicago. She said he grew up poor. She left a note about the high-end, boutique places he likes. No big names. He's all about the personal touch."

Faith rested her head back and stared at the darkening road ahead. If the man spent his childhood in poverty, and now frequented only the finest hotels, they could form educated guesses about his habits.

She shifted sideways and faced Shane. "His appreciation of the finer things probably extends beyond hotels. We know from Darla's shop that he's a snob about coffee. Why not restaurants? And cars and liquor."

Shane checked his rearview and slid into the left lane to pass what might be the world's slowest moving car.

"I'll roll with that," he said. "Check Michelin-rated restaurants in Chicago."

Ah, yes. The *Michelin Guide*. A publication renowned for its rating system that, each year, sent talented chefs and restaurateurs into a state of euphoria if their establishment found its way to the coveted list.

Faith turned front again, scooping her phone from the door compartment and putting her thumbs to work searching for Michelin-rated restaurants in Chicago. And then what? She couldn't simply call the restaurant and read off a list of thirty-one names. Or could she?

The first link to pop up gave her a handy map of Michelin-rated restaurants downtown. "According to this article, there are twenty-one Michelin restaurants in Chicago. One three-star, a couple of twos and the rest ones." She set the phone in her lap, conjured a cover story. "I'm the harried assistant. I think the reservation for my company's annual board dinner was double-booked and," she placed her hand over her mouth for added drama. "Oh, my *goodness*, there are thirty-one board members."

Shane laughed at her antics. "You're going to read a hostess all thirty-one names?"

"How else will I know if any of those supposed board members also made the reservation? At the prices they charge, there's no way a Michelin restaurant wants a double-booking on such a large party."

"True. They'd lose their ass. I'll help with calls after we return the rental. The way Trevor drives, we'll have a few hours to kill. That Boy Scout won't go over the speed limit. I can't blame him. Right now, I'm ready to blow my head off trying to stick to it."

"I knew it was killing you. But don't complain. He

dropped everything to pick us up. For that alone I'm grateful."

She glanced in the side-view mirror. The silver car was gone. To make sure, she peered over her shoulder for a view of the entire roadway. With all the jumping on and off highways and rural roads Shane had done, if they had a tail they'd have spotted him by now.

She hoped. After the incident in the Challenger, her confidence in her observation skills was sorely lacking.

"The silver car," Shane said. "It turned off at the last exit. I don't see anybody else back there."

Satisfied they weren't being tailed, Faith went back to researching the finest restaurants in Chicago. Then she'd start on a list of hotels.

If Brutus was in the city, she'd find him.

14

THE FIRST TEN CALLS TO MICHELIN-STARRED RESTAURANTS netted Faith a big fat zero.

She dropped her phone in her lap. "I've been thinking about Leslie's brother. Sully can probably get him a deal."

Still twenty miles from the rental car place, Shane remained steadfast in keeping to the speed limit. He glanced over at her, his blue eyes darkening before going back to the road. "That requires bringing him further into this. I don't trust him."

"He got us Leslie's address and ran her plate for us."

It turned out they hadn't needed the plate because Leslie had revealed herself to them, but he'd helped.

Shane shrugged. Damned stubborn man.

"All right," she said. "You've said all along he'd sell his soul for a promotion. He's involved in the Alfaro case and we have a potential asset inside Alfaro's compound. You, of all people, know how long it takes to get an agent inside."

When Shane didn't answer, she took it as a victory. "Am I right?"

He gave her another quick glance, curling his lip while he was at it. "You know you're right."

"Can we further agree that someone — say *Sully* — who is ambitious and would sell his soul for a promotion, would find Reynaldo absolute catnip? Reynaldo can help the agency get Alfaro and that's a career-making case. One that might get said ambitious person bumped to the executive floor. Don't you agree?"

He smiled. Oh, yes. She had him.

"Leading questions," he said. "Classic manipulation tactic. Nice. Executive floor or not. He knew we were coming down here. He may have sold us out and you're willing to further involve him."

Back to this? Unbelievable. The man had given them Leslie's address. He didn't have to do that. In fact, why would he risk getting caught doing it?

She shook it off. "Since I can't move you from this line of thinking, how about this? His ambition might be his weakness. He'll be so busy trying to get to Reynaldo, double-crossing us becomes secondary. He'll have to cooperate with us if he wants Rey."

If the man came up with an argument to that, she might anoint him quick-thinker-of-the-century. And he'd deserve it because she'd been pondering positives and negatives to calling Sully since they'd gotten into the car. And she couldn't come up with nearly enough negatives.

"Okay," he said.

Wait. What? She cocked her head. "Okay?"

"Yeah. We're partners. You've made good points. I have one condition."

Ugh. She hated conditions. "What's that?"

"I want to be on the call. He needs to know it's not a kumbaya moment and that I still don't trust him."

Fine. Whatever. She picked up her phone, tapped the burner number Sully had given her. Two rings in, he answered. "What's up?"

His clipped tone wasn't lost on her. She may have just interrupted something. "Can you talk?"

"Hang on." Rustling came through the line followed by what sounded like a door clunking shut. "I'm good. Got a call in five though."

"This won't take long. Shane is here. I'm putting you on speaker." She tapped the button and before either of them could speak, beat them to it. "Let's keep it simple and get right to it. We found the address you gave us and made contact. She had what we think will be useful intel. We're working on a plan now."

"Virginia," Sully said, using her codename. "I have three minutes. What do you need?"

"Fuck the code words," Shane said. "You remember Reynaldo? The brother?"

A few seconds of silence hung heavy. "I do," Sully said. "She wanted him to leave with her. He refused."

"That's changed."

A prominent pause that made Faith's heart go pitter-patter ensued. She waggled her eyebrows at Shane who'd glanced over at her.

"Really," Sully said.

Statement. Not a question. Excellent.

"Yep," Shane said. "She wants a deal for him. If we can't find Brutus, Rey might be able to help."

More silence and then a low whistle from Sully. "He would be helpful. Let me get into it. See what I can do."

"And Sullivan?" Shane said. "Screw us on this and I'll kill you myself."

"Christ," Sully said, his voice an absolute live wire ready

to snap. "I don't have time for this, Shane. I have shit to do. I'm out."

Freaking Shane.

Faith punched the speaker button and lifted the phone to her ear. "Sully?"

No answer. Just in case, she checked the screen. Nothing. *"Well,"* she said. *"That* was fun. You couldn't resist messing with him, could you?"

Freaking Shane glanced over and flashed a winning smile. "Nope. Now, let's see what he comes up with."

HEADPHONES IN, FAITH SAT AT THE DESK IN YET ANOTHER hotel room they'd checked into after arriving in Chicago the night before.

Trevor had kept to the speed limit, making their remaining nine-hour drive a long one. Considering the guy had spent a total of eighteen hours in a car to pick them up, she'd focused on gratitude and used the time to research hotels Brutus might like.

Now, while Shane ran to the bar to check on things, she'd gotten busy calling the establishments on her list.

She glanced around the room. A decent, no-frills one that offered cleanliness and a mildly clunking air conditioner. Over the years, she'd grown accustomed to hotels. Still, her tiny apartment had just started to feel like home and she found herself daydreaming about going back.

Hopefully, when this was over, she'd be able to do that, but she'd learned long ago not to count on longevity. In her world, longevity was a sucker's bet.

She tapped her pen against the veneer desk. The rhythmic tttpp-tttpp-tttpp kept her focused as the call hit the fourth ring.

"Bonaventure Hotel," the operator said, her voice low with a bit of high-brow-snob thrown in. "May I help you?"

This particular establishment housed a Michelin-rated restaurant that was only one star, but, hey, just making the list was an honor. And since the first twenty Michelin restaurants were a bust, she might get lucky on this one. During her research, she'd gone with the theory that if Brutus enjoyed good restaurants and nice hotels, the Bonaventure would be a double-bonus.

"Good morning," Faith said. "Antonio Rivera's room please."

"Please hold."

The clickety-clack of a keyboard sounded and Faith started tapping again. *Come on, come on, be there.*

She cut her gaze to the bright red display of the digital clock. Eight-thirty. She'd been awakened at dawn by Shane turning on the shower and that turned into an epic fantasy about his naked and sculpted body, all those muscles rippling under a hot stream of water, and her mind went all sorts of fun places.

Places that included him on top of her. *Oooh-eee.*

Shane Quinn.

Total stud.

She'd actually managed to fall back asleep for a few minutes and awakened to find him gone.

No note. No text. No nothing.

Her rational mind suggested it had been common courtesy from a man who habitually put others first.

Made sense. To her *rational* mind. The other one? The side belonging to Liz Aiken who'd gotten way too comfortable with people leaving her? Not so much.

No one loves me enough to stick around. And, oh, that bit of nastiness looped in her mind as she lay in bed. It kept at her and at her and at her and at her until she couldn't take the onslaught and figured she might as well get started on tracking Brutus.

Refocusing her mind had helped. Distraction. An excellent friend.

Now, even with the full pot of coffee from room service, this calling not-so-random hotels was getting old. After working through the list of Michelin restaurants, she'd researched starred boutique hotels in Chicago, finding a solid twenty worth calling. Then she had a B list with another batch.

The operation required her to call a hotel, ask for one of Brutus's aliases and then do it again.

And again.

And again.

When she'd gotten through all the hotels, she'd start back at the top with another alias. Soon, she'd need to take a break because even with her voice disguised, the hotel operators would more than likely question having received so many calls in one morning for nonexistent guests.

The hold music stopped. Finally.

"I'm sorry, ma'am," the operator said. "We don't have an Antonio Rivera registered."

Another bust. Faith disconnected and yanked out her earbuds. Definitely time for a break.

The ka-chunk of the lock disengaging sounded and a burst of panic flooded her. She spun her chair, already cursing herself for not having her gun within reach.

What the hell was wrong with her?

Shane, every bit of his hot self, stepped in, quickly closing the door behind him. She blew out a breath, shook off the blood rush.

"Hey," she said.

"Hey, yourself."

He tossed his key on the dresser and moved toward her, his gaze on her in a way that kicked her pulse into high gear for a totally different reason.

Call it loneliness or a lack of human touch, but being in his presence made her want more of whatever he offered.

But his eyes; something was off. The sparkle had flattened.

Could be exhaustion. God knew they'd had an interesting few days. Combine that with interrupted sleep and it caught up fast.

He hooked his thumbs in the front pockets of his jeans and studied her. Yes, the man definitely had something on his mind. "You okay, fella? You snuck out this morning."

And, whoopsie. He wasn't here two minutes and she'd already let that tiny, vulnerable piece of her loose.

"I didn't *sneak* out. You were sleeping. Did you think—"

"I didn't think anything."

Liar.

They both knew it. She rolled her lips in and met his gaze. "Old habits. It's true. They're hard to break."

"I'm sorry. Next time, I'll leave a note."

He'd do that for her. No hissy fit about her needing to grow up. No telling her she shouldn't feel a certain way.

She could love this man.

Probably.

He squatted in front of her. "I'll never run out on you. Ever. If I'm leaving and it's for good, I'll tell you."

"Thank you."

"You're welcome. I expect the same from you. If you're leaving, you tell me. No going rogue." He held his hand out. "Deal?"

She nodded, gripped his hand and shook it. "Deal."

"Good. Now, what have you been up to?"

Just that fast, they were back to business. A shame really, but maybe, after this mission there'd be time for . . . what?

A relationship?

A future?

Picket fences?

Keep dreaming, sister. She grabbed her notepad and held it up. "I've been making calls."

Shane stood. "And?"

"I'm through three of his aliases and none of the top boutique hotels in the city have him registered."

"I guess he didn't become the best hired-gun by being sloppy." Shane pointed at the coffee pot. "This still hot?"

"Probably not. I can order another. Did you eat?"

A lack of food might be the reason he seemed a bit off. He shrugged and she immediately picked up the desk phone. "You need to eat before your sugar crashes."

Already, she'd learned his cues. Oddly enough, she liked it. Recognizing something in someone.

She ordered him a meat-lovers omelet, two scrambled eggs and ham for her and fresh coffee.

"Protein," she said after hanging up. "Can you wait thirty minutes?"

"Yeah. I'm good."

"Okay. If it's not your sugar crashing, what's bugging you? And don't tell me you're fine. You're not. I can tell. Spill it."

He wandered to the bed and sat on the edge, stretching his long legs in front of him. He folded his arms across that amazing chest.

"I'm tired. Thinking too much. Trying to figure out Brutus's next move. I haven't missed this part of the job."

She couldn't blame him. She'd shown up out of the blue

and thrown his carefully crafted life into turmoil. "I brought disruption. To you and your friends."

"You did."

Yikes. Normally, she'd appreciate the bluntness. Normally. At least he didn't deny it. Not that it made her feel any better. "I'm sorry."

He shrugged. "For what? Making me realize I like having someone around? That I miss companionship?"

Talk about blunt. This time, she didn't mind so much. It, in fact, unleashed a silent squeal inside her. Before her Liz persona took over, warning her of all the pitfalls of getting attached, she forged ahead. "I get it," Faith said. "But reality is a bitch. Even if we deal with Brutus, I can't stay in Chicago."

"We don't know that. We haven't confirmed my cover is blown. We have to figure out if Alfaro found you or all of us."

"If it's just me, I'm leaving. I won't risk you. Or Dusty or Trevor. You've built lives, established yourselves. Once we find Brutus, I'll go."

He met her gaze and held it long enough for her to start doubting everything she'd just said.

"I guess," he said, "what I want doesn't matter."

Of course it mattered. But if it meant further risks for him, she wouldn't stay. And she didn't see a way around that.

"What *we* want doesn't play into it. You know that. Believe me, after the last two days, I'd like nothing more than to stay. I have . . . comfort . . . with you. And I've never had that. My grandmother was the closest thing, but even then, I was always scared. Always on edge. I knew she wouldn't leave me, but her health wasn't good and I understood, down deep, she wouldn't live long."

"God, that had to suck. Constantly waiting for her to die."

"It did. But it also taught me coping skills. Life doesn't play fair. We have to move on."

"Walking away is that simple for you?"

She shook her head. "Not on your life, but you and I? We know this game. We knew fieldwork came with sacrifices."

"But we're not in the field anymore."

Foolish, foolish man. "I want it too."

"What?"

"This. Talking. Having someone who understands me."

"So stay. Why leave? We're in this too deep now. Brutus is here. We have to find him and see what he knows. Then we'll eliminate him. Let's focus on that. When it's done, we'll figure out next steps. Can we do that?"

Shane Quinn.

He might be both their downfalls. "I'll stay until we find him. After that, we'll see what happens."

AFTER FINISHING BREAKFAST, SHANE STOOD BESIDE LIZ AT THE desk reading over her list of hotels. She'd handwritten the names alongside the addresses, the letters neat and compact. Compared to his chicken scratch, her penmanship probably earned high marks.

He pointed to the ones with X's, some with multiples, beside them. "These were a bust?"

"So far. Each X is how many times I've called asking for a different alias. I think you should try those hotels for the rest of the names. Eventually, even with disguising my voice, they'll get suspicious."

He eyed the remaining names. "That's a lot of calls.

Could take days if we have to contact each hotel with each name."

"Yep."

He perused the names and tapped one with two X's beside it. The Elm. "This one is a few blocks from my place."

Damn. What a thought that was. Did this asshole even know how close he was to not only Faith, but Shane?

If he did, Shane had to believe they'd both have had a couple of pops to the head by now.

Faith smacked the space bar on her laptop and keyed in her password. A map appeared with large, highlighted X's. She must have been using note-taking software that let her alter PDFs.

She pointed at the map. "After the restaurants were a bust, I went with the theory that if he went into our coffee shop, he might be staying in the area. The highlighted X's are the hotels I called so far."

"What you have marked in our neighborhood, are those all of them on the list?"

"No. Plotting them was taking too long. I thought when you got back you could help me."

"All right." He wagged a finger at the laptop. "How do I use this software?"

She gave him a two-minute tutorial and left him seated at the desk while she continued her calls from the chair by the window.

"Have you checked in with Henry?" he asked.

Why he was worried about her boss, the professor, he had no clue, but he liked the guy and didn't want him left in the lurch.

"I did. I told him I'd be back tomorrow."

Say what now? How the hell did she think she'd be back at work tomorrow? He spun the desk chair to face her and she immediately threw her hand up. "I know. Don't lecture me."

"If you know, then why?"

"Because he gave me a job. And a chance. I don't want to disappoint him. And, hello? I have rent to pay."

"I can help you with that. I have an emergency fund. This qualifies."

"Absolutely not."

"Faith—"

She drilled him with a look that should have blasted him through the wall. "No," she said. "You've done enough. Besides the risks you've taken, you're already out a car — a really nice one — and you paid for this hotel. That's it."

Okay. He could see her point on this, but it was only money and not worth exposing herself any more than they already had.

"You can't go there. You'd put anyone in the area in danger."

"I know that," she said, her voice carrying some heat. "I have a plan, Shane. The summer session hasn't started yet and Henry is leaving town for a week. He left me some folders. I can pick them up and work remotely."

He sat staring at her, letting her know that this was insanity. If she got fired for not showing up, they'd get her another fucking job.

"Don't," she said.

"What?"

"You're about to launch into telling me there are other jobs. Well, guess what. I like *this* job. I'll probably have to leave it anyway, so I'm going to keep it as long as I can."

"But—"

"No, Shane." She sat forward, resting her elbows on her knees and locking her gaze on his. "The lives we have aren't normal. Stress is the only constant. Our brains are hard-wired for extreme situations. The job with Henry is the reverse. It's interesting and quiet and makes me feel . . ." She broke eye contact, stared out the window where sunshine reflected off the building across the street. "Peaceful. It's like being back in my grandmother's living room watching *Wheel of Fortune*. I like that feeling. I *want* that feeling. Brutus or no Brutus, I want control back."

"After we deal with him, you'll have it. If we do this right, you can start over."

She smiled at him. The you-silly-man smile. "Maybe. I can't do what you're doing. My whole life has been about surviving my circumstances. Somehow, each time I think I'm free — whoopsie — everything blows up. I'm done waiting for the future. I'm already tired of running. After this, I'm done. I want a life."

As much as he wanted to rail on her, argue his point that they could deal with Brutus and she could have that future, he kept his trap shut.

He'd been living undercover for two years and every day it sucked. Sure, he reminded himself to be grateful his head was still attached to his body, but she was right. What they were doing?

Not normal.

He let out a breath. Damn the woman. "What's your plan?"

"It's simple. I'm going to campus this afternoon to pick up the folders. As I said, the summer session hasn't started yet. The place will be deserted."

"You're going to walk to the university alone? I hate your plan."

"It may sound dumb, but it got me out of Venezuela alive. I know how to take care of myself."

"Why chance going it alone? Let me help you."

"No."

"Why?"

"Because if something happens to you, I'll go crazy."

"And if something happens to you, *I'll* go crazy."

As arguments went, it wasn't brilliant, but it sure as hell got the point across. She fired him enough nasty looks to bore a few holes in him, but . . . too bad.

"Can I offer an expanded plan?" he asked.

"Do I have a choice?"

He snorted. "Probably not."

WHEN HE WANTED TO BE, SHANE COULD BE A PAIN IN THE ASS.

What Faith had going here was a classic stalemate. An epic battle of wills.

One thing she'd learned in her time with the agency was that banging horns with stubborn men only wasted time when she could finesse her way around the issue.

"Fine," she said. "Tell me your idea."

"I'll come with you. I've lived here longer and know the streets."

He paused, obviously waiting for her to admit it. Fine. She'd give him that. "I agree you know the city better."

"Excellent. We'll move fast, pretending we're joggers. I'll park a few blocks from campus. Then we'll run the rest. I'll wait outside while you slip into the building. If anyone stops you, show them your ID, tell them you were out for a run and needed to pick up work Henry left. Then you get out of there and we hightail it to another hotel. That keeps us on the move until we find Brutus."

As plans went, she'd heard worse. Entering the building wouldn't be an issue. She had a keycard and her staff ID.

When it came to Brutus, she knew enough to understand he worked neat and quick. He opted to walk up
behind his target, put a bullet in their head and calmly
hustle off rather than set up some elaborate assassination
attempt that might cause chaos.

Neat.

Quick.

Given that fact, if Shane went with her and Brutus found
them, he'd have both of them to deal with. Two against one.
And their combined skills gave them a definite edge in the
fight.

"We can do this," he said, clearly feeling the need to
convince her. "It makes everyone happy. You get the folders
and keep your job and we all stay alive."

Before she could respond, he held his hands out.
"Deal?"

"You're a pain in the ass."

"What's your point?"

She laughed. An honest-to-goodness laugh that relieved
all sorts of pent-up tension. "You really *are* a pain in the ass,
but you make me laugh. Deal."

"Good. And ditto."

He spun back to her laptop. "Before you distracted me
with your insane plan to get yourself killed, I was looking at
a location you haven't gotten to yet."

She rose from her chair and wandered back to the desk.
"Which one?"

"Le Meilleur."

She repeated the name to herself, calling on the
minimal French she'd absorbed over the years.

"Le Meilleur," she said. "It's French for 'the best.'"

"Well, that sure as shit fits his profile."

"Where is it?"

He pointed at the map. "A couple miles from Darla's coffee shop."

"If he was canvassing the area, it's possible he just wandered by the Brew and stopped in."

"Of all the gin joints — " Shane muttered the famous line from Casablanca.

"He comes into ours."

"And thank God he did or we wouldn't know he was here."

True.

Faith tapped her password into her phone, Googled the number for Le Meilleur.

Two rings in, an operator answered.

"Hello," Faith said, "Antonio Rivera's room please."

The standard round of keyboard tippity-tapping sounded from the other end. "I'm sorry. We don't have anyone by that name, registered."

That would have been way too easy. "Hmmm," she said. "How about Matthew Ortega? My coworkers are traveling together and I'm not sure which name their assistants booked the rooms under."

"Let me check." More tippety-tapping ensued. "Please hold."

Please hold? What did that mean? Could they have actually found him? She gripped Shane's arm, squeezing hard. *God, God, God. Please.*

"What—"

She put her finger to her lips and then a phone on the other end of the line rang. Once, twice, three times.

"Fourth ring," she whispered and why she whispered she hadn't a clue, but whatever.

"Hang up," Shane whispered back.

She disconnected.

"I think we found him," she said.

"You *think*? Could be another Matthew Ortega."

"Thanks, Debbie Downer."

"Hey. Just saying. We should confirm. And the only way is to put eyes on him. We can do that this afternoon after you get your files. If it's him, we show up at the hotel around six — assuming he sticks to his pattern of dinner at 6:30 — and follow him."

15

AFTER SNEAKING AROUND THE CITY WITH SHANE — AN ODDLY
fun excursion, all things considered — Faith retrieved the
folders her boss had left for her in his campus office. *Their*
office, she supposed. And wasn't that a nice thought that
gave her a sense of belonging? She'd spent the better part of
her life in search of that elusive feeling, but somehow it
always seemed just out of reach. Maybe now could be different. Maybe.

She glanced over at Shane, who'd lowered his window to
snatch the ticket out of the parking garage entry machine.
Maybe.

Ticket in hand, he hit the gas, climbing the first three
levels of the garage before finding a spot.

"Phase two," Faith said, reaching back and storing the
folders on the backseat.

While Shane drove, she flipped the visor down, checked
that the wig — blond — she'd slipped on was straight and
her gun was hidden under her T-shirt. During the ride,
she'd had the unenviable task of dragging a pair of jeans
over her bike shorts. Thankfully, she was short. Shane had

opted to wear cargo shorts instead of running clothes, so he'd avoided the whole quick-change dilemma.

They exited the car and both headed for the stairs, something that typically minimized interaction with other folks who might be waiting for the elevator.

They hit the street level and Shane held the door open. Bright sunshine blinded her for a few seconds until her eyes adjusted. He pointed to his right and she turned, weaving around the pedestrians crowding the sidewalk on a beautiful spring day.

Mission or no mission, walking the city streets with Shane gave her a taste of what life could be. The aroma of freshly baked bread and pastry from the bakery on the corner. The oddly comforting sound of honking cars and garbage trucks. All of it so normal.

She wanted this. Wanted to stroll with Shane, maybe holding hands, while they stopped for fresh brewed coffee. And a doughnut. Nothing beat a fresh coffee roll.

Two blocks later, Faith followed Shane into a side door entrance to the Le Meilleur hotel. The name on the door read Le Café in a swirling gold font that screamed high-class.

Shane, his short blond hair covered by a baseball cap, held the door open for her and met her gaze with laser focus. "You ready?"

She was most definitely ready. "You know it. Watch me work."

They'd gone over — and over and *over* — the plan. She liked to work off script while Shane was downright anal about who said what and when. Another of their differences. Shane, the ultimate team player against Faith, Queen of the Pivot.

But she'd do her best to stay on script. That said, Shane

might have to compromise. After all, this was their pretext, their charade to confirm that the Matthew Ortega staying at this hotel was Brutus. Sometimes things went sideways during recon missions. When it happened, she improvised. A lot.

She scanned the area behind the U-shaped bar where a male bartender messed with the cash register. It gave Faith a second to take in her surroundings. Given the mid-afternoon hour, the dozen tables stood mostly empty. A man and woman dressed in business attire sat near the window engrossed in documents spread across the table. They wouldn't be a problem. The bar stools, except for one patron perched at the end of the bar, were also all open.

The abundance of available stools — a green light if she'd ever seen one — made her choice easy. Part of their plan required her to be the cute, wronged woman who needed the bartender's help. The fact that he was a man helped. Sexist or not, men loved the whole woman-in-distress angle. Every time. It was part of their DNA and she'd learned to tap into the hero complex when necessary.

Taking the stool next to her, Shane picked up the beer menu sitting wedged in a holder on the bar.

The bartender closed the register and faced them. Faith tagged him as mid-thirties. His short brown hair was neat and gelled into place. His face — more rugged than handsome — had interesting angles with a wide chin and deep-set eyes.

He dropped two coasters emblazoned with the hotel logo in front of them.

"Welcome in," he said. "What can I get you?"

Shane ordered a craft beer while Faith stuck with club soda and lime. A minute later, the bartender — Rory, according to the name tag attached to his black tuxedo vest — set their drinks down. "Would you like a menu?"

"We're good," Shane said.

"Okay then. Let me know if you need anything."

Rory turned back to the register, his back to them, but well within earshot. Go time.

"He's here." Faith added an amped-up, rough edge of desperation to her voice that Rory would be deaf not to hear. "I know he is."

Playing his role, Shane patted her hand. "We'll find him."

"The mortgage is three months past due. I can't move my kids again. They've been through enough." She jabbed her finger into the bar. "He has to meet his responsibilities."

Her gaze was fixed on Shane, but from the corner of her eye she spotted Rory's head turn. Not completely looking over his shoulder, but enough for her to know she'd gotten his attention.

"If he's here," Shane said, "we'll find him and call the cops."

"He has money. He just won't pay. His own kids. What kind of man *does* that?"

She paused, drew in a hard breath and thought about the day her grandmother died. The anxiety and fear. The absolute shredding of her system because at eighteen years old she was officially alone in the world. As it did then, her chest locked up. Every time, every damned time she thought about getting that phone call, about the shattering of her life — *again* — the emotion welled up, filling her chest until it might explode.

Now, fully engaged, Rory peered over his shoulder at her.

Come on, Rory. Don't make me put myself through this for nothing.

"Dude," Shane said to Rory, "can we get some water?"

In less than a second, Rory threw ice in a glass, hit a button on the little handheld thingamajig that dispensed beverages and passed her the water.

She took a healthy gulp, the cold shocking her system and sharpening her focus on the task at hand.

She set the glass down again and dabbed at her lips with one of the napkins Rory had finally set in front of them. "I'm so sorry. How humiliating."

"No. It's okay. Believe me. I'm a bartender. This is nothing compared to some of the things I see. Are you sure you're okay?"

"Yes. And if all goes well in a little while, when I find my rat bastard ex-husband, I'll be even better."

Beside her, Shane made an art of clearing his throat. "We're, uh, looking for him. Her ex. He hasn't paid child support in a year. They have four kids."

Rory's jaw dropped. "Come on, man."

"I'm a private investigator," Shane said. "Mike Abrahams. Becky hired me to help find this guy."

Faith bobbed her head. "He's so kind. He's been working pro bono for six months."

The ad-lib earned her a little side-eye from Shane, but he'd have to deal with it.

"Wow," Rory said. "That's cool."

Shane lifted one shoulder. "Four kids and no child support. How can I charge her? Anyway, this asshole moved out of state, but we think he's here for a conference."

Rory eyed them. With any luck, his thoughts had gone exactly where Faith had hoped they would. After all, he was a bartender in the hotel where her rat bastard ex-husband was staying.

"Look," Shane kept his voice low as he peered around the restaurant. "We need help finding this guy." He pulled out his wallet, retrieved a photo of Brutus they'd gotten from Sully and slid it across the bar. "This is him. Matthew Ortega. His hair might be blond now. Have you seen him?"

Before even glancing at the photo, Rory's gaze ping-ponged between Faith and Shane, the panic clearly taking hold. Hotel employees, in Faith's opinion, were like lawyers. Client/attorney privilege and all that. Some of them were vaults. Impossible to crack.

But Rory was also a guy who lived on tips and by the looks of this place, it was a slow day.

Shane dragged two hundred-dollar bills from his wallet and set them under his coaster. "Anything you can tell us would be appreciated."

"Please," Faith said, widening her eyes and softening her voice, playing up the damsel in distress.

Sometimes being a cute, petite woman played to her advantage and she wasn't opposed to using every tool in her arsenal.

Rory's gaze shot to the cash and then to the photo, studying it a minute longer and then . . . "He's here. He's not blond, though. His hair is dark now. Like the photo."

For a second, the words floated just outside her mind's reach. Brutus. *Here.* Warring fight or flight instincts took hold. She peered at the lobby entrance. The man could walk through those doors any second. Then what? Shoot-out in the restaurant?

Run?

No. They'd see this through.

"He's here?" she asked, hoping to hell she hadn't dreamed it. "He probably complains about the food, right?"

Thank you, Leslie, for that bit of intel.

Rory's eyebrows shot up. "Wow. You do know him. He was here earlier and moaned about his lunch. Said the bread was stale. That's nonsense. We get a bread delivery every morning and the owner donates anything that's left at the end of the day."

"He's a food snob. I wouldn't be surprised if there's spit in his food."

"He's a crappy tipper too."

Shane rested his elbows on the bar and leaned in. "Any chance we can get his room number? I'll call the sheriff and have him arrested."

Rory shook his head. "Sorry. I'll get fired."

Dammit. So close. Faith made a show of slouching. Time for the big guns. She thought back to that day in her dorm. The call from Mrs. Tully, who checked on Gram each morning while Faith was at school. Mrs. Tully had found Gram still in her bed. At least she'd died in her sleep. Faith was grateful for that. That Gram hadn't tried to get up and call for help, but collapsed — alone — on the floor.

On cue, tears welled up. She squeezed her eyes closed and the pressure sent waterworks down her cheeks. She swiped and swiped again.

Shane patted her hand again. "Don't worry. We'll have the sheriff get a warrant. It'll take time, but hopefully he won't check out."

All while poor Rory stood there, totally hustled by two people who'd made a career out of hustling people.

Finally, he leaned in. "Hang on."

He turned back to the register and rifled through a

pouch tucked beside it. Faith met Shane's eye and waggled her eyebrows. Yes, she was that good.

A minute later, the bartender swung back to them placing a leather portfolio on the bar. A white slip of paper stuck out of the top.

"Here's your check," he said, making hard eye contact with Faith.

Then he left them, moving on to the man at the end of the bar.

Shane picked up the check and held it between them. Definitely a bar bill.

But not theirs.

This was no mistake. This was Rory earning himself a $200 tip by handing them Matthew Ortega's lunch order. Turkey and Swiss on whole wheat. Side of fruit and coffee. Grand total of $31.82. At the bottom, the guest had printed his name, then signed it, adding his room number.

There it was: Room 232.

Bingo.

DAMN, THE WOMAN WAS DOWNRIGHT SCARY.

After confirming Rory was still out of earshot, Shane swiveled his stool to face Faith.

"Great job," he said. "Although, you went rogue on me with that bit about me working pro bono. We didn't practice that."

"Sometimes that happens. I'm good on the fly."

He wouldn't argue the point, and in the grand scheme, her improvising hadn't been an issue. Still, he wasn't a fan of surprises.

He checked his watch: 4:05. They'd already been sitting here twenty minutes. At any time, Brutus could show up looking for cocktail hour. Shane didn't expect it since the guy liked to lie low, but sitting here? Too much of a risk.

He opened his wallet, grabbed another twenty and stood. He waved at Rory, who watched him set the cash on the bar with the other bills before wandering toward them.

"Thanks for the help," Shane said. "Keep the change."

The bartender eyed the two hundreds. "Thanks, man. That's good of you."

"Maybe it'll make up for my jerk of an ex," Faith added.

Now she was laying it on thick. Shane shot her a look. "Let's head out and make those calls."

They exited via the same door and turned right on the sidewalk where the evening rush of pedestrians picked up.

"If he sticks to his plan," Shane said, "and has dinner at 6:30, he'll either be leaving the hotel or ordering room service before six."

"Two hours to kill."

"I'd prefer he leave the hotel." Faith halted at the corner to wait for the light, then glanced around, making sure they were alone. "We could grab him on the street. Inside is too confining. Never mind the security cameras."

Total agreement there. "If he leaves the hotel, we'll grab him. If it's room service, we have to get into that room. Somehow get him out of the hotel and take him somewhere to question him. We'll get answers and . . . you know."

And how the fuck did killing a man seem like a reasonable ending? It wasn't. But he'd consider it doing the world a favor by eliminating a man known for terrorizing people.

A teenager pushed around Shane, stepping into the street and rather than be overheard, Faith went on tiptoes, kissing his cheek and whispering in his ear. "I can be a drunk woman trying to get into the wrong room. See if he'll open up."

As soon as traffic cleared, the kid darted across the street leaving them alone on the corner. "He'll never open for a stranger. Too disciplined."

The green Walk sign flashed and Faith stepped off the curb, nearly getting clipped by a cabbie making a right on red. Shane grabbed her arm, pulling her back onto the curb until the cabbie cleared out. Close one. Faith? Totally unfazed. The woman might be nuts.

"We know food is his weakness," she said, whispering in his ear again. "The room service waiter. Maybe we use him as a distraction."

He stepped into the street, walking to the other side and drawing her down the side street away from the crowd. He stopped between a dry cleaner and a coffee shop that had closed an hour ago. "What are you thinking?"

"It's bold."

Shane shrugged. "We're spitballing here. No judgment."

"If he's as anal as Leslie said, he'll want food in front of him right at 6:30. If we time it right, we can be in the hallway pretending to be guests and when the waiter comes out, we catch the door before it closes. Then we go in."

It was doable. But . . . "Security cameras are an issue. You'll need to ditch the wig since the cameras already caught you in the bar. We'll get you a hat and keep our heads down. Faces covered."

"We won't be in the hallway long. A minute at most. Does that work?"

He cocked his head, pictured it playing out. "I hope to hell it does."

16

"HIS ORDER IS IN. I JUST SAW IT ON THE COMPUTER."

Rory stood, hands braced against the bar as Shane slid onto the stool he'd occupied two hours earlier. Beside him, Faith, her head topped with her new Cubs baseball cap, did the same. If Rory was curious about her lack of blonde hair, he kept it to himself. Still, Faith could have easily explained it away by admitting she'd donned the wig hoping her rat bastard ex, if she should see him, wouldn't recognize her from a distance.

Apparently the spec ops gods didn't feel it necessary to give them a fucking break by having Brutus leave the hotel for dinner. They'd spent the last ninety minutes on two plans, one that included grabbing Brutus off the street when he headed out for dinner and taking him to the mausoleum for an extended conversation. If the man gave them the information they wanted, i.e., whether or not Alfaro knew Shane's identity — and location — they'd kill him and be done with the piece of shit once and for all. Killing him bought them time to figure out a plan for Faith while Alfaro regrouped.

Plan B, the one they'd hoped not to use but were now forced to, consisted of getting into Brutus's room, escorting him out of the hotel without calling attention to themselves and then taking him to the mausoleum.

In short, it would take a fucking miracle to pull off Plan B. Shane's guess? They'd have to kill him in his room at the hotel. Brutus wouldn't let himself be taken to a secondary location. He'd put a bullet in himself first.

Shane shook off his thoughts and glanced around the bar. Considering the dinner hour, the place hadn't picked up much. A couple of full tables and folks scattered at the bar. *Two, four, six...* Twelve people.

No wonder Rory was appreciative of Shane's earlier two-hundred-dollar tip.

Shane leaned closer to Faith, half whispering so the guy two stools down didn't overhear. "For a Michelin-starred establishment, the place has foot-traffic issues. Or is this separate from the one on the front side of the hotel?"

During their recon of the building, they stopped to check out the menu for a restaurant that shared the front entrance to the hotel.

"This one isn't on the list. Only the one up front. This is considered casual dining. I suppose guests can call room service and order from either menu."

Ah. Now that made sense. And something he should have known had he not been distracted by . . . well . . . everything.

"I thought I told you that," she said. "Sorry. Anyway, I'll use the ladies' room in the lobby and scope out the stairs. Then we can head up. We need a look at the second floor for spots to hunker down."

No kidding, but they weren't taking that chance. It would be their luck for Brutus to step into the hallway for ice. "Let's find out where his room is in regard to the elevator."

"Hang on."

Faith pulled her phone from her backpack. She tapped the screen a few times. "Here we go."

"What?"

"There are pictures on the hotel website."

She held the phone between them. On screen, a photo revealed a long hallway lined with doors and a seating area in front of the elevator bank.

All good, but who the hell knew when or where those pics were taken. "We don't know which floor that is."

She rolled her eyes. "Hey, it's a start."

Rory came by to check on them and Shane dropped a couple of twenties on the bar. Cash was king and he was going through a lot of it.

"Question." He gestured to Faith's phone. "Is this the layout of the second floor?"

Rory checked the screen. "Yeah. Every floor is the same. Just different colors. Are the cops coming for him?"

Um, no. The cops weren't coming for him.

But Shane and Faith were.

Shane lifted one shoulder. "We called the sheriff's office. Waiting on a call back."

Which was a load of crap, but as long as Rory didn't have a friend or relative who happened to be an employee of the Cook County Sheriff's Department, it might fly. Because the truth was, Shane had no idea, not a freaking clue, how one went about having a deadbeat dad arrested.

Rory wandered down the bar to check on his customers and Faith slid from her stool. "I'm hitting the ladies' room."

"Be careful."

Be careful? What the hell did that even mean at this

point? He blew out a soft breath as Faith exited the bar into the lobby area. The minute she was out of his sight, his stomach pitched.

This whole shitshow wore him down. He'd been living with uncertainty for two years now. More or less, he'd gotten used to it. This was different.

This was Alfaro possibly knowing his identity and Shane being forced to pick up his life, abandon his business and run.

Again.

And that pissed him off.

All the time spent building his business and getting regulars who loved his mom's cheddar burgers. Day by day by day gaining — and sometimes losing — customers.

He didn't make huge money, but his profits were up 16 percent so far over last year. If the trend continued, he'd carve out a decent living.

Leaving would, in short, suck.

"Hi."

He lurched from his thoughts to a brunette sliding onto Faith's stool. He almost laughed. Almost. Was this chick seriously going to hit on him? Just as they were about to do a takedown?

"Uh." He pointed to Faith's glass. "I'm sorry. That seat is taken."

"I know."

The brunette looked over her shoulder toward the street entrance, then back at him. In the dim light he couldn't tell the color of her eyes, but they were giant saucers and most definitely spooked.

He swiveled to face her. "Are you okay?"

"Can I sit here a minute? I just got off the bus and I think some guy is following me."

Well, shit.

But — hang on. She could be playing him. Maybe Brutus had spotted them and, like Leslie once did, this woman worked for him?

She checked the door again and came back to him. He sized up her stiff shoulders and pinging gaze. Spooked. If she was playing him, she deserved an Oscar. At least a nomination.

Then again, so did he and Faith.

Liars everywhere.

He'd like to tell her to call the authorities, but the last damned thing he wanted was a couple of cops showing up.

Faith appeared beside him, eyeing the woman. "I'm gone three minutes..."

The woman shook her head, started to stand. "No. I swear. I'm not hitting on him. Someone is following me. I figured if he saw me with someone he'd leave me alone."

Shane glanced at his watch. 6:13. Time to get rid of this woman and get Operation Brutus in motion. He stood. "What does the guy look like?"

"Tall. Dark hair and round glasses. He's wearing jeans and a jacket. Blue maybe?"

"He's outside?"

"He was behind me before I ducked in here. I don't know if he's still out there."

Beside him, Faith gave him the tiniest of head shakes. Her not-so-subtle warning that he shouldn't leave his wingman. How ironic considering her penchant for going rogue.

And, yeah, they were close on time. What was he supposed to do? Leave this woman when she needed help?

"I'm gonna go check this out," he told Faith. "Wait for me."

. . .

The man had lost his mind. This might be their only chance at Brutus and he wanted to play hero?

No sir.

In typical Shane I'm-in-charge fashion, he marched toward the door while Faith's blood simmered to a boil. All that planning and badgering her into promising she'd follow said plans to the letter and *he* goes rogue?

"I'm so sorry," the woman told Faith.

She wasn't the only one. Damned Shane.

But what could she do? After having been attacked by violent men and experiencing that fear, that gut-shredding anxiety, Faith couldn't tell the woman to bugger off.

"It's not a problem."

Yeah, it is.

Pivot. That's what she'd do. She glanced at the door Shane had just exited through and checked her phone.

Getting close. 6:16.

But she'd been working alone for years. She could easily get a jump on things and head upstairs. By the time the waiter brought the food up, Shane would be done with his superhero mission and they'd resume their plan.

Easy.

She tightened her hold on her backpack, hooked her thumbs into the straps and faced the woman. "I'm sorry. I have to go." She gestured to Rory. "The bartender is a good guy. Stay here until it's safe. When my boyfriend—" And how weird was that? "comes back, tell him to meet me upstairs."

The woman bobbed her head. "I'm so sorry. I really am."

Faith squeezed her arm. "It's okay. We just want you safe."

Before leaving, she peered at the street entrance. No Shane.

Dammit.

He'd hate this. Would probably lecture her endlessly about going rogue. Well, so had he and they couldn't lose Brutus. Not when they were so close.

FAITH CLIMBED THE LAST FEW STEPS TO THE SECOND FLOOR with her eyes locked on the hallway door. Assuming there were cameras on either side of the door, she kept her hat pulled low and head down.

Modern security being what it was, they'd match her clothing to images from the bar cameras, but she'd at least try to hide her face in this part of the operation.

Certain things, she couldn't control.

Gun. She pressed her arm to her waist, took refuge in her 9mm holstered there. She'd checked the magazine earlier, replacing it with a full one.

She wouldn't mind one last check, just to make sure that baby was ready to go. With her luck, a security guard monitoring the cameras would see her with a weapon and bolt on up. Plus, she couldn't stand here long.

Thinking, thinking, thinking. Too much of it never amounted to anything good. Not in her world.

Time check: 6:19.

Six minutes to Brutus's dinner delivery and no Shane.

She had to move. Figure out a spot where they'd be in close enough proximity to catch Brutus's door when the waiter left.

Damned Shane. Their perfect cover would have been as a horny couple, groping each other in the hallway because — *oh my goodness, Mr. Security Officer, we just couldn't wait until we got to our room.*

Roll with it.

That's all she'd do. Like every time before.

She opened the door, took half a step and peered down the hallway. No activity. Excellent.

The elevator dinged and she scanned the area. Nowhere to hide. And ducking back into the stairwell would be a giant, waving I'm-up-to-no-good flag.

Another step got her into the hallway, where she slid her phone from her pocket and pretended to read.

The clink of glassware sounded. A waiter with a room service cart exited the elevator and headed the opposite direction.

Was that Brutus's order?

If so, they were early. Of course they were. Why should anything go according to plan?

She remained in her spot, now pretending to send a text while keeping an eye on the waiter. Thirty yards away, he came to a stop in front of a room, glanced down at something on the cart and then knocked on the door.

Go.

Too far. She needed to get closer. Time it just right so when the waiter walked out she'd pop her foot in the door, slide in and once out of view of the hallway cameras, rip her gun from her holster.

No. What if Brutus, after allowing the waiter in, spotted her?

She'd have to time this right, staying far enough away that Brutus wouldn't see her, but close enough to catch that door when the waiter left.

Lord, it better be Brutus's room.

She walked quickly, her steps silent against the carpet.

Where the hell was Shane? Without him the whole op came apart.

But this was her chance. Maybe the only one she'd get to

eliminate Brutus and give herself an opportunity to run. To hide from Alfaro.

Ten yards from the waiter, she slowed and dropped her hand to her side, ready to pull her weapon. *Not yet.*

She leaned against the wall, pretending to check her phone. The door opened and the waiter nodded at whoever stood inside the room. "Good evening, Mr. Ortega," he beamed. "I have your meal."

Bingo, bingo, bingo.

Adrenaline tore through her like water through a broken dam. She eased out a breath, stole a glance at the door.

No Shane. She should wait. Let this go.

"Thank you," a man said, his Spanish accent barely perceptible.

The waiter pushed the cart into the room and her pulse pounded. *Bam, bam, bam.* Focus. That's all she needed to do. Stay on task. Using her thumb, she pretended to answer a text that was nothing more than random letters that wouldn't be sent.

The clink of glasses brought her attention back to where the waiter disappeared inside the room.

She drew a long breath, taking in the stale air-freshened air, let it flow through her nose and out her mouth. If she could finish this...

Freedom.

Finish it.

She gave up on her phone and walked past room 232, pausing two doors down to check her phone again and go through the whole pretend texting routine. Behind her, the ka-chunk of a lock disengaged. She angled back to where the waiter exited the room. Another juicy burst of adrenaline plowed her forward.

The waiter headed the opposite direction toward the elevator.

Go, go, go.

She hustled, quickening her pace. Two more steps and she'd be there. She kept her hand at her waist, ready to pull her weapon. She pictured it. Jamming her foot in the door, sliding through while drawing her gun and ... surprise!

Brutus wouldn't know what the hell to do. Chances were, he wouldn't have a weapon in hand while a waiter brought his food.

She hoped.

She'd keep him at gunpoint until Shane showed up. Which had better be damned fast.

Too much thinking. She could do this. She took the final step, focused on the door — *go, go, go* — and watched it close.

IN AN ACTION MOVIE, FAITH'S PLANNED ENTRANCE MIGHT'VE been Oscar-worthy.

In real life?

She stood in the hallway cursing a closed door.

Regroup. Walk away, find Shane and try again tomorrow.

No. Brutus was right there, on the other side of the door enjoying his gourmet meal. She had him.

And as much as she wanted to be a team player, this was her chance to end this thing. She could still use the element of surprise and hold Brutus at gunpoint until Shane arrived.

All she needed to do was get in. As simple as it was, she'd knock and hope he opened the door. She glanced at the door across the hall. No peephole. Finally, a break. She'd knock, pretend to be housekeeping and — *voila!* – when the door came open, she'd push her way in.

She drew a long breath. Yes, she could do this.

Before lifting her hand, she checked her phone again. No messages. She shot off a text letting Shane know she was going in.

He'd hate it, but he should have considered that when he'd left her in the bar. Text sent, she tucked the phone back in her pocket.

A muffled voice came from the other side of the door and then the handle moved. *Moved.*

Panic shot from her core, sending hot shocks shooting through her limbs. The door flew open. "You forgot salt," a man yelled.

His gaze landed on her and he halted. Tall and dark-haired, he loomed over her, his eyes nearly bugging out. For a second he stood, clearly as stunned as her. Slowly, like a building wave, his features smoothed and a small smile slid across his face.

She'd only seen photos, but this was most definitely Brutus. And, unless she'd completely lost her edge, he'd just recognized her.

17

SCREW THE SECURITY CAMERAS. FAITH RIPPED HER SIDEARM from the holster and pointed it at his head, catching him off guard and sending him retreating into the room. She stepped in, stalking him as walked backward, hands raised in surrender.

Oh, she wouldn't be falling for that. The man was a highly experienced assassin. The bonus here was that she'd surprised him and he more than likely didn't have a weapon on him. He'd have one close though and the farther he got into the room, the more vulnerable she'd be.

"Hold it." She slid her finger over the trigger and aimed between his eyes.

He halted again and another smile revealed straight white teeth he'd probably spent a small fortune on. "I knew you'd be a challenge." The words came in a soft lilt that screamed of amusement. "Thank you. But you won't leave this room alive."

They'd see about that. She returned the smile, reminded herself that she'd survived men like him before. Had, in fact, gutted them with her bare hands.

The plan. Dammit. The plan was to keep him alive and question him. Where the hell was Shane?

That one moment of hesitation cost her because Brutus moved. Three quick steps toward her. *Shit.*

"Stop!"

Too late. In another step, he'd be on her. Forget the plan. She needed to survive.

Now.

In one smooth motion, she pulled back the trigger.

Click.

Nothing. No shot.

What the . . .

A skull-splitting roar erupted in her ears and she sucked a breathe, fought for concentration. The new mag. She'd forgotten to jack the first round into the chamber. Rookie mistake.

Shit, shit, shit.

Upper body hunched like a linebacker, he closed in for that last step, ready to tackle her.

Move.

But the hallway . . . Too tight. Nowhere to go. Trapped. And that was one thing she never tolerated.

Her senses fired, flooding her with the scent of Brutus's cologne.

Brutus. Right there. Do something.

She hurled the gun. Just slammed it right in his face. It hit him square on the nose and bounced off. He reached up, covering his face while half doubling over. Excellent. Just enough room for her to do some damage.

Go.

She stepped in, ramming her forearms into the back of his shoulder and neck.

"Ooff,"

She pushed on his back and drove her knee up — *boom, boom, boom* — three quick thrusts that hit him on his already battered face. Not enough to disable him, but more than enough to shove him sideways into the wall.

More room. If she was to have any chance of surviving without a weapon, she needed space. She bolted by him, into the living room where a loveseat and two chairs filled the open area in front of a glass door. Balcony.

Two floors up. If necessary, she'd jump over the rail. Even Brutus wasn't crazy enough to fire a gun onto a busy street with a load of witnesses.

She hoped.

She spun back. Brutus shoved away from the wall, the amused smile now gone.

"You bitch."

Her mind snapped to a nasty, dank basement and the stench of urine.

Someone knocked on the door. "Room service," came a familiar voice from the other side.

Shane. Finally.

A spurt of relief refocused her.

In that half-second, Brutus was on her again. Charging. She sidestepped but . . . *dammit.* He looped an arm around her waist, hauled her into the air and tossed her to the floor.

The ride sent her hat flying. She hit the floor hard, her backpack and the rug helping to absorb the blow, but her head bounced like a coconut and an explosion of white blocked her vision.

A loud, crash sounded. *Please let that be Shane kicking in the door.* Otherwise, she was toast. Brutus was too big and too strong and he now had her on the ground.

"Hold it," Shane said from somewhere above her.

Pain ripped through her scalp. She reached up and hit

skin. Fingers. Brutus. Dragging her to her feet by her hair. Before she could muster any defense, he slipped his forearm around her neck and locked his hands together. The bulk of her backpack left her at an odd angle and pain shot through her lower spine.

Son of a bitch.

He pulled her close to his body, his hot, nasty breath spraying her cheek. Six feet away, Shane stood in the entry, gun raised.

Brutus tightened his hold, keeping her between him and Shane. Human shield. Of course. And by now, with all the commotion, security would be on the way.

She couldn't think about that. Right now? She needed a weapon. She looked left — nothing within reach — then right. A desk with a folded laptop on it sat just out of arm's reach.

Laptop. If they got out of this and managed to kill Brutus, they'd take the laptop. No matter what, she'd grab it.

She went back to Shane, meeting his eye, making sure he understood what he had to do. "Shoot him," she said. "Don't worry about me. Do it."

More than likely, she'd die in this room anyway. If Brutus went down with her, it would be worth it. No question.

He tugged her closer, the pressure against her throat stealing her oxygen and making her eyes spurt tears. He took a step backward, pulling her with him. "Follow me," he told Shane, "And I'll throw her over headfirst."

Oh, hell no. If she had to die, she preferred the bullet to a broken neck that might not even kill her.

"Shoot. Him," she said, her voice strangled.

Holding her close, he opened the balcony door.

"Shane! Please! Shoot him."

But wait. She was on her feet and . . . *bam*. She kicked

him. A backward blast with her heel right to the shin. He made a noise. A low grunt that indicated she'd inflicted at least a little pain. He tightened his hold, cutting off her air again.

"I will enjoy killing you," he whispered.

Not.

Today.

She thought back to that basement. The stench. The blood. The anger. All of it seeming to rush down her legs, every ounce of power rocketing to her feet. She lifted her foot and delivered another, kick. Same spot. *Kick, kick, kick.* He let out another grunt, but this time, he tipped forward, loosening his hold enough that she tipped her chin down, slipping it partway under his arm. Room. She had a little room. She stepped right, made a fist and whipped her left hand back.

Whether she hit him in the groin — her intended target — she wasn't sure, but it was close enough because instinct tipped him forward and she drove her elbow up and into his chin. She broke free, tripping on her own feet and landing hard on her ass in the balcony doorway.

A shot rang out and she huddled into a ball, covering her head for a second until . . . silence.

"Faith!"

Shane sprinted to the balcony door where Faith scrambled to her feet. "I'm okay." Her head whipped side to side. "Where is he?"

The son of a bitch was on the move before Faith had even hit the floor. "Over the balcony."

"Dammit!"

They rushed to the rail and peered over. Below, a small

crowd on the sidewalk stared up at them. What was wrong with people? They hear gunfire and stand around?

He scanned the sidewalk. No Brutus. At the corner, a man darted through the intersection. The guy had a set of wheels on him. In the time it had taken Shane to check on Faith, Brutus had hauled ass the half-block to the corner. Even if they got to the ground, they'd never catch him.

A siren blared. Not necessarily a response to shots fired at Le Meilleur. In Chicago, it could be anything. But they wouldn't wait to find out.

"Security!" Someone yelled from the hallway, behind the door that had closed after he'd kicked it in.

At any time, they'd realize the lock was busted and walk right in.

Fucking fubar mission might get them both locked up.

What the hell had she been thinking, coming in here alone? He faced her, ready to give her a healthy preview of his lecture.

Sirens.

He latched on to her elbow. "We've gotta get out of here. Can you run?"

"I want the laptop."

She whipped her arm free and ducked back into the suite, grabbing the laptop and a cord plugged into the desk outlet. She stuffed both items into her backpack as she headed back to Shane.

"Good eye. I didn't even see that."

"You were distracted." She pointed at the balcony rail. "I guess we're going over."

"Are you hurt? Can you do it?"

Already, she swung her leg over the rail. "I'm good. Let's roll."

As pissed as he was at her for not waiting, this woman

was a warrior. Laser focus. No wonder she'd survived in Venezuela.

He followed her over the railing, glancing down to where the crowd below gave them a wide berth. They'd make this quick. He gripped the iron spindles, crouched low, hung his feet over and let go. His body plummeted the few remaining feet to the ground. Anticipating the impact, he kept his body loose to hopefully avoid blowing out a knee and hit the ground, sticking the landing.

Before he could even move, Faith dropped beside him. She landed hard, rocking back and he grabbed hold before she went over.

The onlookers continued to disperse. Probably their good sense returning, given the fact that two people who might be carrying guns had thrown themselves over a balcony.

The sirens grew louder. Way too close. "Gotta go."

They hustled to the corner where the bright orange Walk sign flashed. Possibly their only break in this clusterfuck.

Shane pointed left. "Let's get to Michigan Avenue. We'll get lost in the crowd."

18

"YOU WANNA TELL ME WHAT THAT FUCK THAT WAS?"

Shane stood in yet another hotel room — a Hampton they'd checked into because they needed to get off the street. Having no idea if Brutus might be following them, they weaved through pedestrian traffic, circled blocks, hid in a few alleys before deciding they were probably clear.

Probably.

Total shitshow.

Seemingly undeterred, Faith used a tissue to open the laptop. A multitasker. Oh. Goodie.

"Excuse me?"

She heard him. And her tone? That holier-than-thou one he despised whenever he heard it. From anyone.

He crossed his arms. "I told you to wait."

Now she full-on faced him, pushing her shoulders back. For a small woman, she knew how to make herself large. "You certainly did. The opportunity presented itself and I didn't intend to lose it because you had to play superhero."

Superhero? What. The. *Fuck*? And now it was his fault? What was he supposed to do? Leave that woman to get attacked? He never did find the asshole following her. That chapped his ass even more. "You could've waited. We *could've* done it tomorrow."

"Sorry. That wasn't in my plan. What if he checked out? Then what? We'd start from scratch and I'd still be on the run."

"I'm on the run with you."

"But he's here for *me*. We still don't know if he even knows who you are. So, yes, *Shane,* I saw an opportunity to help myself and I took it. Sue me."

She went back to the computer. Total dismissal. Amazing how easily she disposed of people.

"Working alone," he said, "as usual."

Keeping her eyes on the computer, she scoffed. "Don't start with the team player crap."

"We had a *plan*."

"And *you* chose to deviate from it. Seems to me, I was the team player today."

For the first time in his godforsaken life, Shane was speechless. Seriously? She expected him to leave that woman on her own? "Was I supposed to ignore her?"

She swung her head to him, meeting his gaze. "The bartender could have called a cop."

"Call a cop when we're about to assassinate a man one floor up." He snorted. "Brilliant."

That stopped her cold. Good.

"Whatever, Shane. Keep in mind, we got this laptop because of me."

At that, he rolled his eyes. *Queen of the Pivot.* "You're killing me, Faith. I don't give a shit about who did what. We're in this together. I've been straight with you since the second we met. Did I get sidetracked helping that woman? Yeah. That's on me. Knowing what I know now, maybe I'd have done it differently. I don't know. But I never expected you to go into that room on your own. And the fact that you did scares the hell out of me. And it shows me that you don't trust me."

Her mouth opened, but immediately closed. Hell, maybe they were finally getting somewhere. All he knew was this had to stop. And the two of them at odds with each other wouldn't help them find Brutus.

Pressure built behind his eyes. He squeezed them closed and pressed his palms against them. What did he have to do to get through to her? To make her understand they were in this together. No matter what.

"It's not..."

He dropped his hands and looked straight at her, waiting for her to finish. Nothing. "It's not what? Tell me."

She shook her head. Blew out a breath. "I trust you. It's . . ."

The whirring of the laptop's fan broke the silence. She shut it and the room went quiet. He'd wait her out. Maybe finally get an indication of where her mind was.

"I don't know," she said, her voice quiet and, hell, totally defeated. "I'm so used to doing things a certain way. Going it alone. It keeps me focused. Flying solo means not worrying about where my partner is. Today, it frustrated me that I had to think about where you were while our plan was falling apart. That's new and completely uncomfortable for me. I don't know what I'm supposed to do with that."

If he was smart, which he believed he was, he'd tread carefully here. Pretending to understand was useless. Given the short time they'd known each other, she'd bust him on that. Compared to her, he'd grown up in paradise. Perfect family unit.

He made an effort to keep his voice level. "Why do you

have to do anything with it? You, of all people, know that when you're in the field anything can happen. Today was no different."

"It *was* different. You want me to change the way I operate."

He stepped closer and she popped out of the chair sending it rolling back against the wall. *Whoa.* She tilted her chin up. Body language for come-near-me-and-I'll-kill-you. Whatever her thoughts were right now, she did not — in any way — want him closer.

And, since he wasn't in a rush to die, he stayed put. Forced himself not to move. "No," he said. "What I want is for you to open your mind to options *other* than going rogue. You came to me for help and I gave it to you. That was my choice. Now, whether you like it or not, we have to work together. That means we both make adjustments. Next time, I'll figure something else out for that woman. That was my mistake. I'll own it. If we're gonna get through this, I expect the same from you."

MIRACLES.

That what Shane expected. He *expected* her to abandon the one thing — her independence — that had kept her sane most of her life.

And that, she couldn't do.

She cocked her head. "It's easy for you. You're accustomed to a team environment. I'm not."

"You don't give yourself enough credit. Look what you've done. You've been on your own for years. You got out of *Venezuela* on your own. No credentials and minimal money. You did that. There is *nothing* you can't do. You just have to commit to it."

Commit to it. He made it sound so easy. Like all she had to do was decide, hey, I'm going to flip this switch and change everything about me and it'll be easy because I decided it would be.

Good.

Luck.

But even she had to admit something had to change. Her aching skull and neck were proof of it. Her actions today, her insistence on going into that room alone, might have resulted in an innocent man dying.

That would have been her responsibility.

She lowered herself to the king-sized bed. Of course, the king room was the only one available. Ironic and yet another sign that she'd have to figure out how to share her space. It was, in fact, a major *fuck-you* from the universe. She let out a frustrated laugh.

"What's funny?" Shane asked.

"Aside from the universe flipping me off?" She waved it away. "You're right. I'm sorry."

A long pause ensued and she peered up. A slight smile quirked his lips. *Oh, the bastard.* With the mood she was in, it took a strong man to gloat.

"Believe me," she said, "that was *intensely* painful for me to admit." She gave him an all-teeth smile. "See, already I'm learning to be a team player."

At that, he barked out a laugh. "I'm wildly impressed."

At least one of them was. Placing her hands on her knees, she blew out a long breath. "I lost Brutus."

"*We* lost him. But we've got the laptop. We'll call Dusty. See if he can get us into it. He's pretty good with that stuff. If he can't, he'll know someone."

He sat down next to her, the bed giving way to his much

heavier weight. He bumped her shoulder. "We're okay. The day wasn't a total bust. "

Giving her an out. Shane, as usual, doing the kind, compassionate thing by simply moving on. Where the hell had he been all her life? She nodded, but couldn't quite meet his eye.

"He won't go back to that room," Shane said. "If he's smart, which we know he is, he has his arsenal stashed off-site. In case he needed to bolt. That's what I'd do."

She lifted her head and finally met his gaze. "Thank you. You could have been an ass about this whole thing. Drilling it into me about all the mistakes I made."

"I made mistakes too. We're human."

"It's most definitely been a learning experience."

On more levels than she'd like to admit. The first being that she might be falling in love.

"SHANE QUINN, WHERE HAVE YOU BEEN ALL MY LIFE?"

With Faith, Shane was learning, a guy never knew what to expect. Total chameleon this one. One second, she'd jump into the fray, totally unafraid, and the next . . . Well, hell, that was the intriguing part. A guy just never knew what came next.

Kinda like the question she'd just hit him with. Could be a joke. Maybe not.

She sat there, staring up at him with her soulful brown eyes that had pretty much slayed him from the beginning. "Ha!"

Chickenshit answer, but a safe one considering he didn't know where this conversation might go.

"I'm serious," she said. "You call me on my crap and do it

in a way that doesn't make me want to kill you. That alone is a miracle."

He shrugged. "We're different, but the same. Both afraid of losing what we have. Even if what we have isn't optimum. It's ours. The one thing we can control. That first day, when you walked up to me on the street and I saw the faded bruise on your face, it lit something in me. All I wanted was to protect you. I still feel that way." He bumped her shoulder again, smiled down at her. "It's worse now because there are other things I want. Seriously naughty things that my mother would scold me for."

Faith snorted. "Pig."

"Most men are."

"So, I guess we both want what we shouldn't have. I could come up with plenty of reasons to go our separate ways."

He met her gaze, holding it for what felt like a year but was probably only a few seconds. "You've got a list of reasons we shouldn't get involved. So do I. As long as those lists are, I've got an alternate one."

Companionship being number one.

Emotional connection running a close second.

And, yeah, regular sex with a woman who excited him wouldn't hurt.

Beside him, Faith rested her head on his shoulder. Probably more from fatigue than anything, but he'd missed this part of being with a woman. Lately, sex had been more about fulfilling a physical need. Getting that release. He'd get the job done and hit the road before anyone got too attached. Most of the time he felt damned shitty about it.

A selfish prick really, but why spend too much time thinking about it. He couldn't offer anyone a relationship. Relationships required honesty and intimacy. Neither of which were possible. Not with him. *Golly, honey, did I mention I'm not really Shane Quinn?*

Just contemplating living that life exhausted him. At least alone he didn't have to lie.

Truth of it was, he hadn't come across a woman that made him want anything serious.

At least until now. What did that mean for either one of them? He kissed the top of Faith's head, giving himself another minute to not think. To not make himself crazy worrying and what-if-ing everything to damned death.

One day. That's all he wanted. One day of peace.

Then she did it. She reached up, dragged her hand down the center of his chest and curled her fingers into his T-shirt.

His body immediately responded. In a big way. "Uh-oh," he said. "Keep that up, and you'll be in for a long night."

She laughed. "I won't complain."

His mind went crazy, leapfrogging all over the place. Do it, don't do it. Let go, don't let go.

All of this could be stress relief. Two people who'd been on the run and ready to blow off steam.

Bullshit.

He knew it.

Didn't care either.

He dipped his head and she lifted her chin, meeting him halfway. She upped his game by sliding her hand underneath his shirt, her warm fingers sliding over his skin. *Holy shit.* His body erupted into a flaming ball of heat.

He wanted her.

She eased back, drew his shirt up. "Take this off."

"Faith, we're—"

"I know what I'm doing." She lifted the shirt up. "Can we not dissect it? For the next few minutes or an hour or five hours, please, just stop."

For two years, it'd been constant vigilance. Avoiding missteps. Not being reckless.

Now, he wanted reckless. He wanted to be Bobby MacGregor again and take a chance. On something. On someone.

On the worst possible woman he could imagine, but the one woman who understood his hell.

Together, they lifted his shirt over his head and her hands were immediately on him, those fantastic fingers exploring his chest, his neck, his shoulders.

She dragged her thumb over the scar on his right shoulder. "What's this?"

"Bullet."

She kissed the spot. "I'm sorry."

"I was lucky."

She lifted her lips from the spot, then gently bit him.

Oh.

Baby.

He stood, grabbed her hand and brought her to her feet. She slid her hand free and lifted her shirt over her head, tossing it behind her. Then she smiled at him and it was like the brightest sunrise bursting in his chest.

Her bra went next. Unlike in the bathroom in Alabama, where he forced himself to not look at her body, he took her in. Her lean legs and hips. The soft swell of her tits. Her hard nipples.

This woman had beat the crap out of two monsters. And killed them. Little Bo Peep turned badass.

So goddamned impressive.

He ran the backs of his fingers over her cheek. "You're beautiful."

In response, she toed out of her sneakers, bent low to peel her socks off and wiggled out of her jeans and her underwear, the movement somehow insanely sexual — at least he thought so — and making him hard.

Clearly on a mission, she reached for him, going straight for the button on his jeans.

"Time to ditch these. Let me see the rest of this yumminess."

He toed out of his shoes, dropped his pants, kicked them aside and sat to rip his socks off.

His wallet. He'd tossed it on the bedside table behind them. He drew her down to his lap and kissed her long and slow, taking his time, letting his tongue explore hers.

Who knew where they'd be tomorrow? Or in an hour. They might as well enjoy it.

He hooked his hands under her thighs and stood, carrying her to the side of the bed where his wallet and the condom he kept stashed inside waited.

Setting her down, he snatched the wallet up.

Behind him, she ran her hands over his shoulders and down his chest, pressing herself against his back and sending zings of heat shooting in all directions while he dealt with the rubber.

"I love this," she said.

"What?"

"Touching you. Being close."

Again, she kissed his shoulder and — game over. Still in her arms, he shifted to face her. "Should have known," he said. "That first day. I should have known you'd change everything."

FAITH LAY BACK ON THE BED, WATCHING SHANE, ANTICIPATING that moment, that glorious moment when he'd lower himself, drawing closer and closer and covering her much smaller body with his.

She'd fantasized about it. From that first day on the Ferris wheel when she'd snuggled into his side and felt . . . what?

Surrounded by him. Protected.

"I don't want to crush you," he said.

She drew him closer. "You won't. I want to feel you."

He propped himself on his elbows, then kissed her, letting his tongue slide in and out of her mouth, revving her system.

She explored the taut muscles of his back, his rear, his thick shoulders. Anywhere she could touch.

Breaking the kiss, he eased back an inch. "When you touch me, I'm on fire. It's insane."

"I feel it too. Like I can't get enough. All I want is my hands on you. All the time."

"Well, don't ever let me stop you."

He kissed her again, this time crushing his mouth to hers, kicking things up a notch or twelve as he ground his hips against hers, letting her feel the hard press of his erection against her inner thigh.

If the size of that erection was any indication, Shane was about to make her a very happy woman.

She bit him. Right on the shoulder. Just nipped into flesh and he let out a gasp. He liked that. Apparently a lot.

He nuzzled her neck, trailing kisses up and over her jaw until he got to her mouth where he plunged his tongue in again and she forced herself to stay present. To enjoy every touch and murmur. Every slide of her fingers over his body and the euphoria that came with freedom.

"Thank you," she said.

He inched back, met her gaze. "Haven't done anything

yet."

"Believe me. You have."

She opened her legs and he slid inside her. One long, easy move that seemed to go on and on and on.

She let out a gasp and tipped her head back. This moment. This one amazing moment with his weight on her, his body connected to hers for the first time, she wanted to bottle it. Save it forever.

She would love him.

After everything she'd lost, it should have terrorized her. It didn't.

That alone was a gift.

She raised up, pumping her hips, silently begging for more. For him to take her over that amazing edge she hadn't experienced in so, so long.

And, God, the way he moved. Total command of his body. All that strength and control zeroed in on her, making her feel cherished.

"Please," she said.

He nuzzled her neck again "I don't want it to end."

She clapped one hand over his ass, then reared up, sending him so deep inside her that she cried out.

"That's it," he said, picking up his pace, pumping, pumping, pumping. "You're killing me."

She pulled her legs back, crying out again as he managed to push even deeper inside her. He might break her in two, but . . . so good. So, so good.

And then his finger was inside her, pushing her even closer. "I can't hang on," he said.

"Keep that up and I won't either."

They both laughed and the sound, the two of them having fun — *fun* — filled the room.

I will love him.

Shane pumped his hips and plunged inside her over and over again. Friction, the all-out intensity, spun her mind and body into a chaotic swirl.

More, more, more.

For the first time in a very long while, she surrendered. Just let her body take control.

She opened her eyes, found Shane's crystal blue gaze on her. Whatever happened between them, she'd never get those amazing eyes from her mind.

She grabbed his cheeks and pulled him to her, kissing him with everything she had, driving her tongue into his mouth and giving as good as she got.

He broke the kiss, threw his head back and . . . game over. The two of them went over that beautiful edge.

Together.

FOUR HOURS LATER, SHANE STOOD INSIDE THE MAUSOLEUM hideaway with Faith and Dusty across from him in the soccer chairs. Dusty, as usual, had the surfer vibe going with his shaggy hair and scruffy beard.

The guy should be on a beach in Southern California selling T-shirts to tourists. Instead, they were in a filthy abandoned coal mine trying to crack open the laptop of an international terrorist.

James Bond had nothing on this crew.

Dusty pulled the laptop from the cheap backpack Shane had stuck it in three hours ago. They'd delivered it to him via a dead drop at a coffee shop where they'd set it on the floor next to a stool Dusty had commandeered. While they were getting their coffee, Dusty and the backpack disappeared.

"The short of it is," Dusty said. "I can't get into it. Way

above my pay grade."

Dusty had talent with computers, but a hacker he wasn't.

Shane blew air through his lips. "Dang."

Faith held a hand up. "Don't panic."

"I'm not." He faced Dusty. "Options?"

Dusty slouched back, tented his fingers in front of him and shot a glance at Faith, the two of them exchanging some sort of unspoken message that, if Shane were a betting man, probably involved that asshole Sully.

"Don't say it," Shane said.

"Okay," Dusty shot back. "I don't know what else you want *me* to do. I don't have the skills to hack into this thing. Farming it out is the only way and Sully is already in the loop. If not him, there's a guy I know. Former NSA vulnerability analyst. But the more people who see it, the more risk."

"You don't trust him," Faith said.

Dusty met her gaze for a few long seconds. "I don't trust anyone besides Shane and Trevor." He smiled. "Maybe you."

Shane pushed off the wall, did a slow lap toward the door and back. "You trust Sullivan."

"He comes with an asterisk."

Fucking Dusty. "What the hell does *that* mean?"

"He's the least likely to screw me."

"My God," Faith said. "I thought I was cynical."

Shane let out a sarcastic laugh. "You're no slouch in that department, but we might have you beat."

Something he didn't take pleasure in because, Jesus, living his life this way sucked. One day, he'd wake up and not feel instant pressure in his chest. One day.

He paced back to his spot on the wall and propped his foot against it. "We're not bringing the NSA guy in."

Dusty's eyebrows hiked up an inch. "You're agreeing to

Sully then?"

"I'm not *agreeing*. He's the devil we know. In terms of risk assessment, he's the best option." He looked over at Faith. "What do you want to tell him about how we got it?"

She shrugged. "We tell him the truth. Let him decide what to do with it. It's not as if we can say we *found* it. He'll know we got it illegally, but half the stuff I discovered while in the field was obtained by playing outside the lines. If this laptop gets us something we can use, I'm not worried about it."

"All right then. Call him. See what he wants us to do with it."

In a case of déjà vu from just days ago, Faith walked across the open field of the cemetery while speaking to Sully, who was equal parts intrigued and irritated.

The upside? They had Brutus's laptop.

The downside? They'd shot up a hotel room, left a bunch of witnesses on the sidewalk and called attention to a situation they shouldn't be calling attention to.

"Seriously," Sully said. "You people are destroying me."

"Yeah, well, welcome to my world."

At that, he laughed. Something he hadn't done a lot in her experience with him. She'd managed to lighten up the ultra-serious Jonathan Sullivan.

"Okay," he said. "Let me clear this with the brass, but plan on me coming to get that laptop tomorrow. I'll let you know details soon."

She disconnected and turned back to Shane and Dusty, who trailed behind in the dark.

She waited for them to close the short distance, their silhouettes backlit by moonlight. What an interesting pair.

Shane, the broad-shouldered, clean-cut warrior and Dusty, a hippy just off the fuzzy bus.

She waggled her phone in the air. "He's flying in tomorrow."

"Tomorrow?" Shane's head dipped forward. "That fast?"

"Yep. He's half in freak-out mode about us shooting up a hotel room. He's running the trip by the big shots, but told me to plan on it. There's no way they won't want Brutus's files."

"Whoa," Shane said. "Once we turn it over, it's gone. We might be able to use something on there."

She cocked her head. Ye of little faith. "I'm on it, Shane. I told him he has to give us a backup."

"I knew I liked you," Dusty said. "Even I don't have big enough balls to ask for that."

"Please," Shane said. "You *really* think he'll give you a backup?"

And *ohmygod,* she might have to kill him. She understood his sense of loyalty to his friends and his being pissed at Sully for selling out Dusty, but right now? When they were all literally running for their lives? Shane needed to set aside his personal feelings and play nice.

She poked her finger at him. "Don't be an ass. Yes, I *really* think he'll do it. He gave me his word. When it comes to Sully, that might not mean much to you, but I have to believe in something. Have you even *thought* about what this could mean?"

Shane got quiet — too quiet — and took a step forward, meeting her gaze with a hard stare that even in the dark told her she'd hit a nerve.

"I've thought about nothing but your freedom," he said. "I've risked my own freedom — and Dusty and Trevor's too — for it."

Ouch. That stung.

Dusty stepped closer, drawing their attention. "Cut the shit and take a breath. You're both being stupid."

"Stupid?" she and Shane said in unison.

At least they were in agreement on *that*.

"Yeah." Dusty pushed his shoulders back, refusing to back down. "That laptop might link Alfaro to all sorts of nastiness. At the very least, it'll drive him out of power. At best, we'll get him thrown in prison."

This, Faith had to admit, was true. Alfaro in prison? She'd love to see it. "He wouldn't survive a day in there."

"Of course not," Dusty said. "The rival cartels would hang him."

Oh, oh, oh. "And with him out of the picture, no one will care about his revenge. His supporters will distance themselves from him in a hot second."

Shane. She reached for him, wrapping her hand around his forearm and squeezing. "You'd have your life back."

And she'd have given it to him. Instead of complicating things, making him vulnerable, wouldn't it be something if she could free him? Free him and maybe be a part of that freedom.

She'd been avoiding emotional attachments since her mom left her, but the thought of waking up next to Shane — as stubborn as the man was — each morning? She liked it.

A lot.

"She's right," Dusty said. "If we get Alfaro out of the picture, you go back to your family."

She spun and started toward the car on the other side of the field. "Damn straight, I'm right. We'll get that laptop to Sully and see what kind of secrets it might tell us."

19

AT SIX A.M., AFTER A NIGHT OF LIMITED SLEEP FOR BOTH OF them, due to stress reduction in the form of banging the hell out of each other, Shane unlocked the bar's back door.

One thing he hadn't planned for the day was dealing with Jonathan Sullivan. Particularly after only a few hours of sleep. The man tried his patience on a normal day. In this circumstance? He'd need a good combat nap before the meeting later this morning.

The beep of the security system snapped him back to his pre-Faith life and his morning routine of being a small-business owner.

Quickly, he stepped inside and flipped the door lock behind him. After the botched Brutus plan, he had to assume his cover was blown. Something that made being here one of the many risks he'd taken since Faith came along. As with his apartment, he shouldn't be anywhere near the bar. But he had a business to run and employees to pay.

He made a mental note to start cross-training his bookkeeper on the payroll system in case, you know, he got hit by a bus or took a double tap to the head by an internationally known assassin.

What a damned life.

He punched in the security code silencing the BEEP-BEEP-BEEP. Maddening. that sound, but he'd purposely made it loud enough to hear from the kitchen.

Employees wouldn't start showing up for at least another three hours, so he reset the alarm. Just in case said assassin tried to break in.

By the time everyone showed up, he'd be gone. This mission was costing him a boatload in overtime, but if his cover was blown, his staff was in danger.

A week ago, he'd been settled into a normal — at least somewhat — existence. Now, after watching that Challenger explode, he refused to go back to his apartment or Faith's and these fucking hotels were draining his emergency fund.

Just as he got to his desk chair, his phone rang. His mind immediately went to Faith, whom he'd left in that giant king-size bed they'd made great use of. He'd left a note this time. Points to him.

He grinned like an idiot. He couldn't help himself. She made him feel . . . something. Something that, every time he put hands on her, made his chest open up.

Hope did that. Faith believed Brutus's laptop was their ticket to freedom. Their get-out-of-jail-free card. As much as he'd like to buy in, he wouldn't get ahead of this thing. He'd learned to focus on the present and that meant getting his employees paid.

The phone rang again, kicking him from his mind travel. He slid it from the front pocket of his jeans. Trevor. At six in the morning? What the hell?

He punched the screen. "Hey. What's up?"

"Gotta talk to you."

"Okay."

"I'm driving around the corner. About to pull in the alley. Come outside and hop in."

Jesus Hotel Christ. He was *here*? Never once had Trevor come to the bar. Not once. Bad enough Dusty had broken that rule by stealing his goddamned cheese, now Trev too? Since Faith showed up, all the rules had gone out the window. That had to change.

Shane hustled back down the hallway, set the alarm and slipped outside to where Trevor pulled into the alley in a Honda Shane didn't recognize. At least Trevor had the good sense to wear a ballcap.

Shane slid into the passenger seat. "Are you out of your fucking mind?"

"At six in the morning, who's gonna see me?"

"Maybe a psychotic assassin?"

Trevor pulled to the end of the alley and shot Shane a glance before hooking a right turn. "Maybe you should be asking yourself the same question. Why are *you* here?"

"Payroll. Everything is on my desktop. How'd you know I was here?"

"I tracked your phone. And it's time for you to invest in a laptop, my friend."

With all the running he'd been doing, not a bad suggestion. "You shouldn't be here. And the tracking app is for emergencies."

"I needed to talk to you. Privately. I wasn't followed."

That he knew of. Trevor cruised down the block, making a left and then a right down the next alley, weaving through the maze while the two of them frantically checked their mirrors. Nothing behind them.

"You could've called me," Shane said.

"Could have. Like I said, I wanted *privacy*."

And, man oh man, Shane had no doubt about that message. Whatever Trev had to say, he didn't want Faith overhearing it.

Shane rolled one hand. "Say what you have to say."

"You have no idea what you're doing."

Whoa. What the fuck? Shane turned, angling his body to face Trevor. "About?"

"Cut the crap. You know. She's bad news. Everything has gone to hell since she showed up. She'll take all of us down."

"It's not your business."

"It sure the fuck is. You and Dusty made it my business when you decided to help her."

"And that gives you permission to butt into my personal business?"

Trev eased to a stop at a traffic light and took the opportunity to meet Shane's eye. "When it might get me killed? Bet your ass it does. Jesus, Shane. Who the hell are you right now?"

Shane turned front again, gritted his teeth. As much as he wanted to argue, to defend himself and insist Faith was more than a convenient lay, what was the point? Trevor was right. The three of them — Shane, Dusty and Trevor — had been allies for two straight years. More than that, they'd been friends. Family.

Dammit. So many mistakes. Shane wrapped the fingers of his right hand around his forehead and squeezed. How had this thing gone off the rails so fast? He should've walked away. When Dusty sent her to him, he should've walked away.

What a load of nonsense. From that first moment he'd seen those soulful eyes and the bruise on her face, he'd seen something in her. Survival. Desperation. The need for protection. Everything about her that day had triggered him and now he'd put it all on the line.

For her.

"It's not what you think," Shane said.

The light changed and Trevor hit the gas, angling around a cabbie picking up a customer. "I don't know what I think. All I see is my friend, who's spent two years making sure he never slips up, suddenly risking all kinds of crazy shit."

"She's different. She needs help."

"So this is what? You playing hero?" Trev shook his head. "Come on, Shane."

"She gets this life. The constant paranoia and checking your six. All the goddamn time waiting for someone to get the drop on you. She understands what that feels like."

"Now you're in love?"

Whoa. Nobody said anything about love. "Hell no. But I enjoy her company. Yeah, I'll admit that. What's wrong with it?"

"Nothing. If she were anyone else. This won't work. You know it."

He did know it. From the beginning he'd been reminding himself. Particularly now. The very best they could hope for was eliminating Brutus before all of their covers were blown.

"You gotta end it," Trevor said. "Too dangerous."

Shane cocked his head. "For who? You? This is *my* life you're screwing with."

Trevor glanced over at him and snorted. "And this is *my* life *you're* screwing with."

Shane peered out the window where a burnt orange sky promised sunshine ahead. He'd dragged his friends into this mess. Still, the balls on Trevor right now pissed Shane off.

"Fine," he said. "You're right. I shouldn't have involved you. I'll own that. I'm sorry."

What he wouldn't apologize for was Faith. For allowing himself to want companionship.

"I don't want your apology. I want you alive, man. Forget about Dusty and me. Are you willing to risk everything for her? Just walk away from the life you've built?"

Shane let out a sarcastic huff. "It's not such a great life."

"Bullshit. You own a business, got a roof over your head and you're breathing. Beats the alternative."

Maybe. He faced his friend again. "What if I want more?"

"We all want more. You don't think Dusty and I want that? Hell, maybe someday we'll get it. We all deserve a family. In my opinion, not that you asked for it, this woman will wreck you. Probably already has if you're blown."

This conversation was going nowhere and Shane knew his friend well enough to understand they'd never find common ground. Trevor was dug in. And so was Shane. He pointed out the window. "Hook a right here. I need to get back and do payroll."

"So that's it? You're just gonna go do payroll."

"Yeah. I'll think about what you said. And from now on, where Faith is concerned, you and Dusty are out. I won't involve you again."

ACCORDING TO THE WEBSITE, THE CHICAGO HYATT REGENCY had the honor of being the largest hotel in downtown Chicago. Steps from the Riverwalk, the building's location offered short trips to museums, Millennium Park or shopping on the Magnificent Mile.

None of which Faith would be doing today.

Maybe soon.

About to knock on the door of the room Sully had directed her to, she paused with her hand in mid-air. Shane stood beside her, looking every inch the average Joe — and that was saying something considering his size — in jeans, a white T-shirt and a battered Cubs hat.

He held his hands out. "Why the hesitation?"

"Are you ready for this? I mean, to play nice with Sully?"

He snorted. "Ready as I'll ever be. If nothing else, it'll be interesting."

Quite possibly the understatement of the century.

Taking a breath, she prayed she wouldn't have to break up a smackdown and rapped on the door. Seconds later, it swung open. Sully stood there, typically dressed in a freshly ironed Oxford shirt tucked into equally neat khakis. Polished loafers and matching belt only amplified his neatness.

Faith supposed his military habits hadn't quite left him.

His hair though. He might be slacking there because those thick brown locks were at least half an inch longer than usual and grazing the top of his ears.

He smiled down at her. If she knew how to read people, she'd say there might be a hint of relief in that smile.

Not wasting time, he waved them in. "Come in."

Once behind closed doors, Sully extended his hand to Shane. "We've had our differences, but it's good to see you."

Shane, being Shane, grunted, but shook the man's hand. Faith sighed.

They stepped into a suite bigger than her DC apartment and double the size of her current home. Floor-to-ceiling windows she'd cut a bitch for overlooked the downtown skyline. Too bad they weren't here for the view.

On the couch sat another man, maybe early thirties and

wearing John Lennon glasses. His sandy blond hair dipped below his jawline, reinforcing the whole Lennon vibe.

"This is Joel. He's one of our analysts. Joel, meet Faith and Shane."

Handshakes complete, Faith dug the laptop from her backpack and handed it over. "As I told Sully — Special Agent Sullivan — it's password protected."

Joel set the laptop on the coffee table in front of him, then took another laptop from his own backpack.

"I'll take a look. I should be able to get into it."

A man of confidence. Excellent. Faith nodded, then casually slipped an external hard drive from her bag. They'd made sure to pick that baby up on the way over. "I'll need a backup once you get in there."

Before accepting the hard drive, Joel peered up at Sully who gave a slight nod.

He motioned Shane and Faith to follow him to the counter-height table and chairs near the kitchenette on the other side of the room

They took the two seats on one side, leaving the opposite open for Sully. If he tried a power move by taking one of the chairs at either end of the table she might have to blast him.

With two alphas, that would be a hot mess.

Sully grabbed three waters from the mini-fridge and took the seat across from her.

Thank you, smart man.

"Joel is good." He handed over the drinks. "It might take him awhile though. Bring me up to speed — in detail — on how you came to be in possession of the laptop."

"You sure you want to know?"

This from Shane.

Sully gave him a hard, direct stare. *Here we go...*

"I'm sure. And I want the truth. I'll figure out what to do with it later."

Faith held up her hands. Time to state the obvious to Shane and Sully in case the rampant testosterone drowned their good sense. "Everyone here is going to play nice, understood? We don't know what we'll find on that computer, but it could be important. We'll need to work together. No pissing matches because you two are holding grudges."

Sully shrugged. "It's Shane who has the issue."

Sigh.

"*Anyway,*" she said. "The *laptop*. We got it last night."

"You're sure it's Brutus's?"

"Positive. We stole it from his room."

Sully's only reaction was a slight raising of his eyebrows. *Yes, fella, we broke into the man's room.*

When she'd called him from the cemetery the prior night, Faith had given Sully the diluted version of events. Now, if they expected his help, she'd have to tell him everything. Blow by nasty blow.

When she'd finished, Sully drummed his fingers on the table. "You've been busy."

"Trying to get shit done," Shane said, "after the *company* cut another of their own loose."

Not bothering to hide it, Faith kicked him under the table. Hard.

"Ow. Shit. That hurt."

"Good."

She pointed at Sully. "Do not respond to that or I'll kick you too." She faced Shane. "Seriously. Knock it off or I'll boot you out of here."

Sufficiently chastised, he sat back. At least he wasn't pouting.

Sully kept his gaze on her. "Okay. I'll get into what the local PD has on the hotel room incident and bury it. For now, we have his laptop. Maybe it'll contain something we can use against Alfaro. What do you wanna do?"

She cocked her head. What the hell did that mean? "About?"

"About your new identity." He peered over at Shane. "Can you get her set up again? If not, I'll see what I can do on my end."

Wait one second, boys. "Um, hello? I'm sitting right here. Nobody is getting me set up."

Sully all but gawked. "You *have* to leave Chicago. He knows you're here. And now you've really pissed him off by stealing his laptop. By now, Alfaro may even know. He already wants your head. Starting over is the only way."

Faith shook her head. "I'm not running."

The admission sounded crazy, even to her. When she'd arrived in Chicago, desperate for help, all she'd wanted was to hide. To start over, in any way possible, and stay out of Alfaro's reach.

Now? The man clearly knew where and who she was and . . . no. Not running. She looked over at Shane, who studied her with those sparkly blue eyes that somehow gave her, the one constantly on edge, sanctuary.

"Listen," he said and she immediately put a hand up.

Whenever someone started a sentence with that word, it was *not* good. "Don't say it."

"What? That he's got a point. At least get out of town until the heat is off."

So much for not saying it. "And what about you? We don't know yet if you've been compromised."

"I have a business to run."

"Oh, I see. So, it's okay for you to stay, but not me? No. That's not happening. If you're staying, I'm staying."

Across the table, Sully's gaze ping-ponged between them as he clearly tried to figure out if she and Shane were . . . whatever they were. She couldn't call it a relationship. Not that she had much experience there. But they were, well, good.

Really good.

And that was something.

Sully sat forward, drumming his fingers again. A habit she'd seen many times when he pondered a situation. "So, what's your plan then?"

"I don't know. I won't spend my life running. When we found out Brutus was here, we were hoping to..."

She wouldn't say it. Didn't need to. Eliminating Alfaro's assassin helped everyone.

"Whatever," she said. "The plan has changed. I won't live every day on the run. I need to see what's on that laptop. If it's enough to get Alfaro out of power or locked up, Shane and I might both be free."

"Even locked up, he's got power."

"He won't survive a day," Shane said. "The drug lords won't let him. I was inside that compound. Alfaro lets the cartels operate unimpeded. He gets a healthy cut of the profits and everyone is happy. If he's arrested, the cartels know he'll sell them out to save himself. No question."

"Huh," Sully said. "Shane and I finally agree on something. I can't share a lot, but we wouldn't be sorry to see Brutus or Alfaro gone. As you know, they've been thorns in the backside."

"So," Faith drew out the word, "if there's evidence on the laptop, the agency will help us?"

"Depending on what it is, yes. Anything against Alfaro only aids us in getting him out of power."

"Out of power won't be enough," Shane said. "We need him in a Venezuelan prison. If we get that done, it's over for him. And after Brutus blew his assignment with Faith, he's probably next on Alfaro's hit list. He's gotta be in the wind by now."

Over.

God, she could taste it. That one little word gave her hope and a vision of a future. Driving on a summer day, top down on a convertible. Volunteering at a shelter somewhere. Working at the university and living in her little apartment six blocks from Shane's bar. Walking into said bar and ordering one of those cheddar burgers she'd heard about.

No hiding.

A life.

She pushed back from the table, slid off the chair and tucked it back under the table. "Gentlemen, let's just say it. We need that son of a bitch dead."

20

SHANE WATCHED FAITH LEAVE THE TABLE AND HEAD TOWARD the computer geek. "Well," he muttered. "I guess we know where she stands."

Not that he'd had any questions because they'd discussed it. At length. Not specifically killing Alfaro, but they both knew their enemy. That kind of evil never gives up. Never stops looking.

Shane brought his gaze back to Sullivan, whose eyes were pinned to Faith. Interesting. Finally, the asshole dragged his attention from Faith back to Shane.

"I don't blame her," he said. "Are you on board with this plan?"

"Eliminating Alfaro? Bet your ass. Why wouldn't I be?"

Sullivan shrugged. "You're established here. Got a lot to lose."

"More to gain if it means seeing my family on holidays. Get this straight, Sullivan, the way I'm living? I've managed to carve out a life, but it still sucks. Sitting in your DC office, you wouldn't know anything about that."

Sullivan basically turned to stone. No nasty glare. No

locked jaw. No poking his finger. Nothing. The guy gave zero satisfaction for a perfectly delivered insult. What the hell kind of fun was that?

"I may not," he said. "But I wouldn't wish it on anyone. And what the fuck did I do to you that makes you hate me so much?"

Now they were getting somewhere. Shane had waited a long time to nail Sully on this one. "You didn't do it to me. You let Dusty take a grade reduction. You're the one who didn't follow orders and you got a fucking *promotion*."

"That's what you're pissed about? Seriously? Hey, dumbass, my promotion had nothing to do with that op. One successful mission doesn't carry that kind of weight. I've been busting my balls for years. *That* got me my promotion."

"Whatever."

"Yeah. Whatever."

In a truly unfortunate way, this conversation didn't have the climactic appeal Shane had hoped for. Plus, they had bigger problems to deal with than Sullivan being an ambitious career-climber.

Shane waved it off. "Where are we on Reynaldo Everado? According to Leslie, he's ready to deal."

Sully's gaze went to Faith, now sitting on the sofa next to Joel. "Depending on what he has, we're open to it."

Shane dug into his pocket for his phone. "Excellent. Let's get Leslie on the phone. Get this rolling."

"Hang on. What does he do for Alfaro these days? Is he part of the inner circle?"

"I have no idea. When I left, he was a driver. If he still is, I'd say he's part of the inner circle."

"Even after his sister left?"

Here's where the story got good. "No one knew she was

his sister. They're half-siblings. Different last names. She's no dummy. She knew Alfaro wasn't a prince and if things went bad for her, she didn't want Rey taken down with her. When she was still screwing Alfaro, she secretly engineered a meeting with someone on Alfaro's staff. One thing led to another and Rey got a job. If you guys hadn't screwed her, she'd still be a tremendous asset."

Clearly done with Shane's opinions, Sully rolled his eyes, then pointed to the phone in Shane's hand. "We'll never agree on this. Call her. Put me in touch with Reynaldo."

"She won't trust you."

"If she wants her brother out from under Alfaro, she doesn't have a choice."

Shane let out a laugh. "There are always choices. I'll call her, but don't be shocked if she won't talk to you."

"And what? You're inserting yourself in this?"

"Not for a second. I'm telling you what I think."

"Fine. If Leslie won't deal with me, Faith can do it."

This, Shane hadn't expected. Control-freak Sullivan turning over the reins? "You'd do that?"

"You don't trust me." He pointed to Faith. "She does. We work well together. I'll clear it with the brass."

Shane leaned in, drawing Sullivan closer like they were about to share top-secret intel. "You got a thing for her, Sullivan? Because, you know, getting emotionally involved isn't wise."

Juvenile? Yes. Without question. From the beginning Shane had questioned the man's motives. After the last few days with Faith, he was entertaining the idea of possibly having a relationship with her and he wanted answers about her involvement with Sullivan.

"Come on," Sully said, half laughing. "You're not one of

those guys who thinks a man and a woman can't work together without it involving sex, are you?"

He considered that a second. When it came to a woman like Faith, a smart, strong and attractive-as-hell woman?

Yeah, he was most definitely one of those guys.

Not that he'd admit it to this asshole. "You've gone above and beyond to help her while the *company* gave me zero support. What's the deal?"

"And this is your business how?"

"It's not. I don't see her as your type."

"What's my type?"

"The one who's willing to make the political climb with you. That's not her. She wants simplicity. Not a bunch of backstabbers."

"Fuck you. You don't know me. And you sure as hell don't know the type of woman I'm attracted to. As for Li — Faith — she did good work on our country's behalf. She got a raw deal. I'd like to see her come out of this. After that? I don't know. I guess we'll see what happens."

And then the bastard gave Shane a slick smile. Not the I-will-win smile though. This was the I'm-screwing-with-you smile and the ultimate mind-fuck. *Dang, he's good.*

"Unless, of course," Sullivan said, "you have a personal interest in her yourself,"

Yeah. Messing with him. Fine. He wanted to play. Shane would play.

"I do," he admitted. "She's amazing. Dependable, caring. Stubborn as hell. If we both hadn't gotten screwed by the agency, I might even think about a future."

"That'd be a huge risk."

"Ya think?"

Faith chose that moment to rise from her spot on the couch and approach them. Great. Her ears must be flaming.

She stopped at the end of the table, her gaze drifting between them. "I can feel you two talking about me. What's going on?"

"In fact," Shane said, "we *are* you talking about you."

She angled her head at him and narrowed her eyes, a warning that he'd better not have fucked something up. Or said too much. Which he probably had.

"Sullivan wants you to broker the Reynaldo deal."

She blinked. *Blink, blink, blink.* "Wait. What? *Me?*"

"Shane doesn't think Leslie will trust me."

Faith rolled her lower lip out. "Well, he's right about that."

Shane couldn't help it. He gave Sullivan his best smart-ass grin.

"Settle down, fella," Faith told him. "You and I see it from Leslie's side. We've experienced being on the run from Alfaro. Sully hasn't."

Before Shane could launch his argument, she held up a hand. "I'm not defending the agency's actions. All I'm saying is Sully can't understand this life. He hasn't lived it."

"It's settled then," Sullivan said. "Faith will make the call."

At one o'clock, hours after leaving Leslie a message, ordering food and trying to remain relentlessly positive about Joel cracking open Brutus's laptop while constantly checking her phone to ensure she hadn't missed Leslie's call, Faith's cell phone rang.

Leslie. Finally.

She showed the phone to Shane, who sat across from her at the table polishing off the last of his burger. The man sure liked his burgers.

Sully had long since left them alone, moving to the other side of the suite and working on his laptop.

"Maybe she's got something," Shane said.

They were about to find out. She picked up the call before it went to voicemail "Hey," she said.

"Hello," Leslie's sexy-vixen voice came through the line. "I've reached . . . him."

The *him* had to be Reynaldo. "And?"

"He's willing to talk. Depending on how the conversation goes, he will decide his next steps. Given my situation, there are trust concerns."

"Completely understandable."

"Indeed. He will call you on this number at five o'clock your time. His dinner break."

Five o'clock. *Four* hours from now. Shoot. But she supposed beggars couldn't be choosers. And they needed Reynaldo.

"All right," Faith said. "Thank you. Question for you. Is he still a driver?"

"He is. His *boss* will be dining out. At five, he'll be in the restaurant."

Across from her, Shane sat quietly, taking in her side of the conversation.

"Thank you," Faith said. "You've been a huge help. I hope you know that."

"Oh, I know. I'd better get what I want out of this."

Something she'd made clear on their earlier call. Leslie, like Shane and Faith, had two conditions: 1. Her brother's safety and 2. A new identity should her cover be blown while brokering the deal.

Reasonable requests. At least in Faith's opinion. The CIA might not agree.

She glanced across the room where Sully pounded away

on his laptop. Did he have the clout to pull this off? She sure hoped so.

"I understand," she told Leslie. "We're doing everything on our end to make sure that happens."

"Good. Talk later."

The line went dead and Faith set her phone on the table, spinning it one way, then the other.

Shane's big hand came into view, resting on top of hers and stopping the spinning. "What'd she say?"

She peered up at him. "He's calling us at five." She leaned in, lowering her voice. "He wants to feel us out. After we talk, he'll decide if he wants a deal."

"He saw what happened to Leslie. Personally, I think he's nuts for trying this. He'll probably wind up dead before it's over."

Exactly Faith's worry. In their efforts to secure their own freedom, could she live with sacrificing Reynaldo? "Is this right? What we're doing?"

"You know you can't go there. Moral decisions aren't our responsibility. He knows what Alfaro is. Especially if he's his driver."

"He *is* the driver. At the very least, we'd be able to track Alfaro's movements."

"Which makes eliminating him a whole lot easier."

Would the agency do it? Particularly when a presidential executive order from the '70s mandated that no US government employee take part in the assassination of a political leader.

Over the years, the agency worked around that order by changing their terminology. Now, there were no assassination attempts but targeted killings.

And Alfaro, based on his crimes, belonged at the top of the kill list.

"You're right," she said. "I'll tell Sully."

When Shane's eyes got snappy, she reached for him, squeezing his hand. "I'm not cutting you out. When the two of you are together, it's solid tension. We need Sully focused on the deal with Reynaldo."

After a few seconds, he nodded. "The tension is on me. I was dogging him earlier."

Faith snorted. "Of course you were. His actions hurt your friend and you're a protector. I'll work around it so we can get this deal with Rey done. If we focus on eliminating Alfaro, we get our lives back."

That's what she wanted. She probably wouldn't be able to go back to being Liz Aiken, but she wanted her freedom. A life as Faith Burgess.

And maybe a future with the man sitting in front of her.

AT FIVE P.M., FAITH'S PHONE RANG. ON THE OTHER SIDE OF the suite, Joel continued his brute force efforts to crack into the laptop. That man might be headed for sainthood because by now Faith would have put a bullet in the damned thing.

This, however, was his job and on some twisted level he probably found it challenging. A task to be conquered.

All while Sully sat at the desk near the bed and busied himself with calls. Across from her at the dining table, Shane watched CNN on his phone.

She held the phone up. "Blocked number. It has to be him." She poked the screen. "Hello?"

"Hello," a man with a prepubescent sounding voice said.

Wow. Totally not what she expected, but Leslie hadn't mentioned his age. They *were* half siblings. He could be much younger. Maybe a second marriage or something.

"This is José. Is this good number?"

José. The code name Leslie had given them. His English was clear but accented. If necessary, they'd resort to speaking Spanish.

"Yes, this is fine."

She could easily toss the burner phone if things went sideways.

Faith waved Shane to her side of the table. He hustled over, squeezing in beside her and tipping his head close as she held the phone between.

She caught the faded scent of hotel soap from that morning and her mind tripped back to watching him leave the bed they'd shared and grab deodorant and a comb from his bag along with clothes he'd stacked in a neat pile.

All of it completely routine, mundane even. Yet she wanted it. Every day.

She shook the thought away. Later, she'd think about homes and meals together and routines.

"José," she said, "our mutual acquaintance indicated you might be able to help us. If the information is useful, our counterparts are willing to assist in getting you out of the country. If that's what you want."

"*Sí*. Yes. I can't do this anymore. It's too much."

A stab of guilt halted her. This kid had no idea what he was getting into, leaving his home, changing his identity. Starting over. After this, if they failed, he'd be on the run, constantly looking over his shoulder.

She glanced at Shane, who nudged his chin at the phone. "His choice," he mouthed.

His choice. She needed to remember that. She went back to Rey. "All right. We're looking for Gustavo. Do you know if he's been in contact with Alfaro since yesterday?"

"I am not sure. Paolo, the bodyguard, told me today that

things were bad. Very bad. Gustavo not answering texts, calls or emails. More men being sent to Chicago."

"To find Gustavo?"

"To find anyone helping you."

"Does he know about Shane? Who he really is?"

A shouting voice sounded from the other end and Reynaldo let fly a stream of muffled Spanish. Something about leaving early.

"I have to go," Rey said, his voice once again clear. "He's coming. Dinner is off."

Shit. "Wait. José? What about Shane?"

"I have to go. I'll call tomorrow."

Click.

Dammit!

Faith tossed the phone, sending it clattering to the table. So close. So damned close. She shook out her hands, blew a hard breath. She had to move. Pace a little and think. Just as she took a step, Shane gently hooked his hand around her forearm.

"Hey. We're okay. We made contact and he's willing to help. It's a win."

Across the room, Sully spun on the desk chair, holding his hands wide. "Problem?"

"We got interrupted," Faith said. "He'll call back tomorrow. He's in."

From the couch, Joel held his hands straight in the air à la football referee, a giant smile lighting his face. "He's not the only one who's in." He pointed at the laptop. "Paydirt."

SHIT ON A SHINGLE. SULLIVAN'S GEEK HAD DONE IT. HE'D hacked into Brutus's computer.

Shane took a second, let the thought roll over him. His

heart rate kicked up and his pulse slammed because...holy, holy hell...they might pull this off.

Faith hauled ass to the sofa, huddling beside Joel. Shane followed, standing next to her as she pointed to a small blue app on the bottom of the screen.

"Click on that," she said. "Let's see if he has his text messages synched."

Now that would be epic.

Joel clicked. Nothing. Too good to be true.

Sullivan joined them, taking residence on the other side of Joel. "Check his emails."

"And his contacts," Faith said. "What does he have there?"

Joel looked up from the computer and stretched his neck. "Everybody, back off. I'm gonna change the password and hit the bathroom. I need caffeine too."

Wasting no time, Sully moved to the desk phone. "I'll get coffee."

"Great." Joel's fingers flew across the keyboard. "Okay. We're good. Password changed. I'll be right back."

The man left Shane and Faith in front of the computer while Sullivan called room service. Might as well take advantage.

Shane bent low, getting closer to Faith so he wouldn't be overheard. "See if Alfaro's digits are in the contacts."

"You read my mind."

She got to work, clicking a few times and then typing Alfaro's name. Nothing.

"Hang on," she said. More typing. "Ugh. Some are actual names but the others are coded."

"What are you doing?"

This from Sullivan who'd just set the phone down.

Faith pointed at the computer screen. "His contacts are in code."

Had to love her. No explanation and sure as hell no apology.

Sullivan moved around the coffee table and sat next to her. "Are there any emails?"

After a few clicks, Faith shook her head. "Nothing. At all. From anyone."

"Check the trash."

"Nothing."

"Not a surprise," Shane said. "He's a pro. He's not gonna leave incriminating emails. He probably dumped them from his phone."

Faith looked up at him, her dark eyes sharp. "We still have all the files. Don't give up yet."

Shane let out a low whistle. "Easy there. Making an observation is all."

"Hey," Sullivan said. "Everyone relax. We knew this wouldn't be easy."

Joel emerged from the bathroom, spotted Sullivan and Faith sitting in his spot and waved them away. "Let me get in there and work."

"You got it," Faith said. "We need anything you can find on Alfaro, the cartels, money laundering, whatever. And I'll give you a list of aliases Brutus uses."

"Good," he said. "All of you go away. I get twitchy when people look over my shoulder."

At that, Shane laughed.

"He's serious," Sullivan said. "He works better with space. Let's give it to him."

. . .

By nine o'clock, after a heck of a long day, Joel made Faith extremely happy by handing over a backup of Brutus's files. Who knew the intel that might be there? The idea of hunkering down for days to study computer files while Brutus roamed the city wasn't exactly a pleasant thought, but if there was anything, the slightest morsel, that might help them find him — or nail Alfaro — she'd do it.

No question.

She held the portable hard drive up. "Did you find anything?"

"Nothing earth-shattering." He passed her a printout. "A list of folders. The first two look like ammunition and gun purchases. The others made mention of," Joel made air quotes, "'the president,' but I didn't get through them all. "

Sully, who'd received a phone call ten minutes earlier and retreated to the bathroom for privacy, entered the dining area.

Whatever happened on that call had left his skin a not-so-attractive shade of gray. Or perhaps the man was simply dog-tired. They'd left DC before dawn and he'd been fielding calls, emails and texts all day.

That part of the job, Faith didn't miss.

She pointed at the phone in his hand. "Everything all right?"

"Same old, same old." He met Joel's eye. "You about wrapped up? I got called back to Langley. The pilot is getting the plane ready."

Wait.

Hold on just one second. They weren't nearly done here. And could the spec ops world not give her a break? She had Sully's full attention and *now* an emergency comes up?

It'd better be a coup. Or something equally juicy.

Maddening. All of it.

She whipped to fully face him. "You're *leaving*? Now?"

"I have to." Before she could launch into an argument, he put his hands up. "We're on this, Li — *Faith*. I promise you. We have Joel, plus I'll dig up another analyst. You have the backup so you can work it from this end. We'll find him."

Sure. Great. They'd all be sitting around combing through files while Alfaro sent his hit squad to murder them.

Her problems weren't the CIA's responsibility. They'd made that abundantly clear when they'd released her. Old news. Dwelling on it would be a useless endeavor.

"And what about the new team Alfaro sent?"

He stared at her. "We're on that too. Talk to Reynaldo though. See if can get intel on them."

"Faith," Shane said, from his spot at the table, "we can handle this."

His confidence did nothing to ease her angst, but she wouldn't sit around whining about it.

While Joel headed back to the couch to pack up his belongings, Sully focused on Faith. "The room is paid for. You're welcome to stay." His gaze shot to Shane and back. "If you're comfortable."

Oh, Lord. One thing she definitely wasn't comfortable with was telling Sully that she and Shane had been making use of a single bed. Not that it was his business, but when it came down to it, she'd long suspected Sully might have a thing for her. Feelings that, although she enjoyed their friendship, she simply could not return.

To her, Sully was, well, *Sully,* her friend and coworker, and discussing sharing a bed with Shane felt damned icky.

Keeping her gaze on Sully, she nodded. "Thank you. Staying put is probably the smart thing."

"I won't check out. Tomorrow, they'll see you're gone and they'll charge my card."

Avoiding an added expense helped. They'd been taking turns paying for necessities, but it all added up. Big time.

She'd pay Shane back. Every cent. It might take her a few years, but she'd do it.

SULLY HEADED TOWARD THE BEDROOM AREA. SHE STAYED ON his heels, watching as he picked up the overnight bag he'd set next to the bed. Had he even unpacked? Didn't look like it.

Which only reinforced the fact that he'd flown out here, with an analyst, to help her. Would nailing Alfaro help his career and the United States? Of course, but he'd dropped everything for her and if they nailed Alfaro, they'd both benefit.

He leaned across the bed, grabbed his laptop and briefcase, shoved the laptop inside and set it next to the overnight bag before facing her. For a few seconds, they both stood there.

With her blocking him.

"Uh, Faith?" He tapped his watch. "What's up?"

"Sorry," she said. "I wanted to say thank you. You didn't have to help me."

"Yeah, I did. You got a raw deal."

She sure did. "That's the risk of the job. We know that."

"Still doesn't make it right." He picked up both bags. "By the time this is over, I'm hoping you can move on. Make your life what *you* want. Your choices. Your rules."

Her choices.

Wouldn't that be something? It seemed her entire life had been reactions to events put in motion by others. First her mother abandoning her, then her grandmother dying — not that it was Gram's fault — and finally her job at the agency. All of it, whether intentionally done or not, had been decided for her.

Now she wanted different. What that different would be, she wasn't sure, but it included not running from Alfaro.

21

THE FLU.

His damned cook had the flu.

Shane lay on his side in the big king-sized bed, his hand cupped over his phone so the glare wouldn't wake Faith. At some point during the night, she'd pressed herself against his back, waking him up in the process.

Spooning. He'd never been a fan. Today?

Big fan.

He brought his focus back to making sure the bar could open. Friday night was not the time to be short-staffed.

Barely dawn and his day was falling apart. Maybe Stef, the part-timer who covered the kitchen when Derek needed a day off, could cover. She worked at another restaurant on the weekends, though, and with Shane not pulling his weight, they were already screwed.

"Shit," he whispered.

Faith sat up. Boom. Instantly alert.

"What?"

He rolled to his back and dropped the phone on his belly. "Sorry. Didn't mean to wake you."

"You didn't. I've been up since five."

An hour? She'd been so still he hadn't realized she'd been awake. "You should have said something."

She smiled. "I was enjoying the quiet. What's wrong?"

"My cook has the flu."

"Ew."

He snorted. "The bar doesn't care that we're chasing an assassin and a corrupt president."

"Do you need to go? I can find us another hotel and work on Brutus's files there. We should leave anyway."

He sat up, swung his feet to the floor, dug his palms into his eyes and pushed. The damned pressure was insane.

"Hoping my part-timer can cover the kitchen."

"I'm sorry," she said. "I've blown up your life."

He looked at her over his shoulder. The phone's light partially illuminated her face, giving her an ethereal presence that chipped away at his pissy mood.

"We've talked about this," he said. "I could have walked away. It was my choice. I'm okay with that. For all our sakes, we need to close this out."

How they'd do that if Alfaro located him, he wasn't sure. Like Faith, Shane had zero interest in starting over.

Shane stood and stretched his back. "I'll run to the bar, get the kitchen prepped and see if my part-time cook can cover today. Before we leave here, let's find another hotel, something close to the bar. Which sucks since Brutus has already been to the coffee shop, but — "

"You have a business to run. Don't worry about me. I'll lay low."

"I'll drop you off on the way and meet you there when I'm done. That work?"

She whipped the covers off. "It sure does. Hopefully, by

the time you're done, we'll have heard from Rey and I'll have found something in the files."

Yeah, good luck. Chances of all those things happening in the next few hours were a total long shot.

Two hours later, Faith hunkered down in yet another hotel, this one smaller, independently owned and barely a mile from the bar. A bit too close, in Faith's opinion, but they'd been hotel hopping each day and wouldn't be squatting long.

For now, it was a necessary evil so Shane could be close while keeping his business afloat.

The only room available boasted two double beds, a desk she currently utilized, a loveseat, and a giant whirlpool tub her weary body might enjoy.

Combat with Brutus resulted in muscle soreness and stiff limbs. None of which were good on the run.

Back to work.

The tub would have to wait. She peered at the laptop in front of her. So far, she'd skimmed a handful of folders from the list Joel had given her. When skimming didn't result in any hits, she used the find function and searched for Alfaro, Venezuela, United States, CIA and Liz Aiken.

Zippo. Zippo. Zippo. Zippo.

And zippo.

She sat back, stacked her hands on top of her head. Nothing in the files regarding Liz Aiken.

It should have been great. Terrific even.

But if her name wasn't anywhere in Brutus's files, how the hell had he found her so fast?

Then it hit her. An absolute blast that should have knocked her out of her chair.

Cover name.

Dammit.

He must know her cover name. All this time she'd been searching for Liz Aiken when she should have been searching for Faith Burgess.

Total rookie mistake.

She jotted her new initials at the top of the list she'd printed earlier and circled the directories she'd need to go back and search.

Her phone buzzed. Blocked number. For a brief second, she considered letting it go. What if . . .

She scooped up the phone, swiping at the screen. "Hello?"

"Hi." The same high, male voice from the day before, but this time barely a whisper. "It's me."

Reynaldo. Thank God.

"Are you okay?"

"I have little time. This morning. Driving boss. He talked to someone. About Chicago. A restaurant, I think. He said fire."

The words came fast. Mixed with Rey's heavy Spanish accent, Faith wasn't sure she heard correctly. "Slow down. A restaurant *fire*?"

"*Si.*"

Okay. Now that was weird. By now, Alfaro probably knew they'd found Brutus. Or at least that *someone* had found Brutus. Could he be planning on burning down a restaurant the man might be eating in?

That made no sense. Why would Brutus, after being outed, tell Alfaro where he might dine? If anything, he'd run like hell.

Wait.

She snapped her head up, sucked in a hard breath. No, no, no. Couldn't be. But...

"Rey, are you sure he said restaurant? Or a *bar*?"

Because, holy cow, if it was a bar, they had a big problem. *Deep breath*. She needed to focus. *Concentrate*.

"He was on phone," Rey said. "Talking about a kitchen. I heard corner and then tap. I have to go."

She squeezed her eyes closed, visualized slowing the blood rush storming her system. "You heard corner and tap? Was it together? Like Corner Tap or was it broken up? Corner and tap with words in between?"

"Together. I think. *Si*. Corner Tap."

Oh, God. She stood, already moving around the room and propping the phone between her shoulder and cheek. Her mind reeled, screaming commands as she grabbed her gun and holster, securing them to her waist. "When?"

"Good morning!" Reynaldo called to someone on his end then a flurry of Spanish.

"Reynaldo!" she snapped. "Please. This is important."

The line went silent for a few seconds. "I have to go," he said. "I call you back."

Click.

Dammit, this guy.

She lowered the phone, staring at it for a solid five seconds while options whizzed through her mind.

Fire.

Corner.

Tap.

She eased out a breath, forced her brain into focus. One thing at a time.

Could Alfaro be planning to set Shane's bar on fire? Why would he do that? Setting the fire wouldn't benefit him. Why not just kill Shane?

What the hell was Alfaro doing?

The whole damned thing confused her. Unless . . .

Oh no. No, no, no. Could Alfaro know Shane usually went to the bar every morning? Could they be planning on killing him and setting the fire to cover it?

Faith ran.

Just bolted to the door, swinging into the hallway and charging to the stairs, flying down, using the railing so she didn't faceplant. *Get there. Warn him.*

Yes. That's what she'd do. Warn Shane. Tell him to get out until they verified he'd been burned.

Again.

Phone still in her hand, she paused on the second-floor landing. No signal.

She burst into a run, hurling her body down the steps. First floor. Finally. She whipped the door open. To her left was a long hallway to the lobby. To the right? Emergency exit. She pushed through.

Dark gray clouds rolled in and a blast of wind blew her hair back. She hadn't been in the Midwest long, but she'd already experienced the intensity a spring storm could inflict.

She checked her phone. Signal. She tapped Shane's number, lifted the phone to her ear and sprinted down the alley.

The call went straight to voice mail.

Was he kidding? Could the phone be off? No way. That'd be insanity.

"Shane!" she said. "Get out of the bar. Right now. I'm on my way. Rey called. I think Alfaro found you. Get out!"

She clicked off, reached the end of the alley and found herself staring at logjammed cars. The last of the morning rush. She turned left, heading in the general direction of the bar, hoping to find a cab at the corner.

Three-quarters of a mile. That's all. She swung her head left and right. Cars, cars and more cars. A horn sounded. One of those long blasts that set her last nerve firing.

Even if she nabbed a cab, they'd be sitting in this mess.

Six minutes. If she pushed, she'd reach Shane in six minutes.

Her apartment, that cute little space she might never step foot in again was only a few blocks east. Over the last weeks, she'd mapped out every escape path from this neighborhood and knew them well. She hooked a left at the corner. She'd cut down the next block and — *an alley*. A long one that would shave at least a minute.

She gripped her phone. That and the gun were the only things she'd left the room with. Not her knife or cash or even a damned key.

Shit.

Emotions. Always the enemy. She'd been trained better.

She got to the alley. A garbage truck blocked traffic. Easy. She'd squeeze by.

Less than five minutes. That's all she needed to get to Shane. But they'd need help if Brutus or Alfaro's hit squad had already found him.

She stopped running. A quick second. Her lungs heaved and she forced herself to take deep, diaphragmatic breaths while stabbing at the phone. Searching for Dusty's number.

While it connected, she sprinted around the garbage truck.

"Baby girl," Dusty's easy voice came through the phone. "What's up?"

"Get to the bar. I think Shane's in trouble. He's not answering."

"What?"

"Dusty! Please. I'm hauling ass there now. On foot. Meet me there."

"On my way," he said. "I'll call Trev and we'll meet you."

The line went dead. God only knew where either of them were and how long it would take in this traffic. Shane had already said he, Dusty and Trevor lived on opposite sides of the city.

She glanced at the phone, willing Shane's name to appear on screen.

Nothing.

By now, Shane might already be dead.

SHANE STOOD AT THE PREP TABLE TOSSING SALT AND PEPPER into the giant mixture of ground beef and pork. His mom's trick with these babies was getting the ratio of beef to pork right. That's where the flavor came from. Everyone thought it was the seasoning. Some sort of ultra-secret recipe. If they only knew.

Once he had the meat prepped, he'd move on to grinding chicken and turkey. They didn't do as many chicken and turkey burgers, but he still liked to be prepared.

In larger restaurants, they had prep cooks that handled this level of work. In his operation everyone pitched in.

He kneaded the meat, giving it a final mix, the rhythmic, easy motion soothing his battered mind. He glanced at the wall clock: 9:10. He'd be out of here in an hour and the staff could handle the rest. Stef, his part-timer, had saved him, somehow managing to cover the weekend. It would cost him time-and-a-half, but he didn't have much choice.

The sound of glass shattering in the bar area stopped him cold.

What the hell?

He dragged his hand from the raw meat, grabbed the dishrag on the prep table and ran to the swinging double-doors, kicking one open. More glass breaking.

Whump!

A fireball erupted in the middle of the floor, the flames shooting in all directions and — holy shit — a barstool went up in a flashing burst that torched the stool next to it.

He reared back, sprinting the few feet to the wall-mounted fire extinguisher.

Seconds. That's how long a fire took to engulf a room. Particularly one with oiled wood. The whole place might be gone in minutes.

He ran through the doors and the P.A.S.S. method for fire he'd trained the staff on hammered his mind.

Flames shot up the walls. In those few seconds, the fire had doubled.

He pulled the pin, aimed, squeezed and swept side to side.

Should have called 911 first. At this rate, the bar would be gone before the fire department even got there.

He kept at it, spraying in a sweeping motion, aiming at the base of the fire. Barstools he could replace. If it got to the kitchen, forget it. Months of rebuilding.

The register. He'd been too tired to leave the hotel last night to collect the day's cash. First time ever he'd left it and now an entire day's revenue could burn up. He didn't even know how much was in there. Could be thousands, could be hundreds. Either way, it was money he'd need.

Not to mention his mom's blue ribbon from the baking contest. He kept the award on the wall next to the register. He'd removed any identifying features, leaving just a plain ribbon, but every time he went into that cash register, he had a reminder of a good life.

And he wasn't letting it get torched.

He turned toward the bar, shot at the base of the flames. If he could knock it back enough, maybe he'd get there. But he needed two hands for the fire extinguisher. How the hell would he get that register open?

He'd figure it out when he got there.

If he didn't die in the process.

THE BAR WAS ON FIRE.

Her stomach cramping from the run, Faith sprinted the last thirty yards to the Corner Tap as glowing orange flames snapped and licked at the now broken front window.

A crowd of onlookers gathered across the street in front of the coffee shop where the owner, Darla, appeared to be on her cell phone. Hopefully calling 911. Thunder boomed overhead, the sky continuing to darken. Storm rolling in. A good soaking might help Shane.

Could he have gotten out? She scanned the crowd again. Please let him be there.

No Shane.

Back entrance.

He said he used that one most days to get in and out. He might be there. Safe in the alley.

"Darla!" she called across the street. "Have you seen Shane?"

For a second, Darla simply stared at her, apparently trying to make the connection between Faith, one of her customers, and Shane.

"Um, no," she hollered back. "I called the fire department. Is he *inside*?"

Not bothering to respond, Faith cut down the intersecting block, nearly skidding around the corner. She pumped her legs, pushing herself harder, faster. *Get there, get there, get there.*

Cutting left into the alley, she spotted his car parked near the entrance. She reached the door. An old-fashioned one with a glass upper pane that had been painted black and blocked her view inside.

She touched her finger to the knob — no heat — then grabbed it. Locked. She smacked the door, banging her palm against the wood beside the window.

"Shane! It's me! Open up!"

No answer.

Her heart banged against her chest, the panic spewing and lighting her senses. The stench of spoiled food from the dumpster assaulted her. Her gag reflex kicked in and she held her breath, focused on getting the damned door open.

Sirens howled. Not close enough. She had to try.

She slid her gun from the holster, but not wanting to take a chance that Shane might be on the other side of the door, decided against shooting the lock off. Instead, she slammed the butt of the gun through the window, cleared a hole big enough to snake her arm in and skimmed her fingers over the inside handle. No heat, but thick, black smoke filled the hallway, oozing toward her, stealing whatever oxygen might be left.

She'd never been inside, but had peeped in the front window once when she'd been out at dawn after a sleepless night.

Entering from the rear, the bar would be on her left. Kitchen behind it? Had to be.

"Shane!"

When he didn't answer, another burst of panic flooded

her. Smoke continued its snaking approach to the rear door, filling more and more of the hallway.

If she intended to go in, she needed something to filter that lung-destroying smoke.

She glanced down at her long-sleeved T-shirt. Removing it would leave her in a tank top. Zero protection from flames.

Burns she'd recover from.

Smoke inhalation would kill them both.

Tearing the shirt over her head, she covered her mouth, stepped inside and darted through the hallway. Ahead, flames swarmed the bar area and the smoke . . . Lord, her eyes burned.

First door. She opened it. Storage closet. She shut the door again, refusing to give the blaze additional oxygen.

Next door. Office. No Shane.

God help him if he was in the main area.

Before she reached the mouth of the narrow hallway, a bizarre roar sounded. What the hell? A blast of heat halted her then — *poof!* — the far wall went up.

Faith's feet rooted to the floor as the flames devoured the wall in a glorious flash of orange and yellow. Seconds. That's all she had before the entire interior succumbed to the vicious fire.

She had to find him.

Go.

Was he even here? Maybe he'd gotten out.

Had she run into a burning building and he wasn't even here?

No. He'd have answered her calls by now. He had to be here. She ran toward the flames, reached the end of the hallway and there he was, fire extinguisher in hand.

At some point she'd rage at him for being an idiot. Right

now she was so damned happy to see him, her mind tripped to an escape plan.

She lowered the shirt from her mouth. Smoke immediately filled her throat, smothering her air. "Shane!"

He swung to her, his eyes nearly bulging. "Get out of here! I've got it!"

Uh. No. He didn't.

"Are you insane? We need to go! The fire department is on the way!"

"Last night's cash is in the register."

That's what he was worried about. The cash?

He coughed, then lifted one arm, sealing his mouth against his sleeve, the smoke clearly getting to him. She'd been in here less than a minute and felt its effect.

"Forget the money," she said. "Do you *want* to die in here?"

She charged him, grabbing hold of his shirt, squeezing her fingers over the fabric. "Let's go."

He gave the fire extinguisher a shot, spraying it in the general direction of the register. The flames retreated, then roared back, their angry licks snapping at the mirror behind the bar.

Again, she tugged on Shane's shirt and he looked at her, his eyes darkening.

"The money. We need it."

"I know," she said. "But we're not dying in here. Let's go."

She raised her shirt back to her mouth and used her free hand to drag him with her to the hallway.

Whump.

A fireball erupted through a floor vent, swarming the small area. She halted, slamming against Shane, in full command of that fire extinguisher.

Oh my God. Of all the ways to die, she didn't want this to be the one.

Fire snaked up one wall to the ceiling tiles that exploded into a ball of orange.

Shane jumped in front of her, aiming and blasting the ceiling and the walls in a sweeping motion.

"Go!" he said. "I'll hold it back while you run."

"You have to come with me!"

"I will. I'll follow."

Again she grabbed his shirt. "We're staying together."

He continued the sweeping motion, back and forth, up and down clearing a path, momentarily delaying the inevitable, but giving them enough time to run. Just feet ahead, the door welcomed them to safety.

Get there.

That's all they had to do. Just get there.

22

"Go!"

What the hell was Faith doing? She needed to get out. Get out and run because whoever set this fire had a reason. And that reason was, more than likely, Alfaro finding him.

Or Alfaro finding the person helping the woman who'd killed his son.

Either way, she shouldn't be here, putting herself in danger.

A loud crack sounded and Shane spun, body blocking Faith as an exposed beam behind them gave way, one end slamming to the floor.

Holy shit. A second sooner and it would have landed on them, trapping them in this inferno. *Forget the money.*

And the ribbon.

He shifted his gaze from the beam to the walls and ceiling just beyond, now fully engulfed.

He couldn't fight this bitch with a fire extinguisher. It was too big, too violent. He'd have to leave the money and the ribbon behind. Not worth dying over.

Flames devoured the side wall to his left. He shot at it

but — *whump* — the flames doubled, spreading toward the door.

He peeked over his shoulder. Another ten feet and they'd be out. He slid in front of Faith and continued sweeping back and forth, clearing a path as they moved to the exit.

Orange licks retreated.

Now. He ditched the extinguisher. "Run!"

They cleared the back door just before another burst of flames lit it up. Outside, sirens wailed. A thick sheet of rain bulleted down and — thank you, sweet baby Jesus — no pain-in-the-ass onlookers gathered in the alley.

But the sidewalk. He'd bet even with the rain, that sucker was packed. The arsonist might be watching his work. Standing around. Enjoying the show.

He glanced at his car, parked right where he'd left it.

Keys.

Shit. He'd left them on his desk in their usual spot.

Shane pointed right. Away from the front of the building. "This way."

They bolted to the end of the alley, slowing as they neared the corner. A crowd had gathered across the street, some of them tucked under umbrellas and all of them staring up at rising black smoke that meshed with the sea of gray above.

Faith, already soaked, slipped her long-sleeved shirt over her head and grabbed his hand. "Away from the crowd."

From his pocket, his phone vibrated. Still moving, he checked the screen. Dusty. "Hey."

"Where are you?"

"Just left the bar."

"You're okay? Neither of you were answering and I freaked the fuck out. I'm five minutes away."

"We're good. The bar is an inferno." A few seconds of silence drifted between them. "Dusty?"

"Wait. The bar is on *fire*?"

"Yeah. Someone torched it." He glanced behind them, checking their six and not seeing anyone who gave him the willies. "I was in the kitchen, heard glass shatter and the place went up."

"Molotov cocktail?"

"Guessing. Someone is ballsy because they tossed it through the front door window."

"Maybe your security camera caught them."

"Maybe. But do you seriously think they'd make it that easy?"

His friend knew better. If this was one of Alfaro's men, which Shane had every reason to believe, it would be someone whose photo wasn't in a database. That's how the man worked. Everything neat and tidy.

Call-waiting beeped. He checked the screen. Chicago number. He let it go. "Listen," Shane said to Dusty, "we're going back to the hotel. We've gotta get off the street. We'll get our stuff and find another place."

"I'll pick you up."

"No. You can't."

"Shane—"

"Dusty, no. I appreciate it. But you can't be anywhere near us. Not right now. I have no idea what's going on. And we're not risking you. I'm out."

He clicked off and tucked the phone in his front pocket, thankful he hadn't told Dusty their hotel. Hopefully, his friend would get a hold of his good sense and not track Shane's phone.

Thunder boomed and the wind and fat rain slapped his face.

Soaked to the skin, but alive.

He wouldn't complain. He grabbed Faith's hand and picked up his pace, nearly dragging her through the deluge. From his pocket, his phone chimed. *Voice mail.* Probably the cops telling him his business was burning.

Something in his shoulders locked up. Two years of hard work. Gone.

He'd deal with that later.

"He's a good friend," Faith said, using her arm to wipe rain from her eyes.

She'd been quiet since they'd left the bar. For a mouthy woman like her, quiet was never good. Quiet meant too much thinking and that scared the shit out of him. "Yeah, he is."

"And so are you. For wanting to protect him. Especially now, when we could use the help."

He glanced around again. Behind them, a few pedestrians hustled along. Businesspeople trying to control wind-blown umbrellas while carrying briefcases and backpacks. A guy in a baseball cap wearing jeans and a light jacket held his cap in place with one hand and ditched his coffee in a trash can with the other.

Him. Something was off.

Student?

Or some other random innocent person out for a cup of coffee. In the rain? Why didn't he just stay inside the coffee shop, let the storm blow over?

"We're turning right at this corner," Shane told Faith.

"What? The hotel is straight."

"Turn right. We might have a tail."

Being the pro she was, she didn't flinch. Didn't look back, didn't ask questions. She just hooked the turn and they hauled ass. Halfway down the block, Shane checked behind them where coffee-guy crossed the street. Completely ignoring them.

Goddammit. He hated this. The constant paranoia.

"Are we good?" Faith asked.

"I think so."

"Okay. About the fire, the only thing I can think is maybe they don't know who you are. Maybe Brutus has seen me with you and to put pressure on me, they torched your place."

"They burn my business down as a warning to you that they're coming after anyone who helps you?" He shook it off. "I can't figure any of this. Even if they are playing with us, how the hell does Brutus or Alfaro constantly know where we are? This is coming from someone inside. Sully must be flapping his gums."

"Oh, here we go again with Sully."

Shane stopped at the corner, waited for the walk sign and turned left, crossing the street. "He's our only loose end. If it's not him, it's someone he's talking to."

Trevor had just warned him about this. About Faith possibly taking them down.

Faith double-timed her steps to keep up. "Why does it have to be my friend?"

"Ha! You think it's Dusty? Or Trevor? Please. They'd have nothing to gain. Besides, I know them."

"Well, I know Sully." She waved it away. "This isn't helping. Let's deal with what we know. I agree that if Alfaro knew who you were, you'd be dead already. I think this is psychological warfare. It's about torturing me and I'm done with that."

.   .   .

TEN MINUTES LATER, SHANE SLIPPED HIS ROOM KEY FROM HIS back pocket, swiped and pushed the door open. He left Faith at the door and quickly cleared the room. *All good.* He waved Faith inside. She strode past him, her steps slow, almost cautious.

Disregarding the fact that water dripped from every spot on her body, she lowered herself to the bed, keeping her eyes on the carpet and propping her hands on her knees.

"I'm so sorry," she said.

The door shut behind them and he flipped the safety lever before striding toward her.

"Did you set that fire?"

For a few seconds, she continued to stare at the floor, then finally peered up at him, her lips forming a perfect O. "No! Of course not. But I sure as hell brought it to you."

His cell phone rang. Again. He pulled it from his pocket. Chicago number. Eventually, he'd have to answer.

"How'd you know?" he asked Faith. "That I was in trouble?"

"Reynaldo called me. He overheard Alfaro talking about a fire at the Corner Tap. When I couldn't get in touch with you, I panicked. They *found* you. Because of me."

Shane shrugged. "Maybe not me, but the guy helping you. You said it yourself. I'm not usually in the bar this early on Friday. I close on Thursday, so my staff gets the kitchen prepped. Brutus could have told Alfaro there was a man helping you. A man who owns a bar that they could torch as a warning. I still think we have a leak, but the warning idea is feasible."

She let out a sarcastic snort. "I don't get that lucky."

He shrugged. "Let's not assume anything. We have to get you out of the city. Then we'll figure out if I'm blown."

His phone rang again. He ripped it from his pocket. "This has to be the cops."

"Answer it. They'll keep calling. Talk to them and we'll figure out what we need to do."

IN THE INSANITY OF THE DAY, SHANE HAD TO GO BACK TO THE bar. Well, what was left of it anyway. And from what Faith had seen on the news, it wasn't much.

As much as she didn't want him out of her sight, fire investigators had questions and he couldn't *not* go. Doing so would only arouse suspicion.

Still, this was dangerous. Who knew if an assassin was hanging around outside the bar, hiding amongst the gossip-mongers and onlookers, enjoying the show.

Waiting.

For Shane.

Or maybe not. *Maybe* Shane had it right and whoever set that fire didn't even know he'd been in the building. Could she get that lucky?

To have Alfaro merely sending a warning to the stranger helping Faith?

Still, people could have died.

Freshly showered and dressed in dry clothes that didn't stink of charred wood, she finished shoving toiletries, along with the new burner phone Shane had given her from his stash, into her backpack and tossed it on the bed beside Shane's.

She'd assured him she'd find them another hotel, bring all their belongings and text him with the room number. They had to stay mobile, constantly on the move.

Once in the new hotel, she'd call Sully. See if they'd

found anything on the laptop while she'd been running through a burning building.

She slumped to the bed, dropped her head in her hands. She'd done this. Wrecked Shane's already tenuous existence.

No matter how much he argued it wasn't her fault, they both knew it. She should have known better than to crash into his life, expecting help when it compromised him.

Even if Sully — or Dusty for that matter — hadn't enlightened her about Shane's history with Alfaro, once she knew, she should have walked away.

Desperation did that. Made smart women turn stupid.

And she'd never been stupid.

Ever.

This time? Her responsibility.

And running wasn't an option. If Shane *had* been compromised, her leaving wouldn't help him. She had to get him out of it. He deserved peace and she sure as hell didn't intend on spending her life on the run.

She'd rather be dead than live in fear.

She bolted upright, clarity storming her system for the first time in days.

She glanced around the hotel room. No Shane. No partner. No teammate.

Just her.

And everyone *knew* she worked better on her own. Queen of the Pivot. That was her. And pivoting was a whole lot easier when working solo.

Clarity. A beautiful thing.

She scooped up her backpack, carried it to the small desk and slid the laptop out.

Sully hadn't called. If they'd found anything of interest, he'd have alerted her. Or would he? Some of it could be classified and, well, she was no longer part of *that* club. Plus, as much as she wanted to trust Sully, who knew if he'd shared her whereabouts with someone?

Forget Sully. Not a viable option.

No Shane, no Dusty or Trevor. Just her. She could fix this. One call. That's all it would take.

She tapped her password into the laptop and a few clicks later got into Brutus's contacts.

"You want to play, asshole," she muttered. "Let's *play*."

In the files she'd seen so far, whenever Brutus mentioned Alfaro, he'd referred to him as El Presidente. Nothing in a derogatory manner or involving anything criminal. All of it, she'd assumed, had been code for whatever operation Brutus had been tasked with.

Somewhere in here she'd find Alfaro's contact information.

She scrolled the lists, clicking on the A's, B's and C's. Some were names. Normal, everyday names. The others? Code. An odd mix of letters and numbers and symbols.

She'd start with those. Study them for patterns.

Wait. *Whoa.*

That day on the Ferris wheel. Talking with Shane. He'd told her about his relationship with Alfaro's son and getting busted looking at the kid's phone.

The code.

She closed her eyes, brought herself back to that day, sitting beside Shane, staring out over the glistening lake. His warm breath on her cheek. Snuggling. She'd been so content with the human contact she'd almost purred.

The code.

Pieces of conversation came together. Andres in the bathroom. A staff member busting Shane.

Words spelled backward.

Yes. That's what he'd said. The names were spelled backward with symbols in between.

She opened her eyes, snatched a piece of notepaper and the pen from the holder on the desk and started writing.

Matias Alfaro.

Below that she copied the letters of his first name backward.

Saitam.

Next came his last name.

Orafla.

On the laptop, she typed an S into the search bar and was rewarded with a list of names beginning with S. She skimmed any containing letters and symbols. Nothing even close to Saitam.

Maybe this wasn't the correct code. Which would suck on many levels. The first being she wasn't a code cracker.

Before giving up, she typed an O into the search bar. Another list of names appeared, some with symbols and numbers mixed in. She scrolled, quietly whispering the alphabet — *l, m, n, o, p, q, r* — as she went.

There. The names beginning with O-R.

Orab.

Oracco.

OrC9ad&&d7*o

She opened her notes app and copy/pasted the word. After studying it for a few seconds, she deleted the numbers and symbols.

Orcaddo.

She typed it backward.

Oddacro. If that was Alfaro, it was damned good code. She moved on to the next name and repeated the same exercise.

Nothing.

She kept at it, her pulse pounding and her brain barking that this could be a giant waste of time when she should be finding another hotel.

Next name.

After six failures, she considered stopping. Maybe moving on to the S's.

A few more. Her instincts buzzed and she'd never been one to ignore her inner guides.

She scrolled to the next name.

OrT$5afX9*la

What a mess. She did her copy/pasting routine and once again deleted the numbers and symbols.

OrTafXla

Whoa. Her pulse kicked up, her mind racing ahead, which never amounted to anything good. She drew a deep breath. Focused on the word in front of her. The letters were all there. The a and the l. The F. The X and T though? Wrong.

But if she eliminated those . . .

Delete. Delete.

Orafla.

And Orafla spelled backward . . .

Slowly, she typed the word, making sure to get each letter correct.

A-l-f-a-r-o.

Alfaro.

No way. Her slamming heart sent tiny shock waves to her limbs. She shook out her hands, fought the blood rush.

Before she got too far ahead of herself — more than one Alfaro in the world — she moved to the first name in the entry.

n*Sa4Bit3oam.

Again, she removed the numbers and symbols.

nSaBitam.

Shoot. Just as with Alfaro, some of the letters were right. Some not. The capital S and B didn't fit. She deleted those.

naitam.

She reversed the spelling.

Matian.

Matian? No, that wasn't right. But the S?

She put it back in and removed the n.

Saitam.

And Saitam backward? M-a-t-i-a-s.

Matias Alfaro.

She'd found the son of a bitch.

23

FAITH STARED AT THE SCREEN FOR A SOLID THIRTY SECONDS, her mind reeling.

Matias Alfaro.

She'd found his email and cell number.

Call him. End it.

Her cell phone sat on the desk and she zipped a glance at it. Right there. Nearly begging for use.

The old Liz would. Without hesitation, she'd dive right in. The opportunity to stop this madness lay just in front of her.

All she had to do was dial and surrender.

Give up the fight.

Something that never came easy, but Shane's request had been for her to be a team player.

Surrendering made her the ultimate team player.

Her logical mind took over, forming a loose plan. If Alfaro hadn't identified Shane as the man responsible for his son's imprisonment — perhaps he thought Shane was simply some poor schmuck she'd hooked up with — she could turn herself over to him. He'd kill her and that would be that. Revenge complete.

If he hadn't identified Shane.

No way to know. And, wow, the idea of walking straight into a death sentence filled her with . . . something.

Fear, anger, heartbreak. All of the above?

She shot from the chair, sending it wheeling backward and tipping over. Leaving it there, she strode the length of the small room, then spun back, her gaze glued to the laptop.

Ding.

Email.

She hustled back, hoping to hell it was Sully giving her something. Some kind of revelation that would derail her from current thoughts.

She tapped the tiny envelope at the bottom of her screen.

Her horoscope. Telling her to save her outrageous antics for another time.

How incredibly prophetic.

For kicks, she scrolled her emails, making sure she hadn't missed something from Sully.

Nope. No Sully.

She paced the room again, cruising by the bed and Shane's backpack. Because of her, his car — that sexy Challenger she'd loved driving — had been blown to bits. The cops still hadn't caught up with them, probably never would since a dead guy owned the car. In addition, thanks to her, his backup cover was useless and, the ultimate *fuck you,* his business burned.

She did another lap. She could do this. End it for all of them.

Maybe, if she got really lucky, she'd surrender to Alfaro, find a way to kill him and escape.

Yes.

Kill him and run. A bold plan for sure. She even had a man inside with Rey.

A revised plan took shape.

She'd contact Alfaro. Insist on a meeting. If he wanted her dead, he'd have to do it himself.

Sadist that he was, he'd love it.

Then she'd kill him.

How?

She paced another lap. Knife? Gun?

No idea. And she'd have to get by his security. She'd figure that out later. Queen of the Pivot, that was her.

Finally, they'd all be free.

What if she failed?

That option couldn't be ignored. If she confronted Alfaro and he killed her first, Shane would never know if he, Dusty and Trevor were safe to continue their lives as normal. If what they were doing could be considered normal.

She walked back to the desk where her laptop snoozed. Another sign from the universe to take a break and think it all through. Not be so impulsive.

Ignoring her mental bedlam, she smacked the space bar, tapped in her password. Alfaro's contact card sat open, nearly taunting her.

She could do this. She *had* to do this. For Shane.

Failure was definitely not an option.

NEARLY THREE HOURS AFTER LEAVING FAITH AND DEALING WITH the arson investigator's endless questions to confirm that, no,

Shane did not burn down his own goddamn business to commit insurance fraud, Shane made his way back to the hotel.

Apparently, Faith hadn't secured a new room yet because she'd gone silent on him. And what the hell had she been doing while he was getting filleted by an investigator?

Worse, the guy probably wasn't done with him. A financial rectal exam would be next and he hoped to hell it didn't trigger some kind of IRS audit.

He'd been obsessive about keeping his books, but if they dug deep enough, they'd figure out a dead guy — the original Shane Quinn, whom he'd found in a cemetery in Indiana — owned the Corner Tap.

And that, he'd have trouble explaining.

Total cluster.

He swiped his key card, waited for the lock to disengage and entered the room.

Empty. Except for his backpack on the bed. He checked the bathroom where the door sat half open.

No Faith.

He slipped his phone from his pocket, shot her a text and waited. Five seconds, ten seconds, fifteen.

No response. *Okay.* She could be on the phone. Maybe finding them that hotel room. Or checking into said hotel room so she could send him the location.

But hold up here. She'd said she'd take his backpack.

Either she forgot or she'd purposely left it.

Nope, nope, nope.

Not going there. He didn't even want to consider what she might be up to.

Taking advantage of the quiet, he moved to the bed and sat. A few minutes to rest his brain. To shut down the chaos. That's what he needed.

As soon as he hit the bed, his backpack shifted against his elbow. He peered down and nudged it a few inches. A piece of notepaper he hadn't put there stuck out of the front pocket and that couldn't be good. Not the way this day had been going.

He blew air through his lips, checked his phone again. No Faith.

So much for his few minutes of quiet.

"God," he said, "please don't let her have gone rogue."

She'd been so damned good this last week. Total team player. He sensed, down deep, it'd been painful for her. There were times she'd started to argue, caught herself and let it go. Working as a unit, for Faith, went against everything she'd been bred for. She'd been honest about that.

No attachments. No heartache.

Her own twisted theory that had zero chance of succeeding.

He slipped the paper from the backpack, noted the handwriting on both sides.

He skimmed it, his eyes darting over her neat script.

Leaving.

I have a plan.

Let Alfaro think he has what he wants.

Time to end it.

Give you your life back.

Sorry.

Yep. She'd gone rogue.

"Well, shit," he muttered.

He poked at his phone. No response yet.

Fine. He swiped the screen, locating his tracking app showing aliases for phones belonging to Dusty, Trevor, Faith and the burner he'd given her. He tapped the burner and a map with a blinking red dot appeared.

He zoomed in. O'Hare Airport.

Wherever she was going, she intended to fly. Terrific.

He grabbed the backpack and headed for the door. Hopefully, whatever flight she booked wouldn't leave for a while. He'd buy a ticket at the airport going anywhere that would get him through security. Then he'd track her and see what the hell she was up to.

Before he got to the door, he stopped. Sullivan. As much as he wondered about that guy, she hadn't been making a move without checking in.

He dialed the number Faith had given him for Sully's burner. Maybe she'd reached out.

"Hey," Sully said.

"Where's Faith going?"

"What now?"

Shane closed his eyes, forced his brain to first gear rather than fourth. "She's at O'Hare. She left a note about letting Alfaro think he has what he wants."

"What the hell does that mean?"

Shane laughed. Had to. "I was hoping you knew. Dollars to doughnuts she's gone rogue."

"Come on? Seriously?"

"Yeah. My bar got torched this morning. She thinks it's her fault. I got back from a rectal exam with a fire investigator and found the note. The tracking app says she's at O'Hare."

"Shit."

"Exactly."

"Do you need my help with the investigator?"

Of all the things he expected Jonathan Sullivan to ask, that wasn't on the list. He took a second. Let the shock sink in.

"Look," Sully said, "whatever you're feeling about me,

I'm being straight with you. If there's something I can do, I'll try. You've all gotten raw deals. Plus, you did me a favor by helping Faith. I owe you one."

Too much. All of this. It was like a demolition derby in his brain. He moved back to the bed and sat. "The investigator. He's probably gonna look into my financials. They're clean, but if they dig hard, I don't know."

"I'll see what I can do."

Shane let his shoulders droop. Let the tension leave him. Help, he decided, sometimes came from the strangest places. "Thank you."

"No prob. Now, what about Faith?"

"We gotta figure out what she's doing."

"I'll call her," Sully said. "She texted me this morning wanting an update. Maybe she'll respond."

"If she does, tell her not to get on whatever plane she's intending to. Keep me posted."

He clicked off and checked his texts and emails. Nothing from Faith.

He flicked his finger against the phone, tried to think like a rogue CIA agent with abandonment issues. Talk about going against the grain.

The day they'd met, she'd walked right up to him on the street. She'd used her contacts to find him.

She'd problem-solved.

Let Alfaro think he has what he wants.

He dropped his phone on the bed beside him and lay back, staring at the ceiling while he noodled Faith's note.

What Alfaro wanted was her. Specifically, her *head*. Something she wouldn't give him without trying to kick some ass first.

Let Alfaro think he has what he wants.

Could she be planning on flying back to Venezuela?

Putting herself in Alfaro's sights to try and kill him?

"Ah, shit!"

He bolted upright, shot a text off to Sully. *She might be going to Venezuela. Can you find flight reservations for her?*

Without bothering to wait for a response, he scrolled his contacts for Reynaldo's number.

"Jesus," he muttered. "Of all the half-baked and completely brave ideas."

Part of him, the part that appreciated her willingness to put herself in danger, admired her. The other part of him?

That part might kill her.

He shot off a text to Rey, who'd immediately responded that he hadn't spoken to her since earlier that morning. Presumably, when he warned her about the fire.

Maddening as it was, it was exactly what Shane would do. He'd wait until he arrived at the target location and then call. It accomplished two things: It gave her a head start plus it surprised Reynaldo, eliminating the chance to formulate a plan to double-cross her.

As he walked toward the parking garage, he dialed Dusty.

"You good?" his friend asked.

Hardly. "Yeah. Faith's on the move."

"Where to?"

"If my guess is right, Venezuela."

A few seconds of silence stood between them. "Wow," Dusty said. "Just . . . wow. How do you know?"

Shane gave him the summation of her note and tracking her to the airport. "I'm heading to O'Hare. I texted Sully. Hoping he'll find her flight reservations before I get there. If not, I'll fly to New York or Miami and be that much closer."

"Dude, you're killing me. You don't even know where she's going."

"Yeah, well, *she's* killing *me*."

"You're not going alone."

Jesus. This again? "You're out of it."

"My ass. If she's going up against Al — who we think she is — you'll need backup. I'll call Trevor and we'll meet you at the airport."

Trevor. Who'd just warned him about getting involved with Faith.

"I promised him I'd keep you both out of this. I'm sticking to it. This is my fight."

"Blah, blah. If the situation were reversed, there's no way, no *fucking* way, you'd let us do it alone. Whatever flight you book, get us on it. See you at the airport."

As soon as the plane touched down, Faith turned her phone — the burner Shane had given her — on. More than likely, he was tracking her. All she could do was try and stay ahead of him. A flurry of dings sounded. Voicemails, texts, missed calls. All of them bombarding her.

And all Sully and Shane. She tapped on a few of the texts, each escalating in tone due to her lack of contact.

Sorry, boys. Business to transact.

Getting into Venezuela turned out to be infinitely easier than Faith's earlier escape. The various credentials she'd brought from DC assisted her in getting a connection through Miami to Bogotá, Colombia. A three-hour layover led her to a flight to Caracas. Now, after one heck of a long day, Faith stepped off the plane, scanning the terminal for anyone who might be ready to pounce.

Even if Shane and Sully had figured out she'd flown as Barbara Alman, a pediatrician entering the country on a humanitarian aid mission, chances were she'd gotten the jump on them.

Sooner or later, they'd catch up to her, but she only needed a few more hours.

Seeing nothing suspicious, she strolled into the ladies' room and swapped out the business clothes she'd bought on her way to the airport for jeans and a T-shirt. While in the stall, she donned her blond wig, checked it with a compact mirror and deemed it passable. Then she got seriously lucky at the sink and slipped out of the ladies' room behind three women traveling together.

Easy.

Peasy.

Now that she'd arrived, she'd alert Reynaldo and hopefully secure his help in escaping after she assassinated the president of Venezuela.

No one would ever call her an underachiever.

Given the hour — nearly 10:30 local time — she'd find a room at one of the airport hotels and start making calls. First to Reynaldo, then to Alfaro.

She made a not-so-quick stop at baggage claim to retrieve her Rollaboard. Even she wasn't crazy enough to attempt this mission without a weapon and had been forced to check luggage due to the nine-millimeter she'd packed. It helped that Barbara Alman had a license to carry said weapon.

Luggage secured, she stepped out of the airport, breathing in the balmy night air that somehow left her peaceful.

Maybe it was having a plan, a potential end to weeks of stress. She wasn't sure. All she knew was that soon, this would be over.

She hailed a cab, directed him to a Marriott and settled

in for the short ride.

Her phone dinged again.

Shane.

She'd been ignoring him all day. Was it fair? Absolutely not. Nothing she could do about it, but let him know that yes, she was indeed still alive.

Within seconds, he responded, asking for the location of the first dead drop he'd arranged prior to their ride on the Ferris wheel. Something only she'd know.

Shane, in his infinite wisdom, didn't trust anything or anyone.

When she responded correctly, he hit her with a barrage of texts she couldn't — wouldn't — answer. The man's hero complex ran too deep. He'd swoop in and that was the last damned thing she wanted when trying to keep his cover safe.

She tucked the phone into her backpack until she reached the hotel and checked into a single room that looked like a thousand other rooms she'd been in over the years. Bed, television, desk and chair.

She tossed her backpack on the bed, slid the phone out and checked it. Nothing. Good. She set it beside her and lay back, closing her eyes for a brief few seconds.

So damned tired.

Her phone rang.

No doubt who this was. She lifted it — yep — and rolled her eyes. The man was impossible. She tapped the screen.

"Please stop," she said. "I know what I'm doing."

"Faith?"

"It's me and I need you to stop calling."

"Not a chance. I know where you are. I'm in Bogota. Don't do anything stupid."

"How'd you catch up so fast?"

He snorted. "I pretended I was you and thought like a rogue agent. I saw you were at the airport, pieced together your note and figured you were about to do something *bold*."

"Ha. Bold. You mean stupid?"

"You said that. Not me. We caught the last flight out of New York when Sully confirmed you had a reservation as one of your former aliases."

Well, shoot. "That didn't take long."

"I was impressed. Considering I hate him, that's saying something."

True that. "Who's with you?"

"Dusty and Trev."

She closed her eyes. Not just him, but all three of them. Putting themselves at risk for her.

She opened her eyes. "Shane, I'm begging you. Please. Stay away. I have a plan. If it works, we'll both be free. You being here complicates things. Alone, I can pivot."

"You can also die."

"Shane — "

"We're boarding, I have to go. Promise me you'll wait for us."

Something she'd never do. She'd already compromised him. If anything, he'd simply moved up her timeline.

"Faith," he said, filling the silence. "I'll be there in two hours. It's late and you're tired. Wait for us and we'll figure this out together."

The line went dead and she tossed the phone beside her. Forget resting.

She needed to make contact with Alfaro before Shane and crew landed in Caracas.

Damned Shane.

She'd had a plan and he was in the midst of completely

screwing it up.

Well, not happening.

With flying time and transport from the airport, it would take Shane and crew — at the very least — two hours to catch up.

A lot could happen in two hours.

Sully. She'd start with him. She shot off a text sharing the decoded contact information for Alfaro.

If she disappeared, if Alfaro took her hostage somewhere and interrogated her, Sully could track the phone to her location. Assuming the number she had was indeed Alfaro's cell.

Would he do the dirty work himself?

Given that she'd taken out his son, she sure hoped so.

Ten seconds after sending the text, she received a response.

Whatever you're doing, stop.

Sorry, friend. No can do. Time to end this.

Ignoring the text, she hit the bathroom, freed her hair from the wig and washed up with cold water to energize her tired body.

Options were plentiful. Call Rey first? Then Alfaro?

Or wait and call both later.

She'd cab it over to the presidential palace in Caracas. Maybe have the driver drop her off two blocks away and walk the rest, calling from whatever street got her closest to the entrance.

Hey, Alfaro. You want me? I'm at your front gate.

She patted her face dry with a fluffy white towel, breathing in the fresh scent of detergent. Suicide mission. That's what this was.

But if it saved Shane. And Dusty and Trevor?

Worth it.

Plus, she might get lucky. Wasn't she the badass who'd escaped from that hellhole basement?

She lowered the towel, stared at it in her hands. Part of winning a battle meant identifying the enemy's weakness. Alfaro's weakness? His sons.

Once in his presence, she'd torture him with the nasty details of his son's death. At the hands of a much smaller woman no less. That alone would enrage him. Add to that the emotional baggage over losing his child and his focus would be gone.

She'd challenge him. Exasperate him. Force him to show his ever-present minions how much of a tough guy he was.

She'd *own* him.

How she'd kill him with his minions present and escape the palace, she had no idea. As soon as she stepped inside the gate they'd take her gun from her.

Total suicide mission.

No.

She'd make it work. She had to get him alone. That was the only way to succeed.

But how?

She dropped the towel, slapped the light switch and walked back to the bed for her backpack.

As usual, she'd figure it out on the way.

THE CAB DRIVER DROPPED HER OFF NEAR A NIGHTCLUB WITH A blinking, blue neon sign. Given the warnings about Caracas being one of the most dangerous cities in the world, parking on the street was plentiful. Faith strode by the club, where large windows were thrown open and a live band entertained a gaggle of people on the dance floor.

Faith had never been one for the nightclub scene. Too many creeps. Too many people to converse with.

Who needed that monotony when she could be alone with her thoughts and her career and her lack of familial responsibilities.

At least until now. *Now*, she had Shane — and Dusty and Trevor — to free from this mess.

A man wandered from the club, giving her the once-over in her jeans and loose T-shirt that covered the gun holstered at her waist. If she actually made contact with Alfaro, she'd be searched and relieved of her weapon.

At which point, she'd improvise. Hand-to-hand combat might be her only option. Word had it Alfaro enjoyed a roaring fire — in the heat of Venezuela — so a fireplace poker would make a dandy tool.

First, she needed access.

"Pretty lady," the man said, his English heavily tinged with a Spanish accent. "Come inside. Enjoy the music."

Faith kept walking, giving the man a backhanded wave. "No thanks."

Hopefully, that would be the end of it. Shooting a man — this man anyway — wasn't necessarily on her task list.

The guy sidled up to her, walking alongside. Why should any of this be easy?

She stopped and faced him. "Not interested. And believe me, you're not either."

He lifted a hand, possibly to touch her but she wasn't waiting to find out. Been there, done that.

She grabbed his wrist, managed to catch him off-guard and whipped him around, wrenching the arm behind his back.

"Whoa!" he said, letting a stream of Spanish fly.

"Go back inside," she said, giving an extra tug on his

arm, "or I'll snap this arm off. Understood?"

When he didn't respond, she increased the pressure.

He let out a grunt and bobbed his head.

She let go. "Get back inside before you get hurt."

He hit her with a round of Spanish swearing and stalked off, massaging his arm.

Men.

At least this one knew when to quit.

She picked up her pace, checking over her shoulder at the slightest sound. At the next corner, she peered up and saw that a glow lit the evening sky.

Alfaro's palace. At night, it stayed lit up like Disney World. Typically, she hated setups like this. Made breaching so much harder.

Today? She *wanted* to be seen. Wanted Alfaro to know she was at his door, right there for him to pluck off the street.

She kept moving, drawing the humid night air into her lungs. A sense of calm knocked the edge from her fatigue. Warm climates did that. If she survived this and managed to win Shane's freedom, she'd move south. Florida Keys maybe. Beach. Salt air.

Paradise.

A future with Shane was too much to hope for. But perhaps, after a few months, if things calmed down, maybe.

Using the glow of the palace against the night sky as a guide, she made a left at the next corner. Another block or two and she'd be there.

She envisioned the palace's four-block square in the middle of the downtown area. Guards manned each corner, constantly patrolling the ten-foot cement wall. Razor wire topped off the wall just in case someone actually got close enough to scale it.

Main entrance.

That's what she'd go with. For no other reason than, based on her walking route, she'd reach it first. Still, there'd be a bit of *honey-I'm-home!* drama with her entering via the front.

She checked the time on her phone: 11:56.

Shane would be landing any time now and would call. He'd said as much. She silenced the phone and tucked it into her pocket.

Go time.

BEFORE THE FLIGHT ATTENDANT EVEN GAVE PASSENGERS THE post-landing blessing to use their phones, Shane tapped Faith's number on his screen. In his mind, wheels were on the ground. He could make the call.

No answer.

Of course.

He didn't bother leaving a voice mail and dropped the phone in his lap. Across the aisle, Dusty peered over at him. "She ghosting you?"

"Yep." He shook his head, stared down at his phone willing the damned thing to ring.

Dusty leaned into the aisle, prompting Shane to meet him halfway. "Seriously," Dusty whispered. "She wouldn't be crazy enough to confront Al — uh, *him* — alone. Even for her, that's nuts."

After sitting on planes all day and having way too much time to think, Shane wasn't too sure. Assuming they had the plan right, considering she hadn't told them a goddamned thing, it might not be all that kooky.

"Nuts or brilliant? When it comes to his sons and revenge, this asshole loses all composure. She'll play him."

He glanced around at the half-full plane. Trevor sat in the seat in front of Dusty and turned back, his gaze direct.

No more talking.

Even whispering, the guy in front of Shane probably heard them.

Shane waited as the plane damn near crawled to the jetway. Could this pilot not hit the gas?

He picked up his phone. No texts from Faith. One from Sullivan telling him to call when he landed. It'd be one in the morning in DC, but Sully worked for the CIA where 24/7 activity never shocked anyone.

As soon as the plane's door opened, Shane was out of his seat, popping open the overhead and grabbing his backpack. This time of night, folks wasted no time deplaning.

Once in the terminal, he tapped Sully's number and followed the signs to ground transportation.

"Shane," Sully said, his voice surprisingly sharp, "what the hell's going on?"

"Did she tell you her plan?"

"No. Between her flying to Venezuela and sending me a cryptic text with a number for Alfaro she'd decoded, I'm guessing she's about to call him. Please tell me she's not doing that."

Ha. The man had better be sitting down. "If my theory is right, she's doing more than that."

Shane gave Sully the shortened version of his theory that Faith intended to either surrender to Alfaro or possibly kill him. Or both. All to draw attention from him, Dusty and Trevor.

A long sigh came from Sully's end of the phone line. "If I wasn't so pissed at her, I'd admire her courage. Hell, I admire her courage anyway. Damned fool."

Shane knew the feeling. "She sent you his number?"

The idea of Faith sharing intel with Sully before him? It stung. And he was too friggin' tired to hide it.

"Don't get your shorts in a wad," Sully said. "She sent it to me assuming the agency could use it."

The agency. Right. "Send me that number."

"Why?"

"If I can't find her, I'm gonna assume she made contact with Alfaro."

"And what? You'll *call* him?"

"Yes."

"Idiot, why would you do that? We don't even know if he's aware you're involved."

"Even better. Element of surprise and all that. You *know* what he'll do to her. I can't let her go through that. Not for me. Send me the number."

Faith stood on a sidewalk under a swaying palm tree across the street from the palace. She stared straight ahead through the iron gates where expertly placed spotlights enhanced the glow of bright white paint. Between the gates and lights, the palace conveyed exactly what Alfaro wanted. Opulence and power.

Two armed guards stood on either side of the entrance. Behind them another manned a guardhouse with a red tile roof that matched the palace's.

Guards, guards and more guards. Everything about the place screamed untouchable.

They'd see about that.

The guard waved her on, telling her in Spanish not to loiter.

Blah, blah. She stepped off the curb, moving toward him, but leaving ten feet between them. The guard's shoulders flew back. Already, he'd gone to high alert. His buddy on the other side took one step closer and halted. His head was on a swivel, searching all around for another potential threat.

"My name is Elizabeth Aiken."

Just saying the words brought a sense of control. Of reclaiming her life.

"Keep moving," the guard told her, his English broken but clear.

"President Alfaro is looking for me. Tell him I'm here."

The second guard looked over at the first guard, the two of them exchanging a WTF look that, at any other time, would have made Faith laugh.

The guard directly in front of her hollered through the gate, calling two more men to the rails.

This was turning into quite the gathering. Time to get right to the point.

"I'm the woman who killed Luca Alfaro. Tell the president I'm here."

24

IT TOOK AN AGONIZING TEN MINUTES FOR THE GATE TO OPEN. For crying out loud, the man had hunted her all the way to Chicago and now that she literally places herself on his doorstep he takes ten minutes?

Unbelievable.

Or smart.

A tactical maneuver to keep her standing there, under guard, and thinking. Thinking and worrying, thinking and worrying, thinking and worrying.

Alfaro never was one to be underestimated. And she'd fed right into his plan.

That stopped now. She tipped her chin up and took a long pull of the moist, humid air that had relaxed her on the walk over.

I'm doing this.

Time to end it. Time to get her freedom back and Shane's along with it. One way or another, when this was over, she'd be free.

Even if it meant dying, she'd be free.

"Go," the guard told her, pointing at the open gate.

A golf cart, a plain white one — not even a presidential seal — that didn't fit Alfaro's typical flashy style, waited in the driveway with two uniformed guards. One stayed behind the wheel while the other slid from the cart and waved her forward.

She'd anticipated this moment all day. Had made a plan to control her emotions and not lose focus. The adrenaline rush she'd expected? The anticipated pounding head and rapid pulse?

Nothing.

Those first steps through the gate brought only calm control. And that was a gift.

Her escort drew his sidearm, motioned her into the cart, then climbed in beside her, keeping the gun trained on her. Apparently, he'd heard stories about her. Excellent. Alfaro's men knew the chaos she created.

Pushing her luck, she glanced at the gun, then the guard and . . . smiled. One of those sly, you-might-survive-me ones that had served her well over the years.

Why not? It gave her a mental edge. Kept them guessing.

On the short ride to Alfaro's front door she perused the tropical plants and palm trees lining the drive. A massive arched stone entrance and windows lined the front of the palace. All of it stunning and reminiscent of the styles she'd seen while on assignment in France.

Much too elegant for the monster inside.

The cart eased to a stop and her escort slid out, motioning her to the front door. She climbed the wide slate steps and one of the double doors leading inside opened, revealing another guard.

Lots of guards.

She'd expected no less, but seeing them all?

Should have waited for Shane.

She shook it off. The whole point of doing this alone was to protect him. To knock Alfaro off Shane's trail.

And hopefully kill the man. How she'd get out of here once she did that? No clue.

I can do this.

The guard at the door nodded. She took a step closer, pausing for a second to get her bearings before she stepped over that threshold.

Into Alfaro's space.

Straight ahead a large, curved staircase loomed. On either side was a hallway that led to a kitchen and various rec rooms and studies. During her flight, she'd dug up a floor plan online, but who knew what modifications had been made?

Still, it was something.

"Come in," the guard barked. "Hands up."

This was it. They'd search her and find the gun. Something she'd purposely carried because a woman walking the streets alone at this hour was foolish. Something she'd never considered herself to be.

She turned her back to him and held her arms up. "I have a gun at my waist. I walked here."

The guard relieved her of the gun, making no fuss about it. As if it was simply an ordinary occurrence.

What wasn't so ordinary was his dragging his hands over every inch — *every* inch — of her, checking for hidden weapons. He'd done her the courtesy of being thorough but brief.

A real gentleman, this one.

When he reached her ass, he found her phone and slid it from her back pocket.

She remained quiet, allowing him to finish his search

while the guard at the door watched, mildly amused. If *he'd* searched her, she had no doubt he'd be a pig about it.

She slid him her bitch-glare, but decided irritating him wouldn't exactly help her cause.

Search complete, the guard motioned her to the stairs. She took one step, then another across the white marble.

Hard floor. Skulls cracked on that kind of surface.

Maybe Alfaro's skull. Wouldn't that be ironic? Killing the man with his own excellent taste.

Behind her, the guard guided the heavy wood front door closed, the latch catching with a gentle click that fired her pulse.

Inside.

Locked door.

She took a breath, fought to keep her emotions under lockdown.

I can do this.

She climbed the steps, pretending to study the oversized Baroque paintings while surveying the area, mapping out possible escape routes.

At the top, another uniformed guard appeared. *Jesus.* So many guards. All of them armed. She'd known it, but now, seeing them all, the weight of it pressed in.

Second floor. Hopefully, Alfaro would meet with her here. If she could get him alone, she'd kill him and drop from a window, just as she and Shane had done at Brutus's hotel.

The guard who'd brought her upstairs handed her over and then retreated down the steps.

Second-floor guard went left. She followed, her hands already itching for combat. If this guy was stupid enough to let her get out of his sight, he deserved to die.

Her sneakers squeaked against the marble, drawing his

attention. Apparently, *he'd* heard about her too because he halted and waved her in front.

Damn.

She eased her fists open. Probably too early in the operation to kill someone anyway.

Behind her, he called commands. Turn left, turn right.

On her right, a wall of windows and French doors looked out over a courtyard. She'd seen all of that online. The solid doors on the right led to staircases or balconies. The balconies she could drop from, but she hoped to avoid it.

"Halt," the guard said when she reached a set of double doors on her left.

Keeping his eye on her, he grabbed one of the ornate gold handles, flicked it and swung the door open.

Matias Alfaro leaned against his desk, arms folded, an oily, satisfied smile on his smug face.

SHANE HAD BARELY THROWN HIS BACKPACK ON HIS HOTEL room's bed when his phone lit up with Reynaldo's name. On the way over, he'd left the kid a voice mail, but hadn't made any bets on hearing back tonight. Alfaro demanded 24/7 availability from his staff.

No exceptions.

Shane punched up the call. "Rey, thanks for getting back to me."

"She's here."

Bile mounted in his throat. Jesus, she'd turned herself over to a psycho.

He blew out a breath, brought his mind back to finding Faith. "Where are you?"

"At the palace."

Rey's voice was a low murmur. Did he actually live at the palace? Or even on the property?

"You've seen her?"

"No. Boss called. He told me to be ready to drive. When I got here, I asked the guard what was going on. Boss doesn't usually leave so late. He told me a woman — *the* woman, Elizabeth Aiken — was here."

Shane shook his head. Damned fool. She should have waited for them. "Where is she? What room?"

"I don't know. I'm in kitchen. Waiting."

"Listen, Rey, I know what I'm asking, but can you find her? I need specifics."

"No."

The word was an immediate punch. An absolute that neither shocked nor irritated Shane. He couldn't blame the kid for not wanting to snoop around the palace. Getting caught might put him in a grave.

"Rey — "

"I must stay in kitchen. Wait for instructions."

Shane lifted his free hand and pressed his thumb and middle finger into his eye sockets. Between fatigue from the past week, his business burning and Faith pulling this stunt, he needed to get his mind right.

One thing at a time. The rest he'd deal with later.

He exhaled, let his thoughts settle into some sort of controlled chaos.

Right now, he had Rey — sort of. What better person to have on the inside than Alfaro's driver? The one who could communicate all movements?

"Okay," Shane said. "I understand. If he moves her, will you text me? Can you do that?"

"*Si*. What will you do?"

As if he knew? "Working on it. I'll keep you posted."

He disconnected, dialed Sully. His nerves crackled, sending his thoughts spiraling. A vision of Faith strapped to a table popped into his mind and — *shit* — he'd never get that out of there. He paced the room, moving quickly, hoping to burn energy. Once again, he zeroed in on the mission.

Find her. That's all he had to do.

On the second ring, Sully picked up. "What's happening?"

"Just got word from Rey. She's at the palace. I think Alfaro's moving her. Rey is on alert."

"Shit."

"Exactly. We need to stall him."

"Uh, *sure*. Let's do that. I mean, do you seriously think I have the power to make a deal with the president of Venezuela? This is *way* over my pay grade."

"There's got to be something. Talk to the brass. See if we can make a deal. We'll get Andres out of prison in exchange for Faith."

"Now you're dreaming. Even if we could do it, it would take time."

"We don't have time."

Shane completed another lap, working different scenarios, mulling things of importance to Venezuela and, in turn, Alfaro.

Imports, economy, financial markets. Banking.

Oil.

The country's dependence on hydrocarbons wasn't a secret. A whopping 84 percent of that dependence represented nearly $15 billion in crude oil. Mineral fuels were nearly 90 percent of Venezuela's export revenue.

Shane halted, stood stock-still, letting his mind work. "Oil."

"What about it?"

Freaking brilliant, if he did say so himself. "We'll threaten his oil exports."

Sully snorted. "I can't tell my boss to call POTUS and say we need to immediately halt oil production in Venezuela."

"You don't have to. Dusty, Trev and I will do it."

"*What?* You have *lost* it."

Shane started walking again, this time more slowly. A loose plan took shape, odd threads coming together. They could do this.

He waved his free hand in the air. "Shut up and listen. The refineries. We need to disable them. Maybe we cut the electricity or blow a power station."

"Whoa. Slow. *Down.*"

"It could work."

"Yeah," Sully said. "It could. But do we have time for that, considering Faith is with Alfaro right now? We'd have to find someone to get you inside. I'm good, but not *that* good."

Crap. Sullivan was right. Shane reached the windows where the closed curtains swayed from the blasting AC unit below. He held his hand out, let the cold air wrap around his fingers and shoot up his arm.

Relax.

Think about this.

If the refineries were out, what was next. They had to ship the oil by truck and boat.

Shipping.

The ports.

He stuck two fingers in the opening of the curtains and peeped out, seeing nothing but black sky, but he knew what was out there in the distance.

Docks. A bunch of 'em.

He let the curtain go and perched on the edge of the desk. "LA Guairá port is close."

"And?"

Come on, Sullivan. Get on it. "Dumbass, we could take out a dock. Use it as a warning. I'll call Alfaro, tell him if he hurts her, LA Guairá is toast. To prove it, we blow a portion of the dock. Can you get me Semtex in a hurry?"

Semtex BC-HMX, a volatile plastic explosive, was similar to C-4, but more devastating and usable underwater. With Semtex, they could wreck most of a shipping port.

And the double-bonus? Shane, if he had to, could rig the Semtex himself. All he needed was someone to provide it.

Sullivan sighed. "You *can't* be serious."

"Bet your ass I am. We'll place it on a few supports and *boom*. Then we tell Alfaro that unless he releases Faith, more ports and refineries will be blown. If nothing else, it'll buy us some time."

Yes. This could work. Shane pumped a fist. For the first time all day some goddamned hope sparked.

Alfaro's dependence on oil might be just the motivation they'd need. A president would be a fool to risk his nation's top export. Alfaro was a lot of things, but a fool wasn't one of them.

"Give me a few minutes," Sully said. "I'll see what I can do."

"As usual," Alfaro told Faith, "you've surprised me."

He remained leaning on his desk, but lowered his hands, resting them on either side of his body. He wore gray dress slacks and a pristine shirt she had no doubt he'd just pulled from a closet.

His salt-and-pepper hair appeared damp. Whether he'd

showered for the occasion or simply wet it, she wasn't sure, but knowing his obsession with his image, she wouldn't be shocked if he'd taken the time to bathe.

After all, he'd want to be fresh for her beheading.

A quick scan of the spotless office revealed muted lighting that emphasized the richness of dark woods, deep colors and plush, oversized chairs.

Dark, yet elegant.

Like the man himself.

Next to the sofa, the glare of a reading lamp shined on folders stacked on a side table. Other than that, what she could see of the desk and coffee table were clear.

Not a scrap of paper to be seen.

Faith offered him her own smug smile. "By now, I'd hoped you'd know not to underestimate me."

Alfaro's nose twitched. Just a tiny, almost imperceptible movement that let her know she'd hit the mark.

This was an emotional man. Working inside his mind meant knocking him off his game. Forcing him to make mistakes.

Behind her, the guard who'd escorted her upstairs cleared his throat. Without her gun, her chances of taking out both men were slim.

But she'd faced these odds before and prevailed.

"Go," Alfaro told him. "Ms. Aiken and I will talk. I'll let you know when I'm ready."

Talk. Interesting.

And ready for what?

The latching of a door sounded and she assumed the guard had followed orders.

She wouldn't dare take her eyes off of Alfaro. He eased from the edge of the desk, walked around and took his chair.

An oversized one, of course. One fit for the king he considered himself to be.

He pointed to one of the antique guest chairs — eighteenth-century if Faith were to guess — in front of his desk.

"Please. Sit."

She moved to the chairs, noting the two windows behind him. Probably locked.

Seconds. That's all it would take to unlock them, open the window — assuming the windows weren't sealed — and hop out.

She lowered herself into a chair and Alfaro sat back, resting his hands over the armrests.

"Why have you come?"

Why indeed. "I'm done running."

"And? You think I will forgive you? That we will — as you Americans say — settle up?"

She shrugged. "We'll either settle up or I'll be dead. Either way, I'm free."

At this, he laughed. "If I didn't despise you, I'd add you to my staff."

Not if she had anything to say about it. Mirroring his body language, she sat back, draping her arms over the armrests. "Why didn't you kill me on sight?"

"I considered it." He met her gaze, narrowing his eyes. "I want information."

"As you must know, I'm out of the loop."

"Your government abandoned you."

"My usefulness expired."

He tsk-tsked. "No loyalty for the woman who murdered my son? I should be insulted."

Faith concentrated on not reacting. No shocked horror. No gawking. No head tilt.

Zippo.

But, seriously? This guy might be loonier than she thought if he was insulted that the agency cut her loose. Forget the fact that she'd eliminated his son. He wanted her to be honored for it.

"I didn't murder him," she said. "He attacked me. It was self-defense."

Another nose twitch. "My son was an honorable man."

"An honorable man who threatened to rape women."

He pointed at her. "Stop it."

And there it was. The first chink in the armor.

Work it.

She leaned in. "You allowed your son to be involved with drug smuggling for the Liborios, one of the most violent cartels in the world. You cannot have any illusions about his choices. Or his character."

"A woman in your position would be advised to shut her mouth. Or maybe I should fill it?"

Ah, yes. Like father like son, with the threat of sexual assault.

She cocked her head, offered up a small smile. "Considering I butchered your son, you might think twice."

The man locked his jaw so tight it cracked and a sudden burst of adrenaline filled her. Fear mixed with excitement because holy hell, she'd pissed him off. Royally. Now she had to see it through.

"Tell me what happened," he demanded.

"I'm sorry?"

"In that basement. I want to know. Once I do, I'll decide how you die. Maybe *I'll* butcher *you*."

What the hell kind of man wanted the details of his son's violent death?

A vengeful one.

One who got off on anger and depravity. One who used that anger to justify his actions.

She considered it. Telling him would only enrage him further and enraged people, she knew from experience, developed superhuman strength and an ability to focus only on eliminating the enemy.

In this case, her.

She needed him emotional, but not enraged. A fine line.

"His friend came at me first," she said.

"Idiot. He always was short-sighted."

"He assumed because he was bigger and stronger, I wouldn't fight." She waved it away. "Luca heard the noise and came to investigate. By then, his friend was dead."

"You were in the basement?"

Liz nodded. "Yes. That's where they kept me."

"And when Luca came downstairs?"

For the first time in weeks, Liz allowed her mind to go back to that basement. The dank smell, the darkness and dirt. Luca's boots on the steps. All of it filled her mind, made her chest pound. She inhaled, focused on lowering her heart rate.

Control.

That's what she needed. Control and smart choices.

She met Alfaro's gaze. "He saw his dead friend and tried to subdue me. He told me to go ahead and fight. That it would be all the better when he *fucked* me until I bled." She held her hands wide. "Surely, you can't blame me for defending myself."

"Not at all. I blame you for taking my son from me."

"I had no choice."

"There's always a choice. You could have let him live."

Oh, please. *That* would have been fascinating. "He was bigger and fighting hard. You should know that."

"I taught them strength."

"Exactly. It's not as if I could tie him up."

"You're a resourceful woman. There were ways."

"I suppose," she said, "we'll have to agree to disagree. How did you know I was in Chicago? How did Luis Gustavo find me?"

Brutus. She had to know. Had to figure out who burned her.

"My *dear*," he said, drawing the word out as if she were some sort of imbecile. "I have contacts everywhere. Even in *your* country. How do you think I discovered you were working here in the first place."

And there it was. The admission that someone inside Langley had sold her out.

"Who was it?"

He barked out a laugh. "I'd be a fool to tell you."

Alfaro, like every other president, probably had spies all over DC.

"Luis," he continued, "was a horrible disappointment. All he had to do was eliminate you and your lover. When he failed, I had no choice, but to act."

Her *lover*. A nice generic term from a man who obviously enjoyed flaunting his upper hand. Flaunting his ability to find whomever, wherever.

If he knew Shane's real identity, he'd brag about it. No question.

"You had Gustavo killed," she said.

"Of course I did. He knew too much."

Harsh as it was, a tiny bit of relief settled on her. What had she become that a man's death — a violent one, no doubt — pleased her? "My friend," she said. "He's innocent in all this."

"Innocents die every day." He waved it away. "Thank you

for your honesty. For telling me Luca fought and wasn't a coward."

Lord, so twisted.

A blaring ring exploded. Faith glanced at the desk phone. Not that one, but definitely a phone. Alfaro lifted one hip and dug into his pocket for a cell.

Perhaps the number she'd sent Sully was attached to it. Could she get that lucky?

Alfaro's bottom lip jutted out before he poked the screen. "Yes?"

He snapped his gaze to her, his eyes widening. For whatever reason, he'd given up all hope of hiding his emotions.

And then he did the dead last thing she expected.

He handed her the phone.

25

Faith, Shane decided, was batshit crazy.

Had to be.

He walked alongside Dusty and Trevor in the hotel parking lot with a burner phone to his ear. He tossed Dusty the rental's keys. He'd drive while Shane focused on Faith and Alfaro and destroying a shipping port.

As much as Shane admired the solid set of brass ones on the woman, she'd once again gone rogue on him. Hadn't even given him a chance to help her. And it was about more than being a team player. This was a trust issue.

And if he expected any kind of relationship with her, romantic or otherwise, they'd have to work that shit out.

"Hello?" she said.

There was a firmness to her voice, as if she spoke directly into it. No speakerphone.

"Are you okay?"

"Yes."

The simplicity of the word somehow convinced him.

"Good. I have a plan to get you out. Stall him."

"Don't."

Again with a one-word answer. Well, too fucking bad. He'd risked everything by coming here and she'd damn well take his help.

"Give me the phone."

Alfaro's voice.

A shuffling noise sounded and then, "You have your proof," Alfaro said.

He sure did. This whole scenario was screwed, but at least she was alive. And talking. And apparently unharmed.

For now.

"Good," Shane told Alfaro. "She better stay safe."

"Or what?"

Let the fun begin. "Or we start disrupting your economy."

At that, Alfaro laughed. "Impossible."

"You never know who may have insinuated themselves into your business. I mean, I did it myself."

A long pause ensued while Alfaro let that sink in.

Moment of truth. Shane could admit it. Right here, right now, tell Alfaro his identity and the war would be on. Or he could lie. Make up some random name, yet another of his many covers that Alfaro wouldn't know but would wonder endlessly about.

Nah.

After two years of running from this asshole, saying it, actually telling him he was coming for him seemed like a banner fucking idea. If nothing else, it'd blow the guy's mind.

"Who is this?" Alfaro finally asked.

"You don't recognize my voice? You must be slipping. Well, it doesn't matter. It's George."

"George?"

"George Hendrix."

Again Shane waited. Just ahead of him, Dusty and Trev hopped into the rental car's front seats. Shane took the back.

"Where are you?" Alfaro asked.

As if. "You have one hour to release her. If I don't hear from her, you've got problems. One hour, Alfaro."

Shane hung up and nearly crapped his pants because, wow. That was freaking fantastic. To finally take a stand against this fucker.

"Dude!" Dusty hollered. "One hour? We don't even have the Semtex yet."

Shane had just threatened the president of Venezuela and that's what Dusty was worried about?

Each of them needed intensive therapy.

"I'm on it." Shane tapped Sully's name on his phone and on the first ring, he picked up.

Shane didn't bother waiting for any pleasantries. "Where are we?"

"I'm waiting for a call back. We have someone on the ground there. He can get C-4 and possibly Semtex. There's also a SEAL team in the area working another mission."

SEALs were good news, but what a political shitstorm that would be. "Let's not go there if we don't have to."

"You're telling me?" Sully sighed. "Look, Shane, you know he won't release her."

He couldn't think about that. Not yet. One thing at a time.

"That's why we're forcing it. I've been close to this guy. Probably closer than anyone on our side. He loves power and money. Oil brings him both. He'll need to decide if Faith is that important."

The phone line clicked.

"Call coming in," Sully said. "I'll hit you back."

The line went dead just as Dusty pulled out of the lot.

"He's working on it," Shane said. "While we're waiting, we can check access roads to the port."

In the front seat, Trevor had his head down as if reading something on his phone and Dusty glanced over at him.

"What are you doing?"

"Checking my emails. A work thing."

"Fuck that," Dusty said. "Pull up a map of the port. Let's see what we're dealing with."

Shane's phone rang again. Sully. He poked the screen. "What's up?"

"I got you Semtex!" Sully said, his voice full of wonder Shane never expected from straitlaced Sullivan.

He couldn't blame the guy. Shane's own pulse was slamming right now, the excitement lighting him up. He smacked the side of the driver's seat. "Where?"

Sully rattled off an address that Shane repeated so Trevor could enter it into his phone.

"Got it," Trev said. "It's just outside of Caracas."

Shane went back to Sully. "Who is he?"

"An asset we have over there. An arms dealer."

Son of a bitch. An arms dealer. God only knew what Sully had to trade for this. "What's this costing you?"

"Right now, I don't know. It's a favor to be repaid later."

Shane's head dipped. Jonathan Sullivan might have just incinerated his precious career, because Shane's guess was that the guy hadn't cleared any of this with the brass. Not to mention getting in bed with an arms dealer who might kill him. "Oh, man. Obviously, you know what you just did."

"I'll figure it out later. Just get her back."

AFTER HANGING UP WITH SHANE, WHOM SHE'D STRANGLE FOR disrupting her plan, Alfaro checked his phone.

As half-assed as this op might be, it was working. Her goal had been to surrender and get Shane off of Alfaro's radar.

At least until Shane decided to get into the middle of it. Up to this point, nothing in Alfaro's tone indicated he knew Shane's real identity. By placing that call, Shane had sacrificed himself for no reason. And for that, she should kill *him*.

She locked her jaw, brought her focus back to her target, who was busy reading something on his phone. And ignoring her.

Silly man.

Now.

She slid her hand from the armrest, the movement immediately drawing Alfaro's attention.

"What do you have there?"

She shrugged. "What could I have? Your man searched me."

Alfaro narrowed his gaze, studying her for a few seconds before tossing his phone on the desk. Total puzzle, this one.

She always hated puzzles.

"This," he said, his face glowing, "has been a very good day. Not only have you been foolish enough to present yourself, your lovesick boyfriend has come after you. And *he* is the traitor who put my son in prison." He smacked his hands together. "A *good* day indeed."

Opportunity gone, she sat back again, contemplated her next move because, yes, there was always a next move. And then it hit her. If Alfaro hadn't known who Shane was, neither did his inner circle.

As of right now, only Alfaro knew Shane's true identity. If she eliminated Alfaro before he could share the news, Shane would be free.

Lemonade out of lemons.

Alfaro held up his phone. "He thinks he can blow up my port."

What?

Faith dug her heels into the floor, forcing herself to remain still. To keep her facial features neutral even though, holy mother of God, what was Shane *doing*?

As hard as she tried, she must have flinched or given some sort of body language because Alfaro let out one of those annoying fake belly laughs that irritated the crap out of her.

"You didn't know," he said. "Oh, this is glorious."

Glorious, my ass. Faith waved Alfaro's delight away. "He's not blowing up a port."

He pointed at his phone. "I just received a text. George and his compatriots. They are here and have secured enough Semtex to destroy one of the LA Guairá docks."

How the hell did he have this information?

And Semtex?

Sully must have been involved with *that* because Shane scoring Semtex practically the minute he arrived would be a minor miracle.

She'd given up on miracles long ago.

She shook her head. "He wouldn't do that."

"Yes, my dear, I assure you, he would. I have the text giving me the details."

Alfaro definitely had a snitch. But where? Her mind whirled, shuffling through the players. The only person involved, outside of Dusty and Trevor, was Sully. And whomever else he looped in. Someone inside the CIA had burned Liz Aiken. Would they intentionally burn Shane?

For the right price, she knew, people talked.

Alfaro offered her a dramatic sigh. "You Americans. You

think you're the only ones who excel at intelligence gathering. You sit there, with all your wealth and power and look down on *me*?"

What the hell was he talking about?

He jabbed his finger into his desk. *Jab-jab-jab.* "I am a king! I know what my people need."

Letting vicious cartels smuggle drugs and guns across their borders was what his people needed?

Not to mention those same cartels raping women and murdering innocents.

Her mind instantly brought her back to that basement, her senses recapturing the stench of urine and blood and death.

Use it.

She sat forward. "*Your* people need the violence to end."

"Silence!"

"Who's your source? You'll kill me anyway. You might as well tell me."

"No," he shot back. "You'll go to your ugly death wondering."

Mental as well as physical torture. She'd expected no less.

Alfaro's phone chirped. He scooped it up and she shifted her gaze, scanning her immediate surroundings for any sort of weapon.

A large, diamond-shaped crystal sculpture sat on the desk. Had to weigh a good four or five pounds. If she could be quick enough and hurl it at him, it might stun him. Give her time to fly across the desk and hit him with a palm strike.

Before she even moved, he bolted from his chair. "Get up."

Whoa. What was this now? Whatever that text was, it had the man fired up. "Why?"

"Get up! We're leaving."

He strode around the desk, latched on to her biceps, his fingers digging into muscle and sending sparks of pain into her shoulder. Yow. That'd leave a bruise.

She wouldn't give him the satisfaction of wincing.

Not today.

Not ever.

He dragged her from the chair, pulling her to the door. Her feet tangled and she tripped, stumbling against him and knocking him off balance, but he held on to her with that iron grip.

"Guard!" he called.

The door flew open and the same guard who'd escorted her to the office stood there.

"Sir?"

"Take her downstairs and wait for me. I want *one* unmarked vehicle. No limousines. The SUV. We're leaving."

SULLY'S GUNRUNNER, MIGUEL, TURNED OUT TO BE A REGULAR encyclopedia. Not only did he provide enough Semtex to blow a square city block, he gave Shane the motherlode of intel on access points to the passenger terminal at LA Guairá.

Not that the passenger terminal helped them in terms of crippling oil exports, but, according to Miguel, they'd be able to reach the various docks from that entry point. The guards, he assured them, would not interfere.

A total non-shocker considering the guy probably bribed most of them.

The port sat just north of Caracas, bordered by Avenida

Soublette, a main thoroughfare separating the shipping lanes from a hillside stacked with ramshackle homes and businesses.

Shane leaned left from the rear passenger seat and peered through the windshield at Avenida Soublette. Overhead streetlights and lights from the port blazed against the night sky.

"There's the access road," Dusty said from behind the wheel.

He turned onto the dirt road, bouncing and bumping their way across potholes and ruts.

No wonder it was unguarded. People risked whiplash traveling on it.

Shane kept his gaze pinned to the right shoulder where, at any minute, they should find an unlit, abandoned guard station.

Bingo. "That's it," Shane pointed at the wooden shack no bigger than a toll booth. "He said to park behind it."

Dusty pulled around, killing the engine. According to Miguel, there'd be a walking path that led to the docks.

"Are we at all concerned," Trevor said, "that this guy could be screwing us?"

Hell, yes. He didn't know jack about Miguel and, worse, Sully, someone Shane still wasn't sure he completely trusted, had hooked them up.

But they'd come through with the explosives and that's all Shane cared about. At least right now.

Shane grabbed his backpack, now stuffed with bricks of Semtex, detonator cords, blasting caps, fuses and fuse lighters, and slid from the car, closing the door behind him. "My shit-meter is in the red, so yeah, we're concerned. As we should be."

Before Shane could walk by him, Trev held his arm out. "Then why are we risking it?"

"You got a better idea?"

At that, Trevor shut up. Dusty pushed by them, leading the charge. Shane fell in step beside him with Trev taking up the rear.

The whole damned thing was a suicide mission. Prior to leaving the States, Shane had told them this. He'd all but begged them not to come.

Out of some sense of twisted loyalty he didn't blame them for, they'd ignored him.

So yeah, here they were, walking down a dusty road in Venezuela that would probably snag them into a trap.

"Call me fucked up," Dusty said, "but I miss this shit. The rush."

Trev snorted. "You *are* fucked up. But, yeah, I get it."

These two buttheads chose now to get nostalgic?

He shook it off and inhaled the salty air, letting it wash through him and knock his nerves down a notch.

His mind drifted to Faith's battered face that first day they'd met. That's why they were here. For Faith. And anyone else who'd suffered due to the Liborio Cartel or Alfaro's corrupt dealings with them.

They might not be able to stop the madness, but they could save Faith.

"Hey," Shane said, "can we focus, please? We got shit to do."

The quickly hatched plan was simple: They'd each take a couple of bricks of Semtex, place them near the supports on a prespecified dock and blow it.

Said plan had enough holes to sink one of the oil tankers sitting in port, but they didn't have time for a military precision op.

"Go time," he said. "If either of you wants out, this is the time. No harm, no foul."

"I'm good," Dusty said.

"I'm good," Trev said.

"Then let's do this. Hopefully, it'll scare the shit out of Alfaro enough that he'll negotiate."

Trevor looked back at Shane. "And if it doesn't?"

Mary Sunshine. Excellent.

Shane shrugged. "I don't have a fucking clue."

26

Alfaro's guard escorted Faith back to the first floor via the same staircase, his grip firm on her arm. Did he think she'd leap over the railing? Maybe whip out a hidden weapon and light the place up?

At the bottom of the staircase, he pulled her around, making a U-turn and heading down the long corridor she'd spotted on her arrival.

Rear entrance. Interesting. Her mind ticked through scenarios. Perhaps fewer guards out back. There had to be security video. Unless they'd shut those cameras off.

Or they didn't want to be seen driving out the main gate at this hour. Alfaro *had* asked for one unmarked SUV.

The man wasn't stupid. He knew how to erase her.

Except she didn't intend to disappear without a fight. A lesson he should have learned when she'd eliminated his son.

Still holding her arm, the guard moved her through several arched doorways to a large kitchen gleaming with stainless steel double ovens, the biggest stove Faith may have ever seen and a giant marble island.

She skimmed the area, searching for any possible weapon. Not a butcher knife to be had.

The guard pointed to another archway that led to a smaller room with lockers. Staff entrance?

He swung the lone door open, revealing three stone steps lit by an overhead light on the small porch. At the bottom, a black SUV waited in the driveway.

Her mind spun, coming up with scenarios. Hostage exchange? Maybe some deal made with Shane where he'd turn himself in and she'd be set free?

No. She'd done worse. She'd killed Alfaro's son. Far worse than Shane's offense of putting the other son in prison.

This had to be a setup. A chance to kill them both.

Alfaro's snitch had obviously given up Shane's location. That had to be it. Two birds, one stone.

Faith halted, digging her feet into the ground. "Where are we going?"

Not that she expected an answer, but what did it hurt to ask?

"No talking," he told her. "Go."

When she pulled back, he shoved her, sending her stumbling over the steps. She landed hard against the SUV's door, smacking her elbow, but refusing to cry out.

They'd like that too much and she wouldn't give them the satisfaction.

When the guard opened the rear passenger door, she tipped her chin up.

"Get in," he demanded. "The middle."

The middle. Crap.

The *middle* meant company on the other side that would block her in. She'd be trapped in the vehicle.

Run.

Her instincts all but screamed it. Running, she'd become an expert at. She might get a jump on the guard.

Logic took hold and froze her thoughts. Even if she managed to break away, eventually she'd reach the giant wall surrounding the palace.

And then what?

"In," the guard said between gritted teeth.

Pissing him off probably wasn't a banner idea.

She climbed into the air-conditioned cabin praying to whatever god might still be listening to her that she'd get a chance to escape.

A man sat in the driver's seat. A young guy, maybe mid-twenties. A blast of hope exploded inside her.

Could it be Reynaldo? Before the guard could slide in, she leaned forward, pretending to move the seat belt buckle from behind her while she tried to get a look at the driver.

She'd seen pictures of Reynaldo, but who knew how old those were. Still, Rey, she'd noted from the photos, had a mole on the front part of his left cheek by his nose.

The driver, sensing movement turned and faced her, the cabin light illuminating his face and the mole.

Definitely Reynaldo.

Maybe those prayers had already been answered.

He met her gaze, holding it for a long few seconds before giving her the tiniest of nods. She wasn't even sure if it was a nod, but she'd take it as a silent message that she wasn't alone.

"Do you need help?"

His voice was that same prepubescent-sounding one from their short phone calls.

Oh, yes, this was Reynaldo.

"The seatbelt," she said. "I think I've got it."

The guard slid in beside her. "No talking," he said to no one in particular.

Rey faced front and placed his hands on the wheel while the vehicle idled and Faith's mind went crazy on scenarios.

Depending on how much security Alfaro brought along, Rey might be able to help her escape. How, she wasn't yet sure. She'd have to figure it out fast.

Did Rey know where they were going? He had to have an address. Had he texted Shane with it?

Hope once again streamed. Wherever the final destination, Shane and Dusty and Trevor might be there. Then the odds would even out.

Then, they might have a chance.

Another man emerged from the palace. He paused on the steps, speaking to someone inside. He wore black cargo pants and a matching T-shirt that did nothing to hide his muscular frame.

Big guy. *Shane* big.

She'd never win a fight against a guy that big. Could she slow him down? Sure. She might even manage to run, but in hand-to-hand combat he'd crush her.

A second later, Alfaro joined the man on the porch and the two of them walked to the passenger side of the SUV. Cargo-pants guy opened the rear door and Alfaro slid in, squeezing her between him and the guard.

Trapped.

Her throat squeezed in, cutting off her oxygen. She tipped her head back and forced her shoulders down, opening herself up. Forcing her own body to release her. To fight the claustrophobia.

Cargo-pants guy hopped in front and Faith's gut seized. At best, assuming Rey would help her, it would be three on two and something told her cargo-pants guy was former military.

Her odds sucked.

Wouldn't be the first time.

Hopefully, it would be the last.

Rey eased the car into gear and followed the driveway to a service entrance. Rey waved to the guard standing post.

They drove through the gate and Faith's panic whirled again. Between being pinned in and not knowing their destination, she needed to do something. Fast.

She swung her head to Alfaro. "Where are you taking me?"

"No talking," he told her.

To punctuate the statement, he pulled a weapon — a .38 from what she could see — from the door compartment and pointed it at her.

Would the man be insane enough to pull the trigger inside this vehicle? If she pushed him hard enough, probably.

The guard beside her shifted, his hip nudging hers — too close — and the situation hit her full force.

She literally had nowhere to go and the air she'd just fought so hard for disappeared.

Her pulse slammed, the rapid buhm-buhm-buhm echoing in her ears.

Panic, that little beast inside her, wouldn't help her out of this car.

Fight it. She stared out the windshield, imagined Shane waiting for her, the two of them going into battle. And winning.

She could do this. With help she could win.

Queen of the Pivot.

She focused on immediate steps. Alfaro was nuts. No doubt about that. Still, she didn't believe he'd pull the trigger. Not here. Not when he had a thirst for revenge. Twisted fucker that he was, he'd want a show. *He'd* want to drag her in front of Shane and let him watch while they took turns raping her. For him, it would accomplish torturing both her and Shane at once.

Again, two birds, one stone.

But Alfaro didn't know about Dusty and Trevor. Add Rey in and her odds just got a whole lot better.

She'd wait. Stay patient and use this car ride to work out a plan. Eventually, they'd reach a destination and let her out of the car.

That would be her opportunity. If her making-Shane-watch theory held, wherever they were headed, Shane would be there.

Which made screaming an option.

Definitely. The second she got out of this vehicle she'd start howling and alert Shane of her location. Let him find her by tracking the scream.

Gram always said she had a set of lungs on her.

UNDER A BLAZING BRIGHT MOON — JUST HIS LUCK — SHANE stood near the middle of a dock that stretched more than six tankers long.

Per Miguel's directions, they'd followed the dirt road until it dead-ended at a cement barrier and a high chain-link fence that did nothing to keep ill-intentioned guys like them out.

All three of them had scaled the fence and made their way to a walkway and an empty administrative building that Miguel had told them suffered a fire years earlier. To date, the government hadn't done the repairs, leaving this area of the port largely unguarded.

Big mistake.

Big.

Once beyond the building, they'd stayed in the shadows, moving along an access road until they reached rows and rows of shipping containers stacked four high. On the other side of those containers?

The dock where Shane now stood.

Miguel had provided enough Semtex to take out a good chunk of the dock — not to mention the shipping containers — so they'd moved closer to the end. God help them if those containers held explosives. They hadn't planned on *that* much bang for their buck. Plus, injuring civilians or themselves wasn't part of this mission.

Shane reached his target area and squatted. Focusing on his task, he set the duffel containing two bricks of Semtex beside him and glanced to his right where, a hundred yards down, Dusty's shadow moved. He'd be doing the same as Shane and prepping for an explosion that would literally rock Alfaro's world.

He glanced behind him, hoping to spot Trevor, but a cloud shrouded the moon, blackening the area.

Assuming Trevor was in place, Shane unzipped the bag, removed a thick slab of the explosive and set it on the edge of the dock next to the piling. The plan was to damage the support structures and watch the entire section tumble into the sea.

He slid a long length of detonator cord from his bag and shoved it deep into the brick. Then he grabbed the bag and worked his way backward, checking his six for anything he might trip over or a patrolling guard he had no interest in killing. Six feet from the first brick, he placed another hunk of explosive on the dock, linked it to the detonator cord.

Sweat, either from nerves or the heat, dripped down his back and his mind spiraled to Faith, who'd basically handed herself over to Alfaro. What the hell had she been thinking?

He shook it off, concentrated on the Semtex. Distraction during the rigging of an explosive wasn't exactly a good way to survive.

The second batch done, he walked backward, unwinding the det cord again before reaching into his bag for a blasting cap, fuse and fuse lighter. He finished assembling the explosive with a thin wire and started back toward the dock entrance, feeding the cord behind him as he walked. Fifty yards from the explosive, he waited.

At any minute, Trevor and Dusty should be joining him. Above him, seagulls squawked and swooped, diving and soaring in search of food.

If they knew what was good for them, they'd clear the hell out.

Shane's pulse thumped, his foot tapping in time as he waited. *Come on, come on.* Where were they?

Another thirty seconds. That's what he'd give them before risking taking out his phone and basically sending a flare by lighting up the screen.

More seagulls swooped, this time further down the dock, maybe twenty yards ahead. The moon bullied its way through clouds and a sliver of light shined on Dusty moving toward Shane.

Shane waited, letting his friend get within earshot. "You good?"

"Yeah. Where's Trev?"

"Was hoping you knew."

Dusty angled back, scanning the darkness. "He was right across from you. He should be here by now."

"I know."

Dusty handed his det cord over to Shane. "I'll find him."

The last damned thing they needed was the two of them getting lost. Not when security might show up. "We can't split up again. Give him another minute and we'll text. Eventually, someone'll come along and we'll be screwed."

Overhead, the seagulls finally gave up, leaving the slap of water against the concrete dock. Shane breathed in, focused on the salty air hitting his lungs.

Almost there.

At least until a woman started shrieking.

FAITH SCREAMED UNTIL THE IN-SHAPE GUARD GRABBED HOLD of her, put her in a headlock and shoved his hand over her mouth.

"Get me something to shove in her mouth."

The uniformed guard ran to the cargo area.

"Shut up!" Alfaro told her. "Or I'll finally fill that mouth for you."

Dream on, asshole. She'd bite his dick off and spit it at him.

"Here," Uniformed Guard said.

"Do *not* scream," the big guy told her. "Understood?"

She nodded.

The second he lifted his hand . . . "SHANE!"

She'd risked using his cover name because if they didn't get out of this, they'd be dead anyway and it wouldn't matter.

Now at least, if he were here, he'd know it was her.

A nasty rag reeking of gas gagged her. If she puked now,

she'd die. On the list of ways to die, choking on her own vomit didn't make the cut.

Tears bubbled in her eyes. More from the stench and taste than fear, but even badass Liz Aiken had to admit, this whole rag-in-the-mouth thing rocked her.

Please let Shane be here.

"Let's go." Before closing the car door, Alfaro leaned back inside where Rey still sat in the driver's seat. "Stay here. Be ready when we get back."

ZEN MOMENT BLOWN TO HELL, SHANE WHIRLED AROUND, nearly jerking the det cord Dusty had just handed him.

"Jesus, Shane!" Dusty hissed. "Be careful."

He cocked his head and tracked the direction the scream came from. Left. Definitely left.

The sound came again.

Faith, Faith, Faith.

No. Couldn't be.

He faced Dusty again, already handing both det cords over. "That sounded like Faith."

The first time he thought maybe, *maybe* he'd been wishing it in the hole. Second time?

Most definitely her. This time screaming his name.

He ripped his .45 from his waist holster and pumped his legs, sprinting to the general location of where he thought the scream came from.

If he'd tracked the sound correctly, she'd be just on the other side of the stacked containers to his right.

But would she be alone?

Probably not. And what the fuck would they be doing here? Unless Alfaro knew.

Miguel probably.

Just as Trevor suspected.

Of course it was Miguel. He'd double-crossed them. When this was over, Shane might have to hunt down that son of a bitch.

A plan quickly formed. He'd get to the end of the row, take a quick peek and get his bearings.

Overhead, the spotlights shined on the containers. Red, blue, green, all of them mixed in. With any luck, the chaos of colors would make him harder to spot.

The sudden silence, after all that shrieking, made him twitchy. If it was Faith, there'd be a reason she'd gone quiet. He hadn't heard any gunshots.

Suppressor?

They wouldn't kill her. Not yet. Alfaro, if nothing else, was methodical. Vicious and skilled, to boot. He'd let her live until sure his docks were safe.

Ten yards from the end of the containers, Shane slowed, moving closer to the giant stack for cover as he held his .45 in front of him, ready to fire. He paused near the edge, fought to control his breathing and stay quiet after the run.

"Ow! Bitch!" a man hissed.

Right there. The voices were just around the side of the container.

"Sir," another guy said, "are you all right?"

"She kicked me. Grab her."

"Shhhhaaaaane!"

Definitely Faith. And it sounded like she was doing some damage. Good for her. He had to smile.

In the darkness, Shane risked a fast look and a bizarre mix of relief and panic swarmed him, made his skin itch.

Barely ten feet away, two men, one in uniform and one in dark clothing, held Faith's arms while Alfaro stood in front of her, facing her.

Footsteps behind Shane brought him spinning, gun at the ready.

Trevor. Jesus. Did he want to die?

He threw his hands up and Shane held a finger to his lips.

Shane used hand signals, motioning around the side of the giant shipping container.

They should split up. One go. One stay. Possibly surprise Alfaro from both sides.

No. The containers were at least four city blocks long. Too long for one of them to run to the end and loop around. And who knew if he could even access the next row from that end?

"They're here somewhere," someone said from Alfaro's side.

Shane leaned in, got right next to Trevor's ear. "Where's Dusty?"

"Back with the detonators," Trev whispered back. "I told him to wait. Just to make sure."

Shane peered over Trev's shoulder envisioning the area he'd just come from. The blast site would be at least 100 yards away. Maybe 150.

Aside from potential flying debris, that 150 yards would be out of the blast's range.

Helluva diversion.

Handing Trevor the gun, he stepped behind his friend and slid his phone from his pocket, using his body to block the glow of the screen.

He shot a text to Dusty.

Blow it.

The response was immediate. *Blow it? Now?*

They didn't have time for this shit.

Blow it now.

When no response came, Shane tucked the phone away, spun back to Trevor and tapped him on the shoulder, motioning for his gun back.

Ka-boom!

The force of the blast threw Shane flush against the container, the hard steel knocking the wind out of him for a second.

To his left, hellish fire surged upward, lighting up the night sky as small chunks of metal and rocks rained down and Shane covered his head.

"Go!" he told Trevor.

Weapons aimed, the two of them rushed around the edge and halted.

His gaze locked on Faith. She'd maximized the blast by getting her arms free from the two guards who now had weapons drawn. Before the guards could grab her, she drove her elbow into El Presidente's nose.

Helluva woman right there.

Alfaro cried out, his hands going to his face, but Faith pummeled him with a kick to the mid-section, doubling him over.

"Hold it!" Shane said.

The guards whirled, both aiming their guns at Trevor and Shane.

Classic standoff.

Shit.

Shane slid a gaze left, then right, searching for additional guards. Had to be more.

"*The* driver is here," Faith said, jamming her elbow into the back of a still doubled-over Alfaro.

She emphasized the word *the*.

Rey must be here. Had to be.

Alfaro dropped to a knee and one of the guards flinched.

This poor schmuck didn't know if he should help his boss or risk them all getting shot.

Well, Shane would help him with that decision. He pointed his weapon. "Don't move. Faith, leave him. Come over here."

The bigger guard shifted right and Shane fired a shot between the uniformed guard and Alfaro.

"The next one," Shane said, "hits someone. Leave her be."

Faith joined the good guys, standing between Shane and Trevor. "Get behind me," Shane said. "At least until we get you a weapon."

She slid behind him — that alone might be a miracle. For once, she listened.

And where the hell was Dusty? If he'd blown himself up, Shane would . . .

No. Getting distracted with thoughts of his possibly-dead friend would never get him anywhere good. In minutes, the place would be swarming with cops and firefighters dealing with the aftermath of the explosion. From his vantage point, only a couple of small post-blast fires had ignited on the remains of the concrete dock.

Still, there'd be emergency personnel showing up.

And no Dusty.

Wait. There he was. Creeping up behind Alfaro and crew and Shane's relief nearly gutted him. Goddamn, he wasn't primed for this work anymore.

Gun drawn and still out of Alfaro's sight, Dusty moved away from an overhead spotlight to the far end of the row.

Alfaro levered to his feet, wiping his bloody nose with his arm. He lifted his gaze to Shane, then Faith and finally Trevor.

"Here we are," he said. "About to have some fun."

27

SHANE SLID A SIDEWAYS GLANCE AT TREV AND THEN BACK TO Alfaro. The two men took part in a vicious stare down that sent warning flares firing.

Did they know each other?

The big guy moved again and Shane aimed his weapon center mass. The two of them stood, guns trained on each other.

"Shoot him," Alfaro said.

"If he does," Trev said, "you'll be dead in less than a second."

For emphasis, a red dot from Trev's weapon appeared on Alfaro's head.

"Well, well, well." Alfaro held his arms wide. "Aren't you the loyal friend?"

"Fuck you," Trevor said.

Whoa. What the hell?

Alfaro made a show of dragging his focus from Trev — total dismissal — to Shane. "Ask him how I found her."

Nice try, pal. This guy was a master manipulator. Shane

knew this, had spent enough time in Venezuela to have seen it himself. And he wasn't about to be played.

"He's messing with you," Faith said.

"No." Alfaro said. "*He's* not." He pinned Trev with a hard stare. "Shall I tell him? Or will you?"

The distant sound of a siren knocked Shane into action. Whatever kind of bullshit play this was, they didn't have time for it. They needed to get the hell out of here.

"Ah," Alfaro tipped his head up. "My people are here. Excellent. I'll have you all thrown in prison. Just like my son." He gave Faith, still half hidden behind Shane, the once-over. "Imagine what a woman like you would be worth in prison."

He turned to the big guy and laughed. "This is brilliant. It's all coming together, isn't it?"

"Yes, sir."

Alfaro came back to Faith and Shane. "Go ahead. Ask your *friend*, Trevor, how I found you."

And hold up here. Had anyone said Trevor's name?

A flash of light drew Alfaro's attention to an SUV driving around the last row of containers. Probably his driver — Reynaldo? — checking on the situation after the blast.

Boom!

Shane whipped to Trevor, who'd just fired. What the hell was he thinking?

The shot hit a stunned Alfaro dead center in his chest, knocking him back a full step. His mouth dropped open, his hands going to the hole between his ribs and then he let out a wet, gurgling sound before he collapsed to the ground.

Shit, shit, shit.

The big guy flinched, swinging his weapon to Trev, his finger sliding over the trigger and pulling back.

Shane fired. Three quick shots. *Pop, pop, pop.*

A mix of screams and gunshots filled his head and his brain roared, the panic swarming him as the big guy hit the ground.

The remaining guard brought his weapon up, aiming at Shane. This was it. Over. He'd die in Venezuela and his mother would never know. Dammit, everything he had tried to avoid.

Faith. Right behind him.

He turned and shoved her sideways.

Boom, boom, boom.

Another three shots sounded. *Who's firing, who's firing, who's firing?*

The guard's eyes got huge and — boom! — he got a shot off and Shane's heart nearly exploded from the blood plowing through it. The bullet whizzed by his left ear just as the guard dropped to a heap on the ground.

Faith charged at Trevor, on the ground, but levering to his feet. Blood soaked the upper sleeve of his T-shirt and Faith put her hands on his waist, steadying him.

"We have to go," she said. "That's Rey in the SUV."

"No," Shane said, rushing to Alfaro still gurgling on the ground. He aimed his gun. "You're dying. I'll end it for you. Tell me."

"Jesus!" Dusty said, running up behind the crumpled guard. "What are we standing around for?"

"Trevor knows something," Shane said.

"What?"

"Shane, it's *bullshit*." This from Trevor, his voice rising. Panic.

Alfaro coughed and a spurt of blood dribbled out of his mouth. "Not bullshit. He sacrificed you. Saved himself."

Cough, cough.

The son of a bitch was dying. Dammit. "Tell me. Saved himself how?"

"The cartel. Lifted the bounty."

He peered up at Shane, his gaze holding and that smug smile Shane remembered slid into place. "In exchange for her."

Alfaro closed his eyes and an ugly, phlegm-filled wheeze left him. His body went quiet.

No movement.

Red flashes lit the sky and sirens came closer. The SUV's horn blared.

"Shane," Faith said. "Please. We need to get out of here."

Not yet. Not before he had answers. He faced Trevor. "Your bullet is in the president of Venezuela. Tell me what you did or I swear to God, I'll leave you here. We'll get into that SUV and leave you."

Trev's gaze bounced to Dusty, Faith, and Alfaro before finally coming back to Shane.

"They're coming," Shane told him. "And I'm pissed enough to let them at you. If you didn't do it, how did he know your cover name?"

Dusty stepped up next to him. "Come on, Shane. This is crap. It's Trevor. He wouldn't do it."

"All this time, I was trying to figure out how he found her so quick. I knew we had a leak. Knew it! I was blaming Sullivan. But the Challenger. That's been bugging me. How the hell did Brutus know where we were? Think about it. Sullivan had no way of knowing. The only people who could possibly know our exact location were the four of us. You and Trev? *You two* can track my phone."

That stopped Dusty cold. His head whipped to Trevor. "Dude, please. Tell him you didn't do it so we can get the fuck out of here."

The SUVs horn honked again, this time a long blare. "That's it." Shane reached for Faith's hand. "Let's go. Leave him here."

He headed for the SUV, eating up the ground with long strides that forced Faith to triple-time her steps.

"You can't leave him," she said.

"I never sold *you* out!"

Shane halted. Now they were getting somewhere. He turned and marched back, jabbing his finger. "You fucker. What'd you do?"

Trevor reached up, pulled his soaked sleeve from the bullet wound and winced. "Ah, Jesus." He peered back at Shane. "She was blowing everything. Bringing heat on all of us. I wanted her gone."

"And what? You made a deal for your freedom?"

"Yeah. Why not? I mean, if I could get my life back? You'd have done it."

"Trev," Dusty breathed, the shock evident in his soft tone. "What the fuck? We were a team."

Shane stood, half stunned and half—hell, he didn't know. All he knew was that betrayal was an evil bitch that wormed around, chewing up what was left inside him. His ability to trust. To hope for normal relationships. To believe that one day he'd live paranoia-free.

For whatever fucked-up reason his mind went to Andres. The man Shane had betrayed in service of his country. Could this be what Andres had felt?

His stomach twisted. *Trevor. How did I miss it?*

Shane shook his head, pushed his shoulders back. "No. I wouldn't have done it. We had each other. That was it. That meant something to me."

"Shane, please. I *never* told him about you. Just her. I

told him she had a boyfriend who owned a bar. You weren't supposed to be there that early!"

"That's why he set the fire?"

"It was a warning. You weren't supposed to be there."

Now, rage took hold, swarming the last of Shane's calm. This was his *friend*.

He took two steps, his fist ready to do some major damage. After everything he'd done for his so-called friend.

Faith jumped in front of him, body blocking him as she shoved him back. "No. We're not doing this. Let's go."

"It was working," Trevor said. "Alfaro had no idea it was you."

Faith shoved him back again. "He's right."

Now she was taking his side?

He glared at her and she lifted her hands from his chest, holding them up. "I'm not defending him, but it's true. Alfaro didn't know who you were until you called him. He was stunned. After he hung up, he damn near peed himself he was so happy. Now, can we please go before Rey leaves *all* of us here?"

Shane went back to Trevor. "Tell me about the deal."

Trevor's head swung back and forth, back and forth, back and forth.

"You've got three seconds or I swear to God, I will leave you here."

"I got word to Alfaro that I knew where the woman who killed his son was. Told him if he could get the cartel to lift the bounty on my head, I'd tell him. He went for it. That's how he found her so fast. I saw an opportunity, Shane, and I took it."

"I guess you did. It didn't matter that Dusty and I were at risk? All you cared about was yourself."

"I thought I could keep you and D out of it. Then we'd go back to business as usual."

Business as usual. Shane shook his head. "Then you're a bigger fool than I thought." He turned, headed for the SUV. "I'll get you back to Chicago, but then we're done. Don't come near me again."

HOURS LATER, SHANE SAT IN HIS SEAT ON THE C-17 SULLY HAD managed to get them a ride home on, with Faith asleep beside him, her head resting on his shoulder. Rest, he knew, hadn't come easy for her lately. Now? With an entire SEAL team having completed their mission and on board, she'd gone out like a light.

After this, hopefully, they'd both sleep for days.

Two seats down, Dusty snored like a freight train. As dog-tired as Shane felt, his mind wouldn't stop spinning, leaving his body to suffer the wrath.

Everything he thought he knew about his life and the people in it had been turned upside down.

Voices from his left drew his attention to where a couple of the SEALs shared a beer. Whatever their mission had been, they'd obviously succeeded. A woman in jeans and a black button-down, who'd introduced herself as Cheryl when they'd first seen her at the base, broke away from the group, a bottle in each hand.

When they'd met, she hadn't given him details, but he figured her for CIA. Probably an operations officer assigned to whatever mission the team had just completed.

And, damn, he hoped one of those bottles she carried was for him.

On her approach, she eyed Dusty, her gaze holding a few seconds before meeting Shane's.

She halted in front of him and — bless her — held one of the beers out to him.

He nodded. "Thank you."

"Sure." She remained standing, glancing at Faith, then back to Shane. "How are y'all doing?"

Southern accent. Barely there, but there. Carolinas maybe.

"A whole lot better now. Thank you for the ride home."

He lifted the bottle, took a long pull that hit his stomach and turned sour. He was so emotionally jacked up he couldn't enjoy a beer.

"You're welcome," Cheryl said. "Thought I'd brief you. If you're interested."

Oh, he was interested. "That'd be good."

"As you know, Alfaro is dead. The other two guards as well. From what we gathered, the one in uniform worked at the palace."

"And the other?"

"He wasn't on staff. We believe he worked for the Liborio Cartel. We got a hit on facial recognition."

"Where's Reynaldo?"

"Still at the base. He'll be taken care of."

"Forgive me if I'm skeptical."

At that, she smiled, but there was zero humor in it. "I get it. Believe me. But he's a treasure trove of information. I promise you, he'll be safe." She nudged her chin at Faith. "I know what happened to her. Completely unfair."

"It was."

"I also just received word on Trevor Hutchins. He's out of surgery. Bullet was lodged against the humerus. They took it out. He should be fine."

Shane closed his eyes. It was good, he supposed, that

Trev would be all right. No matter the stab of anger and betrayal assaulting him, they had history together.

He'd trusted him. And with so few people in his life, he wasn't sure how to process this godforsaken mess.

All he knew was that anything Trevor had been to him, anything he had felt, was now gone. And that would take a long time to get over.

He opened his eyes, met Cheryl's gaze. "Thanks for the update. What's the spin on Alfaro's death?"

She shrugged. "There's enough linking him to the Liborios that we'll pin it on them."

"They're already one of the most feared cartels. They'll be delirious if the world thinks they murdered the president of Venezuela."

"Exactly."

"Messy though."

"Wouldn't be the first time." She held up her beer. "Thank you for your service. Hopefully, the future will be better now."

The future.

With Alfaro dead, maybe Shane could ease up on the covert shit. Life as Bobby MacGregor probably wasn't possible since he'd built a business as Shane Quinn. But with Alfaro out of power and his only surviving son in prison, anyone who feared that family would be free.

"With Alfaro dead, how long do you think it'll take for Andres to wind up with a shiv in his heart?"

"If he lives twenty-four hours, it'll be a miracle."

Without his father offering favors or guarantees, Andres would be considered a liability. The cartels wouldn't risk him talking, revealing secrets to save himself.

Shane shook his head. What a life.

One of the SEALs hovering over a laptop atop a stack of trunks hollered for Cheryl.

"Duty calls."

Back to the business of saving the world. Good for her.

Beside him, Faith shifted, then winced, her eyes popping open. She stared straight up at him, blinking a few times, clearly getting her bearings.

"Hey," he said. "We're still in the air."

She nodded, then lifted her head, massaging her neck. "I hate sleeping on planes. How long was I asleep?"

"Couple hours."

Her head lopped forward. "Seriously?"

He laughed. "Seriously. Guess you were tired."

"Wow. Have you slept?"

"Nope. Too hopped up."

She pointed at the beer he'd somehow forgotten about. "Can I have some of that?"

He handed over the bottle. "Cheryl just updated me, if you're ready to hear it."

After taking a slug from the bottle, she held it up. "Fire away."

He gave her every detail. The Liborio cartel, Andres's chance of surviving. Trevor. Reynaldo.

All of it sucked. No question. But with each word, answering each of Faith's questions, his body relaxed. As if his mind had finally wrapped itself around the idea of freedom. Of the Alfaro nightmare being over.

Could it be? Seriously?

"It feels weird," Faith said.

"What?"

She shrugged. "I'm . . . I don't know . . . relieved? Hopeful? Normal people shouldn't be hopeful after all that."

"We're not normal."

"Ha. True."

She took another sip of his beer, handed it back to him and he tucked it on the seat between his legs. For a guy who liked his beer, he wasn't interested.

"What will you do about Trevor? He'll probably contact you."

"I'm done with him. Can't trust him."

"How does Dusty feel?"

"The same. We both want to get back to Chicago and pick up our lives again. I need to get the bar opened."

She peered up at him. "And then what?"

"Haven't thought that far."

"You could call your parents, finally."

Yeah. He could definitely do that. "*That* would be good."

He thought about that first bite of his mother's brownies. Damn, that'd be a fine moment.

Brownie fantasy firmly in place, he peered over at Faith. "The bigger question is what will *you* do?"

SHANE'S QUESTION HUNG IN THE AIR. FAITH HAD THOUGHT about it a lot in the last twenty-four hours. Could it be that it was only a day ago that she'd left Chicago, intent on winning Shane his freedom?

Now, she had hers too.

She tipped her head up, kissed his cheek. "It depends on you."

"Nope. This is about *you* and what *you* want."

She thought about that a second. For the first time — ever — she got to decide her next steps. No one telling her where to go or who to be. Just her, figuring it out.

"That's a concept," she said.

"You could go back to being Liz Aiken."

Liz. The warrior. The one who'd fought for every damned thing she'd ever had. The one afraid to get attached to anyone or anything.

Why would she want to go back to that?

She sat up, shifted to face him. "I think I'll stay Faith. Liz's life wasn't so great. Faith has potential. Does that sound crazy? Considering I'm Liz *and* Faith."

"It doesn't. I won't ever be Bobby MacGregor again. I'm Shane now. It's a coping thing. A way to leave all the emotional crap behind."

Yes. He understood. "I was thinking, if it's okay with you, I'd like to stay in Chicago. I have a job, a cute little apartment." She poked his arm. "You're there. And, you know, I kinda like you."

He gave her a flashing smile that ignited something inside her. When they got back, the things she'd do to him. In her apartment. In her bed.

"Does that smile mean you're agreeable to the idea?"

"Oh," he said, "I'm agreeable."

"We could start over. Maybe take a ride on the Ferris wheel again."

"Yep. It'll be our first date."

She sat back, slipped her hand in his, entwining their fingers. "I'd like a date with you. I'd like it a lot."

28

Being a good little soldier, Shane followed the directions of the female voice blaring from his phone and made a left.

Beside him, Faith looked out the passenger window, through the vibrant green of trees in full bloom to the white caps on the lake beyond.

"That's Lake Erie? I've never seen it."

"It is. The cabin is, according to our guide here, half a mile up."

She shifted in her seat. "Even you have to admit this was nice of Sully. I mean, lucky us that he has a friend who owns this place."

"Well, I guess he's growing on me."

Faith snorted and his phone blared again. Shane hooked the turn into the driveway where a gray sedan and a small SUV sat in front of a two-car garage. This so-called cabin? Two stories with a wrap-around porch. If the floor-to-ceiling windows in front extended to the back, they were in for a treat.

Faith pointed out the windshield. "Are you sure this is the address? Why are there cars here?"

He parked and stared at the two vehicles with Ohio plates and a heaviness set in. He shook it off. After today, he'd know which vehicle belonged to whom.

"Shane?"

After killing the engine, he peered over at her wide eyes that screamed of suspicion. Panic. He gripped her arm. "Relax. It's okay."

"Who's here? You know I hate surprises."

"I know. This one, I'm hoping you'll like." He jerked his head. "Trust me. Please. Let's go inside."

Before they reached the porch, she stopped and faced him, her head swinging back and forth. "I'm sorry. I can't. Please. Just tell me who's here."

He'd blown this. In his mind, he figured they'd get here and he'd tell her. Otherwise, she might not have come. And he wanted her here. Wanted her with him.

He glanced up at the door. Just feet away. It wasn't fair to her. Totally selfish move on his part and now he needed to come clean.

"I'm sorry." He gestured to the door. "I should have told you."

"Told me what?"

"It's my family."

Her head lopped forward. "Your *family*? Inside this house?"

"Yeah."

"Why would you keep this from me?"

He shrugged. "I was afraid you wouldn't come." He grabbed her hands and squeezed. "And I wanted you with me. The first time I saw them, I wanted *you* with me. So you could meet them. And they could meet you. All the people I love. Under one roof."

There. He'd said it. He loved her. They'd thrown the word around. *Love ya!* But saying it? The way it's supposed to be said? No. They'd both been too chicken.

She grinned up at him. "All the people you love, huh?"

"Yep. Because, you know, I *do* love you. You'll have to deal with that."

Behind him, the ka-chunk of a door unlatching scraped against his already worn nerves. Shane whipped around.

And saw his mother.

"Bobby!"

She threw her arms open, stepped forward and wrapped him up, her much smaller body folding into his and his chest did that crazy blowing-open thing he'd grown to really like.

And, God, his mother. Her smell, that subtle floral scent she'd been wearing for years. From the feel of her ribs, she'd lost a few pounds on her normally thin frame.

"Mom," he croaked, "eat a sandwich or something."

She snorted and backed away, still hanging on to him. Like him, afraid to let go and shatter the dream.

"My Bobby." Her eyes welled up, but she didn't bother to fight the tears. "To think I've missed you."

"I guess I know where he gets his sense of humor," Faith muttered.

Mom touched his face, cupping his cheeks in her hands while her tears streamed.

Dang, he hated making his mother cry.

"Can I get in here?"

Dad appeared at his mom's side and she gave him an inch or two. "For a second," she said. "Then I want my baby back."

His father wrapped a meaty arm around him, smacking his back. The Dad hug.

"Hey, Pop."

"Son. Good to see you. Finally. We're so happy."

"I'll, um, give you all some privacy."

This from Faith. Like hell she would. Shane looked back just as she retreated toward the car. Running. As usual.

That shit had to stop.

"Hold up."

Shane broke free, hustling toward her before she could escape. He caught her just as she reached for the door handle.

"Please don't," he said, keeping his voice low so he wouldn't be overheard. He dipped his head and smiled. "I want you to meet my family."

"Yes," Mom said, her bionic hearing clearly still in working order. "Let me say hello to the woman who returned my son to me. Whoever you are, I'll love you forever."

"She will," he said. "That's how she is. Please, let her love you." He grabbed Faith's hand, drew her away from the car. "Please?"

She peered up at him with those soulful dark eyes he'd loved from day one. "I'm sorry I surprised you, but, seriously, would you have come?"

Sliding her gaze to his parents, she grunted. "Probably not."

"Are you mad at me?"

"I want to be. But, yeesh, how can I when you just told me you loved me and want me to meet your family?"

"Smart girl," Dad said. "Son, you should have told her. I'd kick your ass."

Shane looked back at his parents, both of them with the

stern look he remembered from his childhood. "Hey, knock it off. Can we get a minute here?"

"No." Faith stepped around him. "We don't need a minute. Your family has been waiting two years to see you." She walked toward them, held her hand out. "Hello. I'm . . . Faith. And I'm very pleased to meet the people who brought this amazing man into the world."

Mom, never being one for formality, blew right by Faith's outstretched hand.

"We're huggers in this family. Plus, I'm so grateful. You of all people deserve a hug. Thank you."

It took Faith a second, but slowly she raised her arms, loosely wrapping them around his mother.

She wasn't used to this. To affection from family.

She'd adapt.

If it killed him, she'd finally understand what it meant to have family.

He met his dad's eye for a second. They were here. With him. Finally.

Add to that, Faith and his mother with their arms wrapped around each other and something inside him, something he'd been shutting away for two unbearable years, let loose.

"Come inside," Dad said. "The whole crew will be here tonight, but your brother is here now. He wants to see you."

"Let's go in," Mom said. "I have brownies in the oven, and today, of all days, I'll be spitting mad if they're not perfect."

Faith. His family. Brownies.

Life didn't get much better than that.

———

THANK YOU FOR READING *CROSSING LINES*. IF YOU WOULD LIKE more romantic suspense, check out **Risking Trust**, book one in the Private Protectors series.

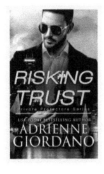

MICHAEL TAYLOR IS COOLER THAN ICE under pressure. As CEO of a private security company, his job means protecting those at risk. But now Michael's the one in trouble—he's the prime suspect in his ex-wife's murder. To prove his innocence, he needs not just a few good men, but one smart woman. If she agrees to forgive him...

Read on to enjoy an excerpt of *Risking Trust.*

RISKING TRUST

BY ADRIENNE GIORDANO

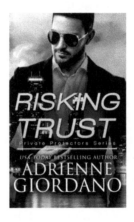

Chapter One

"Mr. Taylor, do you want to make a statement?"

Michael remained still, his hands resting on his thighs, his shoulders back. He'd been in this Chicago P.D. interrogation room for the better part of an hour and hadn't said a word.

"Mr. Taylor," Detective Hollandsworth repeated, "your wife was murdered last night and you have nothing to say?"

Oh, he had a lot to say, the first being he didn't kill his wife, but if he'd learned anything running one of the nation's most elite private security companies, it was to keep his trap shut. "Not until my lawyer gets here."

An alien sensation settled on him. Shock? Disbelief? Maybe even sadness because a woman he had loved, a woman who had once been vibrant and fun and sexy, a woman who had grown into a greedy, unhappy wife was dead. Jesus. He may have wanted to end the nightmare of a marriage, but murder? No way.

In his worst bout of rage he wouldn't have done that to her. Sure they were finalizing a brutal—and costly—divorce, but money he had and if giving up some of it meant getting her out of his life, he'd do it. Simple arithmetic.

Right now, the only thing Michael knew was that these two detectives banged on his door at 8:00 a.m. to haul his ass in for questioning.

He flicked a glance to the two-way mirror behind Hollandsworth's head. The room's barren white walls and faded, sickening stench of fear-laced sweat made Michael's fingers twitch. He'd keep his hands hidden from view. No sense letting his nerves show.

The side door flew open and smacked against the wall with a *thwap*. Hollandsworth and his younger partner, Dowds, shifted to see Michael's lawyer storm in wearing a slick gray suit complete with pocket hanky.

Arnie Stark set his briefcase on the metal table. "Is he under arrest?"

"Not yet," Hollandsworth said.

"Do you have anything to hold him?" Arnie held up a hand and his diamond pinky ring flashed against the over-head light. "Wait. Let me rephrase. Do you have anything to hold him on that I won't shred in the next two hours?"

The room stayed quiet.

Arnie turned to Michael. "Have you said anything?"

"No."

The lawyer jerked his head without dislodging even one strand of his gelled gray hair. "Good. Let's go."

Thank you. Before Michael could move from his chair, Hollandsworth stood. "We're not done."

Arnie stopped in the doorway, spun around and said, "Charge him then."

Again the room went silent and Michael broke a sweat. The idea of being locked up scared the hell out of him. Hollandsworth's face took on the tight look of a balloon about to burst and Michael let out a breath.

Arnie pointed to the door. "We're leaving."

Once outside the police station, the late March wind coming off Lake Michigan slammed into Michael and he sucked in air as if he'd been without it for months. "I didn't do it."

"I don't care," Arnie said. "I'm your lawyer, not your priest. You want someone to hold your hand, I'm not your guy. You want someone to keep you out of prison, that's me."

Not that Michael needed a babysitter, but hell, he'd appreciate his lawyer believing in his innocence. Then again, this particular lawyer was the best in the city. Anyone living in Chicago knew that because he seemed to be on the news every other week touting another win.

"Keep me out of prison. What now?"

"We go back to my office and you tell me every disgusting detail of your relationship with your wife."

"Ex-wife," Michael corrected.

"Not yet she wasn't."

"It's on the four o'clock news," Mrs. Mackey said, pressing the button on the television remote.

Roxann tore her gaze from the declining numbers on the revenue reports and watched as the *Chicago Banner Herald*'s longtime executive assistant, her hair teased and sprayed into submission, switched the channel from CNN to the local news station.

As much as Michael Taylor had wronged her, Roxann couldn't imagine him a murderer. Or maybe she didn't *want* to imagine him a murderer. "Has he been charged?"

"He's only been questioned. I heard from the newsroom that his lawyer got him out before he said anything."

"What about an alibi?"

"He says he was home alone. His doorman saw him go up."

Buildings have back doors.

"I can't believe it. I'd heard they were fighting over money and couldn't agree on a divorce settlement, but still, to kill her?"

Mrs. Mackey shrugged. "I always knew he was no good."

"Eh-hem."

Her assistant whirled to the office door and her head snapped back. Michael Taylor, the man who at one time had filled Roxann with unrivaled happiness, stood in the doorway. Her body went rigid. Literally frozen.

Twelve years ago he ripped her in two, carved out a chunk of her soul and left her emotionally obliterated to the point where she'd made her life so orderly there'd be no room for devastation. Ever.

She had yet to mend that wound.

How much did he hear? She shot out of her chair, sending the blasted thing careening against the wall. He stepped into the office and a tingle surged up her neck.

Michael.

Here.

Now.

"Sorry to interrupt," he said. The sound of his voice, resonant and edgy, had stayed with her over the years. A warm blanket on the coldest January day.

Then she remembered she hated him, despised him with a fury that would level a city block. Her back stiffened, pulling her into immediate battle mode. What could he be doing here?

An explosion of something Roxann hadn't felt in a long time consumed her. She'd spent years preparing a speech that would reduce Michael to a sniveling lump of flesh. Now she had her chance. Twelve years of compartmentalizing. Twelve years of missing him. Twelve years of righteous anger. *Breathe. One, two, three. Stay calm.* Roxann imagined starting at her toes and rebuilding herself bit by tiny bit.

Michael continued to stare, his angular face resembling sculpted rock. She had loved that face. Not quite handsome, but rugged and intriguing. He wore his dark hair combed back and the style accentuated the few wrinkles around his eyes.

Mrs. Mackey glared at him. "How did *you* get up here? Did you even stop at the security desk for a visitor's pass?"

This man left Roxann with enough emotional ruin to fill Soldier Field and her assistant was worried about a visitor's pass? *Squeeze every muscle. More control. Tighter. Rebuild.*

She held up a hand. "He's here now. Let's not worry about the pass."

"I would have gotten a pass if the guard hadn't ignored me for ten minutes. What should really fry you is I made it up eight floors unimpeded."

"Should I have him escorted out?" Mrs. Mackey asked.

A little late for that. Roxann turned toward her desk. "No, but thank you. I'll handle this."

"But—"

Roxann eyed her. "I've got it. Thank you."

Mrs. Mackey offered Michael one last sneer before leaving. Any other time, Roxann would have laughed, but right now? Not so much. She ran a hand over the coil of hair tucked behind her head. Something told her this wouldn't be good.

"So," she said. "This is unexpected."

"That, it is."

The understatement of the century. If someone had told her Michael would be in her office today, she'd have stayed in bed. Sure she wanted the opportunity to skewer him for the destruction he'd inflicted upon her, but seeing him now, a successful businessman whose simple presence commanded the room, took her breath away. Yes, Michael had become better looking with age and according to the media, more dangerous.

She had wanted a life with him and over the years, as she watched from afar, the what-ifs tortured her. He had given himself to someone else, when all she'd ever wanted was for him to give himself to *her*.

For all the time spent obsessing over it, Roxann still couldn't determine why he had chosen Alicia over her.

In place of marriage, Roxann lived alone, worked like a demon and occasionally squeezed in dating men who never managed to capture her interest.

And Michael, the one man who had captured said interest was now suspected of killing his wife.

ALSO BY ADRIENNE GIORDANO

The Prosecutor

The Defender

The Marshal

The Detective

The Rebel

JUSTIFIABLE CAUSE SERIES

The Chase

The Evasion

The Capture

CASINO FORTUNA SERIES

Deadly Odds

JUSTICE SERIES w/MISTY EVANS

Stealing Justice

Cheating Justice

Holiday Justice

Exposing Justice

Undercover Justice

Protecting Justice

Missing Justice

Defending Justice

SCHOCK SISTERS MYSTERY SERIES w/MISTY EVANS

1st Shock

2nd Strike

3rd Tango

STEELE RIDGE SERIES w/KELSEY BROWNING & TRACEY DEVLYN

Steele Ridge: The Beginning

Going Hard (Kelsey Browning)

Living Fast (Adrienne Giordano)

Loving Deep (Tracey Devlyn)

Breaking Free (Adrienne Giordano)

Roaming Wild (Tracey Devlyn)

Stripping Bare (Kelsey Browning)

Enduring Love (Browning, Devlyn, Giordano)

Vowing Love (Adrienne Giordano)

STEELE RIDGE SERIES: The Kingstons w/KELSEY BROWNING & TRACEY DEVLYN

Craving HEAT (Adrienne Giordano)

Tasting FIRE (Kelsey Browning)

Searing NEED (Tracey Devlyn)

Striking EDGE (Kelsey Browning)

Burning ACHE (Adrienne Giordano)

ACKNOWLEDGMENTS

As with every book, there are people to thank. Writing the acknowledgments page is always fun for me, but this time it feels just a bit sweeter. *Crossing Lines* has been in the works for nearly five years and finally being able to thank the folks involved is gratifying.

Milton Grasle, this book wouldn't have happened with you. Thank you for always (no matter what) answering my calls and emails. Thank you more for opening your home to me when this book was simply a nugget of an idea. Your insight helped me shape Shane and Liz/Faith, and I'll be forever grateful. Thanks to my pal Misty Evans for all the early brainstorming help. I'm lucky to call you my friend.

To Elizabeth Mackey, cover artist extraordinaire, thank you, thank you, thank you for crawling inside my brain and giving me the cover I dreamed of for this book. Your talent is enormous! Megan Records, thank you for your patience while I finished this manuscript. Your editing is always spot-on and I know the work is better because of you.

Then there's Martha Trachtenburg, a copy editor who saves me from making a fool of myself each time she catches an obscure detail I've missed. Even when I want to scream, I'm always thankful you 're part of my process.

To my friend and beta reader, Liz Semkiu, thank you for always making room in your schedule for an early read of my books. I so appreciate it! Thanks also to my Review Crew for being part of the team that makes a book happen. You guys are the best!

As usual, thanks to my husband and son who make me laugh every day and talk me down when the words won't come. I love you.

A NOTE TO READERS

Dear reader,

Thank you for reading *Crossing Lines*. I hope you enjoyed it. If you did, please help others find it by sharing it with friends on social media and writing a review.

Sharing the book with your friends and leaving a review helps other readers decide to take the plunge into the world of Shane and Liz/Faith. I would appreciate it if you would consider taking a moment to tell your friends how much you enjoyed the story. Even a few words is a huge help. Thank you!

Happy reading!
Adrienne